Blooming Prairie

T0312889

Part of the Abercrombie Trail Series by Candace Simar

Abercrombie Trail, 2009

Pomme de Terre, 2010

Birdie, 2011

Blooming Prairie, 2012

Other titles by Candace Simar

Farm Girls, co-authored with Angela F. Foster, 2013

Shelterbelts, 2015

BLOOMING PRAIRIE

Candace Simar

To Keith,
Thanks for dreaming with me

First Edition, August 2012
Second Edition, August 2015

Printed in the United States of America

Originally published by North Star Press of St. Cloud, Inc.

Represented by Blue Cottage Agency

www.bluecottageagency.com

Acknowledgments

Many offered encouragement and assistance with *Blooming Prairie*. I'd like to acknowledge the following: Martha Burns and Teddy Jones for their insightful online critique; Angela Foster and Claudia Lund for their editorial assistance; Publicist Krista Soukup for her tireless efforts on my behalf; Beverly Abear for writing time by her fireplace; and the good folks at North Star Press for taking a chance with an unknown author.

The enthusiastic response to the Abercrombie Trail Series amazes me. Thank you for spending time with my characters. Words fail to express my gratitude for your gracious support and generous enthusiasm.

Manga takk!

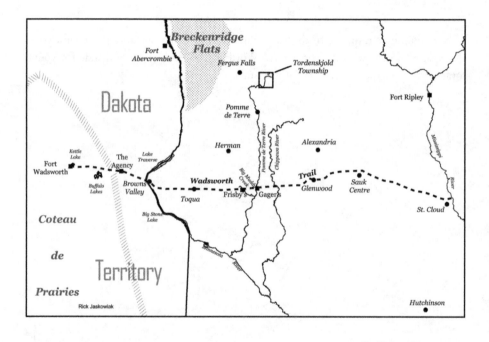

Prologue

1876

THE SOUND OF MONEY. Dagmar Estvold heard the squealing wheels of the oxcarts as the first rays of morning sunlight pressed through her bedroom window. The squawking wooden wheels could be heard for miles and were a reliable indicator of when the hungry men would arrive at Pomme de Terre seeking hot food and warm beds.

Dagmar wore a clean black dress with braided hair wound tightly into a silver crown around her head. Onion soup simmered on the stove. The smell of baking biscuits filled the room. Dagmar wiped rough hands on her gray, second-best apron, hitched up her skirt, and climbed a wooden stool with stiff knees. She reached for her good teapot from the corner shelf.

She must hurry. The oxcart traffic dwindled every year since the advent of railroads into western Minnesota. It would not do to miss out on the little business that remained.

"Ox carters coming!" Ole called from the door just as her hands grazed the china pot.

Startled, Dagmar twisted toward her son's voice. In doing so, she lost her balance and knocked the teapot from the shelf. The teapot, her only keepsake from the Old Country, had belonged to her mother.

Dagmar lunged to catch it, her breath caught in a spasm of fear. Dear God, not the teapot! Dagmar grasped the blue china spout as she fell off the stool and slammed to the floor, landing hard on her left side and hip, but holding the teapot high out of danger. A white bolt of pain shot through her leg and back.

"Good God, Ma!" Ole rushed to her side, swinging his good leg forward between two padded crutches. He wore homemade overalls with the right leg sewn shut below

1

the knee joint and a faded army blouse. His face etched with concern and his brows knit together into a single yellow line above his blue eyes.

"The teapot," Dagmar groaned. "Take it."

"Damn the crockery." Ole pried it out of her hand and placed it on the table. "Are you all right?"

Dagmar tried to move but stifled a scream. "My leg." Her head swirled. "And back." Bleak realization washed over her. "Take the biscuits out of the oven." She felt herself slipping out of consciousness. "And fetch your pa."

The leg was broken in two places but Dr. Cormonton declared her back only sprained. Dr. Cormonton's pale-blue eyes squinted beneath bushy white eyebrows. He had served in the War of Rebellion and attributed his wheezy voice to a war injury. He splinted her leg with lengths of boards secured with strips of old sheeting. The pain was unlike any Dagmar had ever known. Worse than childbed, worse than the time she had sprained her ankle.

But not as bad as losing her children, she quickly corrected herself. Nothing compared to the pain of losing her babies to fever or her oldest son, Emil, in that terrible War of Rebellion.

Her husband, Anton, and Ole moved a cot into the main room of the inn, between the iron cook stove and washtub. Dagmar could not bite back a scream as the men lifted her into bed. Anton's anxious face hovered over her, his long nose almost in her face. He was starting to bald and wore rough trousers and a homemade shirt missing a top button. Sweat stained his shirt and his barn shoes tracked cow manure across the clean floor.

"Now then, Mrs. Estvold," Dr. Cormonton said. "You're laid up for the summer and maybe longer, depending on how you mend." He pulled on his rumpled jacket and retrieved his floppy felt hat from a peg by the door. His threadbare trousers, held up by suspenders, stretched around his bulging middle with gaping buttons.

"Can't," Dagmar said. "It's the busy season."

"You'll stay in bed and let these bones mend," Dr. Cormonton said, "or end up crippled." He placed a gentle hand on her arm and said in a kinder voice, "Send the men to Gardner's. He has plenty of room."

"Over my dead body," Dagmar said with a snort. "I wouldn't send a dog to that place."

N.W. Gardner owned a store and hotel in the village of Pomme de Terre, just a mile north from the old fort. The town had grown up around the gristmill on the Pomme de Terre River. After the Civil War, the army had need of soldiers for the western Indian campaigns and mustered Fort Pomme de Terre out of service. Since then, the stockade had been used for firewood and the buildings at the old fort had fallen into disrepair. Dagmar labeled Gardner's new hotel as a low-down effort to put the Estvolds out of business.

"Listen to the man," Anton said. "This is serious."

Counting the undone tasks like a banker his money, Dagmar tried to sleep. The washtub overflowed with dirty linens from the upstairs beds. The garden partly planted. Brooder hens to be separated from the main coop. The spring cleaning half-done. Dust coated inside log walls beside smudged windows. Berries and pie plant ripe for jam.

"The ox carters." Ole woke her from a fitful sleep. "Should I lay the spoons?"

She bossed from her bed, telling Ole how to serve the bubbling soup. Which pickles to use. Reminding of the honey jar. The biscuits too brown on top and burned on the bottom. Dagmar's head swirled from the laudanum Dr. Cormonton insisted she take.

Ole, one-legged since the War Between the States, struggled to carry items to the table while using his crutches. He slopped soup and spilled tea on her good cloth. As she watched the men swarm through the door and shovel food into their mouths, Dagmar realized the inn could not function without a woman at the helm. Anton and Ole were busy enough without the added burden of the inn. Stones to pick, spring work, the new fence needed in the barnyard.

Last year's crops had paid off the note on the plow. Grasshopper-damaged harvests to the south and west created an unexpected market that the Estvolds used to their advantage. Ox carters hauling goods to the Herman railroad stations and mule teams heading west kept them busy. Immigrants flocked to fertile land in western Minnesota. Last summer required a sack of flour a day to keep the travelers fed. The first profitable year since the 1862 Indian war. Another good year would pay the remaining bank note.

They would breathe easier with the note paid—at least keep the wolf away from the door. That's all anyone could ask for in such hard times.

But then Gardner's move to steal their business. The snake. The low-down louse. The short little storekeeper did not hesitate to hurt other people in his effort to climb to the top.

Dagmar turned her thoughts away from her predicament and focused instead on those who might help. There were few she felt close enough to ask a favor. Even fewer in a position to leave everything during the busy summer months.

"Ole," she said. "I need you to write a letter when you're done with the dishes." She settled back on her pillow and sent a desperate prayer for help. Only one name came to mind. Dear God, let her come.

1

I T SEEMED SHE HAD BEEN TRAVELING FOREVER.
Serena Brandvold Gustafson set aside her crocheting and pulled her reticule onto her lap as the locomotive screeched westward across Minnesota. It was late afternoon and they must travel all night to reach the town of Herman, where the Estvolds would collect them to go on to Pomme de Terre.

Serena opened the black bag and removed three letters. Two were in neat envelopes addressed to Mrs. Serena Gustafson, Burr Oak, Iowa. One was a folded piece of brown wrapping paper.

Soot blew in through the open window and messed her hat. Troublesome, but better than the stuffy air and fetid smells of the car. Serena adjusted the snood over the thick bun at the back of her neck and anchored her hat with a long hatpin. She fanned the back of her neck with the envelopes.

She should have taken her sister's advice. Jensina advised braided hair for traveling. "It will be cooler with the hair off your neck." Her sister had no qualms about stating opinions. "You're amiss to drag the girls all the way to Minnesota."

Out of stubbornness, Serena had twisted her long golden hair into a fashionable bun and covered it with an elegant crocheted snood, a gift from Auntie Karen. Now sweat collected under her hair and dripped down her back. A crown of braids would have been cooler.

Serena took a deep breath, unfolded the first letter and read again the words from her friend:

I'm down flat in bed for the busy summer season. I need a daughter and
you are the closest to one in my life. I understand if you can't get away.

When Serena needed her, Dagmar Estvold had been there without judgment. Serena, bereft after her baby's death, beside herself with anger and grief after losing her husband, had no one to turn to but Dagmar. Serena remembered Dagmar's kind arms,
soothing words, sharp tongue and the cooking odors that clung to her shapeless dresses.

No matter the cost, Serena would answer Dagmar's request. Though old enough
to be Serena's mother, Dagmar had proven to be a true friend.

Besides, it was an opportunity to return to Pomme de Terre and settle her business.
She still owned the farm Gust had purchased. Selling the land would provide cash in
hand to make a new start somewhere. She and the girls would strike out on their own.
Maybe to St. Paul or Iowa City.

She opened the second letter and reread its contents. This letter was from someone
she did not recognize, N.W. Gardner of Pomme de Terre.

I am interested in purchasing your Pomme de Terre property and will pay
top dollar.

"Mama," Maren said rubbing sleep from her eyes. "Are we almost there?"

Maren, Serena's daughter, and Kersten Brandvold, Serena's little sister, shared the seat
next to Serena on the dirty train. They wore matching brown gingham dresses fashioned from
an old dress belonging to Serena's mother. The brown cloth made them look washed out and
freckled. Blond braids stretched almost to their waists, more like twins than niece and aunt.

"Not until morning." She handed them flatbread from her bag. "When you're finished, tend your knitting." Serena tucked the page back into its envelope. "You'll have
time to turn the toes of your stockings."

The girls grumbled but obeyed. The clack of their needles joined the chug of the
engine. Serena smiled. They were good girls—but sometimes a handful.

Serena had been with child when Gust died. She and her mother had both given
birth in 1864. Serena mothered her little sister, Kersten, since that terrible day when
their mother died from fever. Kersten only six years old. Serena kept house for her father
and the girls. They had been mostly happy.

But things changed after her father died in 1875, and Jensina and her man took over
the home place. Jensina suffered sick headaches. Serena and the girls stayed to help her.

Lately, Serena had grown very tired of living with her sister's family. She wearied of
working in another woman's kitchen, caring for nieces and nephews. She was sick of being

dependent on someone else for every scrap of cloth and morsel of food. Most of all, she disliked the way the older girls were treated— more like servants than family members.

It's not as if Serena were without options. Her brother-in-law, Julian Gustafson, had been trying to court her since her father's death. He had thrust the brown paper note into her hands as she boarded the riverboat.

Julian was a kind person, a decent man who had taken over his father's farm and cared for his widowed mother. The Gustafson farm sat next to the Brandvold home place in Burr Oak. Serena unfolded his note.

It would give me great joy if you would consent to be my wife. I'm sure Gust would have wanted this. I will take care of you and be a father to his daughter.

She fanned herself with all her might.

Serena doubted Gust would champion such an alliance. In fact, Serena was certain Gust would prefer she live out the rest of her life in widow's weeds. He had been selfish that way, and possessive.

No, Gust would not want her to marry his younger brother. Julian was a slow-moving, soft-spoken man. He reminded Serena of a plodding ox. She hated to hurt him but from previous conversations, Serena knew that Julian and his mother welcomed only Gust's daughter into their home.

Not her sister, Kersten.

Serena reached out and patted her little sister's head. She had promised her mother that she would raise Kersten as her own. She would go nowhere without her.

Besides, Serena had put herself under Mrs. Gustafson's scrutiny once before and knew better than to repeat that mistake. She couldn't imagine living in the same house as her mother-in-law. The old lady would probably outlast them all.

Serena balled the piece of brown paper to throw it out the window but instead smoothed it out and placed it along with the other letters into her reticule.

Serena straightened the folds of her black skirt and furtively looked around to make sure no one was watching. Then she wiped the dusty tops of her button shoes on the backs of her pantaloons and picked up her crocheting.

Wasted time was a wasted day. Her mother had taught her that lesson.

Serena recounted their journey as she crocheted. First up the Mississippi by riverboat with its turning, splashing wheel. Maren had complained of stomachache most of the way. Even leaving the boat for the cars in St. Cloud gave the poor girl no respite. Time and again, Maren lunged for the cuspidor near the exit. Sometimes she reached it in time.

Other passengers avoided them, moving to seats farther away in the sparsely filled car. Serena did not blame them. Perhaps they feared sickness or fever. She thought to explain Maren's traveling weakness, but felt helpless to the task.

Only a disheveled old man dressed in filthy animal skins seemed not to notice Maren's stench and splatters. He kept his seat directly ahead of them.

"Sistermine," Kersten whispered, "tell us the story about the brown bird."

Serena's heart melted. They were still children, after all, and Serena had never been able to deny them anything.

At least that is what Jensina said.

Jensina was quick to judge. Serena pushed back the guilt that came with the harsh thought. Jensina's children were babies. Maren and Kersten, just twelve, carried more accountability.

"I'll tell the story if you tend your knitting," Serena said with a serious tone. It would not do to indulge in idleness.

"The little brown bird sang in the forest." Serena laid down her handiwork and rubbed her daughter's thin shoulders that almost poked through the faded gingham. "It sang with all its heart though no one noticed or cared."

Kersten's needles slowed, her stitches loose and uneven. Kersten always struggled with neatness.

"Its song so ordinary that it blended with the whisper of wind until it was lost to all but the most careful listener."

"The wood thrush?" Maren turned her needle and began another row of even, gray stitches. Maren was meticulous with her work, every stitch to perfection.

Serena continued the epic saga of the little brown bird whose story had comforted the girls since they were tiny tots. Serena smoothed Kersten's braided hair, tendrils curling around her face in the summer heat and humidity as the story droned. "And the little brown bird felt so envious of the songbirds that it decided to quit singing altogether." The story finally ended with the little brown bird discovering the value of its ordinary voice.

Serena picked up the crocheting again, remembering her first trip to Pomme de Terre. She stabbed the needle into the woolen loop with all her strength, trying to forget the misery and grief she had carried with her so long ago.

"Why is everything black?" Kersten elbowed her way on top of Maren for a better view out the window.

The trees along the tracks stood bare and black though it was June, usually the greenest month of the year. Fields lay stripped and forlorn. Not a spot of color anywhere except in the blue sky and scattered ponds.

"A prairie fire, maybe." Serena pulled the squabbling girls back to their seat. "Be good now or I'll give you a *chiliwink*, a slap alongside your head."

"It's hoppers, ma'am," the old man in the seat ahead of them said with a polite touch to the brim of his shapeless hat. His face was one big wrinkle. He turned sidewise in his seat to converse. "Real bad these parts."

A cold chill settled in Serena's chest as she noticed a strange crawling movement. Crunching sounds louder than the roar of the locomotive filled her ears as the wheels crushed the hordes of grasshoppers crawling on the iron rails. One flew in the open window and Serena slammed the window closed, slapped the insect to the floor and squished it with her shoe.

"The swarm landed and laid eggs last year," the man said. "Hatchlings can't fly for weeks. Crawl around and eat everything until they sprout wings."

"Icky!" Maren said with a wrinkled nose. "The grasshopper smells funny."

"They lay eggs before they fly away." He scratched his head and turned back to face the front again while speaking over his shoulder. "Whole thing starts again next year."

The train labored though the engine chugged and smoked. Serena rubbed the back of her hand over the sooty window and looked out at the blackened fields.

"Why are we stopping?" Maren and Kersten sat up, their knitting abandoned in their laps. "Are we there?"

"Not yet," the old man said and pointed to a man getting off the train. "Watch now."

The brakeman lugged a bucket alongside the cars and threw handfuls of sand in front of the wheels.

"It's hatchlings," the man said and wiped his nose on the back of his sleeve. "Make the rails so slippery the train can't get traction. Slick as ice."

The engineer climbed back in the engine, they resumed their journey, and soon pulled out of the desolation into the green of normal Minnesota. Serena feasted her eyes on lush grass and swaying trees. No movement anywhere except a doe and twin fawns against a backdrop of breeze-blown grass.

"They're unpredictable," the man said. "Swarm some places and leave others alone. Farmers feeling the pinch with things gone sour everywhere these parts."

Old memories of other troubles thickened in Serena's throat. How Indians burned their wheat while she hid in the basement, terrified they would discover her. Baby Lena buried along the trail to Fort Snelling. Gust's lies and deception. Killed by Indians. Tommy Harris and the soldiers at Fort Pomme de Terre. Dagmar's son killed in the War of Rebellion and another maimed for life. All Serena had so carefully pushed away these past thirteen years rushed back to her mind. Each detail like a sharp knife between bone and marrow.

The stifling heat cooled as night settled in. Serena opened the window, letting in the sooty smoke of the steam engine. Maren dozed and Kersten rested her head on the armrest. Serena leaned back against the horsehair seat. She hadn't intended to sleep but woke as the train slowed with screeching brakes and hissing steam. The sun was just creeping over the eastern horizon.

Other passengers gathered their bags and belongings. Serena reached a hand to steady her hat. Her hair was a mess and her throat parched.

Kersten's pale cheeks carried smudges from the sooty engine and her eyes glazed with sleep. Serena reached for her handkerchief, spat on its corner and rubbed the child's face.

"*Nei!*" Kersten squirmed away from the handkerchief and turned her face. "I'm too big for spit baths!"

"Maybe," Serena said, "but you look like a *skraeling*, a dirty Indian." She grasped her sister firmly by the chin and scrubbed. "What will the Estvolds think?"

"I don't feel good." Maren's blue eyes dulled and a tinge of green painted her lips.

"Think about something else." Serena dug into her reticule for a small hand mirror. "We're finally there." She tucked yellow strands of hair into her snood and anchored her hat. "That's better." Serena placed the mirror back into her bag and straightened her shoulders.

Maren lunged toward the spittoon as the train lurched to a complete stop. Vomit splashed across the front of her dress and down the aisle between the seats.

"*Stalkers liten!*" Serena reached again for her handkerchief. "Poor little one!"

The passengers in the back of the car hesitated, as if they could not decide if they should walk through the mess or wait for rescue. The old man gathered his pack and with complete disregard, walked across the wet floor. Serena followed, lifting her black skirt and reticule with one hand and pulling Maren, dismayed and sodden, with the other. Kersten straggled behind.

"Phew!" Kersten held her nose.

"Your best behavior, now." Serena stretched her neck to see out the door. "Both of you—and no nonsense." No sign of the Estvolds.

"I want to go home." Maren burst into tears. "I'm sick."

The old man turned to help Serena down the steps of the train. Blue eyes, as blue as her own, looked up from a face tanned nut brown. His eyes scanned her form quickly with what appeared to be approval. "Looks like you could use some help, ma'am." He lifted both girls down from the high metal stairs.

"Thank the gentleman, girls." Serena felt her face flush. She was a widow woman traveling alone with young children. He had been kind and considerate but she hesitated. He looked and dressed like a savage. "We have not been introduced, sir."

"My friends call me Old Hen." He removed his hat with a flourish. Gray hair fell in sweaty tendrils across his leathery face and a gap-toothed smile. "Short for Henry Brown."

"*Mange takk*, Mr. Brown." Serena scanned the depot. Neither Anton nor Ole Estvold was in sight. Perhaps they hadn't received the letter telling of her arrival time. She swallowed a desperate feeling. She had no money for a boarding house. "I'm afraid my daughter is a poor traveler."

They stood on the wooden platform outside the depot. The town of Herman sprawled around them with muddy streets, shabby houses, and the sounds of early morning. Dogs barked, a rooster crowed, chickens scratched in the dirt, and cows grazed in the ditches. Two hogs rolled in a mud puddle. A strong odor emanated from a rotting manure pile next to a sod barn.

"Where you headed?" Old Hen said.

"We will visit Mr. and Mrs. Estvold at Pomme de Terre." Serena brushed away a fly caught in the veil of her hat and dabbed a scented handkerchief to her nose in an effort to avoid the stench of the village. "At the inn."

"I'm heading that way," he said. "Know Anton and Dagmar right well."

"Mama," Maren pulled on Serena's arm. "What if they don't come?"

"My team is at the livery." He scratched his thinning hair and pushed the stray locks behind his ears before replacing his hat. "You can ride with me."

"But the Estvolds." Serena felt her lips quiver. She bit them and swallowed hard.

"Anton's nobody's fool," Old Hen said with a chuckle as he picked up Serena's satchel. "He's an old injun-fighter from way back." He hawked and spit on the street. "Only one decent trail to Pomme de Terre. We'll meet him if he's on his way."

Serena looked around one more time. She finally nodded.

"You ladies wait in the depot while I fetch my rig." Old Hen hefted the heavy satchel up on his shoulder. "Be back to pick you up."

Serena had the same sinking feeling she had known when she lived at Pomme de Terre, that she was losing control, dependent on strangers, in over her head. *Dear Jesus*, she whispered. *Let it turn out all right.*

"Sistermine." Kersten tugged at her sleeve and wiggled. "I have to go."

They used the facilities behind the small depot, a stinking outhouse with buzzing flies and a stack of corncobs. Afterward they went into the women's waiting room and headed for the pail and dipper on the edge of the ticket counter. The water tasted warm and brackish in Serena's mouth.

"Icky!" Kersten said.

"Best manners, now!"

11

The clerk behind the counter wore a green brimmed visor and wire-rimmed spectacles. His trousers bagged around his middle, held up by red suspenders. A gold watch chain drooped out of his pocket. He licked the point of a lead pencil and scribbled furiously in a ledger. A strong smell of hair tonic and body odor emanated from the man, and Serena wondered why he wore a visor in such a gloomy room.

"Excuse me." Serena resisted the urge to replace the handkerchief to her nose. A pig squealed from the street and a cowbell clanged. An Indian walked by the window carrying a dead deer across his back. A ripple of fear made Serena step closer to the ticket counter. Serena clutched Kersten's hand with all her strength, keeping her eyes on Maren at the drinking bucket. Indians kidnapped children—she knew that for a fact. During the uprising, the two Larson girls had been taken and only one came back.

The man did not look up from his work.

"Sir." Serena raised her voice. Maybe he was hard of hearing.

"Heard you the first time." The man licked the tip of his lead pencil again and tucked it behind his ear. He turned green eyes upon her and a too-familiar smile. "May I be of assistance, ma'am?"

Serena took hold of Maren's hand and stood as tall as her five-foot-two-inch frame allowed. "I expect Mr. Estvold from Pomme de Terre to collect us." Tears gathered in her eyes and Serena willed them away. She was a grown woman with responsibilities. She and the girls were capable of reaching their destination.

"Nobody asking," the clerk said. "But you could leave a message in case they do, Miss . . ."

"Mrs.," Serena said firmly. "Mrs. Gustafson."

* * *

TRUE TO HIS WORD, OLD HEN brought his team and wagon to the depot. The mules were a strange pair, one large and one small, one black and one spotted. The smaller one brayed, tossed its head and looked at Serena with wild eyes. White spittle dripped out the sides of its mouth, and it stretched a pink tongue, showing yellow teeth. Serena stepped back and pulled the girls with her.

"Don't worry, ma'am." Old Hen pulled with both hands on the lines. "Grant and Sherman aren't easy on the eyes but they'll get you there safe and sound." The mules lunged, and Old Hen set the brake. "Should be at Anton's by suppertime."

Serena climbed on the seat beside Old Hen and the girls scrambled into the wagon bed and perched on flour barrels and crates of supplies destined for Pomme de Terre.

"I've been working mules for years," Old Hen said. "Driving with the mule trains to Fort Abercrombie. Come, Sherman! Come, Grant!" He jerked on the lines until the mules settled into their traces. The road north was a dusty trail, corduroy in its bumps and ridges. "And Fort Wadsworth. Smaller loads to Perham or Pomme de Terre."

"Mama." Maren pointed toward some little girls alongside the road. "They're playing hopscotch."

"It's not polite to point," Serena said and reached into her valise for needles and yarn. "Here's your knitting. No sense wasting the whole day." The girls settled into their knitting much like the mules settled into their harnesses.

"Progress on every corner." Old Hen spoke against the musicality of stepping animals and creaking harness. "New store and hotel in Pomme de Terre. Houses and farms everywhere. Of course the soldiers are gone, followed the Injuns to Dakota."

Serena crocheted as Old Hen entertained with stories about the Pomme de Terre storekeeper who hauled lumber all the way from Sauk Centre to build his new hotel and his unsuccessful efforts to make Pomme de Terre the county seat of Grant County.

"Is there a storm?" Kersten poked Serena's back. "It's getting dark."

A dark cloud stretched across the southern sky behind them.

"Not grasshoppers!" Serena put a hand to her throat. The crops were green, the area smug with prosperity.

"Just pigeons, ma'am." Old Hen examined the sky and slapped the lines across the backs of Grant and Sherman. "Grasshoppers come in whirling clouds, glittery when the sun reflects off wings. Passenger pigeons stretch across the low sky in dark waves. If you listen, you'll soon hear them."

The daylight turned into darkness. It was as if a huge blanket draped overhead.

"So many," Kersten said. "Are you sure they're doves?" The birds overhead chattered, shrieked and clucked. "They don't coo."

"Takes hours for a flock to fly over." Old Hen hawked and spit. "If you watch close, girls, you'll see how they ride each other's backs when they get tired. Take turns."

"I'm scared," Maren said.

"Nothing to be scared of, little lady, unless you have a crop in the field ready for harvest," Old Hen said. "They'll strip a field of grain. But they're mighty fine eating. These doves are good news to poor folks shy of meat."

They plodded north toward Pomme de Terre in the shadow of the flying birds until the flock veered northeast and flew away from them. The sky lightened. The mules carried them north as the noon sun beat down upon the lonely trail.

"How do you know Anton and Dagmar?" Old Hen's voice startled Serena, who had been thinking about Baby Lena and her unmarked grave east of Hutchinson.

"I own a farm in Pomme de Terre." Serena felt an unwelcome quiver on her lips and bit down hard before speaking again. "At least, it used to be a farm."

Old Hen chewed on a toothpick a long moment. "Gust Gustafson your man?"

"Did you know him?"

"Heard of him." He paused another long moment as if he measured his words. "I was at Pomme de Terre during the uprising." He spat tobacco juice in the weeds along the trail. "Knew the Salmons."

Serena had forgotten the names of the people who had sold them the farm. The Sioux had killed the Salmon's son. Gust, foolish in his pride, bought the place and bragged what a good deal he had made.

Gust hadn't figured the farm would cost him his life.

"Buildings may be burned," Old Hen said, "but your place is close to town, a nice piece of land."

The rocking wagon and afternoon heat lulled Serena almost to sleep.

"You taking up farming?" Old Hen clucked the lines.

"I've had an offer," Serena said after a long pause. She wished he would just let her crochet in peace. "I may sell the place."

"Then, ma'am," he said with a dry chuckle. "You'd best pray." Sherman kicked at a biting fly and lunged out of step, causing the wagon to bounce and jerk. "Injuns say grasshoppers are heading this way."

"When?" Serena forced her voice to remain neutral. She had waited too long.

"They don't say when," Old Hen said. "Just said they're coming." He pulled hard on the lines and turned the team away from a sinkhole on the trail. "Injuns know such things." He wiped his face with the back of his sleeve. "Know more than white folks."

Old Hen rambled on about a black trader named Lying Jack and his Sioux woman, Many Beavers. Serena had trouble keeping her thoughts focused on the conversation. Instead she thought again of her need to make a change in her life, to try something different, to make a life for her girls.

A panicky feeling clutched her throat. Although Serena did not know exactly what she wanted, she knew one thing for sure. She would not live the rest of her life in her sister's house.

2

E VAN JACOBSON SNIFFED THE SWEET FRAGRANCE of hewn wood as he daubed a
mixture of ashes and mud into the gaps between the logs of his new cabin. A
late spring storm had dumped a heavy load of wet snow, collapsing the roof of
the old dugout, making the new cabin a necessity. As Evan worked, the patches of sunshine piercing between the logs darkened one by one, until he worked almost in darkness.

His worn clothes carried almost as much mud as the cabin. Flies bothered and Evan
left a print of mud with every slap. He reached into the mud bucket at his feet and scooped
a handful, careful to keep his red beard away from the mess.

When he reached to fill the last hole on the back wall, Evan gasped in surprise
and jumped back.

Two brown eyes stared at him through the crack.

Then two more brown eyes lined up beside the first pair, and then another. His
son, Gunnar, had brown eyes like his mother, but the other boys carried eyes like his, as
icy blue as a Norwegian fjord.

Evan took a deep breath and lifted his gun from its pegs over the doorway. The
Chippewa were back at summer rice camps on Otter Tail Lake. He shouldn't have been
surprised they would visit his Tordenskjold claim, but Red Men had a way of sneaking
up on a person when least expected.

Evan stepped out into the spring sunshine of late morning and walked behind the
cabin where three Indian boys spied into the crack between the logs.

"*Velkommen!*" Evan lowered the gun to his side. They boys stepped back from
the cabin wall and eyed him. They didn't look dangerous, but Evan was glad that his wife,
Inga, was busied at the lake. Indians, even peaceful ones, scared her to death.

The young Indians, maybe in their late teens, wore leather breech cloths and beaded moccasins. Black hair tangled down their backs, loaded with cockle burrs. They stared at him with the curiosity of young fawns.

The tallest boy held a bow in his hand with a quiver draped over his shoulder. The shortest boy was fatter than the others and had a droopy eye. The middle boy carried a knife in a leather sheath. None wore eagle feathers, proof they had not yet killed an enemy in battle.

The boys murmured to each other as if they didn't know what to say. Evan smiled to reassure them and tried to remember Indian words he had learned at Crooked Lightning's tipi. Of course, Crooked Lightning had been Sioux and these were Chippewa. The Sioux were banished from Minnesota since the 1862 massacre and his friend, Crooked Lightning, hanged in Mankato.

The boy with the bow and arrows gestured toward the trail going northeast and made motions of picking berries and eating them.

"Berries?" Evan nodded his head to show that he understood.

There was more gesturing and pantomime but the meaning was lost to Evan. Something about a stew pot, he thought. The boys jabbered a little more and then pointed to the gun in his hand.

Evan shook his head firmly. "No trade for gun."

They pointed to Evan's gun again and made motions imitating berry picking. Evan shook his head again. "No trade for gun. I need gun for hunting." He pantomimed shooting into the sky and picking up game.

The boys nodded solemnly.

The fat boy pointed to a shirt hanging on the clothesline, belonging to their oldest son. Gunnar would need it for confirmation—if he ever memorized the Catechism.

Evan shook his head. They had nothing to spare. He wracked his mind for something to trade. He wanted no problems with his Indian neighbors. Trade generated good will. At least that's what the Mormon Saints in Clitherall said. They had been living in peace with the Chippewa for years.

A red bandana handkerchief hung on the clothesline alongside the clean shirts. It was all Evan could come up with but he hated to part with it. He reluctantly took it down and handed it to the tallest boy. "Trade."

The boys smiled and talked among themselves, then gestured toward the cow in the pasture, making milking motions with their hands and rubbing their stomachs.

Evan nodded and motioned for them to wait. He hurriedly fetched the milk jug from the dugout next to the cabin. Thank God for the faithful cow that kept his children in milk with enough extra to placate the natives.

Evan tipped the jug and pantomimed passing it to each boy before taking it back into his arms. He must explain that they could not keep the crockery.

The boys drank, passing the jug back and forth until it was empty, belched loudly and then returned the jug. The tallest boy pantomimed a howling wolf and then reached down to show a small size. He repeated the pantomime and tapped his chest. Evan determined the boy's name was Little Wolf. He wished he could know for sure. The other boys went through similar gestures but he couldn't figure out what they were trying to say.

Evan watched them fade into the forest. One minute they were there and the next they melted into the trees. He must tell Inga about the visitors but he didn't want to upset her on such a happy day.

They would sleep in their new house that night. How pleased Inga would be after two winters in the dugout. They would move their few possessions and furniture this afternoon. No window glass, but a stretched hide would tide them over until after the harvest when they could afford such luxury.

The dwelling, only twelve feet by twenty, felt clean, bright and spacious as a castle after their dugout. The sleeping loft, thatched roof, planed wooden floor and log walls pure luxury after living like gophers. Of course, he reminded himself, five growing boys and a baby daughter added enough noise and commotion to fill any space. At least the loft provided a bit of privacy.

To the right stood the old dugout. Straight down the slope in front of the cabin, lay the narrow lake and beyond the lake the meadow that served as western boundary of their homestead in Tordenskjold Township. To the left stretched a narrow field with a fenced garden area and a patch of corn planted right up to the house. A path snaked through the trees to their Danish neighbor, Milton Madsen. Behind the cabin, out of his view, was an open meadow and beyond that a hardwood forest.

Plovers warbled and a swallow battled a cowbird in the clear blue sky. The May sun blazed straight overhead. Perfect growing weather.

Evan counted heads to make sure his family members were where they belonged. The Chippewa were friendly. There was nothing to worry about but Evan had thought the same about the Sioux before the uprising. *Nei*, he knew to use caution in his dealings with the Red Men, friendly or not.

Inga washed clothes at the lake. She knotted her faded wash dress and full-length brown apron in a feeble effort to keep her skirts out of the icy water. As she bent forward to wring the clothes, her bonnet flopped forward into the lapping waves. Christina, the new baby, napped on a blanket in the shade of a tag alder.

Ragna, their foster daughter since the Indian Uprising, washed clothes at a sandy spot just down the shore from Inga. Her brown hair contrasted with Inga's blond braids.

Ragna wore no bonnet or kerchief and made no effort to keep her dress out of the water. She wore a short apron tied around her waist.

The twins scrubbed clothes on the rocks. Sverre and Lewis, identical nine-year-olds, had yellow hair that reflected the sunshine until it seemed they blazed like burning match heads. They wore homespun overalls with rolled up hems, without shirts or shoes. Bony shoulder blades stuck out behind them like small wings.

Five-year-old Sigurd dragged Fisk, the gray cat, by one hind leg toward the water. He had brown eyes like his mother's and light brown hair curled around his shoulders like a girl. He must speak to Inga about cutting his hair. Sigurd had lost his hearing in his left ear after a bout of measles two years back. Thank God his life had been spared. Sigurd seemed a little slow but otherwise looked healthy enough. Too thin, of course, but what else could be expected after two years in the wilderness and a long, hard winter.

Fourteen-year-old Gunnar and twelve-year-old Knut, dutifully hoed in the garden patch, their required rows almost finished, and looked longingly toward the water. Like their brothers, they were dressed in homemade overalls without shirts or shoes. Gunnar's dark curly hair and swarthier complexion resembled his real father who had died before he was born, long before Evan had met Inga. Knut resembled Evan with reddish hair, long face, and taller frame.

Beyond the dugout barn, a team of oxen, Goldie and Ryder, plodded in the meadow. The remembrance of his horse, Steel Gray, traded for the oxen, brought a sharp stab of regret. Oxen were needed for the hardest of fieldwork, that tilling of virgin land.

The milk cow grazed in the meadow golden with spring buttercups. The animals paused to nuzzle the fresh grass, their bells clanging with each movement. The cow's bell tinkled brighter than the ones worn by the oxen. Marsh marigolds bloomed in the low places, their cheery yellow blossoms a splash of color against new grass.

"Make Sigurd stop!" Sverre pointed toward his brother. "He'll drown the poor cat."

Instead of scolding, Inga called out a cheerful admonition to be kind to the good cat that kept rats from the grain bin.

A warm feeling flushed Evan's neck and cheeks. The long winter had finally ended. They were on their own place with a half-acre land under cultivation to meet the requirements of Congress. Evan and his boys had tapped sugar maple trees to trade syrup for seed. The crops were planted and as yet, no grasshoppers had taken it. They had enough food to get by, and the children were mostly healthy. Inga and the new baby were both doing well. The cow recently freshened with a new heifer calf.

Though they had lost crops to the grasshoppers in Alexandria, they had fared better since their move to Otter Tail County three years ago.

By God, maybe luck was not always bad.

Evan would wait to tell Inga about the Indian boys. They would be back soon enough, and he hated to mar the joy of this day.

Instead, he fastened an old horseshoe above the door, ends facing upwards to hold in the luck, just as had been on his father's house back in Norway. As he hammered the nails, Evan prayed a simple prayer. Lord, help us make it.

They needed all the luck they could muster.

Milton Madsen and Anders Vollen rode into the yard on a big, white mule just as Evan finished nailing the horseshoe over the door. They rode bareback, both men on the same animal, their long legs dangling almost to the ground.

Milton, the older man, was in his early forties and dressed in a blue army blouse and tall boots. A slouchy hat covered long greasy hair. His sharp gray eyes were the only thing about him that did not languish.

Anders, the younger man, was blue-eyed and handsome, tall and lanky. He went bareheaded, wearing plain trousers and a blouse with sleeves rolled up to the elbow. His smile showed a chipped front tooth and his left hand a missing tip on his pointer finger.

"*God dag!*" Evan tucked the hammer into his pocket. "Good day!"

Anders leapt off from behind Milton and greeted Evan respectfully although his eyes searched for Ragna.

"She's at the lake." Evan pointed his chin to where Ragna stood shading her eyes. Her face glowed bright as sun on water. She lifted her hand and waved.

"For God's sake." Milton climbed off the mule with a clumsy thud. "Kiss her, boy, and get it over with." A grin softened his harsh tone. "Don't know what to think about young men these days." Milton wiped his sweaty brow with the back of his forearm leaving a wet stain on his blue shirt as Anders raced down the slope to Ragna. "Can't wait to tie the knot."

"*Betre pengelaus enn aerelaus,*" Evan said. "Better unmarried than badly married."

Milton laughed and prattled about the benefits of being single. Evan listened half-heartedly as Anders swept Ragna into his arms. The little boys gathered around the couple, whooping and cheering at their open display of affection, so foreign to their stoic Norwegian culture. Sigurd tugged at Ragna's apron until it pulled off in his hands.

The lovers made Evan feel much older than his thirty-five years. The couple would marry as soon as Anders finished his cabin. The sadness of Ragna's leaving left a dull ache behind Evan's eyes. He had promised her father that he would care for her. He hoped he had done enough.

"Are you listening?" Milton handed Evan a folded *Skandinaven* newspaper and a slim envelope. "Picked up your mail at Dollner's Store. Charlie says more gold strikes in the Black Hills."

"*Mange takk.*" Evan read the spidery, unfamiliar penmanship on the envelope: Evan Jacobson, Tordenskjold, Minnesota. The envelope bore no return address. "Many thanks. Sorry to keep you from your work."

"Skipping work is the best part of getting the mail." Milton's laughter boomed across the yard. "I'm tired of farming. Might join the gold miners."

"Stay for dinner, Milton?" Inga strode toward the cabin lugging a basket of wet clothes, her long braids hanging down her back. "It's almost noon."

Milton carried the heavy basket over to the line stretched between two trees. "I'm counting on it." Milton said. "I'm sick to death of my own cooking."

Evan was thankful for good neighbors. Milton homesteaded south of them and Anders's claim was on the other side of Milton's along Long Lake. Milton led Whitey to the water as the boys clamored around him. Sigurd wore Ragna's apron tied around his neck like a cape. Sverre carried the cat. Lewis climbed onto the mule's back.

Anders and Ragna walked up to the cabin hand in hand, eyes only for each other, Anders lugging another basket of wet clothes with his free arm and Ragna carrying Christina. Ragna laid the baby on a blanket in the shade. Together, Anders and Ragna hung the laundry on the clothesline, brushing up against each other at every opportunity, oblivious to all else.

"Can we be done now, Far?" Gunnar called from the garden. "We've almost finished."

"All right, just this once," Evan said. The two boys whooped toward the lake, stepping out of their overalls and jumping into the icy lake, splashing Milton and their little brothers.

"The sun's overhead and we've barely finished the wash," Inga said while twisting her braids into a bun at the back of her neck and fastening them with a wooden comb. "And the boys like wild Indians. I hope they don't wake the baby."

It was the perfect opportunity to tell her about their Indian visitors. Evan fingered the envelope in his hand and thought longingly of the newspaper. He would wait until tomorrow to tell her. It wouldn't hurt to wait a while longer.

Inga stirred the *groet*, porridge, on the cook stove that, since yesterday, sat outside. They had already moved the metal stovepipe to the new cabin and must move the stove soon. Milk pans lined the table and Inga removed the wooden strainer before pouring fresh milk into a pitcher. Her face flushed with heat and scurry. Her wet skirts dragged around her legs. How beautiful she looked, in spite of a missing front tooth. Inga was lucky with only one gone—some women said a tooth for every child.

Evan slouched in the shade of an elm and slit the envelope with the tip of his pocketknife. He unfolded flimsy sheets of paper and read:

> Dear Evan Jacobson,
>
> You may not have heard of my transfer to Fort Wadsworth, Dakota Territory, where I am Chief of Procurement. It is a good fit for this old storekeeper. Supplies come by mule team from the railroad at Morris but I have need of a special shipment from Cold Spring, Minnesota, to be freighted along the Wadsworth Trail. Many drivers have left for the gold fields and I find myself shorthanded.
>
> Please reply by post.
>
> Yours Truly, Captain John Van der Hoerck
>
> Fort Wadsworth, DT

Regular money. Something to refill their coffers after a run of bad luck. Money to buy a team of mules, another heifer, or a bred sow. Driving the stage was the best job he ever had. Of course, mules were different than horses, but surely he could learn how to manage them.

Captain Van der Hoerck had captained Fort Abercrombie during the Indian Massacre. How good of him to remember their former acquaintance.

But teamstering? Out of the question. He was a homesteader and must remain on his claim or lose it. There remained corn to tend, the potato field, haying, the vegetable garden, and stones to pick on the south field across the lake. Their larder was near empty, and he must supplement their stores with fish and small game. More trees to clear and land to break. The boys needed shoes before winter. He must build a granary to store his wheat. Besides, he had five growing boys who needed guidance and a new baby girl.

After the grasshoppers took his crop on the rented farm by Alexandria, before they had moved to Tordenskjold, Evan and Milton had hired out to the Mormon settlement in Clitherall. Inga miscarried while he was gone. He couldn't leave Inga alone again. Especially now with Ragna getting married.

"What is it," Inga said.

"Nothing important." Evan tucked the letter into his shirt pocket and stuck the newspaper into the waistband of his britches.

"How's the daubing?" Inga set the iron kettle of mush on the table, slapped a pesky deerfly buzzing around her hair. She wore her work apron and everyday dress made of feed sacking, faded and frayed. The hem of her skirt flopped heavy and wet around her legs, collecting sand and dirt from her walk up from the lake.

"Done," Evan said. "We'll sleep in our new place tonight."

"Husband!" Tears glistened Inga's brown eyes. "*Manga tusen takk!*"

"You're welcome."

"*Jeg, elsker deg.* I love you." She wiped her eyes with the corner of her apron and placed a chapped hand on Evan's arm, leaning close to kiss his whiskery cheek.

The sun blazed overhead in a clear blue sky. The fragrance of spring and green grass filled the air along with the smell of cooking food. A chorus of meadowlarks sang from the field as the children laughed and shrieked in the water. The new cabin stood completed, its squared logs topped with a thatched roof, fully chinked, and the metal stovepipe sticking out as smug proof of prosperity.

Evan's throat thickened. They were no longer cotters, renters, but landowners, finally making a mark in this new country.

If only everything would go well for them. If only the grasshoppers would stay away, the crops prosper and the children stay healthy. His yearning was like a prayer. Dear Lord, help us make it.

"*Jeg lengter etter dag.*" He glanced toward the lake to make sure Milton and the boys were not watching. Evan reached for his wife and pulled her closer. "I long for you."

Inga pulled away. "Evan!" She colored red as the scarlet tanagers in the trees. "It's broad daylight." She turned back to the porridge and reached for the pitcher of milk. "There will be plenty of time for that later." She flashed a sassy smile that showed her missing tooth. "Tonight in our new cabin."

* * *

"THE SAINTS COME TOMORROW." Anders lifted a cup of milk to his lips and took a long swallow. "Everything is ready."

"How many men?" Inga leaned across the table and refilled Anders' cup. Concern crept across her brow.

Christina let out a howl, and Inga hurried to pick her up and brush a tormenting fly off her baby face. Inga brought her back to the table and settled the baby at her breast. The wails changed into greedy slurps.

Evan knew that Inga planned to bring the customary noon dinner for the house-raising. It was spring starving time, the stretch between last year's harvest and the new crop. He had netted suckers in the creek and flicked his whip to kill blackbirds and plovers—not bad eating when there was nothing else. Inga and the boys prowled the woods for fiddleheads, wild onions, dandelions, lamb's quarters, and morel mushrooms. Evan was tired to death of wild nettle and elm leaf soup. They weren't eating high off the hog, but they weren't starving either.

They had it better than most because of Ragna's contribution to the family larder. Ragna had worked for a Mormon woman the previous two years in exchange for the metal stovepipe, badly needed for the dugout. Mrs. Sevald gave Ragna her remaining supplies before returning east after her husband's death. The half-sack of flour, tin of wheat berries, pail of beans, and other smaller items came as gifts from heaven. They had enough grain to keep them in *sopp*, mush, until the garden started.

The fresh heifer allowed Inga to make cheese again. The winter had been hard on the animal, but she was looking better with fresh grass again. Milk was once again abundant.

But groet and milk wouldn't do for a cabin raising. They were completely out of flour, meat, sugar, and coffee. Their pockets were empty. Several times Inga had reminded Evan to go hunting but other tasks demanded his attention. Now he was caught flat-footed. *Alle ting treng si tid.* Everything needs its time.

"The preacher will be in Tordenskjold next Sunday." Anders reached for Ragna's hand and held it tight while looking at her with such longing that Evan felt embarrassed. "I'll have my cabin finished by then."

Evan had agreed that the young couple could marry as soon as Anders finished his cabin. He had refused to allow the wedding if Ragna must live in a dugout. Evan felt he owed Ragna's father that much, at least. No man wanted to see his daughter start out in such a hard place.

A knot settled in the back of his throat. Ragna, even married, would be no farther than a stone's throw south along the shore of Long Lake. It wouldn't be so bad.

"A May fourth wedding suits us," Anders said. "While the preacher is here for Sunday preaching."

All eyes turned to Evan. He looked at Inga who shrugged her shoulders and forced a wan smile. Ragna had been a daughter to them since the uprising. Her help, especially with the new baby, eased Inga's many burdens. By law, Evan could keep her another year until she reached majority. Any money she earned would be his.

But they wouldn't stand in the way of Ragna's happiness for any price. She looked at him with pleading brown eyes that reminded Evan so much of Lars Larson, her father killed in the uprising. Evan remembered how it felt.

Evan's heart melted and he swallowed hard. "A Sunday wedding it is."

"*Skal.*" Milton raised his noggin of milk. "Although a summer wedding seems a poor choice." He drank and wiped his mouth with the back of his hand with a smirk. "The longest days of the year have the shortest nights, you know."

Milton laughed loud and long at his own joke, continuing with plenty of teasing directed at the bridegroom with the rosy face.

"Why is it a poor choice for a wedding day?" Knut's face knotted. Of all their children, Knut was the deepest thinker. He always tried to understand. "The weather is always good."

Evan frowned at Milton. "Your Uncle Milton is teasing. There's nothing wrong with a wedding any day of the year."

"Knut," Inga said, "remember your Catechism. Marriage is a holy ordinance."

"But young man," Milton said with a wag of his finger in Knut's face, "if you're smart, you'll pick the winter solstice for your wedding day." He winked at Evan. "You'll understand when you're older."

They finished their simple meal and plotted the rest of the day. Milton agreed to help move the cook stove into the cabin, a heavy chore necessary before it rained. Water on the hot firebox might heave the iron and ruin their valuable possession. Anders offered to break sod on the south field. Ragna and the boys would follow the plow and gather rocks. Sigurd must herd the cows and keep them out of the planted areas. Anders would stay for early supper but must leave to ready for tomorrow's cabin raising.

Anders hitched up the oxen to the makeshift plow made from a cottonwood tree and headed to the field. Gunnar and Ragna pulled a sledge attached to a long rope to carry the stones. Gunnar stood almost as tall as Anders, and Knut was taller than Ragna. The twins ran ahead of the others, always full of energy. Inga changed Christina's soakers and took her into the dugout for her nap.

They were growing up too soon.

Milton motioned with his chin toward the new cabin.

"Let's do it now."

Using stout oak branches slipped under both ends of the stove, the men lugged it to the cabin where they set it down with a clatter.

"My God, it's heavy. Solid iron, made to last," Evan said.

"We should have kept Anders back from the field to help with the lifting," Milton said while wiping his face and struggling to catch his wind. He slumped to the ground in the shade of the ash tree. "I need a breather before I rupture myself."

"Only a minute," Evan said.

Unlike Milton, he had a large family and no time to dawdle. He must hunt for tomorrow's feast. What he wouldn't give for a nice young buck. The Clitherall Saints once hunted elk around Long Lake, but Evan had seen no trace of them. Evan allowed himself the luxury of daydreaming about an elk stepping into the prairie behind the cabin. He would raise his old Danzig rifle and shoot it squarely between the eyes, providing enough meat for a feast.

A mess of squirrels would at least be meat on the table. Or fish. Maybe muskrats, if nothing better showed itself.

"News," Milton interrupted in a serious voice. "Old Man Dollner says hoppers southwest of Pomme de Terre, Maine Township, and Pelican Rapids." He spat in the weeds next to him. "Did you read the headlines?"

"*Nei.*" Evan pulled the newspaper from his waistband with shaking hands. "I didn't take time to look at it." Grasshoppers Invade and Destroy Crops. "Dear Jesus. I was hoping the hard winter had killed off the eggs." Evan's heart sank. "Why didn't you tell me?"

"Anders." Milton reached for a blade of grass and stuck it in his mouth. "Didn't want to steal his thunder." He spat. "Or worry the women."

A dark mood settled, robbing Evan of his earlier optimism.

They discussed whether it was worth investing in crops as they placed the branches under the stove and hefted it over the threshold. They puffed and groaned as they placed it square on the hearthstone and connected the stovepipe.

"I want to see the grasshopper damage for myself." Milton slumped to the floor in silence as they caught their breaths and listened to the gentle cowbells, blackbirds, and breezes rustling the leaves of the trees around the cabin. The cabin smelled of fragrant new logs and the fishy smell of lake. Evan swatted a fly buzzing around his head. Fisk, the gray cat, rubbed against his legs. He reached a hand toward its furry head as it purred a greeting.

"Thinking of taking a little sashay over to Pomme de Terre." Milton spat the chewed grass. "I'll leave after the house raising and be home before the wedding."

"You might stay at the Estvold Inn," Evan said. "Good people."

A sharp longing to go along flitted across Evan's brain but he pushed it away with all his strength. He had a family. Responsibilities. It was fine for Milton to meander around but he had work to do.

"Rain coming." Milton pointed through the open door to a dark line of clouds on the southern horizon. "Good thing we moved that stove. Fields could use moisture."

Evan's mind whirled dark as the clouds, worrying he would not be able to provide for his family if there were another grasshopper invasion.

"By God," Milton chortled and jumped to his feet. "Listen! That's no storm—it's a flock of pigeons coming our way."

A wave of relief washed over Evan and he chided himself for his lack of faith. God had sent the Israelites a flock of quail in the wilderness when they hungered for meat and now He sent pigeons to them in their hour of need.

Passenger pigeons would be a fine dish for the cabin raising and a grand wedding supper as well. *All mat kjem ikkje pa eitt fat.* All food does not come upon one single dish.

3

RAGNA LARSON RAN TO HER FRIEND, Bertha Wheeling, and hugged her around the neck. Bertha was petite and blue-eyed with blond hair that curled away from her bun. She wore a faded calico dress that did not disguise her advancing pregnancy.

Bertha had come with her husband to the frolic, as she called it, to build Anders's cabin. The house would stand on a small rise beside the lake. Tall ash and poplar trees shaded the spot. Anders had plowed a small garden plot just south of the house ready to be planted as soon as the danger of frost was past.

The meadow beyond the garden was one great flower garden, filled with prairie crocuses, cowslips, liverwort, and jack-in-the-pulpits.

About a dozen Mormon men from the Branch of Zion settlement gathered to build the cabin. Anders had taught two winters at the Branch of Zion School. Their work was part of his wages.

"Bertha!" Ragna patted her friend's protruding belly and lowered her voice to a whisper. "When is your lying-in?"

Ragna felt an awkward pause when Bertha said the expected date and explained that a new midwife had moved into the settlement, the wife of the new school teacher.

"I'll be married," Ragna said with a forced laugh. "Too busy to come, even though I'd love to be there."

Neither mentioned Bertha's sister, Josephine. Ragna had tended Josephine's lying-in the winter before last with tragic results. Everyone assured Ragna that Josephine's death hadn't been her fault. Ragna still had nightmares about that horrible day.

"Ragna!" Auntie called from the makeshift food table beside the lake where she nursed the baby. "Start the fire."

"I have a surprise." Bertha waddled toward the wagon while Ragna gathered dry sticks from the wood pile and started a campfire. Ragna could feel Anders's eyes upon her from his perch on the growing walls. She flashed him a shy smile when she thought no one was looking.

They were finally getting married. She felt like a foolish girl. Even though she was almost twenty, she wasn't sure what it all meant. She only knew she loved Anders with all her heart and that it was time to leave Uncle Evan and Auntie Inga and live a life of her own. Ragna added a spoonful of butter to melt in the hot cast-iron pan.

"Look!" Bertha lugged a wooden box filled with food stuff. "Everyone sent something."

"What's this?" Ragna and Auntie gathered close to exclaim over the wild honey, molasses, maple sugar, salt, cornmeal, saleratus, buckwheat flour, dried fish, and dried peas.

"It's a pounding for your commencement party," Bertha said with a tinkling laugh. "A pound from every family at the Branch of Zion as you commence married life."

"How can I thank you?" Ragna's voice choked. She would have hugged her friend except the smell of burning butter made her scurry back to her task. "*Mange tusen takk,*" she said, pulling the pan from the fire. "Many thousand thanks."

Ragna browned a pile of pigeon breasts, placing them in Auntie's Dutch oven. The Mormons were good neighbors. None had helped like the Saints. Because of them, she and Anders would have a start at housekeeping.

"Anders," Ragna said when Anders came close enough to hear her over the pounding of hammers. "See what Bertha brings from Clitherall."

Anders's face lit up. "*Mange takk!*" He thanked Bertha and then the work crew, shaking hands with the sweaty men, taking their friendly jabs about being a bridegroom while Ragna finished browning the birds and covered the Dutch oven with hot coals.

They were starting out at the bottom rung. Anders owned a frying pan, two plates, two spoons, and two tin cups. Ragna cherished an old tin teapot that belonged to her real mother, found in the weeds after the uprising.

Her hope chest included an old trunk partly filled with two quilts and a set of embroidered dishtowels that Ragna had made while staying with Marta Sevald. Marta was an artist with embroidery and had given her a tablecloth and pillow cases. She would be most careful, she decided, and use them only when company came. Anders had built a rough table and a rope bed. Auntie and Uncle had nothing to spare.

Ragna's Alexandria farm, inherited from her father, was ruined by grasshoppers. Maybe someday she and Anders would live there but only if the grasshoppers left. Like all settlers, she was land poor.

But today they would eat like kings.

* * *

RAGNA BLEW A STRAY PINFEATHER STICKING to her nose. A mountain of passenger pigeons lay in Uncle Evan's old dugout. Her hands and arms fuzzed with down. At this rate, she would be plucking feathers all day.

The dressed birds went directly into tubs of cold water. Pigeons fed the work crew at the cabin raising the day before and they would feed the wedding guests tomorrow. Uncle Evan had situated a meat rack over a slow fire. Auntie Inga dried extra pigeons for winter, hanging the birds from the rack by a thread so that air could circulate freely around them.

Uncle Evan and Milton had discovered a nesting tree where thousands of passenger pigeons flocked. Uncle Evan said they found it by following the sound of breaking branches and shrieking birds. "No need to waste ammunition." Uncle puffed as he dragged a huge bundle of birds to the butchering tree outside the dugout. "The Good Lord sent a feast and we needed only stout clubs to claim it."

The temperature climbed with the sun, and Ragna was thankful for the shady elm that shielded her from its direct rays. She piled the downy feathers on a burlap sack stretched out beside her, the feathers saved for pillows and featherbeds for their new home.

Their new home. Ragna flushed and pulled feathers even faster.

"Ragna!" Sigurd pulled on her apron. "Look what I found." In his arms he held a brown spotted puppy with floppy ears and a wet nose.

"Where did you get it?" Ragna wiped her hands and reached out a hand to pet the soft head of the small animal. It closed its eyes and whimpered. Ragna's heart melted. She took it into her arms and held it tight. It wiggled with joy and licked her hand with its rough tongue.

"Over there," Sigurd pointed to the cabin door. "By the basket." A birch bark basket holding a good measure of bracken ferns lay on the stoop.

"Fetch your *far*," Ragna said and looked around the yard. No one was in sight although she had been standing at the butcher tree all morning. The basket looked Indian. A cold shiver went through her and she clutched the puppy closer to her bosom.

The family swooped around her, the boys clamoring to hold the puppy, Auntie Inga examining the basket on the stoop.

"I traded with some Indian boys," Uncle Evan said with a scratch to his long beard. "Gave them that red handkerchief and a drink of cold milk. Didn't understand they meant to give a dog." He took the puppy from Ragna's reluctant arms and examined its underside. "A female at that."

"Beautiful," said Auntie grudgingly, poking a finger into the basket. "I wonder where they found them. It's early for wild asparagus." Ragna could tell Auntie was upset by the tilt of her chin. "I don't like Indians coming around."

"She'll be a good watch dog even though she's flea ridden," Uncle Evan said. "It was a good trade."

The boys were supposed to help with the pigeons after they finished pulling weeds in the garden, but no one wanted to return to their chores after seeing the new puppy.

"Keep it away from the pigeons and the meat racks," Auntie said. "And away from the baby." She threaded a large needle and pushed it through a dressed bird, then knotted the string around the rack allowing it to hang over the smoky fire. "I won't put up with any nonsense."

"What will we name it?" Sverre said with a lisp.

"Sigurd found it," Uncle Evan said, "and I think it only right that he would name the dog."

They discussed possible names while Ragna returned to plucking the birds. She must keep at it or the job would not get done.

"Muskrat," Sigurd said. "She's brown like a river rat."

"We'll call her Musky," Uncle said. "But first we give her a bath."

Uncle Evan and the boys headed toward the lake with great excitement. Ragna tackled the dead birds. If only she could get away by herself and have time to think about the decision she was making. She plucked and, as she worked, gazed over the sparkling lake.

The water of Long Lake reflected the bluest of skies, blue the color of Anders's eyes. How good he was. Love throbbed in her chest. He was all she had dreamed a bridegroom to be.

But a dark shadow floated along the periphery of her vision. This day before her wedding should be happy. But alongside the happiness, came a deep sadness.

Uncle and Auntie were like family to her—but not her real family. Her parents had been killed in the massacre along with her baby brother and sister. Raw grief spilled over into tears. Ragna had thought the sadness was finally gone. Maybe it would never leave.

Ragna forced her thoughts to the wedding as she dropped a naked bird into the tub of water and grabbed another pigeon.

It was really happening. Tomorrow she would become Mrs. Anders Vollen. It must be wrong to feel so lonely for her mother on the eve of such joy.

Anders's cabin stood proudly on the shoreline of Long Lake. She pictured its squared logs fresh and fragrant, topped with a thatched roof. Anders had planted a handful of popcorn on the roof, laughing and telling her that in the dead of winter they would climb up on the roof to gather enough for a batch. The chinking wasn't quite finished but the door was tight. No stove, but a rock fireplace in the corner. Not big, but just the right size for starting out. It would be like playing house.

Ragna tried to imagine keeping house on her own, being a woman, a wife.

"Don't dawdle, Ragna." Auntie Inga stripped clean soakers from the clothesline with such a jerk that the clothespins flew in all directions. "And careful with those feathers—they'll fill a pillow." Auntie always bristled under pressure of company coming. "Boys! Hurry with that dog so you can help your sister."

The words jerked Ragna back to the present and brought a choke to her throat. She always thought of the boys as brothers but Auntie Inga rarely named her as their sister. Tears sprouted from her eyes and dripped onto the bird in her hands.

"What's wrong?" Auntie grasped a bird and plucked feathers with great energy. "Are you sick?"

"*Nei.*" Ragna shook her head. "It's nothing." She wiped her face with her upper sleeve and started another pigeon.

They plucked feathers in silence, the only sounds the whispery ripping of feathers from carcass and the plunk of naked birds dropped into the water.

"I remember my wedding day back in Norway," Auntie said as she reached for another pigeon. "When my parents died, I made the decision to marry Gunnar and come to America." She plopped the stripped bird into the tub and reached for another. "I was never happier. Gunnar and I had loved each other since childhood. But at the same time I was never sadder."

Ragna looked up in surprise and forgot to pluck feathers. Fisk rubbed against her legs and scrounged in the gut pile.

"I hated that my parents weren't there to share my happiness." Auntie blew a stray pinfeather from her lips. "And it was a big decision to make without guidance."

Auntie was usually reticent in sharing about her past. Her first husband, Gunnar's father, had died shortly after their marriage. Auntie had been forced to marry a stranger, an evil man who had been unkind to her. Then after his death she had married Uncle Evan.

"I hated to leave my brother in Norway—even though Trygve entered military service." Auntie grasped another bird and plucked feathers furiously. "I felt I was abandoning him. He'd be all alone in Norway without parents or sister."

The boys flocked around them as noisy as the pigeons in the nesting tree. "Ragna, let the boys take over. Thread these birds to hang on the meat racks. Sverre and Lewis, pluck feathers." Auntie Inga reached for the butcher knives and handed them to the older boys. "Gunnar and Knut, dress them out and Sigurd, you keep that dog away."

They worked with a murmur of complaining and bickering, the cat pouncing each time entrails plopped on the gut pile, Musky growling and fighting for her share.

Ragna would be leaving them. Of course, she would only be down the shore, but she would never again live with these brothers. Tears started again.

"Don't cry," Gunnar said with a concerned look. She and Gunnar had always been close. "We'll help you."

"I'm not crying," Ragna said and sucked in her breath and held it. After a long moment she let it out. "Just a speck in my eye."

"Why do you have to get married?" Sverre lisped. "We want you to stay here."

"Don't be foolish," Knut said. "Marriage is a holy sacrament and honorable for all men." Knut read for the minister and was always quoting from Martin Luther's Catechism. "Ragna will promise before God to love, honor and obey Anders for the rest of her life."

Obey. Ragna swallowed hard. She loved Anders with all her heart but it was scary to make such a promise. The last two winters she had cared for Marta Sevald's sick husband. Marta had followed her husband into the Mormon religion against her will. She had not wanted to leave her Catholic faith.

During the long winters, Marta had taught Ragna the prayers of her childhood. Ragna tried to imagine what she might do if Anders refused to let her follow her desire to learn more about the Catholic religion. He said he didn't object. Maybe he would change his mind once they were married.

Suddenly her world went dark as two strong arms surrounded her from behind and callused hands covered her eyes.

"Anders!" she whirled around and as he pulled her into a hug, her worries vanished.

"I couldn't stay away, little sweetheart," he whispered into her ear. "*Du betyr sa mye for meg*. You mean so much to me."

"Anders," she started to say but he put his fingers to her lips.

"Tomorrow you'll be my bride . . ." his whisper tickled her ear.

"If you're here," Auntie interrupted in a stern voice. "You'd best sharpen your knife and help dress these birds." Only the sparkle in her eyes proved she was teasing. "There's a wedding tomorrow."

4

SERENA STRAGGLED UP TO THE INN as the sun dipped in the late afternoon sky, dragging her valise with one hand and pushing the girls forward with the other. She was exhausted after her long day of travel. Her hat drooped over one eye and she stepped on her skirt, ripping out the hem. It was supper time.

Only a few splintered timbers remained of the old stockade that had guarded the Pomme de Terre army post during the Indian war. The inn stood in the middle of the old stockade, looking abandoned.

A young girl herded a flock of honking geese toward a raw-looking pen next to the inn. A dirt path snaked between the buildings and stretched toward the old Abercrombie Trail. Serena's farm lay a mile and three quarters east of the old fort, through the woods. A little farther if they went on the trail. The Village of Pomme de Terre had grown up around the grist mill about a mile north of the old fort site.

Serena remembered how scared she had felt when she and Gust had first moved to Pomme de Terre. Memories flooded in, thick and smothering. So long ago.

"Mama, I want to go home." Maren leaned back into her mother's skirt, almost pushing her off the dirt path.

"Be good now." Serena set her valise on the ground and pushed up her hat, refastening it with the hatpin. "We're finally here." She straightened her skirt. Hens scratched in the weeds, cows lowed from the nearby pasture, and the geese honked. From the trees behind came the sounds of Minnesota summer—orioles singing, crickets chirping, and the breeze rustling through the branches. Also the squealing noise of ox carts.

The inn, a barnlike structure, carried a faded sign: ESTVOLD INN, BED AND BOARD $2.

A short man wearing an angry scowl blustered out of the inn, slamming the door behind him. He hesitated on the stoop when he saw Serena, changed his expression to a fawning smile and tipped his bowler hat. He was dressed in dark trousers held up by suspenders, a white shirt, blue bow tie and shiny black boots. A waxed mustache rested on his upper lip and though he looked as if he had stepped out of a store window, there was something unclean about him. Serena pulled away.

"Ma'am." A sickening stench of stale tobacco and something resembling rotten meat came out with his words. "Lovely day, today." His eyes lingered a fraction of a second too long on her bosom. "And lovely ladies."

"Good day." Serena brushed past the man and knocked firmly on the inn door. Through the corner of her eye she glimpsed the man replace his hat and stride toward the village.

"I said get the hell out of here!" Dagmar Estvold screeched and something bounced off the other side of the door. "You dirty snake!"

"Dagmar!" Serena had forgotten Dagmar's tendency to profanity. "It's Serena."

Complete silence.

Serena knocked again, cracked opened the door and stepped inside, keeping the girls behind her. Dirty dinner dishes covered the table and sprawled across the kitchen. The smell of sour milk and urine filled her nostrils. The cook stove smoked in the corner and Dagmar lay sweating on a rumpled cot next to it. Dirt and cow manure stained the puncheon floor.

"Now I'm embarrassed." Dagmar grimaced as she raised her head off the soiled pillow. "We thought you were coming next week." She wore an ancient white flannel nightgown, stained with spilled coffee and blueberry jam. Her white hair wild around her face like a dandelion gone to seed and her face grooved with worry lines. "I'm a foolish *gammel kvinne*, old woman."

"Who is he?" Serena dropped her valise beside the wall, away from the messy table and dried manure.

"The bastard trying to run me out of business." She smoothed her hair and straightened the blanket over her nightgown. "The devil, N.W. Gardner," Dagmar said. "Wants me to close down the inn. Says I'm getting too old to keep up." She mopped sweat from her face with a soiled handkerchief. "Said he'd buy me out." The tears started again and she wiped them with her hands. "You're here now . . . that's all that matters."

Serena's mouth dropped open and she closed it with a snap. N.W. Gardner's letter burned in her reticule. "Maren Rose, this is Mrs. Estvold." Serena nudged the girls toward her friend. "And my sister, Kersten Gunda Brandvold."

Maren looked at her shoes and curtsied, suddenly shy. Kersten May reached out to shake Dagmar's outstretched hand but looked at Maren's curtsy, drew back her hand, and made a curtsy, too.

"Don't worry," Dagmar said. "I won't bite." She laughed shrill as a rain crow, the old sound that always made Serena smile. "And call me Bestemor, Grandmother. I've always wanted granddaughters. We'll pretend while you're here."

Serena removed her hat and tied an apron around her soiled traveling dress. Those squealing sounds were oxcart wheels heading toward Pomme de Terre and getting louder. She had best get to work.

"Girls, clean off the table." Serena pushed her sleeves up and gingerly poked a hand into the dishpan of cold water. Skiffs of greased floated atop the dirty water. Flies buzzed around her head and tangled in her snood. "There's work to do."

* * *

B<small>Y THE TIME THE OX CARTERS PULLED</small> into Pomme de Terre, the screeching sound of their wheels was head-splitting in volume. Serena had cleaned the kitchen and swept the floor. Clean dishes lay on the table and a pan of cornbread baked beside a crock of beans. Water boiled on the stove, ready for coffee grounds mixed with raw eggs. Serena had never cooked for a batch of men before, but Dagmar was quick to give directions.

"Serena, do you need kitchen wood?" Anton poked his head in the door. He looked older than Serena remembered and what hair he had left had turned completely silver. He wore patched overalls and a lumpy hat. His long face drooped into wrinkles behind a full beard and mustache. His eyes were ice blue, almost white. "Water?"

"Both," Serena said.

"Mama." Maren tugged at her skirt. "Can we go out and play? Bestemor says there are new kittens in the hay barn."

"Chores first." Serena pushed strands of loose hair behind her ears. It was almost dark, well past suppertime, and she had only dozed in the train the night before.

But the ox carters didn't come.

Serena heard them talking and shouting, the bellowing of their oxen, the rattle of traces as they unhitched the wooden carts. But instead of coming to the inn, they tramped toward the new hotel in the village.

Ole crutched into the room from the fields, a confused look on his dirty face. "Good day, Mrs. Gustafson." He tipped his filthy cap. "Pleased to meet you." Sweat darkened his yellow hair and dripped in dirty rivulets down his dusty face. "We didn't expect you until next week."

He was tall and good looking, but Serena couldn't see past his folded pant leg. His deep bass voice surprised her. It sounded like the low note on a fiddle.

"Where are the men?" Ole said.

"We've been robbed, pure and simple." Dagmar balled her fists and struck the mattress beside her. "That no account Gardner. He was over today and tried to buy us out. Must have told them we were out of business."

"Settle down, Mother," Anton said entering the kitchen door with a full armload of firewood. "You'll set yourself back over nothing."

"Nothing!" Dagmar snorted. "That lying snake." She glanced toward Maren and Kersten and crimped her lips into an angry line. "We've been in business for almost twenty years. And now he's trying to cut into our trade."

"I'll see for myself," Ole said with voice lowered. "There will be hell to pay if he's up to some shenanigans." He reached for a military holster hanging from a nail by the door.

"*Nei!*" Dagmar placed a hand on her throat. "No guns."

"Don't worry, Ma." Ole balanced on his crutches wearing a face set hard as rock. He fastened the gun belt around his waist. "It's only for show. Even Gardner wouldn't shoot a cripple."

"I'll go with you." Serena surprised herself by her words. Surely the presence of a woman would prevent violence. And she must speak to Mr. Gardner about her land.

"I'll handle it," Ole said.

"Please, I'd like to go along." Serena removed her apron and reached for her hat. "Girls, stay here. I'll be right back."

Dusk settled around them as she and Ole walked to town. She had left Pomme de Terre before the end of the war. Dagmar had written of Emil's death and Ole's injury. Ole was about her age, younger than his brother who had been killed at Fredericksburg.

They followed the same path that she and Gust had walked the night of the Christmas Ball. Bror Berg had danced the Halling that night in 1862, his feet a flash of movement as he leapt and kicked the hat from the pole held high in Serena's hands. She had worn Dagmar's gray dress and danced the night away. How young they had been.

"You needn't come along, Mrs. Gustafson," Ole said. "I know what I'm doing."

Serena felt the color rise in her cheeks. "I know. But I'd like to stretch my legs and see the village." She forced herself back to the present. "Please call me Serena."

"It's good of you to help us." His voice sounded calm and easy, but his face was a mask of steel. The muscles of his jaws worked and he moved his crutches with steady resolve. "Ma didn't rest until she knew you were coming."

Ole looked a combination of his parents with the eyes of his father and smile of his mother. Ole had the take-charge attitude of Dagmar. She couldn't imagine how terrible it must be for him to be without a leg.

"Ma says you lived here." He placed his crutches carefully on the path and swung his good leg forward. "While I was in the army."

"It was hard times," Serena said. The sun was a half circle against the horizon and the air filled with the calls of plovers and meadowlarks. A hissing white goose chased a rooster. "We prayed for you." Her voice caught. "All of you boys."

His silence spoke his skepticism. She wished she had not mentioned the prayers but surely he realized that his survival was a miracle. One legged or not, he was alive, though she remembered only too well how the surgeons at Perryville doubted he would make it.

"Your mother read your letters to us," Serena said. "I feel like I know you from them."

"You don't." Ole jabbed his crutches deeper into the grassy path. "No one does."

They walked in silence as a rider on a white mule rode toward town from the east. Serena strained her eyes to see if she might know the man. He didn't look familiar. She thought of the people she had known from before, trying to remember what news Dagmar had sent in her letters.

The hotel stood raw and new, a barn-like structure built with sawed lumber. Gray paint splashed the bottom half. A ladder propped against the wall beside empty buckets and dirty brushes. A herd of goats chewed weeds by the door. Serena stepped over their droppings. A mangy dog peeked out from beneath the porch and growled a warning. A hand painted sign boasted: BEST FOOD IN POMME DE TERRE, BED AND BOARD $1.95.

"Damn him." Ole said with a growl. "Undercutting our price."

"You're not really going to shoot him, are you?"

Ole shook his head. His lips turned into a grim smile. "I have a better idea." He pushed the door open and leaned against his crutches to allow Serena to go in ahead of him. "Only a blind man would avoid your table."

Conversation and the clank of cutlery ceased as they stepped inside the door. Every eye was upon Serena except a young black man balancing heaping plates on a round tray.

To the left a high table stood next to the wall with a leather-bound ledger lying open beside inkwell and quill pen. Ahead, a grand staircase led to the upper floor. To the right sprawled an open room filled with tables of rough looking men, some halfbreeds wearing Indian clothing, many with bright sashes tied around their waists.

"Hello, boys." Ole's voice eased across the silent room, his voice as calm and deep as a church bell. "Seems there's a rumor going around that the Estvold Inn is closed." His voice like honey though Serena felt a thread of iron running through it. "I'd like to introduce our new cook." A few men whispered and Serena's face flamed. She wished she could hide under the floorboards. She shouldn't have come. "Mrs. Gustafson is helping out until Ma is back on her feet."

Mr. Gardner hurried down the wooden staircase with a clunk of boot heels, his face florid, nervously fingering the pocket watch chain hanging from his vest pocket. He took a stub of cigar out of his mouth. "What's going on here?"

"Nothing." Ole pivoted on his good leg to head back out of the hotel. "Just correcting a misconception." He opened the door for Serena while leaning on his crutches.

About a dozen men, still waiting for their late supper, scrambled to their feet and followed them out the door, jostling to walk closer to Serena, some starting conversations.

Serena looked back at Mr. Gardner, wondering how she might talk to him about her land, and almost bumped into the rider they had seen coming toward Pomme de Terre, who watered his mule at the trough.

He was dressed in an ancient blue army blouse faded almost white and boots run down at the heels. A slouchy military cap covered dark curls graying around the ears. He was older than Ole, maybe closer to forty. Good looking, Serena thought, with his warm brown eyes.

"Excuse me, ma'am." He touched his hat and nodded toward Serena. "Is this the Estvold Inn?"

Ole motioned with his chin. "Down the path." Ole repositioned his crutches to shake his hand. "We're heading that way."

The man reached for the reins on his mule. "I'm Milton Madsen from Tordenskjold." He tugged at the mule's halter but it refused to budge. "Come Whitey, don't be so stubborn." He pushed against the mule with his shoulder, but it held its ground. Mr. Madsen pushed again with enough force to make the animal move his legs. While the animal shifted his weight, he pulled hard on the halter and the animal followed. "Damn a stubborn mule," he said, "excuse my French, ma'am."

"I'm a friend of Evan Jacobson," Milton said as they walked across the village. "He said to look you up."

Serena remembered Mr. Jacobson, the stagecoach driver who had rescued so many during the massacre. When she returned to Burr Oak, he had made sure she met the riverboat on time, staying with her until it was ready to debark down the Mississippi.

"How is Mr. Jacobson?" Serena said.

"He's fine, ma'am," Mr. Madsen said. "Shall I bring greetings to him and his family?"

"Yes," Serena said. "Please tell him Mrs. Serena Gustafson sends best wishes."

Ole pushed ahead of them, and Serena could tell from his scowl that he was angry. Why, she did not know. Maybe he was angry about Mr. Gardner. Or temperamental about his war wound. Gust had been the same about his crippled leg, always touchy and overly sensitive.

Mr. Madsen chatted about his journey to Pomme de Terre, the threat of grasshoppers and the beauty of the spring trillium. Ole didn't say another word.

When they reached the inn, Ole removed a stubby pencil from his pocket and changed the sign by the door: ESTVOLD INN, CLEAN BEDS, GOOD FOOD $1.90.

Serena hurried to serve the meal. With so few boarders, they would be eating leftovers for a week.

5

EVAN TOOK A DEEP BREATH AND TURNED his thoughts back to the preacher's words, away from the old memories. Ragna and Anders stood before the Lutheran minister, under the shady elm beside the cabin. The butchering table covered with Inga's best cloth served as the altar.

Milton Madsen had slipped into the yard as the ceremony started. Evan was anxious to hear what he had learned in Pomme de Terre, but there was no time to ask. Elijah Wheeling was there with his missus. Syl Wheeling and his family arrived from the Mormon settlement in Clitherall, along with several of Anders's former pupils. Anders had taught the winter session of school at the Branch of Zion settlement. Charlie Dollner rode in on an old mare.

The sun through the elm leaves reflected off Ragna's face. How beautiful she looked. No resemblance at all to the tear-stained and lousy-haired little girl he had rescued after the uprising. Anders kept a protective hand on her elbow.

Inga and Ragna had reworked an old tan dress of Marta Sevald's into a suitable wedding gown, tucking and stitching until Ragna looked like a fashion plate. Ragna carried a bouquet of blue flags gathered from the slough. She wore a daisy chain on her brown braided hair. How proud her father would have been.

"Who giveth this woman to be this man's wife?"

"I do." Evan stepped forward. As he spoke the words of relinquishment, Evan realized he had fulfilled his promise to his old friend, Lars Larson. He had done his best to care for Ragna and now she was Anders's responsibility.

Evan sat down and took Christina on his lap. Inga squeezed his arm and wiped her eyes on her best handkerchief. Anders stood tall and handsome in his Sunday suit. His face, tanned dark as an Indian, made his eyes blue as crystals underneath hair bleached white by the sun.

They were a good match. Evan felt certain of that. Steady and educated, Anders was solid through and through—and of Norwegian heritage. Surely, Ragna's *bestemor* would approve if she knew the young man. Ragna's father, Lars Larson, gone so many years, would also approve.

Through good and bad times, Ragna had never failed to be a loving and dutiful daughter. The realization brought a hot tear to Evan's eye. Her leaving closed the door on a chapter of his life.

Evan prayed a desperate prayer that the young couple would do well in life, that they would find happiness and avoid suffering.

"You may kiss the bride," the minister said. Perhaps the exuberant young man kissed his bride a little longer than was good manners, but no one cared now. They were married. Inga had watched like a hawk, worrying about bed courting and sin of all kinds. All that now in the past.

Milton pushed forward to kiss the bride along with a good deal of elbow poking and hand shaking of the groom, threatening to steal the bride and throw a chivaree. Gunnar and Knut smacked kisses on their foster-sister's cheek. Ragna swooped little Sigurd into her arms and kissed him on the nose. Lewis and Sverre stayed close to her as if reluctant to let her out of sight.

Bertha and Elijah Wheeling surprised the wedding party with a cake. Large and flat, the cake boasted red currants and a dusting of maple sugar across the top. Inga wept for joy when she saw it and reverently added it to the food table already laden with baked pigeon, hard-boiled eggs, dandelion greens, and cottage cheese dressed with wild onions. A pitcher of buttermilk stood beside a glass of wild violets.

"Just think." Inga wiped her eyes "A real cake." She fussed over Anders's plate, touched Ragna's shoulder and sniffed back tears.

"Uncle Evan." Ragna tapped him on his arm, interrupting his thoughts. "Aren't you going to kiss the bride?" She hugged him around the neck and kissed his cheek. "*Mange tusen takk.*" She brushed his red beard away from her face.

Evan thought to tell her what a good daughter she had been to them but words like that did not come easy for him. He leaned over and kissed her forehead.

"Howdy!" Lying Jack, the Negro trader, called out as he and his missus rode up to the cabin on mules weighted down with bundles of trade goods, interrupting Evan's conversation with Ragna. "Looks like we is just in time for a party."

Evan squeezed Ragna's arm and walked toward the trader, looking around to see if anyone objected to the trader or his Indian wife joining the festivities. He should have known his good and decent neighbors would welcome them. Lying Jack was trusted in the community and his wife, Many Beavers, once married to Crooked Lightning, had rescued Ragna during the uprising.

"Hello, Mr. and Mrs. Yack." Evan always pronounced J's as Y's, the heavy Norwegian brogue a hindrance in the new world. "Yust in time for wedding cake."

"Congratulations to you young folks jumping the broom." Lying Jack's booming laugh lightened the mood and livened the conversation. Lying Jack pushed a whole bag of coffee beans into Ragna's hands. "Now let's cook coffee."

* * *

Evan watched Anders and his new bride leave hand in hand, walking alongside the lakeshore on their way to their claim. Anders toted a gunnysack of Ragna's clothing and their few wedding gifts. Ragna carried a basket of leftover pigeons, enough for their breakfast. The southwestern sky, colored pink and purple, made a picture-perfect backdrop for the newlyweds. A chain of herons circled and landed on Long Lake, joining a family of loons and a pair of swans. Bitterns sang amidst a chorus of spring peepers, their *oonk-a-lunk* call contrasting with the croaking frogs. Clouds of mosquitoes swarmed out of nowhere.

One by one, the other guests left, hurrying back to cows and chores until only Milton and Lying Jack remained. Knut and Gunnar dragged their feet toward the bawling cows anxious to be milked, the twins not far behind. Inga and Many Beavers washed dishes, dumping the dishwater on the tomato plants. The baby and Sigurd already slept in the big bed in the new cabin.

Evan lit a smudge for the mosquitoes. He purposely averted his eyes and thoughts from Ragna and Anders. He felt glum already and dreaded Milton's report about grasshopper damage. The men sat in the smoke, their only relief from the horrid insects, using logs as stools.

"Now then," Evan said. "Tell us."

"Hoppers terrible in Stearns County." Milton fanned smoke away from his face with his hat. "And the southwest part of the state." Milton edged away from the smoke.

"And I hears," Lying Jack dropped his usual bantering tone, "they landed in St. Olaf and Tumuli Townships."

"*Nei.*" Evan's heart dropped. St. Olaf and Tumuli were close.

"The wind carries them." Lying Jack said. "According to my woman's people."

"Maybe we'll be lucky," Milton said.

Evan thought to say something cheerful, something to encourage the others, but nothing came to mind. He glanced at the horseshoe over the door and hoped it would hold the luck they needed. Evan added another leafy branch to the fires. Thick smoke billowed, burning his eyes and throat.

They discussed the newspaper articles about locusts in Minnesota, Dakota Territory, Missouri, and Nebraska.

"Folks giving up and heading back east," Milton said. "Can't feed their families."

"Big news is that the government changed the law," Lying Jack said fanning the smoke away from his face. "It's in the papers. A man can work away from his claim in these hard times without losing his stake."

Evan let out a sigh of relief. Thank God. It was what had bothered him the most. To leave his claim for a paying position would have meant losing it. Without that worry, he could take Captain Van der Hoerck's offer. Regular money. He must if the hoppers were at Tumuli. Surely, the job offer was the outstretched hand of God, an answer to prayer.

As the other men conversed, Evan made his decision. He would write to Captain Van der Hoerck and accept the job. The old horseshoe over the door might not be enough to keep them. Teamstering would put them back in the black and see them through this stretch of bad luck.

Inga wouldn't like it. He had no other choice.

Betre aa sitje med visa enn gaa med haapet. Better sit with certainty than walk with hope.

6

RAGNA VOLLEN KNELT AT THE LAKE, rubbing soft soap into Anders's smelly socks—well not exactly socks, she corrected herself with a smile. In the summer, Anders wrapped his feet in cotton strips rather than wear heavy knitted wool.

She had saved the laundry for the hottest part of the afternoon, hoping for respite from the heat. She swirled the long cotton fabric in the cool water, thinking how she was a *kjerring* now, a married woman, responsible to keep her husband fed and clothed. Ragna wrung out the cloths and hummed a little melody her mother used to sing. She reached for a soiled shirt, dipped it into the water and rubbed soap into the stains, scrubbing the cloth on a rock.

Their cabin was cozy with its stone and mud chimney, thatched roof and adzed logs. The single room smelled like fresh oak and though the floor was packed dirt sprinkled with sand, Anders promised to lay floorboards over it the next winter. Anders had fashioned a table, benches, and a bed frame. The embroidered tablecloth from Marta decorated the table. Hand-made quilts and embroidered pillowcases lay on the bed.

Best of all, the lone window had real glass, Anders's wedding gift to her. The thick glass allowed only a hazy blue and green image of trees and water, but Ragna loved the colors and light. It would have been enough to have only the cabin. Since the Indians had stolen her during the massacre, Ragna had been afraid of windows. Not this window. Not with a husband to protect and keep her safe.

Her home. No longer an outsider staying where she didn't belong.

A bubbling spring at the north edge of their lakeshore provided clean fresh water. Anders boasted that the spring was strong enough to stay open all year round. Lucky, they need not dig a well. They bathed and laundered in a patch of sugar sand farther south on the shoreline.

Ragna was wringing out the wet shirt when something caught her eye in the trees next to the house. She startled, looked again, but saw nothing. Maybe a deer. It had been like gray fog slipping through the aspen. She squinted and shaded her eyes to see better. Maybe the wind. Then a gray rabbit hopped out from the trees and across the open ground.

"You're a lucky bunny," Ragna said with relief. "If Anders were here with his gun, you'd be in the stew pot and your skin sold to Lying Jack next time he comes around."

The sound of her own voice reassured her and she returned to the small pile of dirty linens. Ragna felt almost indolent at the reduction of her workload. Auntie's dirty clothes piled high. Ragna's bread lasted for days with only the two of them at the table. The mending caught up—something she had never seen in all her years living with Uncle and Auntie. She wondered how Auntie Inga was doing without her help and stuffed back a guilty twinge.

She was married now and living her own life, Anders's wife with responsibilities of her own. She would be perfectly happy if only her friend, Bertha, lived closer. At least they could write letters. Ragna vowed to write that very evening.

Of course there was a never ending list of tasks. Wild strawberries ripened in the far meadow. Tomorrow she would spend the day picking June berries along the slough.

Willow branches were the right size for weaving baskets and Creeping Charlie threatened to take over the garden patch. Ragna had plenty to do.

As she swished an apron in the water, something moved in the trees again.

Her heart pounded and she held her breath. Coming from a large family, Ragna had never been alone. Even before the massacre, Ragna was always with family members. A sudden memory intruded into her mind of how she and Birdie were taken by the Indians. It had been a quiet day, too. And hot, like today.

She took a deep breath and turned her thoughts away from the Indian Uprising with all her strength. That was long ago. She was imagining things.

Then another flash of shadow. Ragna felt eyes upon her. Maybe a wolf. Something was there. Or someone.

She didn't know what to do. Going to the cabin would bring her closer to the trees. Anders scythed hay in the south meadow beyond the hill, opposite the trees and the house. He might think her a Nervous Nellie. That's what Gunnar would call her, anyway.

"Mrs. Vollen." Anders waved from the top of the hill.

Anders! She leapt to her feet and ran to meet him, holding her wet skirts high. The meadow bloomed yellow and purple under her bare feet and dragonflies and bumblebees flitted among the blossoms. It was as if he came as answer to her unspoken prayer.

Ragna wrapped her arms around Anders's sweaty neck and he swung her around until her wet skirts fluttered. "You're home early."

"I missed you," he said. "Couldn't stay away a minute longer."

"Why call me missus?" She struggled to catch her breath, laughing. "I'm still Ragna, you know."

"Not to me." Anders put her down on the ground but kept her in his embrace. "Back in Norway, only the noblemen's wives were named missus." He kissed her neck and held her tighter. He looked at her with those bluest of eyes and her heart melted. "You don't mind, do you?"

"So now you are a nobleman."

"You can't deny that I have a bigger farm than Old Man Bergerson back home."

"Well, Mr. Nobleman, then it's true." Ragna pulled away and straightened her apron. She ran down the slope clutching her skirts in one hand and stubbing bare toes on clumps of weeds. "Last one to the lake is a rotten egg."

Anders ran past her, pulling off his shirt as he ran. By the time she reached the water he already swam, his clothes scattered on the sand. "Come join me, Mrs. Vollen!"

"It's daylight," Ragna said, looking at the trees. "What if someone comes?"

"No one's around." Anders ducked under water and came up with a spout of water. "Obey your husband, Mrs. Vollen," Anders said with mock severity. "The water is lovely."

Ragna hesitated. She dearly loved to swim and was hot and sweaty from the race down the hill. She glanced back at the trees. Nothing there. Surely she had imagined everything. With a final look around to make sure no one was in view, Ragna stepped out of her dress and dove into the lake.

The water like a silken caress.

* * *

THEY HAD ALMOST FINISHED EATING. Anders looked handsome with his wet hair curling around his ears and his shirtsleeves pushed above his elbows. How blessed she was to be his wife. She had never been so happy. She thought to tell him about being afraid but hesitated. She didn't want him to worry.

Ragna reached across the table for the pitcher. Bread and cream again. Someday she would really cook for Anders— pork chops and stewed apples, roast beef and mashed potatoes. They were lucky that Uncle Evan supplied them with milk until they could afford their own cow. She should be grateful.

A shadow fell across the table. Ragna looked up, screamed and dropped the pitcher, splashing cream over the table and onto the floor. Anders leapt to his feet. An Indian flattened his nose against the window glass, looking in at them. The Sioux Indian who had kidnapped her and Birdie had looked in through the window the same way.

It was as if her nightmare became reality.

She pushed away from the table and hid her face in Anders's chest. "It's all right," Anders said. "Don't be afraid."

Ragna reminded herself to breathe. Holy Mary, Mother of God. There was nothing to worry about. The Sioux were exiled to Dakota long ago. Only friendly Chippewa lived in Otter Tail County. Even so, her breath came in small gasps and her heart fluttered in her chest.

Anders reached for his gun resting on hooks above the door. "I'll take care of you." He gave her a reassuring smile, opened the door, and motioned the Indian inside.

The Indian stood a head shorter than her husband, squat and muscular, with long black hair tied back from his face. He looked around the cabin with curious eyes. He was about the age of Uncle Evan and wore leather britches without a shirt. A small bag hung around his neck by a strap. Beaded moccasins dressed his feet. He smelled like rancid grease and dirty hair.

He carried a dead gray rabbit and a dripping-wet beaver carcass.

"Have a seat." Anders pointed to the bench by the table. The Indian looked at him without answering or sitting.

"Are you hungry?" Anders made an eating motion with his hands to his mouth and pointed to the table.

The Indian's eyes glittered, and he pointed to the partial loaf of bread. Ragna's heart sank. They had so little flour. Anders picked up the loaf and handed it to the Indian, who thrust the game into Anders's hands.

"*Mange takk*," Anders said with a friendly nod and put the dead animals on the floor by the table. Ragna noticed a tightening around Anders's mouth, the way his jaw worked, and knew he was more concerned than he would admit.

The Indian said something in his language and pointed to himself. Anders said the name, "Migwans." The Indian repeated the name, patting his chest and then pointed to Anders.

Anders touched his chest and said, "Anders."

Time stopped and it seemed the savage had been in their house forever. Maybe he would never leave. Of course, he was there to trade. He didn't wear war paint. Anders would protect her. Holy Mary, Mother of God, be with us now and in the hour of our death.

"Anders," The Indian said and pointed at Anders. The Indian's face relaxed until Ragna thought he might smile, but Migwans kept his mouth in a straight line. He pointed at Anders and repeated his name, then pointed at Ragna. She froze and felt helpless in the gaze of his glittering eyes.

Anders stepped closer to Ragna and put his arm around her. "Missus," he said at last. "This is my missus."

"Missus," Migwans said and pointed at Ragna. "Anders." He pointed at Anders. Then without further comment, he strode out of the cabin. Ragna and Anders watched him disappear into the trees like a shifting shadow.

"*Mange takk,*" Anders said though the Indian was too far away to hear. Ragna noticed a faint tremble in Anders's hands and heard the relief in his voice. He closed the door and set the bar, leaned against the doorframe, replaced the rifle on its hooks and pulled her close.

"I saw him," Ragna told her husband about the movement in the trees. She blushed to think he watched them bathe in the lake, watched her undress, saw her dive into the water.

Anders listened but didn't answer. Perhaps he thought of their swim, too. He returned to the supper table and spooned the soggy bread into his mouth.

Ragna looked at the window, hoping with all her might that Migwans would not return, knowing that he would. The cozy little house that seemed so perfect suddenly left her vulnerable and afraid.

"Lying Jack pays thirty cents for a beaver pelt," Anders said in a too-jolly voice. "Can you cook a beaver tail, Mrs. Vollen?"

7

I EXPECTED YOU'D NAME HER LENA CHRISTINE." Dagmar lay in the cot with the quilts kicked back for the heat, her leg stretched out before her, splinted and wrapped. Her knitting needles clicked as she worked on a mitten. "After your first child."

Serena punched the bread in the kneading bowl. With so many men to feed, she was forced to make a batch every day. Why, the day before she sat thirty-six men at the midday table. She glanced over where the girls folded clean towels.

"I had planned to name her Lena," Serena said and turned the dough with the heel of her hand. "But I had a dream."

"What kind of dream?" Dagmar reached toward her leg with the knitting needle, scratching beneath the bandages.

Serena looked again toward the girls. It wasn't something she wanted to talk about in front of her daughter but she had little choice. It was clear that Dagmar wouldn't let up until she answered.

"I dreamed that Lena Christine came to my bedside and whispered in my ear." Serena rolled the dough, added a little goose grease to her hands and kneaded it some more. "Asked me not to give her name to anyone else."

The words lingered in the room and Maren stared at her with an open mouth. "You mean you almost named me after my dead sister?"

"Lena Christine was our mother's name," Kersten said.

"Lots of children are named for older siblings already in heaven." Serena rubbed more goose grease on her hands. "Don't worry, Maren Rose is your name."

"Smart not to dwell in the past," Dagmar said. "To move into the future without dragging along the weight of yesterday." She stretched the knitting needle to scratch her toes.

Serena dug deep into the dough with the heels of her hands.

"It's high time you get on with living," Dagmar said. "Find yourself a new man."

Serena felt a flush of anger creep up her cheeks. She had almost forgotten how blunt Dagmar could be, rude actually. It was midmorning, and Serena had been up since the first rooster crow. She had fixed breakfast, butchered a pullet hen and washed a load of dishtowels and sheets. Dagmar should offer gratitude instead of criticism.

"Gust wasn't worth all these years of mourning," Dagmar said. "Don't remember him as better than he was."

A strong urge to defend her husband welled up in Serena's throat. This was the last straw. She thumped the dough with all her strength.

"Girls," Serena said. "Time to play with the kittens." As an afterthought, she added, "Dump the slop pail on your way."

As the little girls raced toward the barn, Serena considered a response. Dagmar was a sick woman, laid up with little else to occupy her thoughts. But the old woman had overstepped herself. Her private life was none of Dagmar's business.

"Gust was the father of my child," Serena said at last. "Please don't speak ill of him in front of Maren again." She pounded the dough with a clenched fist.

"It's time you marry." Dagmar said. "If you were my daughter I'd say the same." She wiped her sweaty brow with a crumpled handkerchief and pressed it to her chest. "As your mother would if she were alive."

Serena thought to tell her that only the past week she had received a marriage proposal when Ole clattered into the room with an armful of kitchen wood. He dropped the sticks into the wood box, pulled two letters from his pocket and placed them on the table.

"Mail for you, Serena. Mailman says a mule train is heading this way from Georgetown." He drank deeply and put the dipper back into the bucket. "We'll have a full house for midday."

Serena turned the dough and kneaded it without comment. A pot of chicken soup simmered on the stove. She would churn the butter while the bread baked. She forced herself to focus on the work rather than Dagmar's comments.

"I was just telling her," Dagmar said, "that it's high time she found another man."

"Mother!" Ole's face turned red from the neck up.

"She's a young woman with plenty to offer," Dagmar said. "And look at you, Ole, single all these years."

"That's enough!" Ole's face set into a scowl.

Serena turned her back to them to hide her red face, and divided the dough into greased bread pans. She wanted to run but there was no place to go.

"Apologize, Ma," Ole said. "I mean it."

"I'm sorry," Dagmar said with a sniffle after a long pause. "I'm just a foolish old woman with too many opinions."

Serena set the yeasty pans on the table where the morning sun could warm them. She washed her hands and picked up the letters. One was in Jensina's ornate scribble. The other was from Julian Gustafson.

She stuffed both letters into her apron pocket and left to gather pieplant from the garden, any excuse to get away from their peering eyes.

> Dear Serena, Mother is ill and going down fast. It's a bad fever.
> She's asking for Maren Rose. Please come home. Julian

It was as if a spider's thread reached out to snag her, even from this distance. Whenever she was with her husband's mother she felt stifled, smothered, and invisible.

Impossible. She wouldn't return to Burr Oak quite yet. She crumpled the letter and stuffed it back into her pocket.

Jensina's letter chatted long about the children, the family, and the crops.

> You must come home before the garden comes in. Surely you realize our
> need during this busy time and your responsibility towards us.

Serena stomped her foot and let out a small scream. She was not their slave. Just because she did not have a husband did not make her less of a person. She would not go back to Burr Oak. Not yet.

* * *

JUST AS THE BREAD CAME OUT OF THE OVEN, the muleskinners straggled in, sweaty and tired. Their conversation was about the grasshoppers to the north, south and west, speculating on when they would arrive in Pomme de Terre.

Their conversation caused Serena a niggle of worry. She must talk to Mr. Gardner about her property. As she served the soup and sliced the bread, she made plans. She would walk over to the hotel, ask for Mr. Gardner, and tell him of her intent to sell.

If only she knew about land values.

"Mrs. Gustafson," one of the men said, "we asked for butter."

Serena hurried to refill the dish, embarrassed to be lost in the clouds. Without the help of the girls, she ran her legs off to keep everyone served. Ole tried to help, but his clumsy crutches got in the way. Dagmar dozed in her bed and for once kept quiet.

After the dishes were finished, she would visit Mr. Gardner.

8

EVAN HAD PUT OFF TELLING INGA about the new job but could delay no longer. He sent the little boys to chase blackbirds away from the garden and found Inga in the cabin churning butter. He told her the news as simply as he could, hoping she would see the sense of his decision, see it as the hand of Almighty God.

"You're doing *what?*" Inga looked at him with a blank expression and forgot to push the dasher.

"I'd be a crazy man to turn down regular money in such times." Evan had known Inga would be upset, but he had no other choice. Providing for his family was his priority. "*Betre aa boye seg enn stoeyte seg.* Better bend than bump."

"But the family." Inga jerked the dasher, tossed the cover aside and drained bluish buttermilk into a crock. "The hay . . . and wheat." She lifted the glob of butter with a wooden paddle and placed it in the carved bowl dedicated only to butter making.

"The boys will do the chores and Anders will help with the hay," Evan said. "Milton will harvest the wheat if I'm not back in time." He hated feeling defensive about his decision when he knew he was doing the right thing. "Captain Van der Hoerck didn't say how long the job would last."

Inga's face set hard as stone and she raised her chin, a sure sign that she was angry. "You'll lose it all if you're not on the claim." Inga used the paddle to work out the buttermilk still in the solid butter, every motion an angry jab. She pressed the butter against the sides of the bowl and poured cold water over to sweeten it while Evan explained about the changes in the law.

"The law is changed, so I can leave without penalty."

"Then maybe I'll leave, too," Inga drained the butter, added a pinch of salt and worked it in using the paddles again. She gathered the butter into a large lump and plopped it in the butter dish with more force than necessary. "Find a paying job and leave home without a thought for the children."

"That's not fair." Evan clenched his jaw. "I'm thinking about the children—that's why I'm taking work."

"Then go." She grabbed the butter dish and headed for the root cellar in the old dugout. "We'll manage without you." She stalked out of the cabin, not looking back.

Evan sighed. Nothing was easy in this world. Teamstering was a golden opportunity, not what they had planned, but an open door nonetheless. *Betre foere vis en netter var.* Better wise beforehand than aware afterwards.

Inga would get used to the idea.

"Far," Knut said sticking his head over the edge of the loft with his fingers keeping place in his Bible. "Are you leaving us?"

Evan was surprised to hear his son's voice. It was the middle of the day. Knut should be out in the potato patch instead of reading. Knut was the studious one in the family. While Evan hated to discourage reading habits, he needed to be fair as well. "Did you finish your chores?"

"I traded," Knut said. "Gunnar's hoeing my row in the garden, and later I'll help him with his Catechism."

Knut had his work cut out for him if he would teach Gunnar the Catechism. Gunnar was thick-headed when it came to reading or study of any kind. But give him a foot race or a chance to arm wrestle, and that boy could compete with grown men.

"Are you going?" Knut's brow wrinkled into a frown. He had the large forehead of Evan's people.

"Just for work," Evan said. "Teamstering to Fort Wadsworth in Dakota Territory." He didn't know how much he should tell his son. "Grasshoppers, you know."

"We'll be all right," Knut closed the Bible and climbed down from the loft. "I'll take care of things while you're gone."

He looked so serious that Evan had to smile. "I know you will."

* * *

Mosquitoes kept them awake into the night. Evan added green branches to the smudge fire alongside the cabin perimeter and returned to bed. Inga turned her back to him. He could always tell when she pretended to be asleep.

He lay awake, tormented by the heat if he closed the door but tortured by mosquitoes if he opened it. It seemed he had just dozed off when the sound of rhythmic pounding filled the cabin. Loud wailing came from the direction of the lake.

"What is it?" Inga sat up with a start and stifled a scream with the back of her hand. "Dear God, Indians!"

Evan struggled into his britches, reached for the ancient Danzig muzzleloader from its place on the wall, and poured shot and ball into its barrel. Then he cracked open the door and stared out into the darkness. Only the stars and the weak glow of the waning moon. Wild singing and pounding drums came from across the lake, the sounds magnified over the water.

"Are they on the warpath?" Inga whispered with breathless voice.

"*Nei*," Evan said. "Just carrying on."

"How do you know?"

There was no way he could know for sure, but the Mormons told how the Indians gathered and danced in the woods. Some heathen custom of their religion.

"They're across the lake. Minding their own business."

Evan pulled the skin away from the window opening, just enough for him to see out over the water. No Indians in sight though the drumming grew louder and the singing more frantic. He pulled Inga closer to his side and they stood together, not talking, listening to the Chippewa.

"Mor," Knut called from the loft. "What is it?"

"Go back to sleep," Evan said. "The Indians are having a little powwow, that's all. Nothing to worry about."

Although Inga did not say a word, he felt the blame, thick enough to cut with a knife. He had hoped to leave the next day. He didn't know how Inga would cope without him.

"I know you have to go," Inga said at last. Undulating wails continued in the frenzy of the drums. "But I'm afraid." She straightened her spine and lifted her chin. "I won't be caught unprepared if something bad happens while you're gone." She sniffed hard and clenched her fists. "You can go, and with my blessing . . . but build a coffin first."

Just the thought of coming home and finding one of his children dead and buried almost crumpled his resolve.

"My parents always kept an extra in the *stabbuhr* for emergencies," she said. "We'll do the same."

Ululating wails pierced the night even louder. Inga pressed closer into his side. Evan wondered if the Indians would come screaming with raised scalping knives. He fought back old terrors. The sights and sounds of massacre.

"I'm afraid." Her voice small in the darkness.

"Then I can't go." Evan pulled her into his arms and they stood a long while in the darkness, the wailing songs and incessant drums almost loud enough to drown out the pounding of his heart.

"You have to." Inga's voice a whisper. "The grasshoppers . . . we'll lose everything unless you take this job."

Dear God, what could he do?

The answer fell into his mind like a key opening a lock. Anders and Ragna could stay with Inga while he was gone. The newlyweds had no livestock and little land under cultivation.

They must all make the best of it, but it didn't mean it would be easy for any of them. His chest twisted at the thought of leaving Inga and the children. No matter how he justified it, *borte er ikkje aa vere heime.* Away is not at home.

9

RAGNA LET THE FIRE DIE OUT AND SWARMS of mosquitoes whined down the chimney into the cabin. Mosquitoes tormented unmercifully with the door open. She started a small fire in the fireplace, just enough to discourage the blood-thirsty insects, but it made the cabin even hotter.

Anders slept swathed in a sheet to protect against the mosquitoes and Ragna slipped into bed beside him. She dozed into a fitful dream about her sister, Birdie. In her dream, they draped Baby Evan's clean soakers over hazelnut bushes to dry. Birdie was too short, and Ragna scolded her for dragging the clean cloths in the dirt. The sound of drums intruded into her dream and Ragna bolted upright into that limbo between waking and sleeping.

"Anders!" She jumped out of bed, reached for her shawl and peered through the window. Syl and Milton had threatened a chivaree. But instead of their neighbors coming to celebrate their wedding with yells and whistles, she saw only the milky glow of the moon refracted in glass.

Her knees weakened. She grabbed onto the side of the table for support. "Wake up. Indians!"

Her husband slept like a stone after working all day in the fields. She called his name again and shook his shoulder, thinking the whole time how worthless he was in an emergency. The drums pounded loud enough to wake the dead and yet Anders slept through them. He had promised to protect her. For the first time in her married life, she realized he might not.

"Get up!"

He struggled to his feet and pulled on his britches. The drumming was louder now. Ragna froze with terror as the wailing started. Surely any minute, Migwans would swoop down upon them painted for war.

Anders reached for the rifle and peered through the window, rubbing sleep from his eyes with his free hand.

"Can't see a thing," he said, "but it sounds like they're close by." He opened the door. Mosquitoes swarmed inside with a swooping bat. The drumbeats and singing blared louder with the door open. He was only outside a moment before he hurried back in, and then closed and barred the door. Anders slapped mosquitoes off his neck and reached for the broom. He opened the door and chased the bat outside.

"They're across the lake." He held his gun, leaning his back against the door, slapping mosquitoes off his chest and arms. "Some kind of Indian ceremony."

"What can we do?" Her voice squeaked in the darkness.

"Go back to bed," Anders said with a yawn. "As long as we hear the drums, there's no danger."

"And if the drums stop?" Ragna's heart throbbed in her chest. Every drumbeat prodded old memories of being kidnapped by the Sioux.

"The Saints said the Indians dance and sing for days at a time." Anders peered through the window again. "They're not hurting anyone." He stifled a yawn. "Don't worry. I'll take care of you." He placed the gun across the table and climbed into bed wearing his britches. "It won't do any good to stay up all night."

Soon Anders's heavy breathing told her he was asleep. Fear pushed in from all sides, almost smothering her. A wave of disappointment washed over her. She could not depend on Anders for protection.

She dropped to her knees beside their bed. "Holy Mary, Mother of God." She reached for Marta's rosary given to her as a wedding present. She fingered the beads as she recited the prayers. "Blessed are thou among women and blessed is the fruit of thy womb, Jesus." The ancient words a hedge against the terror of the night.

* * *

THE DRUMS DIDN'T STOP.

Ragna spent the entire night on her knees. Anxiety overwhelmed her whenever she stopped praying. She walked through the valley of death. She determined not to be afraid, but old memories fueled a tornado of unrest. She was too afraid to sleep. Though Anders slept close beside her, she felt alone.

As the sun lightened the eastern horizon, she gathered all her courage and peeked out the cabin door. Smoke curled beyond the trees across the lake. Drums still pounded and the singing did not end. The air fresh and moist on her face, the sound of robins and meadowlarks blended in with the Indian cries. No one in sight.

She was afraid to use the privy. Any moment she expected painted Red Men to come streaming out of the woods. Ragna barred the door, added wood to the fireplace and put water on for coffee. Her mind focused on the prayers.

"I've plenty to do around the cabin," Anders's voice made her jump. She hadn't realized he was awake. "I'll not go to the fields today."

He pulled on his shirt and boots and picked up his gun. "I'll walk you to the outhouse."

Afterwards, Anders fetched a bucket of water from the spring and an armful of kitchen wood. Ragna held her breath until he returned to the house, then threw her arms around his neck and sobbed. She could not help herself. She had more happiness than she ever thought possible and now suddenly that happiness was like a thread so easily broken.

"It's all right," he whispered in her ear. "I won't leave you."

She prayed the Our Father under her breath as she sliced the bread. She thanked God for her husband, for their cabin, for their health and future. Repeatedly she recited her blessings—that Crooked Lightning had rescued her, that she had survived the Indian war, that Auntie and Uncle had raised her, that God had sent Anders to her, and Marta Sevald had taught her the prayers.

It was as if she built a hedge around them with prayer. Surely, God would keep them safe if she kept prayerful.

She kissed Anders on the top of his head while she poured coffee. How good of him to stay inside with her. She felt such tenderness toward him. If it were to be their last day on earth, she would at least demonstrate how much she loved him. Her last words would be of utmost kindness.

It was all she could do in the shadow of the drums.

Her anxiety increased as the throbbing intensified, the wailing voices louder and more insistent. She couldn't eat. Ragna paced back and forth across the small cabin, looking out the window, trying to block the sounds of the Red Men.

"Now then, Mrs. Vollen." Anders placed a slab of wood on his lap. "Can you guess what I'm making for my beautiful wife?" The carving knife gouged a curl of wood and released a whiff of fresh oak. He worked the wood, encouraging Ragna to converse. She knew he was trying to make her forget what was going on across the lake.

"I don't know," Ragna said. "Maybe a mangle?"

"Now what would you do with a mangle, Mrs. Vollen?" Anders cast a sly grin.

Ragna teased. "I wouldn't dream of returning it." Norwegian suitors traditionally presented prospective brides with a wooden mangle to smooth wrinkled clothing. A returned mangle meant a marriage refusal.

"It's not a mangle." Anders shaved more wooden curls from the board before him. "I already have my bride."

The drums pounded and Anders carved. Every so often, Anders would ask her to guess what he was making. It wasn't a cupboard door or a sign for their door. It wasn't a bread plate.

Ragna couldn't focus on anything but the drums, the wailing, and her prayers. Finally, she took the rosary out of her apron pocket and knelt again by their bed. It grew hotter as the sun climbed the sky even though they let the fire burn out in the fireplace. Sweat poured down her face and dripped down her back. Anders's face flushed in the heat.

Anders propped the door open with a block of firewood, but Ragna could not bear it.

"Please," she said. "Keep it closed."

Anders obeyed and returned to his carving.

"I've finished." Anders held up a carved wooden washboard. "All finished but the final sanding."

"*Mange takk!*" Ragna had never thought to own one. It felt exactly right in her arms. "It will save me many an aching back."

"Good." He stood up and stretched his legs, picked up the gun and opened the door. "We can't stay inside forever." Light spilled in with a welcome breath of freshness although the drums and wailing sounded much louder. Anders scanned the clearing around the cabin, the lake, the pathway that led north to Milton's.

"Come, we'll go to Evan's. It's better than being prisoners in this cabin."

Guilt washed across Ragna. She had not once thought of Auntie Inga. Of course, she and the boys would be terrified. "I'll pack a change of clothes." She bustled around the house, wrapping the loaf of bread in a dishtowel, tucking the coffee bag into her deep apron pocket and reaching for the half-filled sack of flour. Going to Uncle Evan's was the perfect plan. Safety in numbers, surely. The relief almost giddy.

"We'll stop for Milton," Anders said. "Take him along."

Ragna looked at their little cabin, the washboard on the table, the window glass. It might be gone when they returned. Maybe burned like her father's house. She sniffed back a tear and reached for the rosary. She picked up her bonnet and shawl. Then the new washboard.

CANDACE SIMAR

"Leave the bread." Anders said. "Indians might see it as a sign of friendship and leave things alone."

Ragna could not bear the thought of Indians going through their belongings. She swallowed a sob.

"It's convenient to be without livestock." Anders propped the gun across his shoulder and carried the partial sack of flour in his hand. "We're lucky, Mrs. Vollen," he said with forced gaiety and reached for Ragna's hand. "Poor people have less to worry about."

The drums pounded louder as the sun reached its zenith. Desperate wailing sounded as Anders and Ragna scurried down the trail toward Milton's place. Anders held her hand and Ragna resisted the urge to cover her ears and scream. Instead, she prayed another Hail Mary and concentrated on the path beneath her feet.

How good it felt to reach the woods, out of sight of the shoreline. Then she remembered how Migwans skulked in the trees. Panic welled within her and she dropped Anders's hand and ran down the footpath.

"Ragna," Anders said. Fanatic ululations sounded over the waters of Long Lake. "Wait up."

Ragna was too afraid to stop. She ran as fast as she could. Anders caught up with her. They ran until they reached Milton's door. Ragna doubled over with pain in her side, trying to catch her breath, looking back to be sure no Indians had followed them.

No sign of Indians other than the wailing songs across the water accompanied by the incessant beat of the drums.

10

I	T'S RAINING," DAGMAR SAID from her bed. "Hear the drops on the roof." S e r -
	ena scrubbed the last cooking pot from the noon meal. Chicken fat congealed and
	floated on top of the dishwater. She heard Dagmar but paid little attention. As
Serena scalded the pot with boiling water from the stove, she planned a visit to Mr. Gardner. She would go in spite of the rain and take the girls along. She didn't care to be alone
with the man.

In the weeks she had been at Pomme de Terre, Serena had procrastinated selling
her land. She couldn't explain it if she tried, but every time she thought to speak to the
prospective buyer, she changed her mind.

Not today. Today she would speak to the man in spite of any distraction. Kersten
and Maren stacked eggs in a basket for trade at Gardner's Store. A perfect excuse to walk
to the village.

"I worry for the wheat," Dagmar said. "A hard rain might set it back."

"Look!" Maren's voice made Serena turn around.

Dagmar raised herself to a half-sitting position in her cot in an effort to see out
the kitchen window. "Good God, not hail."

It was as if a blanket covered the sun. Grasshoppers swarmed over the ground and
outbuildings. They clattered in the stovepipe. They crawled under the door.

Serena scooped them with the dustpan and fed them into the kitchen fire. One
squirted tobacco juice, its fetid excrement, on her hands. They crackled and stank in the
blaze while she hurried to scrub her hands in the wash bowl.

"It's grasshoppers." Maren left the egg basket and sat on the edge of Dagmar's bed, taking her gnarled hand in her smaller one. Maren's face gleamed white against the dark wall of the cabin.

"It's dark as night." Kersten wiped tears with the back of her hand and moved closer to Serena.

Serena's dreams of Iowa City and St. Paul washed away as surely as the chicken fat had melted in the boiling water. She would end up back in Burr Oak with her sister's family. Or be forced to marry Julian. Despair washed over her.

Pomme de Terre brought nothing but bad luck. It had been hellish in 1862 and now it was again in 1876. Surely cursed of God.

Anton struggled into the inn, slapping hoppers away from his face and brushing them off his arms. He slammed the door and looked toward the cot where his wife lay.

"Chewed holes in my shirt." Anton stomped the grasshoppers with a sickening crunch, then tossed them into the stove renewing the stench that made Serena sick to her stomach. "It's the worst of luck with the wheat looking so good."

"Damn it," Dagmar said through clenched teeth. Sweat dripped down her pale face and her gray hair swirled wild around her head. "We'll lose it all." She threw her arm over her face and wept into the inside of her elbow.

They stood in the kitchen in the darkness, the stove blazing with burning hoppers, the only noise the chewing of grasshoppers and Dagmar's weeping.

Ole pushed into the room, his crutches slipping on crushed locusts. He collapsed to the floor in a clatter. Serena reached to help him up, but his angry glare made her step back. Anton secured the door while Ole grabbed the side of the table and pulled himself back upright. Serena reached for the fallen crutches and handed them to Ole. The crutch padding was filthy and sweat stained. He didn't look at or thank her.

Serena grabbed the broom and swept grasshoppers as if her life depended upon it. The stench of burning hoppers gagging, the grinding sound of the horde of chewing insects loud as a thunderstorm.

"We've got to do something," Ole said. "We can't just sit here. They're in the wheat." He clenched his hands on the rungs of his crutches and his eyes became black holes in his face.

Serena envisioned how he had looked during the war. Like a mad man, angry enough to turn the artillery on advancing uniformed soldiers without hesitation. Her thoughts quickly went from dying soldiers to Gust being killed by arrows on their Pomme de Terre farm.

"Maybe a smudge." Anton, bent and frail, looked older than his years. "We've nothing to lose by trying."

"Then don't just stand there." Dagmar's voice screeched in exasperation. "Start a smudge before it's too late. By God, I'll go out and do it myself!"

"Don't be foolish, Mother." Anton lit the lamp. "Rest yourself."

The men left carrying the lantern. More grasshoppers swarmed in through the open door.

"Girls." Serena forced her voice back to a normal timber although the roar of the hoppers continued outside. "We'd best get busy." Her limbs felt numb and she wanted only to crawl up in the loft, go to bed and cover her head.

Her mother had a solution for every situation, big or little. Serena followed her example. She grasped the broom and began sweeping the hoppers that scattered across the kitchen floor. They were nasty things, unpredictable in their leaping and flying, with sharp wings that cut into the flesh. Worst of all was their horrid odor.

"There is work to do."

11

T HE DRUMS POUNDED THROUGH TWO long nights and one day along the shores
of Long Lake, then abruptly ceased the morning of the third day. Evan climbed
out of bed and checked to make sure the boys still slept in the loft. He glanced
over to where Milton, Anders, and Ragna stirred on floor pallets.

The silence reverberated through the trees and over the water—the silence louder
than the drums.

"What now?" Inga's face chalked white beside him.

"I don't see anything," Evan said.

Milton and Anders struggled into their clothes and joined them at the doorway.
They reached for their guns and checked to make sure they were armed. All eyes fastened
across the lake where the drumming had stopped.

"What is it?" Knut said from the loft. "What's happening?"

"Nothing," Inga said. "Please lie beside the baby in our bed."

"You've a clear view of the lake." Milton's tone reminded Evan that he had been a
soldier in the War of Rebellion. "But you're blindsided to the rear of the house."

Milton stepped out of the cabin and walked around back. Evan felt more vulnerable without the former soldier with them. How easily the cabin would burn. Maybe
they should move to the old dugout—safer than a log dwelling in an Indian attack.

Evan stifled a remembrance of the burning Larson cabin during the Indian Massacre and took a firmer grip on the old Danzig muzzleloader.

"We must set guards," Milton said as he came back into the cabin. He wiped his
sweaty face with the back of his sleeve and hitched up his trousers. "Anders, watch from

the top of the hill behind the cabin. Sit on the east side of the rock pile and keep your eyes open, especially to the north."

Anders hugged and kissed Ragna, who sniffled great sobs. "Be careful," she said.

"A warning shot if you see anything." Milton shook his hand and opened the door for Anders to leave. Anders scanned the clearing and hurried up the hill, crouching down to make himself less of a target. "That leaves us to watch the south," Milton said.

Evan's mouth turned to dust. He could not afford to be a hero. With six children, he could take no chances.

It was as if Milton understood without explanation. "I'll go," he said. "Keep the children inside."

They waited all morning but nothing happened. The sun climbed higher in the sky, but the Indians never came. The boys quarreled in the loft, complaining of the heat in the closed cabin, while the baby fussed and refused to nurse. Ragna mended Sigurd's shirt.

"I want to be with Anders," Ragna said as the afternoon turned to evening. They had let the fire die out, and Inga planned a cold supper of cottage cheese and milk. "Let me take his supper to him."

Evan shook his head, remembering her mother's fate during the uprising.

"I'll go," Evan said. "You take my place until I get back." He handed the gun to Ragna, told her where to stand and reminded her how to fire the ancient muzzle loader.

"Anders!" Evan balanced the heaping bowl in his hands while climbing the uneven ground. "Don't shoot. I'm bringing supper."

"I thought you'd never come," Anders said and handed the gun to Evan. "I'm starving." He reached for the bowl and spoon.

Evan scanned the horizon. From this higher vantage point he could see across the lake. No smoke rose over the trees. He could see Milton standing guard on the south end of the property, just beyond a clump of birches. All was quiet. Evan had just decided there was nothing further to worry about when two horses and a pack mule came over the crest of the hill. One was an Indian.

The other was Lying Jack.

"Halloo!" Lying Jack said when he saw the men holding guns by the trail and held out his hands in front of him in mock defense. "Don't shoot! We come in peace!"

They greeted the trader. "See any Indians?"

"A bunch of old peoples and childrens heading north to their summer camp on Otter Tail Lake."

Anders and Evan looked at each other in relief.

"Trouble?" Lying Jack climbed down from his horse and held the reins as it nibbled long grass by the rock pile. A striped gopher scurried out of its hole and ran into the bushes.

"Guess not," Evan said. "Drummed two nights and a day and almost scared the women to death."

"Nothing to be ascared of," Lying Jack said with a big grin and a slap on Anders's back. "They's just stirrings up the young bucks to makes war on the Sioux."

"But the Sioux are gone," Anders said. "None left in Minnesota."

"They's heading west of the Pomme de Terre River," Lying Jack said. "Out Dakota way. They young bucks haves to make war before they can get married or wear feathers." He spoke a few words to Many Beavers in her language and she climbed down from her horse and led them toward the house. "Don't you worry none. Them's fight will be western of here."

Evan remembered the curious faces of the Indian boys who had looked through the cracks in the logs. He tried to imagine Little Wolf, the oldest of the three, painted and on the war path against the Sioux. He hoped he would come back alive.

12

THE NEXT DAY, RAGNA FOUND UNCLE EVAN under a shady elm near the old dugout where he cleaved boards from a rough log. Not easy without a sawyer's tools, but Uncle could do anything he set his mind to do. At least that's what Ragna thought. It was pleasant in the shade with the fragrance of wild roses blooming along the path and a soft breeze blowing in from the west.

Auntie Inga had used Ragna's flour to bake flatbread for Uncle Evan's journey. She hardboiled two dozen eggs and tucked a precious packet of dried pigeon breasts into the bundle he would carry.

Uncle must walk to Herman where he would catch the train to Morris. At Morris he would meet the teamsters heading to Fort Wadsworth in Dakota Territory. It was a long journey, and Uncle hoped to ride with the mailman out of Dollner's store. The mailman drove a two-wheeled cart and sometimes had room for an extra rider.

Uncle Evan had said he must finish a final task before he left, even though the morning was passing and the Indian scare had delayed him several days.

It had rained during the night and long worms curled in the dirt. Night crawlers, according to Milton, were good for fishing. Ragna reached down and gathered them into her apron pocket. The feel of the slimy worms, gritty with dirt, made her shudder but she knew Anders would be delighted. Perhaps he and the boys would have time to go fishing later in the day. Her mouth watered at the thought of fresh fish fried in salted butter.

Anders and the boys were making hay in the meadow, the twins and the older boys jumping on top of the stack to trample it down as Anders pitched more hay to the top.

Their laughter and screams wafted up the hill.

"What are you building?" Ragna spoke more to get a conversation started than wanting to know. She had missed her uncle more than she would admit.

Uncle Evan straightened up and rubbed the small of his back. His long red beard carried flecked strands of white. He looked at her a long moment before he answered.

"A precaution only." He picked up the wood plane from the toolbox and rubbed it across the rough lumber. "Your Auntie asked me to build it. You know how she worries." He planed a long curl of fragrant wood. "It's a coffin."

Ragna stepped back in horror. An image of Auntie's dead baby flashed into Ragna's memory. The baby had been as small as a mouse, though perfectly formed. Anders and Ragna had buried it in the family cemetery at Alexandria, wrapped only in a dishtowel.

But this coffin would have done no good for the baby's burial. It was built for someone much older. She pictured Gunnar, always the reckless one, lying in a coffin, and pushed away the unwelcome image.

With every stroke of the plane, Uncle voiced a concern. Anything might happen while he was gone—Indians, sickness, accident, drowning. Ragna must take care with the children when they played around the lake.

"Nothing will happen, Uncle."

"I pray to God you're right. But if it would," he straightened again and pushed closed fists into the small of his back, "use your judgment. You have a good head on your shoulders, and I know you'll do the right thing. And if something happens," his voice broke and he paused a long minute, "get word to Dollner's Store. The mailman will take a message to Fort Wadsworth." Uncle fitted two rough boards and hammered them together with a ten-penny nail. "Captain Van der Hoerck will know where to find me."

"We'll be fine," Ragna said although she wasn't sure she spoke the truth.

"Inga needs your help with the baby." He mumbled the words over several nails held between his lips. "I'm depending on you." He hammered another board.

The hideous wooden box took form before her eyes. Ragna swallowed hard.

"Is this a funeral?" Milton said suddenly beside them. Ragna had not noticed him ride into the yard but she saw his white mule by the house. He spoke in a loud, jolly voice. "I didn't think to bring my good hanky."

"Uncle Milton," Sigurd ran from the cabin to meet him with Musky running at his heels. Milton scooped up the boy in both arms and held him over his head while the puppy jumped on his legs and chewed the bottom of Milton's trousers.

"Thank God I got here before you left." Milton juggled the giggling boy and patted the dog's head. "Change of plans."

"I don't understand." Uncle Evan said with a scratch to his thinning hair.

"Captain Van Der Hoerck sent word to Dollner's store." Milton swatted Sigurd's bottom and shooed him off to play with Musky. Anders and the other boys waved from the field and headed toward the house. Auntie Inga came out wiping her hands on her apron.

"What about?"

"He wants you at Cold Spring by the twenty-fifth of May," Milton said. "Meet the teamsters there instead. They're short a man and need you real bad." Milton tucked his thumbs in his galluses with a pleased look on his face. "Puts you on the payroll at least a fortnight sooner."

"But that's the day after tomorrow," Auntie Inga said. "Evan can't get there in time."

"If only I had Steel Gray." Uncle nailed an end piece that connected the larger boards. "Should never have traded him."

"Goldie and Ryder are nothing to sneeze at," Milton said. "I'll let you take Whitey in exchange for the use of your team while you're gone."

* * *

RAGNA SMILED A GREETING AS ANDERS and the boys came in from the hay meadow, Anders sweaty and covered with hay chaff. Ragna didn't dream Uncle's conversation might affect them until she heard Milton speak Anders's name.

"Anders can ride along to return the mule."

Ragna tried to protest, but nothing came out of her dry throat. They were barely wed and now her man would be leaving. The Indians might come back, painted this time.

Anders didn't ask her opinion but joined the discussion without as much as a look in her direction. Ragna would stay with Auntie and the children.

Milton, with military experience, would stay at Uncle's farm to protect the women and children. He would sleep in the dugout. Uncle Evan and Anders would ride double on Milton's mule. Afterward, Anders and Ragna would stay in the dugout until Uncle Evan returned in the fall. They discussed crops, hay, the fields needing work, where to pile the gathered stones, and the care of the animals.

Uncle Evan would settle with them after he was paid.

Anders never consulted her before making the decision.

* * *

"GOLDIE HAS A NICK ON HER FLANK from Ryder's horn." Uncle Evan opened a wooden box from the corner shelf. "Treat it with this." He handed Ragna a small metal can of ointment labeled Udder Balm. "It heals any wound on man or beast." Uncle hesitated and spoke carefully. "Spare the animals as much as you can."

"We will," Anders said. "Don't worry about a thing."

Uncle reached again to the top shelf where he took down four silver dollars. He put two into his pocket and gave the other two to Inga. "For emergencies."

Sigurd climbed out from behind the wood stove and held onto his father's leg. Musky chewed on Uncle's wooden clog. Fat tears rolled down Sigurd's cheeks. Auntie's lip quivered.

"I'll be back in four days," Anders said as he reached over for a kiss. Ragna pulled away. "A week at the most." He seemed happy to leave her. She felt like crying. He could have asked her opinion.

"Milton will take care of you," Anders said. "You've nothing to worry about."

Ragna and Auntie Inga watched the men leave on the mule as Milton herded the boys to the lake for a quick swim before returning to the hayfield. Anders waved from his perch on the back of the mule.

Auntie crossed her arms tightly in front of her stomach and crimped her lips hard.

Ragna thought longingly of their little cabin. Instead of being a grown up taking care of her own house, she was back staying with Auntie, and she and Anders would sleep in the filthy dugout filled with centipedes and spiders. The unexpected change made her feel like a child again.

She didn't like it. Not one bit.

13

DAGMAR PROPPED HERSELF UP on her elbows to look out the window. "They're letting up a little." Her face looked florid and puffy. Dagmar was so worked up by the grasshoppers that Serena worried her friend might have a stroke.

Serena looked out the window, too, and her heart sank. Dagmar may think it was letting up, but Serena knew the opposite. Though grasshoppers weren't swarming, they now crawled over every inch of ground, eating everything in their paths. The grasshoppers were there to stay.

The situation was worse than before. Smoke rolled over the garden patch where Anton and Ole tended smudges. Serena could tell even from this distance that smoke did not dissuade the hoppers. Maybe smoke attracted more.

"Sistermine." Kersten's arms wrapped around Serena's waist. "I'm scared."

"I'm scared, too," Serena whispered in her ear and kissed the top of her head. "But don't tell anyone. We have to be very brave."

"Remember what our Tommy Harris said back in the Indian War?" Dagmar said in her high-pitched voice that always shrilled when excited. "That God is always with us to help in our hour of need."

"He did say that," Serena said. "That nothing is too broken for God to fix." She looked again out the window. The ground was a roiling black mass, the sound of grinding grasshopper jaws loud enough to be heard indoors, like a clattering train engine.

"Let's pray then," Dagmar said. "Like Tommy taught us." She patted the side of the bed and motioned Kersten and Maren to join her.

Serena looked out the window at the glowing flames in the garden. Anton and Ole stood nearby with buckets of water as fire burned the garden patch. Serena knelt beside Dagmar's bed. It seemed a wasted effort but it couldn't hurt. Serena had to do something.

They prayed for protection, help, and deliverance from the locusts. Serena prayed a silent prayer for guidance concerning the sale of her land. Only God could rescue her now. The land surely had fallen back to its value during the Indian War. Back then its value was nothing.

Anton and Ole clomped into the inn with their heavy boots. Ole went directly to his room and slammed the door. Anton removed his cap and walked over to the stove where he shook the coffee pot before pouring a cup. His face drooped. "It's useless." He slurped his coffee. "We burned the garden, but maybe the potatoes will be spared."

"Nothing left at all?" Dagmar's voice a shrill whisper.

"*Nei*," Anton said.

"Not a kale plant nor a cabbage?"

Anton shook his head. "Don't worry, Mother," he said. "We've weathered worse than this. We'll make it somehow."

Ole opened his door and propelled himself over to his mother's bed, jabbing angry stabs into the puncheon floor with his crutches. He shared his concern that the grasshoppers might find their way into the haybarn to get the hay crop. They debated the barn's tight door and shutters.

"I've got to make sure they don't get in," Ole said as he pulled up his shirt collar to keep the hoppers from falling down his back. "Damn them, anyway."

Anton drank his coffee and covered his neck and face with an old scarf before returning to continue his battle against the hoppers. He gathered them into burn piles, raking without end in sight. The insects flew up in his face, scratching the soft parts around his eyes, chewing his clothing and hair until they finally drove him back inside.

"It's no use." Anton stood by the window, watching the destruction of his efforts. His face looked hollow-eyed, his gnarly hands locked and interlocked together.

"Bestefar." Kersten tugged at his shirtsleeve. "Are you afraid?"

"*Nei*," Anton said with a start. "Of course not. I'm planning a new ax handle, that's all. I've just the right piece of ironwood tucked away for such a day as this."

Kersten went with him into the lean-to where the firewood was kept. They returned with the branch in hand.

Anton and the women stayed inside all afternoon, the women tending knitting and sewing while Anton whittled the ironwood into a smooth handle for his ax head. They kept the cook stove going to discourage hoppers from getting into the house through the stovepipe. Every so often there would be a clatter of wings and legs on the stovepipe, a hiss and then their putrid smell when another landed in the firebox.

"Ole's had it hard," Dagmar said. "Losing his sisters so young, a brother to the fever and then another in the war . . . and then his leg." She put a handkerchief to her nose and sniffed. "Now this, just when we were getting somewhere."

"Now, Mother," Anton said. "We've much to be thankful for. We won't burden our friends with our troubles."

They knitted and crocheted in silence. Serena helped Kersten cast off from the finished stocking. She searched her mind for topics of conversation that might turn their minds away from the bleakness.

"Milton Madsen," Serena said, "you know, the man from Tordenskjold, said he's a friend of Evan Jacobson."

"The stage coach driver," Anton said. "Knew him well."

"Didn't he marry the Ericson widow?" Dagmar turned her needle to begin another row. "Such a sad story."

They conversed about the young woman who had lost her man on the ship coming over and was forced to marry a stranger to keep from being sent back to Norway.

"I wouldn't do it," Kersten said with a grimace. "No one could make me marry someone I didn't know."

"It was difficult," Serena said as she dug her crochet needle into the rows of yarn. "But when that husband died, she and Evan were free to marry."

"How come you never got married again after Far died?" Maren said. The knitting needles stopped clicking and all eyes turned to Serena.

Serena gave her daughter a stern look and grasped for another topic. "I had hoped to sell my land to Mr. N.W. Gardner while I'm here this summer."

"You'd sell Hungry Hollow to him?" Dagmar said with a gasp. "He wants to own the whole township."

Serena sat up straighter and poked the needle into the yarn on her lap. "I've never known the land to have a name."

Anton looked at his wife and then answered with a shrug. "The place has a reputation for bad luck." Anton tossed a finished axe handle into the pile and reached for another. "First Salmon's son . . . and then your man killed." He shaved a long curl of sweet wood off the ironwood limb. "And the fire."

"And now the grasshoppers." Serena's voice sounded barely above a whisper. There was no denying it. Pomme de Terre was bad luck. Hungry Hollow, a perfect name for the land that had taken so much from her.

Her Auntie Karen had read the coffee grounds before she and Gust had set out after their wedding. The grounds predicted death and destruction. They had been right.

If only Auntie Karen were here to read the grounds again.

"Dagmar," Serena said. "Would you read the coffee grounds?"

"Not today," Dagmar said. "Another time maybe."

"You don't get out of it that easy, you old troll," Anton said. "Girls fetch me a cup of coffee and we'll see what the grounds tell us."

The girls squealed with delight and poured another cup of coffee without using the strainer. Anton drank it down and wiped stray grounds from his long mustache. He handed the cup and saucer to his wife with a flourish.

"I'm not up to it," Dagmar said. "We've better things to do than cling to the old superstitions from Norway. Tommy said it wasn't godly."

"That may be, Mother," Anton said, "but today you'll read the grounds."

Dagmar shrugged and turned the empty cup upside down on the saucer and twirled it three times. "The trouble with coffee grounds is that we've got to take what they say." A grasshopper clattered in the stovepipe and hissed in the stove.

Serena's heart beat faster and she held her breath as Dagmar turned the coffee cup right side up and peered inside at the pattern of grounds clinging to its rim and sides. Dagmar looked a long time and finally pushed the cup away. She turned her mouth into a frown.

"What is it?" Kersten said. "Tell us, Bestemor."

Dagmar didn't answer. She placed a hand on her upper chest and sighed a deep sigh. Serena felt a chill go through her. It couldn't be good or Dagmar would volunteer what she saw.

"Tell us, Mother," Anton said, and Serena heard a strange edge in his voice.

"It's silly," Dagmar said with a forced laugh. "It's nothing to worry about."

Serena strained forward to look into the cup. Auntie Karen had taught her the meaning of a few patterns. Serena recognized a clump of grounds at the bottom, separated completely from other grounds higher on the sides of the cup.

The coffee grounds clearly showed a grave.

14

EVAN AND ANDERS BEGAN THEIR LONG JOURNEY. Just south of Leaf Mountain, only a few miles from home, the mule planted its feet and refused to climb the steep hill ahead of them. Evan nudged the mule with his heels, but it held its ground. Evan slapped the reins but it refused to go forward. Anders finally climbed off Whitey's back and pulled hard on the lead rope with a few chosen cuss words. It was no use.

The mule refused to budge.

"I'll push from behind," Anders said and began walking to the rear of the animal.

"*Nei!*" Evan said. "Whitey will kick you into next week."

Evan climbed down and rubbed the animal's ears, slipped a bit of carrot from his pocket and allowed it to eat from the palm of his hand with its long yellow teeth. Then with a deep sigh, Evan began the long trudge up the hill on foot.

"We can't walk all the way," Anders said. "What's the use of a mule if it won't let us ride?"

They must spare the mule as much as they could. Especially in such hilly country. Evan slipped one foot out of his wooden clog and dislodged a pebble. His feet hurt already and there were many miles to travel.

Betre halt enn fotlaus. Better limping than footless.

Anders forged ahead in long, easy steps, seemingly without effort. *Age*, Evan thought. *To be young again.*

"I've been thinking," Anders said, breaking the silence. "Farming is a lot of work." Whitey brushed a blue fly off his hind quarters with a flick of its coarse tail. "Maybe I should go back to teaching."

"At Clitherall?" They paused at the crest of the hill and enjoyed the view before them as they caught their breaths. Green hills, leafy elms and blooming purple phlox. No sign of grasshoppers.

"*Nei*," Anders said. "They brought in a new teacher, someone of the same religion. With a college education."

Anders spoke of his decision to go into farming and admitted he hadn't thought it through carefully enough. As Anders talked, Evan was reminded of himself in his earlier years. Looking back, Evan saw things more clearly. If only he had been wise enough to buy a farm in the beginning. He should have tried harder to get started. Made a decision and stuck with it.

"Ragna's farm is a leg up. The hoppers can't last forever," Evan said after a long pause, biting back advice. "And you've a good start in Tordenskjold." Anders busied himself with Whitey's bridle, making Evan wonder if he was even listening. "A few more years and your claim will bring a tidy profit." Evan knew he was saying too much but could not stop the flow of words. "You'll never get ahead working for someone else."

"Maybe I'm not meant to be a farmer," Anders said. "I've worked more than a year and have only a start of a haystack and a poor corn patch to show for it. Of course, the cabin took most of my time this spring. I'll get another cutting of hay, maybe two if I'm lucky, but at best I'll trade only for a cow."

"What does Ragna say about this?"

"I've not told her."

Evan mounted Whitey's back. *Av skade blir ein vis og ikkje rik.* From harm one gets wise and not rich. Anders would have to learn on his own, as he had done. He stuffed down a worry for Ragna.

It felt good to rest his feet on the way down the long winding hill.

"You riding?"

"*Nei*," Anders said. "I'll walk." He grinned. "Let the old men ride."

Evan could have pummeled him.

* * *

THEY RODE ACROSS COUNTRY to chop a day's travel off their journey. Flies tormented in the shade of the Big Woods and as the day turned into evening, swarms of gnats and mosquitoes surrounded them. Tag alder whipped against their legs as Whitey carried them through the forest on a winding trail no bigger than a footpath. Owls hooted and a wolf howled somewhere nearby. A gray shadow slipped through the trees around them.

"It would be safer to sleep at the farm." Anders wiped his forehead with the back of his arm and took a drink from an old canteen he carried. "Could lock Whitey safe away from wolves in the barn."

"Can't. This shortcut took us ten miles away from the farm."

"I'd like to stop and see the old place." Anders replaced the cork in the canteen. "Milton says hoppers don't always stay."

Evan would also like to see how Ragna's farm was doing. He would dig up a lilac root for Inga from the old patch. It was a bitter reminder of what it meant to work for another man. Evan's time belonged to another.

"We'll camp as soon as we get out of these woods. We'd be eaten alive by mosquitoes in the trees."

"I'll stop at the farm on the way back." Anders picked several wood ticks from his sleeve and flicked them into the brush alongside the trail. "Take the long way home."

Evan bit back an admonition for him to hurry home and forget other errands. Indians might return. The corn needed cultivating and no telling what mischief the boys might find. Anders should know these things without being told, should carry his responsibility more seriously.

Evan had a sudden longing to forget teamstering, return to his family, and reclaim his life. A gloomy mood, dark as the shade beneath the towering pines settled over him.

Evan pushed down the sad feelings that threatened to overwhelm him and made an almost unconscious decision to make the best of things. "Did I ever tell you about the people I met along the Abercrombie Trail back in my early days of driving the stage? Why Big Barn Jensen put his wife in a shack while his Jerseys lived in a mansion of a barn." He would talk only about the days before the uprising, before the slaughter, before things had turned sour. "And Old Man Schwarz had an entire field cleared by a cyclone that uprooted a stand of trees hundreds of years old."

"I've never seen a twister."

Evan entertained the younger man with stories of old friends and acquaintances. When they finally reached an open meadow, they set up camp, started the smudge fires to keep the mosquitoes at bay, and tethered the white mule close enough to share the smoke.

Above them a million stars scattered across the open sky, reminding Evan of his sea journey from Norway. Back home in Tolga, mountains blocked much of the view. How surprised he had been to discover open heavens above the Atlantic Ocean. He drifted again on the ocean in his dreams, rocking back and forth on the sailing ship, sleeping on deck to avoid the stench and confinement of steerage, a salt breeze in his face.

"Can I ask you something?"

Evan startled awake. "What? Is something wrong?"

"Nothing wrong," Anders said. "I'd like to know more about Ragna's father." Loons called from the river and nighthawks swooped across the sky, dipping and diving for mosquitoes. Bats soared overhead. An owl hooted and Whitey stomped and whinnied. "Tell me."

Evan pushed himself up on one elbow and tossed a green leafy bough into the fire to build up the smudge. A steady whine of mosquitoes surrounded him, and he pulled the blanket over his arms and shoulders. He hated talking about the massacre but someday this young man would share Evan's memories with Lars's grandchildren. Lars deserved at least that much. Evan took a deep breath and breathed a silent prayer that he would say the right thing.

"Lars was a good man, honest and a hard worker, a churchman who lived out his beliefs. A good father and faithful husband." Evan pushed away the longing to return to the ocean voyage of his dreams. "You don't find too many like him. Decent and good hearted. He always made me laugh."

"And during the uprising?"

"He trusted his Indian neighbors, the Chippewa." Evan sorted through the stream of memory that flowed through this mind. "The Sioux raided along the Abercrombie Trail, right through this country." The mournful cries of wolves sounded from the forest, and Whitey quit chomping grass to listen, his ears turned toward the sounds of potential danger. "It was harvest time and folks were in the fields. The Sioux came without warning. Killed Lars and his missus . . . and baby." He swallowed hard. "The girls taken."

"He didn't have a chance," Anders said.

"*Nei,*" Evan said after a long pause. Smoke swirled around. He didn't know if the smoke was any better than the mosquitoes. "Crooked Lightning tried but rescued only the girls. Even so, only Ragna survived."

"Thank God," Anders said with a voice thick with sleep. "I'm lucky to have her."

"You are indeed lucky."

The wolves sounded farther away and Whitey resumed pulling the tufts of grass within reach of his tether, stomping his hind legs against the mosquitoes and swishing his tail. Evan thought Anders was asleep when he spoke again.

"God, I hate being away from her," Anders said. "I'll take the shortcut home and stop at the farm another time."

Evan smiled. The pull a woman had on a man. He knew it well. He hated leaving Inga. The children, yes, but especially Inga. He thought what she would be doing at this hour. Sewing maybe. Or reading. He imagined how she looked with her hair down her back and her face in the candlelight.

Inga was strong and healthy. They finally had their daughter. The boys were getting old enough to help around the farm. He had a paying job. Although he knew little about mules, he expected he could learn. His wage would get them through the winter even if they lost their harvest to hoppers. By God, life wasn't all bad.

Evan was just drifting to sleep when a sudden thought bolted him awake again. Lars had thought the same before the Sioux took everything from them. Lars had thought himself safe because of his friendly relations with the Chippewa. Evan might be making the same mistake. The Chippewa went to make war on the Sioux. The Sioux might return to make war on the Chippewa. Heaven help the poor settler found in their way.

Anders's heavy breathing told Evan his traveling partner finally slept.

Evan rolled to his other side and pulled the blanket over his head. The memories, once stirred were slow to dissipate. It wasn't fair that he had been sleeping so soundly before Anders woke him. Now Anders slept like a stone, leaving Evan to wrestle with the old recollections and the new worries.

He was thinking about Lars as he drifted to sleep. In a dream, his old friend beckoned him from the shore of a rushing river. Lars's face glowed with health and happiness. Never had Evan seen a river so startling blue or grass as vibrant as what grew beside the surging water. "Hurry!" Lars said in Norwegian. "What's taking you so long?"

Evan woke and wondered if the dream were a sign. Perhaps Lars called to him from beyond as a warning. He tossed another leafy branch into the fire. He sighed and settled back on the hard ground. It did no good to dwell on the past. It was over and done and not worth getting upset about.

Dagen som er gaatt, faar ein ikkje igjen. The day that is gone, you will not get one more time.

Thank God, Evan thought as he drifted into a restless sleep. Once was enough.

15

RAGNA SAT AT AUNTIE'S TABLE, reworking an old pair of Uncle Evan's trousers into a garment suitable for Gunnar. Gunnar had grown so much that his old pants were splitting at the seams. She would then rework Gunnar's worn trousers into something Knut could wear. With money so dear, it was the only way to keep the boys covered.

Betre berrfoett enn bukser. Better barefoot than without trousers, Uncle always said.

Ragna snipped the cloth and tucked the sewing scissors into her apron pocket for safe keeping. Auntie hated sewing. Someday Ragna would buy a sewing machine to lighten Auntie Inga's load. But the expense of getting started! She listed the things they needed with each stitch: a cow, oxen, plow, harrow, hay knife, cook stove, and supplies for the winter. It would be a long time before she could hope to save money for a sewing machine.

It was late morning, almost time for noon dinner, and Ragna left the door open to catch the light. She threaded her needle, holding it up toward the doorway to sight through the eye. From where she sat, she could see Sigurd herding the cow in the meadow with Musky at his heels. The tinkling bell jingled a homey, comforting melody. Auntie and the boys hoed potatoes and pulled weeds in the carrots and beans. Christina slept in the shade next to the garden.

Since moving home, Ragna slipped easily back into the routine of daughter. She hurried to stitch the seam before she must stop to fix the meal. Milton had left early with the oxen to begin the tedious job of turning new sod on his northern field. He had packed a lunch and said he would be gone until evening.

With each pull of thread, Ragna thought of her husband and wondered when he would return home. He had been gone three days now, three long days, and even longer nights. She expected him soon, tomorrow at the latest. But one never knew about traveling. A thrown shoe on Whitey, a twisted ankle, a hundred delays might happen. She steered thoughts away from the time Anders left to buy flour for the Mormon Saints and stayed away all winter. That wouldn't happen now that they were married.

"Missus," a deep voice spoke from the doorway as a shadow fell across her sewing.

Migwans stood at the door holding a brace of prairie chickens. Ragna clattered to her feet and stifled a scream, dropping the trousers on the floor. The Indian was dressed in the same greasy skins. A louse crawled across the top of his hair. His eyes fixed on her, and she felt her skin turn to gooseflesh beneath his gaze.

Ragna willed herself to remain calm. *Dear God, help me.* The rifle hung over the door, out of reach. She gripped the scissors in her pocket and straightened herself to her full height. *Dear God, keep the family away from the house until he leaves.*

He held out the birds with one hand. "Missus." He thumped his chest with his other hand and said, "Migwans."

She frantically thought of what she might give him, surely he came to trade. A dish of eggs sat on the dry sink alongside a gourd filled with cottage cheese. A few parcels of dried meat and fish hung from hooks in the ceiling but they were desperately needed for winter supplies.

She reached for the eggs and held the dish toward him. Migwans grinned and laid the birds on the table and reached for the eggs, taking as many as he could carry in both hands. He snooped around the cabin.

Ragna wondered why he did not leave. He had what he came for. He seemed to be looking at the bed. Then at her. A great wave of panic washed over her. He sat on the edge of Auntie's bed and bounced up and down, holding the eggs in his hands, childlike in his actions. He said something to her in his language. He bounced again.

Migwans stood to his feet, broke an egg into his mouth and dropped the shell onto the floor, moving the remaining eggs to his other hand. He swallowed and wiped his mouth with the back of his arm, a glob of yellow yolk still on the corner of his mouth, and reached out to touch Ragna's hair.

She swallowed a wave of panic. He fingered the collar of her dress and brushed the back of his hands on her cheek. Ragna gritted her teeth and stepped a full step away from him. His eyes never left her face.

She gripped the scissors tighter in her pocket. She would not succumb to heathen advances. She backed toward the door, closer to the rifle. Uncle always kept it loaded.

Migwans said something else in his language and walked out the door as suddenly and quietly as he had come, then vanished into the bushes alongside the house.

Ragna reached for the rifle and held it tightly to her bosom. Auntie and the boys busied in the garden. They hadn't seen the savage. Ragna's chest heaved and her mind raced. She could have been killed. She might not have seen Anders again. Waves of relief flooded her until her body trembled.

She might not have lived to bear their child.

Ragna held her breath and counted backwards to her wedding date. Her monthly was late. She had never been late before. She let out her breath and touched a hand to her womb. She had not realized she was pregnant until that moment. It was as if the fear had clarified her thinking.

A baby. She knew it was true. A girl to be named after her sister, or a boy named after his father. Tears slid down her cheeks and a warm glow settled deep in her chest. A baby. She, so long motherless would now mother a child of her own. Thank God, thank God. She could not hold back the tears. She did not know if she cried for fear of Migwans, relief that he left, or joy over the new baby. She propped the gun against the wall and dropped her head onto her arms.

"Ragna," Anders said from the doorway. He hurried and knelt by her side. "What's wrong?"

Ragna flung her arms around his neck and sobbed into his shoulder. He smelled of mule and dried sweat.

"Tell me." The timbre of his voice changed to anxious concern. "Did something happen?"

She tried to answer but was crying too hard. She was too old to act this way and though she tried to pull back the overwhelming emotions, she couldn't do it. Finally, she pointed to the prairie hens on the table.

"Indians?" Anders said. "Were they here?"

She nodded and hiccoughed as she tried to swallow the tears. "Migwans."

"Did he hurt you?" his voice hardened. "So help me, if he laid a hand on you . . ."

"He didn't." Ragna said between sobs.

Anders pulled her into his lap and held her as she might hold Sigurd after a bad dream. She wiped her eyes on the hem of her apron.

Auntie Inga and the boys came through the doorway. Everyone stopped talking when they saw Ragna's tears. Ragna gulped and tried to compose herself.

"What's wrong?" Auntie said.

"Indians were here." Anders looked at Auntie Inga with an accusatory glance. "Where's Milton? Didn't anyone notice?"

Ragna told how Migwans startled her and his request to trade. She tried to get up from Anders's lap to lay the spoons but he pulled her closer.

Ragna hoped Auntie would not disapprove of such public intimacies. Auntie busied at her work. "I hate them skulking around," Auntie said. "Are you sure you're not hurt?"

"I'm fine." Ragna blew her nose. "Just scared."

Ragna did not tell how he sat on the bed or how he touched her face. It was far too early to mention the baby. She must be certain before she told anyone about the baby.

"I'll get him," Gunnar said with a scowl and picked up the rifle. "He won't be back again."

"*Nei*, put the gun away," Auntie said. "I mean it."

"Migwans came in friendship," Anders said. "Dress the birds and we'll feast tonight."

"I don't want Indians coming around," Gunnar said. "Far wouldn't like it."

Gunnar put the rifle away and picked up the birds. Ragna gave her favorite brother an encouraging smile as he dragged out of the room.

"Can we have the feathers for a war bonnet?" Lewis said with a lisp. "We'll pretend we're Indians."

"First gather the eggs," Auntie said. "Look in the haystack."

The twins and Sigurd grabbed the basket and raced from the cabin, whooping like Indians.

"Knut, please water Whitey and let him wallow a bit," Anders said. "He's worn out."

"And take the bucket," Auntie said. "We're running low."

Auntie bustled around the stove, piling kitchen wood into the firebox, adjusting the damper. She poured water into the kettle.

"You were smart to give him the eggs," Auntie said. "He could carry them without taking our dishes."

Anders squeezed her tighter, his arms wrapped around her waist and his face buried in the top of her hair. Ragna could feel his heart pumping against her back. When Auntie turned toward the stove, his hands slid up the sides of her chest.

"If we expect to continue to trade with the Indians, we'll need extra gourds or cloth sacks." Auntie asked about Uncle Evan's job, their trip, news from outside.

Auntie headed toward the dugout to fetch the milk jug. As soon as she was out the door, Anders pulled Ragna closer and kissed her face and neck.

"Anders!" Her face burned. "We're not alone." She wanted him to stop, but she didn't want him to stop. The boys might come in. Auntie would be back soon.

"I missed you, Mrs. Vollen." He whispered into her ear. "You're all I thought about while I was gone."

The little boys brought the egg basket with three speckled eggs lying in it. "That's all we could find." Auntie returned as Knut brought the pail of water.

"Ragna and I are going home for a while." Anders stood to his feet and reached for Ragna's hand. "We'll be back by dark."

"Don't you want to eat?" Auntie frowned and plopped the eggs in the boiling water. "It's almost ready."

"Can we go with you?" Sverre tugged at Ragna's skirts. "Please?"

"*Nei,* you boys have chores," Auntie said.

"Just a quick meal," Anders said with his eyes only on Ragna.

Ragna's heart thumped. She couldn't wait to have her husband to herself.

16

SERENA WASHED DISHES AS SHE WATCHED the fires through the window. Ole and Anton raked a row of wriggling grasshoppers into a burn pile in front of the inn. Ole struggled to maintain his balance while leaning on one crutch and working the rake with the other. Ole wouldn't give up, Serena had to admit.

Farmers burned entire fields. Rolling smoke rose from all directions— yet the ground crawled with hoppers. They covered the sides of the buildings, chewed the leaves off trees, and consumed every weed and blade of grass. Everywhere was the stench of burning hoppers and smoldering fires.

Grasshoppers had only been in Pomme de Terre a few days but it seemed like forever.

The sky was blue and if one looked only upward, all seemed in order. Serena considered what Tommy Harris would have said about such a lofty thought and the sermon he might have written around it. Tommy Harris had been a soldier with dreams of becoming a Methodist preacher. His practical faith buoyed them through hard times.

But Tommy never became a preacher. Renegades killed him the same day they killed Gust. Serena sent a quick prayer for his widow and daughters. They would be a little older than Maren and Kersten.

Serena reached for the last dirty pan and called the girls to wipe dishes.

"How many grasshoppers are there?" Maren said as she picked up the dish towel. "A thousand?"

"More than that," Serena said. "A thousand times a thousand, then a thousand times more. Maybe numbers don't go that high."

"Like the stars?" Kersten polished a plate. "Numberless, beyond measure."

A grasshopper found its way into her clean dishwater. Serena bit back an oath and scooped it into the fire where it sizzled and smoked. She refused to compare a dirty locust with a glittering star. They were ruination, destruction.

"It seems we can't get ahead," Dagmar said. Her voice lacked strength and sounded as desolate as the outside landscape. Grasshoppers clattered down the stove pipe and flew into the window glass. Dagmar's cot creaked as she shifted her weight. She had complained of chest pain earlier that morning and her face looked gray and drawn. "Just when we get a toehold, something pushes us down again."

"Would you like some tea?" Serena said.

Dagmar had been unusually quiet all morning. As Serena poured the tea, Dagmar clutched a hand to her breast and cried out.

"I'm calling the doctor." Panic welled up in Serena's chest. She didn't know how to help her old friend.

"*Nei*," Dagmar said but her voice was hardly a whisper. "I'm fine."

"Maren," Serena said. "Fetch your *bestefar*. Tell him we need the doctor."

Dr. Cormonton was seeing patients in Fergus Falls, something he did every Wednesday.

Anton and Serena hovered over Dagmar until the doctor returned that evening. He placed a stethoscope on Dagmar's chest and frowned.

"Sometimes a broken bone causes other problems," Dr. Cormonton said in his wheezy voice. "Humors, clots, apoplexy, or hysteria." He rummaged in his black bag.

"What can be done?" Anton sat beside her on the cot and clasped her hand in his. He seemed to have aged, his face haggard, his eyes rheumy and red. Dagmar languished on the pillow, grimacing in pain whenever she moved.

"Enough pillows to keep her almost sitting up in bed," he said. "Loose all tight clothing and apply cold water to the head and warm water to the feet. Give only cold water to drink."

Anton fetched another pillow and propped it under his wife's head.

"And medicine." Dr. Cormonton handed Anton a paper of powders and instructed how much and how often it should be given. "It's bitter as gall," he said. "You'll take it, Dagmar, and no fighting about it."

Dr. Cormonton shook hands with Anton and headed out the door. Serena and Ole followed outside and stopped the doctor in the front yard. Choking smoke drifted across the yard and grasshoppers crunched underfoot.

"She looks bad," Ole said. He clenched his jaw and set his lips. "Tell me plain. Is she going to make it?"

"She's had a heart attack."

Serena gasped. A heart attack was a death sentence. She wasn't ready to lose Dagmar yet. The thought of it weakened Serena's knees.

"She's almost sixty! Just think. Not many reach such an age." Dr. Cormonton started down the path. "It's useless to tell her and maybe easier on her heart if she doesn't know. I'll stop again in the morning."

Serena and Ole stood on the path, speechless in the aftermath of such bad news. Ole slumped all his weight onto his crutches. Tears gathered in Serena's eyes. How could she manage without her old friend?

Swanson's fat goose chased grasshoppers and scooped them down as fast as it could swallow. They needed a million geese.

"By God, she's had a hard life." Ole's voice turned bitter. "Coming to America and starting over in this wilderness. Indian wars. Losing her children. Except for me—the cripple."

"She may have had a hard time," Serena said straightening her spine to its full height and wiping tears from her eyes with angry jabs of her hands. "But she saw a miracle in her life."

"What would that be?"

"You." Serena wiped more tears from her cheeks. "We prayed for you—and you came home again. It was the greatest joy of her life."

"How do you know?"

"She told me. Said you were raised from the dead."

Swanson's goose chased more grasshoppers. Serena brushed a few off her apron and another crawling in her hair. The sun slipped behind the western hills. Soon the mosquitoes would be too thick for anyone to be outside.

"We'll close the inn until she's better."

Serena's heart sank. Of course. The noise and fuss of the men would be too much for Dagmar now.

"Do you want us to go home?" She hated to ask but maybe he felt she and the girls caused too much commotion.

"Nei." Ole's face showed surprise. His deep voice sounded gentler, quieter. "She asked you to come. Please stay."

The next morning after breakfast, the grasshoppers swarmed up from the ground with a horrible clatter and gathered into a great swirling cloud.

Serena ran outside and watched in astonishment as the chattering horde churned and twisted, almost like a cyclone in the sky. The swarm traveled east, a glittering mass that was soon out of sight.

Thank God and good riddance.

17

E VAN ARRIVED IN COLD SPRING JUST IN TIME. He breathed a sigh of relief when he found the muleteers by the saw mill on the Sauk River, just outside of town.

Grasshoppers were bad in the region and farmers had nothing to harvest—except trees. The millworks did brisk business, evidenced by stacks of logs changing into rough boards and screeching saws. The smells of pine pitch and pungent oak sawdust. Smoke from a smoldering slab pile hung low over the valley.

Three huge supply wagons waited in front of the mill, one piled high with bricks from St. Cloud and another already loaded with rough lumber from this millworks. Evan was a poor judge of volume, but he figured two and a half to three tons of boards on the wagons and each hitched to a team of twelve mules. It seemed enough bricks and boards to build a whole city.

A cluster of men stacked boards onto the third wagon. Evan went over to introduce himself, nervously trying to remember the American words. As he drew closer, he wiped his sweaty palms on the sides of his rough trousers.

Evan stared in disbelief. It couldn't be true. One man had a crippled right hand and wore stained overalls and a ragged shirt. Greasy hair hung ragged around his hawkish face and crooked nose. Rotten teeth showed gaps. As Evan's heart sank, the man caught sight of him and leapt off the wagon.

"Well, look what the cat brung in," Ted Green said whooping and pounding Evan's back. "I thought you'd be hung by now, an old horse thief like you."

When Evan had first come to Minnesota, he had been tormented by Ted, another hostler at Fort Snelling. Evan had rarely known anyone so inept at caring for animals and yet here he was, driving one of the mule teams.

Evan had hoped never to see the bully again.

"Huzzah," Ted said. "I never thought to see you doing an honest day's work. Thought you'd be a big farmer by now."

Words evaporated on Evan's tongue and he stuttered a reply, feeling again like the greenhorn Ted had known. Ted, with his know-it-all manner, hadn't changed a bit.

"If you can't talk American after all this time," Ted said, "you might as well go back to Sweden."

"Not Sweden," Evan said finally getting the words out clearly. "Norway."

"Get back to work, Ted," an older man said, clearly the boss. The load of boards almost reached the top of the wagon.

Ted slunk back to his work.

"You must be Evan Jacobson." The man was dressed in buckskins and a cap made from a coon tail. "Call me Old Hen. Captain Van der Hoerck asked me to show you the ropes. Spoke real highly of you. You'll ride brake with me."

Old Hen gave Evan a brief explanation of the cargo they would carry to Fort Wadsworth and the mule teams. When the load topped the wagon, the other men joined them.

"I'm Jeppe Johansen." One of the men stretched out his hand toward Evan. He spoke with a Danish accent and Evan let out a sigh of relief. At least he wouldn't be the only foreign-born man on the crew. The Danish language, similar to Norwegian in many ways, meant Evan could converse comfortably without the burden of remembering English words. "And this is Zeke Allen, Martin Mortensen, and Homer Perry."

The other men were Yankees, about Evan's age, maybe a little younger, wearing rough workman's clothing and heavy boots. Evan was the only one in clogs.

"The Danes, Jeppe, and Homer, are off to the gold fields after this trip," Ted said. "You'll get their team after they're gone."

"Captain Van der Hoerck decides that." Old Hen turned his shoulder away from Ted and faced Evan more directly. "Let's get on the road."

Zeke Allen mounted a tall bay mare and rode ahead of the wagons. It seemed to Evan that he must be in charge of choosing the best trail for the train.

Ted climbed on the back of the left, rear mule hitched to his wagon. He tucked a bullwhip under his arm. Martin rode the wagon seat behind him, operating the brake. Ted maneuvered his team to follow directly behind Zeke, snapping his whip and cursing a blue streak.

"Eat my dust, Swede!" Ted snapped the long bullwhip over his leaders until they lurched and ran, almost dislodging the lumber stacked on the wagon.

"That man will be the death of me," Old Hen said. "The fact that he has a job shows how desperate the army is these days. Too many men killed in the war. Countless off to the gold fields." His mouth turned into a decided frown. "Ted has not a lick of sense—but you know if you've worked with him before."

Evan relaxed. At least the others knew which way the wind blew. He admired the team of jacks, nine brown and three gray. "I've worked only with horses."

"You've got to remember that a mule isn't a horse." Old Hen hawked and spit alongside the iron wheel and reached for a plug of tobacco from his pocket. He offered it to Evan. "That's the first lesson of mule whacking."

"*Mange takk*," Evan said and his mouth watered at the thought of tobacco. It had been almost three years since he'd indulged in tobacco, not since the grasshoppers took his crop in Alexandria. Inga would be disappointed if he took up the habit again.

He sighed and succumbed to temptation. A man needed some comfort. "*Tusen takk*, a thousand thanks."

Jeppe and Homer's rig followed Ted's team and Old Hen and Evan pulled up the rear. Old Hen rode the left rear mule. Evan sat behind him on the wagon seat, feeling useless and ignorant.

"It's called riding the eleven-nigh-wheel horse," Old Hen said. "See this ring on the back of my saddle? It attaches the strap to the brake bay with a snap hook."

Up to this time the mules had been sleepy in their traces. "Do-sa-doe your partners," Old Hen called with a snap of the twenty-two-foot whip. The mules suddenly woke up and got in their collars. "Allemande left." The long chains stretching from the leader to the wagon drew taught. Old Hen shouted and yanked the brake strap, releasing the break from the ratchet. "Promenade all!"

The animals pulled in unison and the caravan was underway.

Old Hen pointed out how the mules were hitched to single and double trees, and then latched to the long chain running the length of the team. This chain was hitched directly to the wagon.

"See this rope line?" Old Hen pointed to a rope strung through the collar ring of each left-hand mule up to the leaders. "This is the jerk line. Used more than the whip to give orders." Old Hen demonstrated. "A steady pull on the jerk line turns the team to the left. A few sharp jerks turns it to the right."

"Nothing to it," Old Hen said. "You'll catch on in no time."

Evan's head swam trying to remember the straps and ratchets, and wondering what in the world was a do sa do.

"Square dance calls," Old Hen said and laughed until his shoulders shook with mirth. "I like music and trained my team to dance calls." He reached for the whip and snapped to over the leader's head. "Promenade all!"

Evan admired the rippling muscles of the team and how they pulled together to move such a huge load across the prairie. But he had learned a few things during his years of driving a stage and something bothered him.

"How do you manage a sharp turn?" Evan said. "It would seem that the chain would trip the mules closer to the wagon if the leaders start turning."

"Excellent question," Old Hen chuckled. "Van der Horck was right. You are a good hand with animals."

He went on to explain that the first two mules, the leaders, were trained to obey the jerk line, the muleskinner's call, and the whip. Then came the pointers, sixes, and eights—specially trained pairs that knew to leap over the chain when the mule train turned a corner. They were trained to vocal commands. Finally the wheelers, the largest and strongest of the mules, were the last pair in the train. "A trained team, like this one, is like a well-oiled machine. Every animal trained to a specific place in the team and valued for its work."

They drove into a prairie blackened by grasshoppers. Evan's stomach knotted and ached. He knew too well what folks were going through.

Just ahead, sounded a sudden crash, braying and kicking of mules hooves against wood. Old Hen pulled back on the lines and set the brake. "Dang it all," he said. "What's that wastrel done now?"

"Nothing serious," Ted called back, loud enough to be heard over the bray of mules. "Broken wheel, is all."

"Damn!" Old Hen slapped his gloves against his pant leg. "We've barely started and Ted's broke down."

"A muleteer can't push a mule team faster than a mule thinks reasonable," Old Hen said. "They'll keep a steady clip but they're not runners. Push them too hard and they'll stop and put up a fight."

The drivers gathered around Ted's wagon. Lumber slipped off the corner with the broken wheel into a mess of boards and knotted ropes. They debated whether or not they should return to Cold Spring for a new wheel, try to fix the one they had, or leave Ted to figure it out and follow later. Jeppe suggested they turn the bullwhips on Ted to teach him a lesson.

"I know this country," Evan said. "Bror Brorson lives over that hill. He's handy with a forge."

It was decided that Jeppe and Evan would take the busted wheel to Bror's for repair while the others stayed behind to reload the wagon.

"I should be the one sent to fix the wheel," Ted said in a whiney voice as Evan and Jeppe climbed the rise. "I always have to do all the heavy work."

"He's not worth a tinker's damn," Jeppe said. "Always making trouble."

Only the tops of the trees showed green. Nothing grew in the fields. As they walked, they stirred up whirring hoppers that flew in their faces and slammed against their arms and legs.

A crowd of ragged children, accompanied by a white female dog, ran to greet them. It looked like the dog had a new litter of pups from her full udders swaying beneath her belly. The number of children proved how long it had been since Evan last saw his old friend.

Bror showed himself at the barn door, looked toward Evan and stepped out into the sunshine, wiping his hands on his pants.

"Is that you, Evan Jacobson?" he said with a wide grin of white teeth against his dirt-streaked face. "You are a sight for sore eyes!"

They shook hands. Evan introduced Jeppe and explained their situation.

"Agnes," Bror called to one of the older girls. She had big teeth and red hair braided tight on both sides of her freckled face. "Tell your mother we've got company."

Bror examined the wheel and agreed to splice it with a metal brace. "It won't be a permanent fix, but it should get you home." They negotiated a price and Jeppe went back to Old Hen to fetch payment while Evan helped with the wheel.

He and Bror caught up with the news of their families as Bror fired up the forge. Bror was surprised to learn of Ragna's wedding and rejoiced with Evan over the news of five healthy sons and a baby girl. Bror boasted seven children. He was sorry to learn that Evan would not have time to stay for dinner.

"My first day on the job." Evan said. "Can't spare the time although I'd love to."

"Agnes!" Bror called again to his oldest daughter. "Tell your mother to bring the coffee outside."

Bror added more dried wood to the forge and examined the damaged metal supports around the wheel. "Must have been driving like a crazy man to hit a rut hard enough to spring the wheel this bad."

"You've figured it out," Evan said. "Looks like the hoppers are bad around here."

"God only knows what we'll do if things don't turn around." Bror held a band of metal into the hottest part of the flames and twisted it around the broken rim. "Government gave us seed for this year's planting but it's already lost. We've been saying special prayers at church."

"They ruined my chance of buying the farm we were on," Evan said after a pause. "I'm homesteading in Otter Tail County now. Took this job to keep the wolf away from the door."

"Our prospects were dark before." Bror's fire roared red hot. "But now they're all blackened up."

Bror's missus brought a kettle of boiling coffee and a plate of cold pancakes smeared with molasses.

"Nice to see you again," Evan said. "You have a lovely family, missus."

Mrs. Brorson looked nothing like the young army widow Evan had introduced to his friend before the uprising. She had filled out, as to be expected. A fruit-bearing tree was stockier than a sapling.

"They're turning into wild Indians." She poured coffee, slopping it over the lip of the cup. "They're in need of schooling." Mrs. Brorson walked back toward the house and said over her shoulder, "Something not found in this wilderness."

"Agnes," she called. "Mind your little brothers by the well."

Bolstered as much by his old friend as by the coffee, Evan hoisted the wheel to his shoulder to carry it back to the team.

"What did your missus mean about schooling?"

"A neighbor taught school in her cabin the past few years but died of the smallpox."

Evan pondered the reality of the situation. Anders might welcome a teaching job but that would leave Inga and the children without help.

Bror and his children walked with Evan until they met Jeppe on the path. Jeppe handed the payment to Bror.

"*Mange takk*," Bror shook his hand and Evan was surprised to see tears in his friend's eyes. "I appreciate the work."

"*Byte skal vere til bate for to og ikkje for ein.* Barter is to favor two and not just one."

"Come again when you can stay longer," Bror said. "Bring the family."

While the men replaced the repaired wheel, Ted made the motions of checking the harness on his team. The animals shied away from him, one kicking him in the shin. Ted let out a stream of curse words and made a kicking motion toward the offending mule. Ted stomped toward the working men.

"What took you so long, anyways?" Ted said. "We've got to keep our noses to the grindstone."

Old Hen shook his head and motioned Evan back onto the driver's seat. When Old Hen was back on the eleven-nigh-wheel horse, he maneuvered his team to the front of the caravan, behind Zeke, with an allemande left.

"You'll eat my dust all the way back," he said to Ted. "Promenade all!"

18

AS THEY WALKED THE PATH to their cabin, Anders entertained Ragna with tales of his trip to Cold Spring. They stirred a drumming grouse, and a covey of prairie chicken skirted in front of them. When they were over the hill, they paused and kissed, looking over their shoulders to make sure no one lingered in the shadows to see them.

Anders pointed out a gray wolf skulking in the tag alder. Ragna felt the hair rise on the back of her neck. Anders talked of hunting the wolf and selling its pelt to Lying Jack. "He's giving two dollars and fifty cents for a wolf skin."

"That's a lot of money," Ragna said, trying to sound braver than she felt. "What would you buy?"

"I think I'd buy my missus a fancy hat," Anders said.

She leaned back against a tree trunk, its bark rough through her dress. The heat and humidity made their skin sticky.

"*Jeg har savnet deg.*" Anders' voice husky in her ear, his breath tickling. "I've missed you." His kisses weakened her knees. "Are you sure you're all right?"

"*Ja.*" Ragna felt fine now that he was back. She would never again be all right without him near. She had thought she understood what being married meant. She had not known at all.

"We're almost home." Anders took her hand and pulled her toward their cabin.

It stood as they had left it. The weeds and grass tall around the doorway, the meadow filled with yellow daisies and flaming Indian paintbrush. Red winged blackbirds and orioles warbled in the plum thicket, and beaver swam in the lake, pulling branches behind them toward their den. The water reflected sky as blue as Anders's eyes. Everything grew lush and green. The heavy snows of last winter made a bountiful summer—at least in the places without grasshoppers.

"Thank God," Anders said with a look of relief. "I thought the house would still be here but I wasn't sure."

They pushed the door open and walked into the house, as stuffy and hot as a fire-box. Anders propped the door to air it out. The bread loaf was gone from the table and a nice pat of maple sugar wrapped in a leather hide sat in its place, covered with an upside down bowl to keep it safe from mice.

"Sugar!" Ragna refused to think of Indians entering their house, looking at their possessions, taking what they wanted. She imagined Migwans's rough hand on her cheek and busied herself to forget, straightening the cloth, dusting crumbs off the table.

She planned how she would tell Anders about the baby, how pleased he would be, how it would seal their devotion forever.

"Come for a swim, Mrs. Vollen," Anders said with an outstretched hand toward her and bright eyes fastened upon her. "I stink like an old mule."

* * *

IT WAS LATE AFTERNOON BEFORE ANDERS got around to leaving for the hayfield on the south prairie. The field lay beyond the grove of trees, out of sight of the house.

"Are you sure you won't be afraid if I leave you alone?"

"We'll lose the carrots unless I thin them out a little," Ragna said. "And the cucumbers need watering."

Anders would be back soon. She had nothing to fear.

As she knelt in the garden, she recited the entire rosary, at least as much as she could remember without fingering the beads. Maybe Anders would have a wolf pelt for Lying Jack, or beaver skins. Soon Anders would have enough hay to trade for a cow. She would make butter to trade at Dollner's Store. When she saved enough money she would purchase a pair of hens and a rooster and start their flock. And then a couple of pigs.

How happy they would be once the baby made them a real family. She must write a letter to Bertha and share the good news. Bertha's baby would soon be here. They would be new mothers together, if only by letter.

Anders did not return though the sun drooped into the western sky. Ragna finished the carrots and the cucumbers, then hoed the potatoes. She looked in the direction where Anders should be coming. Nothing was in sight but the covey of quail strutting through the long grass. Auntie would be waiting supper.

Ragna decided to walk toward the field. Anxiety forced its way into her chest until her heart thudded against her ribs. She was being foolish. He could cut hay all night without finishing such a large meadow. She looked behind her as she climbed the hill, back at the house, at the garden plot, hoping the wolf they had seen earlier had gone on his way.

Their own place. She was a married woman. It was too good to be true. She reached down and gathered a handful of Indian paintbrush, the scarlet flowers brilliant in her hand. She would give the flowers to Anders and tell him about their baby. She couldn't keep the secret any longer. He would look at her and pull her again into his arms.

No sign of Anders as she pushed through the grove—but she smelled smoke. Maybe a neighbor burning a slash pile. The path snaked through the trees on an old game trail, clearly marked. The trees shaded from the afternoon sun. An owl hooted in the sweeping branch of an ancient oak. Someday she would bring their baby to this spot, maybe pack a picnic for their family.

She thought to call Anders's name but hesitated. There was no Indian danger. She had nothing to fear.

A grasshopper flitted into her face as she walked out of the trees. She brushed it off with a startled squeal. Ahead of her the prairie crawled with hoppers. She dropped the flowers. A wall of fire burned across the hayfield.

"Sweet Jesus," she said. "Not again, Lord. Not again."

Ragna picked up her skirts and ran toward the only dot not blackened prairie, Anders's white shirt. Instead of fragrant grass and blooming wild flowers, the ground lay desolate. Sounds of grinding jaws filled the meadow, as loud as the chirping frogs or calling birds.

Her husband sat like a gravestone with his shoulders slumped and his feet straight out in front of him. His face a stony mask. Grasshoppers crawled over his back and legs.

"Anders!" She ran faster, crunching on grasshoppers, brushing them off her face and out of her hair.

"Damn it all," he said when she knelt down beside him and began brushing the hoppers off his back and chest. "Damn, damn, damn." Anders gritted his teeth until his jaw muscles bulged.

She had never before heard Anders swear.

The haystack was their currency for a cow. Now it was gone and no hope of a second crop. *Holy Mary, Mother of God, pray for us now and in the hour of our death.*

"It will be all right, husband," Ragna said. She tried to remember what Auntie had said to Uncle Evan when the grasshoppers came. She must have said something to comfort him, but all Ragna remembered was how they changed everything.

"I set a fire but it's too late. All for nothing," Anders groaned and his appearance frightened Ragna, haggard and pale with smoky streaks across his sweaty face, with the expression of a desperate man. "Only a fool gambles with God."

"Surely you don't think God sent this to punish you."

"I took a wrong turn. I should have gone on to schooling when I had the chance," Anders said with a new, bitter edge to his voice. "I could have worked my way through if I had tried."

"Husband," Ragna touched his face and he jerked away.

"I'm through with farming." He cursed again, a string of Norwegian swear words that made her blush. "I've had enough."

Ragna pulled back in surprise. Every dream she had dreamed for them included a farm, either this claim or her father's land in Alexandria. She had never considered another kind of life. They had their own place, they were just getting started.

"Abraham Lincoln made it all the way to the top without a formal education and I thought I could do the same." He ground his teeth and clenched his fists. "Old Man Bergerson told me I had the potential to become a professor."

Ragna's throat constricted. He regretted their marriage. Her heart bowed under the weight of it. She tried to put her arms around him but he pulled away.

"I didn't listen." Anders got to his feet. "I never listen."

Her father had boasted about the good black dirt of Minnesota calling to him from across the ocean. She swept grasshoppers off her skirt and wiped a squirt of tobacco juice with the hem of her apron. The nasty stain would be hard to wash off.

"It's only one season, Anders," Ragna said. She got up from the ground and brushed the smudges of dirt and ash off her apron. "It's a setback. We'll be all right."

"Let's go." Anders started back on the path, crunching on locusts with every step. "I've had enough."

He didn't take her hand or wait for her, but strode ahead without looking back. Ragna hurried to catch up with him, lifting her skirts to go faster, the grasshoppers slippery beneath the soles of her shoes.

A thought flashed through Ragna's mind, something she had never before considered. How her mother had felt when she saw the Indians swoop out of the woods and kill her husband and baby. She must have felt as if her world was ending.

And then it had.

19

DAGMAR DID NOT IMPROVE. Serena tended her as best she could but it seemed her old friend failed more every day. The grief of it weighed on Serena's heart like a stone.

"Can the girls come to the barn?" Ole stuck his head in the doorway from the front stoop. "They can gather the eggs and play with the kittens while we do the chores."

Serena pushed her sleeves above her elbows and tackled the pie crust before her on the table. She might as well bake since they had to keep the stove fired. The rhubarb pie would be a special treat, something to encourage their spirits.

Serena hesitated. *Stalkers liten*, Maren and Kersten deserved a little fun.

"Please, Sistermine?" Kersten said at her side. She wore such a hopeful look that Serena couldn't refuse. She finally nodded and the girls cheered, tore out the door in a flurry of bare feet and petticoats.

"*Mange takk!*" Ole said before leaving with the girls.

Serena craned her neck and watched them walk toward the barn—at least Ole walked, swinging himself forward on his rag-wrapped crutches. The girls ran. She heard them laughing. Ole was good to the girls, Serena had to admit. Kersten and Maren both blossomed when Anton and Ole took time with them. If only Julian had been as attentive to both girls.

Serena had not answered Julian's letter. She felt guilty but at the same time liberated. She would not get caught again in his mother's clutches. He said she was dying, but Serena did not believe it. Surely the old lady would outlast them all.

"Where are the muleteers?" Dagmar said from her rumpled cot. Her voice sounded weary and weak. Her face wore a haggard, bloated look. "They should be here by now."

Serena wiped sweat from her face with the back of her hand.

"The mule trains will come." Serena rolled the pin over the dough, fashioning a neat circle. She lifted it into the pie pan and carefully cut the edges to fit. "Don't worry."

"I never knew you to be a liar, Serena." Dagmar said with a twisted look on her face. "You're making only one pie."

Serena did not know what to say. Of course Dagmar would notice the amount of food cooked.

"Tell me the truth," Dagmar whispered. "Where do I stand?" She coughed and gasped for breath. "I'm dying, ain't I?"

Serena wiped her hands on her apron and went to her friend's side. "Do you need a drink of water?" She considered what Dr. Cormonton had said. If she were Dagmar, she would want to know the truth, even though painful. She owed her friend at least that much.

"It's your heart," Serena said at last. "You've had an attack. It doesn't look good."

"I knew it," Dagmar said in a voice barely above a sigh. Gone were her boisterous tones. The outspoken woman had shrunk to a whisper. "How long do I have?"

Serena shook her head and reached for her friend's hand.

"I have something to say," Dagmar said with great effort, puffing with exertion.

"Hush now," Serena said. "You'll set yourself back."

"I'll say what I want," Dagmar said with a flash of old energy and raised her head off the pillow. "Hear me out." Then she clutched her chest and lay back down. She gasped several breaths.

"God sent you to me," Dagmar said. "Not just now," she waved her hand weakly, "but back during the uprising." She took a deep breath and closed her eyes. "You think I helped you . . . you were the one who saved me."

"Don't be foolish," Serena said with a laugh. "I wouldn't have survived without you."

"Listen." Dagmar puffed a few minutes, struggling to catch her breath. "I had lost my way. Fallen into a pit so deep I doubted I'd ever climb out."

"Rest now," Serena said. "We'll talk later."

Dagmar grasped Serena's arm with the sharp fingers of an old woman and pulled her closer. "*Nei!* Listen to me." She breathed slowly until she gathered enough air to speak again. "I cursed God . . . my little ones dead, the boys off to war, the massacre."

Dagmar coughed and held her chest. Serena lifted Dagmar's head and put a cup of water to her lips, the doctor had said only cold water. Dagmar lay back on the pillow and breathed hard.

"Then God sent you . . . and Tommy Harris," Dagmar whispered and held her hand to her breast again. Her face grimaced with pain and she stifled a small cry. "Good Lord, it feels like glass breaking in my chest."

Serena stroked Dagmar's forehead, feeling the wrinkled skin beneath her fingers, pushing the strands of silver hair away from her friend's face. She thought Dagmar slept and was about to go back to her pies.

"Ole's a good boy," Dagmar said. "Not like Gust." Her voice trailed off. "He's fond of you."

Serena couldn't believe her ears. Her friend must be worse than she thought to speak such foolishness. The doctor was coming soon. She must tell him that Dagmar was out of her head.

"Hush now," Serena said. "Rest."

Dagmar gripped Serena's arm again and raised her head from the pillow. "I see it." Her eyes burned like two blue suns.

"You're mistaken." Serena laughed a nervous laugh.

"Promise me," Dagmar said with a desperate look. "Be kind to him for my sake." She gripped harder. "He's all I have left."

"All right," Serena pulled away from Dagmar's death grip. "I promise."

Tommy Harris, the young soldier from the uprising, had wanted to be a preacher after the war. He urged all of them to trust God and believe for miracles. His own miracle hadn't come. Tommy was murdered by Indians the same day Gust was killed.

Serena wondered what Tommy Harris would say on this day when Dagmar lay on her death bed, the grasshoppers ruined the crops, and her chances of selling her farm were gone. She remembered Tommy's earnest face and the way he had urged her to seek God's will for her life.

It was easier said than done.

20

EVAN AND THE MULE TRAIN TRAVELED the old Abercrombie Trail until Sauk Centre where they veered west toward Glenwood. Evan tried to memorize the things Old Hen had said: eleven-nigh-wheel horse, brake bar, snap hook, saddle ring, ratchet, and jerk line. He felt he would never learn.

Evan looked back at the Abercrombie Trail until it was out of view, remembering the days gone by, thinking the old times were simpler.

"These rigs are nothing compared to what used to haul across the Wadsworth Trail, before the railroad came to Morris," Old Hen said with a fresh chaw of tobacco. He passed the plug to Evan.

"I cannot repay you until I collect my wage." Evan's mouth watered and he tucked his trembling hands under his legs.

"I'm not worried," Old Hen said and pushed the plug toward him. As Even took a chaw, Old Hen described the four-ton loads pulled by twenty-four mules and guarded by flanking cavalry. "Those were mule trains. Mule whackers could flick a fly off the leaders with the switch of a wrist." He pointed his chin back toward Ted with a frown. "Not like nowadays."

"Any Indian trouble at Fort Wadsworth?"

"There will be," Old Hen said. "The government will never let the Sioux and Cheyenne keep their land now they've found gold on it. You mark my words." He spat to the side of the wagon, sending a brown streak of tobacco juice into the dirt. "There'll be bloodshed before it's over. Especially with the likes of General Custer in charge."

Evan recalled how Crooked Lightning said the white man would not stop until he owned the whole world. The truth of Crooked Lightning's words weighed heavy.

"There's always fighting between the Sioux and Chippewa." Old Hen spat again over the side of the wheel and wiped his mouth with the back of his hand. "West of the Pomme de Terre River is Sioux country and east is Chippewa. They clash around the river—you got to keep watch lest you find yourself in the middle."

"Chippewa drummed for three nights and two days near our place in Otter Tail County," Evan said, "on their way to fight the Sioux."

They talked about Indian wars, troubles in the past. The conversation shifted to the Uprising and Abercrombie Siege. Evan didn't like talking about it.

They rode in silence for a long while. Evan watched the surefooted way the team planted its feet, sturdier than any horse he had known.

"Tell me about mules." Evan leaned back to listen. He'd much rather talk mules than Indian wars. "I want to know everything."

"They can kick," Old Hen said with a chuckle. "You don't want to get crosswise with them." He pointed his whip at the lead mule, a gray jack. "Now a jack looks mean because he stands his ground." Old Hen pointed at another. "Even the smaller ones will stand and fight rather than run like a horse will."

"That means they're smart," Evan said. "Not just run away like a chicken with its head cut off."

"It's all about personality," Old Hen said. "Take it slow and don't push a mule against its will."

They camped southwest of Sauk Centre, Old Hen complaining that Ted had caused them to get behind schedule and they would never catch up. They ate a hurried meal as Old Hen ordered the night watch schedule.

Evan was to stand the midnight watch. He rolled out his blanket by the fire and stretched out to get some sleep before he would have to be up again. The bugs troubled until he rolled himself in the blanket. Then it was too hot to sleep. Evan had to admit, he had grown soft in his years on the farm. He remembered his side of Inga's bed and wished he were there.

It seemed Evan had just fallen asleep when a deluge of cold rain slapped him awake. He pulled the blanket over his head. Thunder crashed and jagged lightning bolts lit the sky. The smell of rain swept through the campsite along with sheets of water. Strong winds toppled the coffee pot hanging over the fire and scattered tin plates and cups. Mules brayed and men swore.

"Good Lord," Zeke said. The men huddled against a big rock standing alongside the trail. "Get away from the trees."

The storm passed, and it was Evan's turn to keep watch. He built up the fire and hung his wet stockings and shirt on a nearby bush. It seemed the rain brought out every mosquito that lived in Minnesota. He scrambled into his extra shirt and socks, miserable in his wet trousers, trying to keep track of the mules and horse.

Zeke told of a post office near Durkee Place on the northeast bank of Westport Lake. They would drive by the next day and Evan determined to have a letter ready for Inga. Only regular mail would keep Inga from worrying. While he stood watch, he wrote about their first day on the road and sent greetings from Bror. He debated whether or not he should mention the school teacher opening in Cold Spring. He wrote until his eyes almost closed in sleep, then stood up and walked around in an effort to stay awake. Finally it was time for Jeppe to take over. Evan touched his shoulder and called his name.

Jeppe yawned and stretched. "Guess it's my turn."

Evan shivered. The drenching rain chilled his bones. He wrapped into his blanket and tried to find a drier spot of ground. Before he knew it, morning broke. None had slept well and the men were sullen and surly over breakfast.

"You act like it's my fault the mules busted our wheel," Ted said in a whiney voice as irksome as any mosquito. "I get blamed for everything. Old Hen, you know it were an accident that held us up."

Old Hen downed his coffee and walked away without responding. The others finished their mush and hurried to get back on the road. No matter who was at fault, the fact remained that they were behind schedule. Evan prayed a quick prayer for his family's well being.

They shared the Wadsworth Trail with other travelers. Miners heading west passed the lumbering wagons in their hurry to reach the gold fields. They waved as they rode by, greeting the muleskinners and boasting of future riches. Sometimes covered wagons came from the west toward them. These travelers were beaten down, discouraged, and barely looked their way.

"What's the matter with you?" Ted called out to a man riding on a black gelding. The man's boots were falling off his feet and his trousers showed more patch than cloth. "Why so glum? Didn't you find gold?"

"Those with gold ride the cars," he said. "Take my advice and stay home."

They nooned by the Durkee place on the northeastern bank of Westport Lake. It was the only stopping place between Sauk Centre and Glenwood, according to Old Hen, and close to Norman Shook's post office.

"I'll ride over with the letters," Zeke said, "if you boys will do my share of camp swamping."

"Some folks get all the breaks," Ted said. "I should have been the one to ride over to the post office. Why does Zeke get out of all the work?"

Zeke was the only one with a mount and it made sense to Evan that Zeke would post the letters.

"His woman is having a baby," Martin said. "He promised her a letter every day."

"Shut up!" Jeppe said. "Or I'll shut you up."

Ted sputtered but backed down when Jeppe pulled his bull whip from the wagon box. Jeppe snapped it and gave Ted a look that spelled stink eye in any language.

"I didn't mean nuthin," Ted said. He slunk away from the men although he wasn't finished watering the mules. "It's not my fault."

"Blowhard," Jeppe said. "I've had about enough of him."

* * *

A PAIR OF ROUGH LOOKING MEN RODE toward them just east of Lake Amelia, riding good horses and carrying side arms. They swept hard eyes over the freight as if they were judging whether or not it was worth the risk of robbing them. Evan felt uneasy and wished he had his old muzzle loader.

"You folks going far?" the skinnier of the two said from atop his dappled mare. He wore a dusty wrapper and black felt hat. His face was as sharp and lean as a meat cleaver.

The other man fixed dark eyes on the mule teams, the weapons, and the cargo. He wore an old rebel army jacket and tall leather boots. His scruffy beard grizzled with white around the edges and his dark hair peppered gray. He wore a large felt hat with a wide brim. He rode a gelding, black as the ace of spades, with a white patch on its nose.

"None of your concern." Old Hen placed a hand on his Sharps buffalo gun by his side, grasped his bullwhip with the other. "You'd best be on your way."

"Wait a minute," the first man said, stretching the syllables until it seemed he'd spoken a whole lot more than a few words. "Me and Clay ain't looking for trouble."

Old Hen snapped his whip over the lead mule. "Allemande left!" The crack sounded loud as a rifle shot. "Promenade all!" The team stepped out on the trail, every mule pulling against the harness.

The men sat on their horses and watched them leave.

"You two heading to the gold fields?" Ted called out as his rig drove past the men, still astride their mounts.

"We're mighty fond of gold," the sharp faced man said. He laughed a horsey, silent laugh. "Why do you ask?"

"Take me along," Ted said. "I'm sick of slaving my life away."

Evan didn't look back at the men until the mule train was a good half mile away, his heart beating hard against his ribs, a strange fear tangling his emotions and causing him to breathe hard. When Evan finally allowed himself to looked back, he let out a sigh of relief. The men rode east away from them.

"They'll be back," Old Hen said with a hard look around his mouth. "If I ever saw trouble astride a horse, it was those two highwaymen."

"I suppose with all the building going on, our cargo is valuable."

"Hell, yes! Do you know what a good mule brings?" Old Hen snorted. "A trained team and wagon is worth more than gold. You'd think they could scrape together some kind of military escort to protect their investment." Old Hen spat a steady stream of tobacco over the side of the wagon in disgust.

Evan thought of how he might defend himself against an outlaw. It seemed he couldn't think of a single thing except stay out of their way. Hard to do with three tons of freight in tow.

"Is there an extra gun?" Evan said at last. "I'm bare naked without one."

"Rifle under the seat," Old Hen said. "I'm getting too old for this kind of shenanigans." Old Hen looked back over his shoulder. "No sleep again tonight."

They traveled a long while, sweating through the heat of the day. A covered wagon ambled toward them from the west on the dusty trail. On the white canvas of the old Conestoga was painted a huge grasshopper and underneath the words, HE WON.

The man driving the oxen looked skinny and patched, as did the haggard woman beside him. Her belly swelled with another baby and she held a small boy on her lap with a wet rag to his head. A brood of too-thin children walked barefooted beside the wagon.

"Hello!" Old Hen said. "Where do you hail from?"

"Sleepy Eye," the man answered. "Grasshoppers drove us out."

"Where you headed?" Old Hen said.

"Anywhere they ain't," the man said. "Hoppers can't be everywhere."

"What's wrong with your boy?"

"He bounced off the wagon at the Chippewa Creek crossing," the man said with an anxious look toward his wife and child. "Almost fell under the wheel—but I think he'll be all right."

Old Hen reached into his rucksack and pulled out a tin can of beans and another of beef. "Here, take this."

"We don't need charity," the man said though Evan could see his chin quiver and the hungry look in his eyes. It was as if the missus held her breath.

"Not charity," Old Hen said quickly. "You'd work for your supper. Your children could do the camp chores. We've got ourselves in a little trouble and could use an extra man to stand guard tonight. Camping at Chippewa Creek if you wouldn't mind backtracking a ways." Old Hen paused a little. "Better yet if you'd travel with us to Glenwood. We're short of man power this trip."

"I'm your man." An eager light came into the man's face. "Name is Mitch Yokum." He called to his children in a high-pitched, excited voice. "Climb up in the wagon. Hurry now." He pulled his covered wagon behind Ted's mule team at the end of the cavalcade.

They made good time and arrived at Chippewa Creek about an hour before dark.

"Ma'am," Old Hen said to Mrs. Yokum. "It'd be most helpful if you'd cook while you're with us. Feed your children first so they'll be out of the men's way."

Evan turned his face away from the naked relief on her face.

"If you'll make extra biscuits and flapjacks for our cold lunches, we'll trade canned goods for your trouble."

Her face crumpled into sobs and she thanked Old Hen over and over.

Evan couldn't bear to watch. He hurried to unhitch the mules. Why in another circumstance, that woman could be Inga. Or Ragna. How thin the line that separated those who had from those who didn't.

Old Hen was a fine person and a magnificent hand with mules. Evan vowed to learn all he could from the man. If he must be away from his family, he could at least do his very best.

Evan thought of the letter he would write Inga. He would tell her about the muleskinner with the heart of gold. Inga would admire the old man, rough as a cob on the outside but soft as a lamb on the inside.

"What are you doing?" Ted said later while Evan was writing the letter. He leaned closer as if to read for himself.

"A letter home to my missus," Evan said.

"I've a wife at Gager's Station," Ted said. He straightened up and puffed out his chest. "The prettiest little wife you ever did see."

"That's nice," Evan said in an effort to shut him up and continue his letter. "I've six children."

"Then quit sulking," Ted said. "You'd best keep the flies off or you won't last a week with this outfit."

"Ted," Evan said. Anger boiled up in him and he lashed out in unusual bluntness. "Shut up for once in your life."

Ted stalked away, his legs stiff with anger. Evan sighed. He said what he meant even if Ted didn't like it.

Altfor noert er lite kjoert. Too sensitive gets nowhere.

21

SOMEONE KNOCKED ON THE DUGOUT DOOR where Ragna and Anders slept. Ragna poked Anders in his side but he didn't awaken. It was black as a grave in the dugout, damp and cloying. Ragna pulled a scratchy blanket over her shoulders and stepped onto the cold earthen floor with bare feet, hoping no centipedes or spiders would touch her.

"Ragna!" Auntie Inga's voice sounded on the other side of the door. More knocking on the heavy wood.

Something must be wrong.

Not a shard of light showed through the shuttered window. It must be the middle of the night. When she opened the door, Ragna startled to hear the Indian drums pounding again.

Auntie Inga stood wild-eyed in her nightdress, holding a lighted candle in one hand and the butcher knife in the other. The reflection of the flame framed her face in golden light and matched her yellow hair flowing free and long down her back.

Clouds skittered across the face of the waning moon and night hawks swooped in the sky. An owl hooted nearby and loons echoed across the water. A bittern pumped its song. And above all these normal sounds of night, the incessant rhythm echoed across the lake. How could Anders sleep?

"Come to the house," Auntie whispered. "It's the drums—can't bear to be alone."

Ragna looked past Auntie's worried face toward the direction of Milton's claim. He had promised to come if there were any signs of Indians. Perhaps he didn't consider the drumming as trouble, but Ragna's skin turned to gooseflesh as wailing voices joined the sounding drums. She looked down the shore, half expecting to see smoke and flames above the tree line where their cabin stood.

Our Father, which art in heaven. Hallowed be thy name.

The drums continued all day. Auntie kept the children inside behind barred doors and made Anders lock the livestock in the barn. He shook his head but obeyed.

"They're having some kind of feast," Anders said. "They're not after your chickens."

It was the most he had spoken since finding the grasshoppers on his fields. Gone was the sparkle in his blue eyes that Ragna loved. Gone was his hopeful enthusiasm. His voice soured flat and hopeless.

Anders took his gun and left the cabin, careful to close the latch behind him. Ragna watched through the partially open shutter and saw him trudge toward the barn. Anders's feet plodded, his shoulders slouched. If only Uncle Evan were here to counsel him. Uncle always knew what to do.

"We'll take turns standing watch at the window," Auntie Inga said. She took down the muzzle loader and fiddled with the powder horn.

"Stop," Gunnar said with alarm. "You'll kill someone."

Gunnar took the old Danzig muzzle loader from her hands and returned it to its place over the door. "Don't worry. There'll be plenty of time to fetch the gun if Indians come across the lake."

"Why can't we go outside?" Sverre held the wiggling Musky in his arms. He and the puppy were seldom apart. Sigurd's face ran with sweat and looked red as the coals in the firebox. "It's too hot in here."

"Don't you hear the drums?" Auntie Inga said in a sharp voice. Sweat beaded on her upper lip and she tried to settle Christina on the breast. "You'll stay inside until I say it's safe to go out again."

Musky ran underfoot as Ragna cooked porridge. "Shoo!" Ragna motioned for Sigurd to take the dog to the side of the room. Auntie was already in a bad mood and would not tolerate any commotion.

The dog jumped out of Sigurd's little arms and nipped the hem of the baby's blanket, tugging until it ripped.

"That's enough. Out he goes," Auntie said in exasperation. "The Indians can have him for their stewpot."

"*Nei!*" Sigurd pouted and sprouted tears. "Not my dog."

Ragna hoped Auntie might relent at Sigurd's tears, but Musky wrapped his small mouth over the corner of the door frame and gnawed bite marks into the wall.

"Out!" Auntie Inga held the baby to her breast with one arm and cracked open the door with her other. She pushed the little dog outside. It scratched on the door and cried. Sigurd fussed until Auntie gave him a *chiliwink*, a slap on the side of his head.

"Knut," Auntie Inga said. "Fetch the Bible."

Ragna wondered what was taking Anders so long in the barn. Auntie Inga was fit to be tied and it seemed the drums were louder, wilder sounding.

Ragna pulled her chair to catch the light from the partially opened shutter and picked up the never-ending task of mending. Gunnar, with dreams of raising rabbits and growing rich, whittled pieces for a rabbit hutch as he stood watch at the window. Sverre and Lewis practiced sums on the slate. Auntie sat on the edge of the bed and nursed Christina. Sigurd sat on his mother's feet and sucked his finger.

"I'll read about the locusts in Psalm One Hundred and Five." Knut positioned himself to get the most light and turned the ancient pages of the Norwegian Bible until he found the right spot. "He spoke and the locusts came, grasshoppers without number; they ate up every green thing in their land, ate up the produce of their soil."

"What's a locust?" Lewis said, looking up from the slate. Instead of sums, Lewis had drawn Indians instead. Feather-covered Indians danced across the black surface holding tomahawks and dripping scalps.

"It's another word for grasshoppers," Auntie Inga said.

Ragna bit a thread with her front teeth and rethreaded her needle for the next patch on Sverre's trousers. "I've heard enough about grasshoppers to last a lifetime," Ragna said. "Read something more cheerful."

Knut turned the pages. "He that dwelleth in the secret place of the Most High shall abide under the shadow of the Almighty."

"That's better," Ragna said. "Psalm Ninety-One."

"Milton's here!" Gunnar whooped. "He's putting Whitey in the barn."

"It's about time," Auntie said.

Ragna jabbed the needle into the cloth and pricked herself. "Ouch!" She sucked the blood from the wounded finger. The room was so hot she felt she might faint.

Milton pushed through the door bringing a whiff of fresh air and increased Indian sounds. Musky tumbled inside, underfoot and in the way. Sigurd squealed with delight. Milton closed the door but then propped it wide open.

"Good God!" he said. "You'll suffer heat prostration without a little air."

The cooler air coming in through the open door made her feel more hopeful.

"Anything to eat for a hungry man?"

Ragna put the mending aside and dished a large bowl of groet, covered it with cream and set it before their guest.

"Now that looks good," Milton said. "If you weren't a married woman, Mrs. Vollen, I'd snatch you up myself."

"We expected you sooner," Auntie Inga said with a tight-lipped smile. She motioned for the boys to come to the table. Ragna could tell by the tilt of her chin that

Auntie was most disgusted with their neighbor. Auntie had said before that Milton was unreliable and footloose.

"I fetched the mail," he fished an envelope from his shirt pocket and placed it on the table in front of Auntie Inga. "Then thought I'd see for myself what the Indians were doing."

"What did you see?" Lewis said while Auntie carefully slit the top of the envelope and slipped out a sheet of paper.

"Hush now. It's a letter from your *far*." Auntie's voice quavered until she passed the letter to Ragna and motioned for her to read aloud.

Dearest Inga and family, this will be short as I've had a long day and must take my turn at guard duty tonight. Our cargo is of valuable timber and the mules and wagons even more so.

We had a breakdown near Bror Brorson's place in Cold Spring. Bror fixed the broken wheel so we had a little time to visit. Grasshoppers have hit that area real hard and I could tell they're having a bad time of it. He sends greetings.

I'm learning mules. Old Hen is a master muleteer. We are near Westport Lake, a sandy place, and I am able to post this letter before we leave. My love and prayers are with you all. Tell the boys to mind their mother and behave themselves.

Love, Evan

p.s. Bror says Cold Spring is in need of a teacher. Please tell Anders.

Ragna folded the pages and handed them to Auntie. Odd that Uncle Evan should send word to Anders about a school opening.

"The Indians were all dressed up in feathers and finery," Milton said. "I watched them dance from the top of the hill." He blew on a spoonful of porridge and shoveled it into his mouth. "They're nothing to be scared of."

"Then why make all this noise?" Auntie said. "Let decent people live in peace and quiet."

"They have their ways." Milton finished his groet and headed for the door, carrying his rifle. "Young bucks need time to brag about the scalps taken."

"Mr. Madsen!" Auntie Inga said. She used her chin to point to the little ones lined up around the table, listening to their conversation. "Please!"

Milton shrugged in an apologetic manner. "Where's Anders?"

"In the barn," Ragna said.

"Barn's empty," Milton said. "Didn't see him."

"Maybe he went to the dugout," Ragna said. "Or out to our cabin." Her throat constricted with fear. "Come, Milton, help me find him."

When she stepped away from the safety of the cabin, Ragna's skin crawled with the thought that Indians might be watching from the trees. She breathed a prayer of thanks that Milton was there to protect her.

She worried about her young husband. He was despondent and had a gun. A shadowy memory of a neighbor taking his own life after losing a wheat crop reared its ugly head in her mind.

"Milton," Ragna said. "Grasshoppers took our fields."

"No!" Milton said. "When did this happen?"

"Yesterday," Ragna said. "Anders is real worked up about it."

She thought to tell Milton about his announcement that he would leave his claim and return to teaching but she felt disloyal to mention it. A phrase from her wedding vows sifted through her thoughts, "love, honor, and obey."

The dugout stood empty. Musky followed underfoot and Ragna picked her up and carried her. The dog licked Ragna's face until she felt strangely comforted. She held the pup close and let it nuzzle her ears and neck until it chewed the collar on her dress. Ragna slapped its nose and put it down. It tangled in her skirts until she picked it up again.

The barn stood empty and quiet, except for the oxen lowing in the stalls with the swish of their tails and grinding cuds. The barn, another dugout, nestled into the side of a hill with a slatted wall built across the front opening. The barn felt dark and cool, rank with the odors of cow manure and earth.

Ragna turned to leave but Musky jumped out of her arms and ran to the base of a small haystack in the corner. The little dog barked and scratched into the hay.

"Who's there?" Milton said and pointed his rifle toward the stack. "Come out at once."

"Hold your horses." Anders stood up from the back side of the haystack, brushing sprigs of hay and chaff off his shoulders. "I'm just taking a little snooze."

"What are you doing out here?" Ragna felt a rise of irritation. "I was worried!"

"Couldn't take another minute of that crazy woman in there," Anders said. "Locking up those boys in a house as hot as a Finnish sauna." He shook his head and pursed his lips. "She's off her rocker."

Milton laughed loud and long. "She's that all right," he said. "Like a mother hen keeping her chicks under her wings while the hawk is flying around."

They sat in the hay, grateful for the coolness of the dugout barn. The drums and wailing intensified. Blue tail flies buzzed around the animals.

"Hoppers got you," Milton said. "Sorry to hear it."

They discussed the location of the fields, the direction of the winds, whether or not Milton's fields were in danger.

"I worked like a dog for nothing," Anders said pushing his blond hair away from his face. Ragna noticed his need of a haircut. She had not cut his hair before and the idea of it made her face flush. "The first haystack would trade for a cow. Second stack would feed that cow through the winter." He bit into his thumbnail and spat it onto the ground beside him. "Now I have nothing to show for my work, nothing to live on next winter."

"I'm not wasting a whole day because of Inga," Milton said. He reached for the ox yoke and led Goldie and Ryder out through the door of the barn. They blinked and bawled in the sunshine. He rubbed his hand over the scrape on Ryder's back, almost healed with the help of the Udder Balm. "I'm working the north field. Fire a shot if the Indians attack."

Ragna rose to leave but Anders pulled her down beside him.

"I'm sorry, Ragna," he said. "I'm not cut out to be a farmer." He looked into her eyes and Ragna felt her opposition melt. "What if I can't provide for you?"

"Did Uncle know you were thinking about giving up farming?"

"I told him while we traveled to Cold Spring. Why?"

"He sends word that Cold Spring is looking for a teacher."

A look of astonishment came on Anders' face. "Are you telling the truth?"

"Of course," Ragna said. "Why would I lie about such a thing?"

"I was praying," Anders said. "Just now, in the haystack, I asked God to show me a school that needed a teacher."

As they laughed and hugged and kissed, Ragna remembered how Mrs. Brorson had been the first to tell her about praying to the Blessed Mother.

"But our claim," Ragna said.

"Who would even know we're gone? We'll teach the winter sessions and come back in the summer."

"But where will we live?"

"The way I see it," Anders said, "if God sends us a school, He'll certainly direct us to a place to live."

"Can I tell you a secret?" Ragna couldn't wait. Even though she knew it was too early to say anything, the glorious news wouldn't keep another moment. "I think there will be a baby sometime next winter."

Anders looked at her for a moment and then broke into a whoop. He picked her up and twirled her around the barn. The joy in Ragna's heart was greater than the pounding drums.

22

DAGMAR'S BREATHING KEPT SERENA awake all night. Dagmar gasped for air like a fish on the shore. Serena propped more pillows, but it provided little relief for her friend.

Anton fanned Dagmar's face with a small wooden shingle but Dagmar was hungry for air and there was nothing to do about it.

Serena hoped the girls would stay asleep. They needed their rest and were too young for the deathwatch. They would face such sadness soon enough.

"Dagmar." Anton cradled his wife's work-worn hand to his grizzled face. "Old girl."

Serena turned away from the raw emotion. It was too hard to watch. And too familiar. Serena had sat with both her parents and Auntie Karen at their passing. For the first time she thought it lucky that Gust had been taken quickly. It would have been worse to watch him suffer.

Tommy Harris always said that the will of God often felt wrong in the present but in looking back, one could see His wonderful plan.

Maybe he had been right but it hadn't seemed like it at the time of Gust's death, or now at Dagmar's passing.

It was just before dawn, and the dark heaviness of night pressed down upon them. Night birds sang and coyotes yipped in the distance. A whippoorwill started its mournful call. No light showed over the hill. How still it was.

Ole stomped around the kitchen as if jabbing his crutches would somehow give his mother relief. "We've got to do something."

"There's nothing to be done," Anton said.

"I'm fetching Dr. Cormonton." Ole smashed his hat onto his head and stomped out the door, his crutches loud on the wooden floor followed by the softer clomp of his single boot.

"Let the poor man sleep," Anton said with a shake of his head. "He can't do nothing."

Serena propped another pillow under Dagmar's head and turned the wet rag on her forehead. She was about to spoon a bit of broth made of beef knuckle when the breathing stopped. Dagmar groaned and the rasping ceased.

Serena held her breath and stepped away from the bed. Just when she thought it was over, Dagmar gasped again.

Anton kissed Dagmar's swollen face. "Oh, Dagmar," he said in near whisper. He spoke in Norwegian, though he usually spoke English. "Old girl." He smoothed her hair and held her puffy hands. "Did she tell you how we came to America?" Anton never took his eyes off his wife's face.

"When did you come?" Serena picked up her crocheting and sat in a chair on the other side of Dagmar's bed, across from Anton.

"Back in the earliest days of Minnesota," he said. "Before it was even a territory." Dagmar moaned and Anton stroked her cheek. "We met in the Old Country," he said. "She kept my mangle." He pushed her hair away from her face with great tenderness. "But I was a hired man and she was a housemaid at a neighboring farm. The nobleman where I worked didn't like me. Refused to hire Dagmar for the house or let us have a cottage. Just spite, you know."

"So you came to America." Serena pushed the crochet hook into the loops of thread.

A wind blew around the corners of the inn, a lonesome sound. Far away a wolf howled. The moon glowed through the window glass. A mouse scurried in the corner and a burning log settled in the stove box with a thud.

"I quit the farm and worked on a fishing boat out of the Lofoten Islands until I earned passage. Broke our parents' hearts when we left." Anton straightened his back. "We had to beg the Lutheran priest for permission to leave."

"Don't know to this day how we ever got it," Anton said. "We were confirmed but I wasn't a church-goer. Maybe he was glad to see the last of me."

Dagmar groaned and picked the air as if she were plucking apples from a tree. "Hush now, Mother," Anton said. "Hush, my best girl."

Serena threw down her crocheting and ducked into the stairway, tears streaming down her face.

"Sistermine." Kersten sat on the top step. "Why are you crying?"

"It's too early to be up," Serena said. Serena motioned for her sister to sit on the bottom stair beside her. Serena pressed her tear-stained face into Kersten's hair. It smelled of smoky fires and sweat.

"Bestemor is leaving us." Serena choked a small sob as Ole and the doctor came in through the side door. "She's going to heaven to be with the angels and our dear parents. Her children wait for her."

"But not Ole!" Kersten said in alarm. "I don't want Ole to go to heaven."

"Don't worry, little sister," Ole said from the kitchen with a sleepy Dr. Cormonton in tow. "I'm not going anywhere."

Ole settled himself in a chair beside his mother's bed and motioned Kersten to come over. He pulled her into his lap and she rested her head on his chest.

Dr. Cormonton listened to Dagmar's heart and shook his head. "There's nothing to do but keep her as comfortable as you can." He left another bottle of laudanum and went home.

Time dragged and Dagmar lingered. Anton carried the sleeping Kersten back into the loft where Maren slept. He came back down and knelt beside his wife's bed and laid his head on her pillow. He was asleep almost at once.

Serena added another stick of wood to the fire and put the kettle on for another pot of tea. She picked up her crocheting and sat next to Dagmar's bed.

"How long can she last?" Ole said in a whisper as he took a cup of tea from Serena's hand. "She's a stubborn one."

"She's a true friend," Serena said. "Back when we first came to Pomme de Terre, she befriended the smoke from our chimney before she even met me." Serena wiped a stray tear from her cheek. "Came to our house on a terribly cold day because she didn't see smoke."

"Did you run out of wood?" Ole blew on the scalding tea and took a tentative sip.

"Gust had gone to Chippewa Station, leaving me home alone." Serena tried to speak of the harrowing experience in a positive fashion. "I was afraid the Indians would see my smoke—and so I let the fire die out."

"Alone during the Indian war?" Ole pouted his lips. "What was your man thinking?"

"Your mother said that I looked like an American flag with my blue eyes, pale face and red nose." Serena smiled a sad smile. "I loved her from the very first. My God, how I needed a friend."

"They broke the mold after they made her," Ole said.

"My baby died during the uprising," Serena said. It was something buried deep in the past and she rarely spoke of it, the incident still too painful. "Your mother understood."

They sipped tea and listened to the sounds of Dagmar's breathing. "What will you do?" she asked.

Ole's face hid in the shadows and she imagined how he looked, his square forehead, and blue eyes.

"I don't know." Ole paused and his voice gentled in the gloom. "Pa is getting on in years—unable to keep up with the heavy work. It's hard for me to farm with one leg."

"What about the inn?"

A rooster crowed from somewhere outside the building and the first glimmer of light showed over the eastern horizon. Another day. Serena knew it would bring nothing good. She thought of the coffee grounds and the predicted grave.

"We missed our chance," he said after a long pause. "Should have started up a store years ago." He took another sip of tea. "Now Gardner has the leg up."

Serena felt a wave of panic sweep over her. If the inn closed, she would have to make plans for something else. It was too impossible. Too hard to consider. She pushed it out of her mind.

"I've thought of the gold fields." Ole drained his cup and reached for the teapot. "Oxcarts have dwindled to nothing and the mule trains will go the way of the oxcarts once the railroad gets here. Have to find something else to do."

Dagmar grew restless, picking at the air, mumbling as if she were trying to speak to them but saying nothing intelligible. Anton woke and spoke her name. Dagmar tried to get out of bed, struggling with her splinted leg, thrashing until her covers tangled.

"Ma," Ole said with fat tears rolling down his face. "Lay still now. You're sick. We won't leave you."

Dagmar cried out and grasped Ole's hand. She coughed and gasped for breath. Serena ran for a cool rag while Anton tried to give her a sip of tea. She choked and gasped. The death rattle sounded in her chest.

Dagmar finally slipped into a restless sleep.

"Dear God," Anton said. "Why doesn't she just go to sleep?"

"I can't stand to see her this way," Ole said. "Folks say death is cruel but they're wrong. Death is kind. It's the end to suffering."

Serena sat in silence. Life was never easy. Birth, a long agony, messy and difficult, and death a bitter struggle to the end. In between it felt mostly the same—messy and difficult with a rare bit of joy now and again.

Serena considered her life and wondered what she had accomplished. She may have another fifteen years. Most people didn't live past forty-five or fifty.

She must live. She rejected the gloomy thoughts of death and thought instead of Maren and Kersten. If she were to die, they would be sent back to Burr Oak to become

Jensina's servants. Maybe Julian would take Maren. He would be good to her, Serena knew, but the girls were like sisters. They shouldn't be separated.

Dagmar had been right. Serena must let go of the past and move forward in her life. It was hard to know exactly how to do it.

Anton went out to check on the stock. Perhaps he left to weep. Whatever his reason, Ole moved into his father's place by Dagmar's bed and promised to stay with his mother until Anton returned.

"You need some rest," Ole said after a long silence.

"So do you," Serena said.

He put his face close to his mother's ear and whispered something that Serena could not hear.

"Do you want me to leave you alone?" Perhaps he wanted privacy but did not know how to tell her without appearing rude. Maybe she had overstepped.

"*Nei*," Ole said. "Of course not."

Serena's heart rate slowed back to normal.

"Tell me about Hungry Hollow," Ole said. "I've heard only bits and pieces."

"Oh." Serena's heart quickened. She didn't know where to begin.

"You don't have to," Ole said, "if it's too hard." He looked at her with concern. "It's none of my business."

"It's all right. I've not spoken of it for a long time." Her voice trailed off. "Gust got in trouble with the government. Claimed greater losses than what we had." She tiptoed through the words that would explain the situation and yet not cast blame on her husband. "For more reparation money . . . then bought the farm to get away from the investigators."

"I hadn't known that," Ole said in a steady voice.

"I didn't find out until just before he died."

"Killed by Indians."

"We were on our way back home." Serena choked and took a deep breath. "He made a last trip out to the farm to gather his tools. Your ma wouldn't hear of me going along." She wiped tears off her face. "Saved my life by making me stay back."

"Did you love him?" His voice almost an accusation in the darkness.

She considered the question, measuring the hardships and the joys they had shared in their short years of marriage. Gust's sharp nose always reminded her of the map of Minnesota sticking out into Lake Superior. The way he shed tears over Lena when they buried her on the road to Fort Snelling. "Yes," Serena finally said. "I did."

Anton returned from outside and their conversation stopped.

At sunrise, Dagmar still lingered when Kersten and Maren crept down the stairs in their nightgowns.

"Mama," Maren said. "What will happen to Bestemor?"

Serena didn't know what to say. She couldn't imagine Dagmar as an angel with her shrill laugh and bawdy sense of humor.

"Come here, girls," Ole said. "Bestemor is sick and tired." He patted his lap and both Maren and Kersten climbed up into it, their long legs dangling almost to the floor. "See how she struggles. She's trying to say goodbye but all of her strength is needed to cross over to the other side." His voice cracked. "She's sad because she loves us but has no choice."

"The Good Lord calls her," Anton said. "As He'll call each of us someday."

They sat in silence. Serena thought to make breakfast but it seemed wrong to leave her friend's side. Dagmar's chest rose and fell with each ragged breath. Anton did the milking but hurried back inside when he was finished.

The morning passed as they all kept vigil. Serena thought to send the girls upstairs to get dressed but couldn't bring herself to disturb them from Ole's lap. He was a good man. Like his parents in so many ways.

Dr. Cormonton stopped by at midmorning. He took one look at Dagmar and shook his head. He was about to leave when Dagmar took a shuddering gasp. They all looked at her, waiting for the next breath.

It never came.

* * *

ANTON BUILT THE COFFIN. Serena didn't see his tears but the grief on his face brought tears to her eyes. He rummaged for a clean sheet in the cupboard and spread it over a layer of Sweet-scented Bedstraw leftover from refilling the mattress ticks. He carried the coffin to a bench against the wall, out of the sun's heat.

Serena washed her dear friend's body. How small she seemed, and frail. While alive Dagmar had seemed as big as a giant with her outspoken ways and defiant attitudes. Serena dressed Dagmar in her best dress, arranging the lace collar and covering her with a shawl. Serena combed and braided Dagmar's long gray hair and tenderly wrapped the braids around her head, pinning them with a wooden pin.

She and Anton lifted Dagmar into the coffin.

Dagmar looked nothing like herself. Her jaw hung slack to one side and her face looked bloated. Serena folded Dagmar's gnarled hands over her chest.

The girls wept until Serena put her foot down. "That's enough." It was wrong to allow the girls to indulge in such selfish behavior. "There is work to do." Death was part of life and that's all there was to it. "She's gone and no amount of crying will bring her back."

Serena recalled how Dagmar worried about the lack of cake at Gust's funeral. "Come now, girls," she said. "We'll make a cake." Kersten dried her tears and fetched the mixing bowl and wooden spoon.

Maren, still sucking great sobs, broke four eggs into a dish and slid them into the mixing bowl. Kersten beat them into a yellow froth with the wooden spoon until her arm grew tired. Then she passed the bowl and spoon to Maren. Serena added sugar and butter.

"We have no time to indulge in grief." She added a scoop of flour to the batter. "A woman must carry on. I know it's hard, but that's how it is."

Ole stomped around, even more angry than usual, and then busied himself with stock. Serena opened the window and aired the room. She stripped the cot and asked Anton to move it back upstairs where it belonged.

Serena thanked God Dagmar's struggle had ended.

As luck would have it, the Lutheran minister was gone and not expected back for several days. He had a side business of making bars of hard soap to supplement the meager contributions of his parishioners. He sold his wares to Van Dyke's Store in Alexandria. With this heat, the body must be buried at once. There could be no delay in the funeral.

The townspeople gathered around the grave on the windswept hill where Tommy Harris and Gust already slept. The once beautiful meadow lay blackened and forlorn.

Several people shared recollections of Dagmar's life. She had helped many during a crisis or encouraged them during hard times. Serena hung on every word, wishing she had known her dear friend better than she had. Olaus Rierson, the Icelander from Chippewa Station, stood before the group like a wild-eyed Viking with his florid face and white hair and beard.

"Dagmar Estvold was one to stand by in trouble." Olaus' tears dripped into his white curly beard. "Back during the Pomme de Terre siege, she wore a man's hat and fired a gun with the best of us." He blew his nose with a honk. "She killed one red devil for sure, maybe two, if the truth were told."

A neighbor woman read a psalm and led the group in singing the old Norwegian hymn, "*Jeg ved mig en Soevn i Jesu Navn*, I Know a Sleep in Jesus' Name."

As the familiar melody sang out over the little cemetery, Serena pondered each word.

"I know of a sleep in Jesus' name, A rest from all toil and sorrow; Earth folds in her arms my weary frame and shelters it till the morrow; My soul is at home with God in heaven, Her sorrows are past and over."

As the clods fell onto the pine box, Serena sent a desperate prayer for guidance to the God who lived in the blue heavens, the one who cared for Baby Lena and her parents, Auntie Karen, Tommy Harris, Gust, and now Dagmar. Those she had depended on were leaving one by one. There was no one left.

Her tears were not only for Dagmar.

As she walked away from the grave with the girls flanked on either side, Mr. N.W. Gardner approached her. He wore a fancy suit with a gold watch chain draped from the watch pocket. He carefully stepped over a mud puddle to protect his shiny boots.

"Mrs. Gustafson," he said with a tip of his hat. "My condolences."

"Mr. Gardner," Serena answered with a stiff smile.

"I'll come right to the point," he said. "I'm interested in buying your property at Hungry Hollow. I understand your husband paid fifty dollars for the property and I am prepared to match that offer. Generous in these hard times."

Serena's heart sank. She owned eighty acres of fertile soil along the Pomme de Terre River. A wooded forty meant a steady fuel supply and the river guaranteed water. She had hoped for ten times that amount.

"No, thank you," Serena said. Her chest ached, and she remembered what Dagmar had said about Mr. Gardner trying to buy the whole town. She would not give it away. "I've decided not to sell."

"You surprise me, Mrs. Gustafson," he said. "I stand corrected. I was under the impression you wished to sell your property."

The mourners trickled toward the inn. Serena must hurry to serve the cake. She had no time to waste.

"Then I have another proposition," he said. "My cook has taken off for the gold fields." Mr. Gardner twirled his mustache with his thumb and forefinger. "I am prepared to offer you employment."

Serena must not have heard correctly. "Excuse me, sir?"

"I am prepared to offer steady work now that the Estvold Inn is no longer in business."

"You are mistaken," Ole said, suddenly at her side. "The Estvold Inn resumes business tomorrow."

"But surely you are in need of rest in your time of bereavement," Mr. Gardner said. "I'm prepared to offer an acceptable wage, Mrs. Gustafson. And living arrangements for you and the girls at my hotel. There's talk of a school starting in the fall. Pomme de Terre is a growing burg and will be only more prosperous once the railroad arrives."

"She has a position," Ole said. Serena saw the sides of his jaw working and knew he was angry. Anger rose up in her, too, as a flush spread up her neck and cheeks. She could handle her own life. She didn't need him barging in. "And a place to live."

"If you'd prefer," Mr. Gardner turned his shoulder to Ole and spoke directly to Serena. "You might tend my store. More suitable for a lady than scullery drudging."

"I said, the lady has employment." Ole braced himself on his crutches and glared at the storekeeper.

"Then good day," Mr. Gardner said with a tip of his hat. "Don't hesitate to contact me if your plans change."

Mr. Gardner walk away from the cemetery under Ole's steely gaze.

"I thought you said you would close the inn." Serena felt like a little girl, others making decisions about her life. She would have liked to have asked the wage Mr. Gardner might offer. She clenched her hands together until her knuckles cracked.

"I've changed my mind." Ole stalked away, jabbing his crutches into the dirt path through the blackened pasture. "That hotel is no place for the girls."

23

EVAN AND THE MULE TRAIN CROSSED the Red River Trail the next day. Glenwood lay before them at the bottom of a steep hill, built along the shores of Lake Minnewaska. Pelicans and blue herons splashed their wings in the clear water. A flock of geese arrowed across the sky and glided onto the blue water. Mallards, cormorants, and egrets fluttered in the lake. Evan wished he could join the birds and wash away trail dust and the stink of sweaty mules.

"Ride the brake to hold back the load," Old Hen said while pulling hard on the lines and turning half around to show Evan how to do it. A wild screeching of wooden brakes on iron wheels filled the air, and Evan's arms almost pulled out of the sockets with the pressure. "Allemande left!"

"Easier to go down than up," Evan said, trying to be positive.

"Depends on what you call easy," Old Hen said. He spat over the side of the wagon. "Hang on."

Evan's shirt soaked wet with sweat as the wagon swayed under the pressure. He refused to consider what might happen if the teams behind them lost control and plowed into them from behind. Old Hen seemed not in the least perturbed.

"Bow to your partners." He called to the leaders and pulled back the lines until his biceps bulged. He spat to the side and held his whip over the wheelers ahead of him, not flicking it but just holding it even. "Promenade all!" Old Hen said and the team stepped out.

Evan had never seen ballet dancers but had once read about them in *The Skandinaven*. He doubted any ballerina was as graceful as the jacks mincing down that hillside. The leaders held up their heads and eased the great boat of lumber down the hill. Evan's heart thudded with the beauty of beast and wagon.

They pulled over to wait for the other teams at the bottom. Evan jumped down from the wagon box and wiped his forehead with the back of his sleeve. "Beautiful, just beautiful." Evan pumped Old Hen's calloused hand. "Mister, that was some driving."

Old Hen brushed off the compliment with a shrug. "We'd best check the harness. Going down steep inclines sometimes tangles the chain."

They were checking straps between the pointers and sixes when Ted pulled up beside them in a cloud of dust.

"You drive like an old man," Ted said. "I thought we'd never get here." He jerked the lines and cursed his team, hurrying them to the edge of the water with the load swaying from side to side, in danger of tipping over.

Jeppe, Zeke, Martin and Homer unhitched the teams and led the mules to water. The mules splashed like young foals, snorting water and swishing wet tails over their backs for the flies. Old Hen and Evan gathered needed supplies from the wagons, and Ted busied himself doing nothing, as usual.

* * *

Cursing men. Gun shots. Stomping and braying mules. Somewhere a crying child.

Evan scrambled to his feet as the camp erupted into chaos around him. At first he thought he was home and Indians were attacking the cabin. He rubbed sleep from his eyes and regained his bearings, then slipped into his wooden clogs.

A shadowy form shifted through the brush. Evan reached for his rifle. His duty was clear. He must secure the mules.

The air weighed heavy with fog, dampness clung to Evan's feet and legs. It was just before dawn, not light enough to see. Evan tripped over a root, sprawling on the dewy ground amid loud braying and thudding mule hooves.

Evan jumped back on his feet and reached for a mule's halter, taking great care to avoid coming up behind it. The last thing he needed was a kick in the head. He rubbed the mule's head between the ears. "*Naar enden er god er allting godt,* all's well that ends well." The mule nuzzled his nose under Evan's beard until Evan dug in his pocket for a few kernels of grain.

"Thank God." Old Hen joined him in the middle of the herd. Old Hen's hair stood wild about his head and he had jammed his hat on sidewise. His trousers hung by a single gallus. "The mules all here. Freight unmolested."

"What happened?" Evan said. "I saw someone walking through the trees."

"A mule's as good as a watch dog." Old Hen said. "They got wind of the robbers and warned the camp." He pointed to a crumpled mass beside a tree. "Looks like this one didn't know any better than sneak up behind a mule."

Evan bent closer to see in the early dawn darkness and recognized the man with the sharp face, or what was left of his face. He lay in a pool of blood.

Evan's stomach roiled at the sight of the dead man. "Where is his partner?" He remembered the sullen look of the dead man's companion.

"No sign of him." Jeppe puffed after running around the perimeter of the camp. "Or Ted, either. We found Mr. Yokum knocked out by his post. You should see the goose egg on his head."

"Did Ted take Zeke's horse?" Evan said. "He wouldn't have gone on foot."

"The horse is here," Old Hen said. "Even Ted knows horse thieves get hung. Must have ridden the dead man's mount."

Evan stayed with the herd in case the robbers tried again. The sun inching across the sky burned off the early fog. He led the teams to the lake, holding Old Hen's rifle ready.

"Water them real good," Old Hen called from the campsite. "It's a long ways to the Pomme de Terre River."

It was a glorious Minnesota morning. Evan felt most hopeful as he herded the mules to drink at the water's edge. They had survived an outlaw attack and the leader was dead. Surely things would only improve. A pair of loons danced over the water with flapping wings, crying out their haunting call. Blackbirds sang and robins warbled from the grove alongside the lake.

A small flock of sandhill cranes stood in a nearby field until a red fox startled them. They flurried into the air in a commotion of wings and sharp cries, leaving the disappointed fox standing below. They flew so high that they looked like tiny specks circling round and round, their distinctive throaty cries echoing over the settlement.

The town still slept but roosters crowed from all directions. The people of Glenwood soon were up and about.

Evan thought of Inga and the children, worrying the boys might forget their chores, hoping Inga was able to keep the weeds out of the garden and that the baby remained healthy. So many things could happen while he was gone.

Zeke said Tory Thorson managed the post office in Glenwood. Evan scratched out a quick note to mail before leaving town. It didn't feel like enough, but there was work to do.

Mitch Yokum crawled to the shore of the lake and bathed his sore head in the cool water. "By God, they snuck up on me." He dipped water over his head and then drank from a cupped hand.

"Did you see who it was?"

"No, the mules grew skittish and everything went black."

Evan pulled the halter of a jittery mule, crooning softly in Norwegian and led it back to its tether. He measured its grain ration before returning to the other mules.

"I was drove out by hoppers in Alexandria," Evan said to Mr. Yokum, choosing the American words carefully. "Know what it's like to lose everything."

"You're lucky to find work."

"*Ja*," Evan said.

"After I lost the first crop, I took a job in the Sleepy Eye Milling Company," Yokum said. "But after a couple of years the mill shut down. No wheat. Government sent seed but the damn hoppers took that, too. There's nothing left. Thirteen years' work down the drain."

They talked about the grasshoppers and their destruction. Yokum hadn't known they stretched all the way down to Texas.

"What's a fellow to do?" Mitch Yokum said. "Where do I go to get away from them?"

"I'd head to timber country," Evan said. "They like open prairie."

"Thank you kindly," the man said as he stood back on his feet, still holding his hand to the lump on his forehead. "Have a brother who works in a logging camp. Might head up to St. Croix and find work in the pineries."

After a hurried breakfast, they hitched up the teams and started back on the road. They had lost time and must make it up if at all possible.

"Ted's left us in a lurch, damn his shiftless hide," Old Hen said. "I'm moving Martin to driver. Zeke will ride the brake for him."

Mrs. Yokum fried a stack of flapjacks two feet high for them to bring along for cold lunch.

"Take enough for your family." Old Hen divided the stack of pancakes and gave half to the woman. He added a few cans of beef and a small sack of potatoes. "Thanks a lot, ma'am."

The woman drove their wagon. Yokum held his head in his hands at her side. They traveled east toward Sauk Centre. Evan waved to them from the freight wagon as they passed by. "Good luck!"

"We'll need it," Yokum replied.

Their children straggled alongside the wagon. They looked even skinnier in the morning light with their bony backs and shoulder blades. Only their horses wore shoes.

Evan released the brake as Old Hen pulled to the front of the caravan. Old Hen called out a brisk, "Allemande right." The mules snapped to attention. "Promenade all!" And the mule train started out.

Evan calculated how far it was to the St. Croix River Valley in eastern Minnesota, almost to Wisconsin, and how sore the Yokum children's feet would be by the time they got there.

He couldn't help the Yokum children but he could help his own. He would watch for a basswood log and carve clogs for his boys in the evenings. He could bring new shoes home to his family at the end of the journey. He sighed.

Alle monner drar. Every little bit helps.

24

THE DRUMS CONTINUED INTO the evening but Anders refused to stay in the cabin. "Inga drives me crazy with her worry."

Instead, they borrowed Uncle Evan's writing desk, a carved wooden box filled with writing supplies, and carried a lighted candle into the dugout—a cool relief after the house. Ragna always felt safer in a place without windows.

The only furniture was the rope bed built into the wall of the dugout. Ragna, afraid of centipedes, made the bed so their feet were toward the wall and their heads toward the center of the room.

The milk jug sat in a bucket of cold water from the spring. A cheese cloth drained cottage cheese into the milk pans on the shelf.

Auntie Inga had put down a barrel of eggs in June. The lime solution made the entire dugout smell of whitewash, but the eggs would stay fresh for winter use. Auntie always said June and September eggs were the best to store—she planned another barrel in the fall.

"Someday we'll have eggs to put down for the winter," Ragna said. "I'll fry eggs every morning. Even through the coldest of winter."

"We surely will," Anders said. "And smoked hams and dried beef." He put the candle in its holder. The earthen floors and walls absorbed the feeble light. "And sacks of potatoes and crocks of lard."

"And I'll bake blackberry pies and rosettes." Ragna twined her arms around his neck. "And grow fat and lazy from eating all the good food you provide."

"And my belly will hang over my britches." Anders kissed her neck and nuzzled her ear. "And everyone will say that Mrs. Anders Vollen is the best darn cook in Tordenskjold—and the prettiest."

Ragna pulled away, laughing, and picked up her knitting. She did not need light to knit and sat on the dark side of the bed to allow Anders the candle for writing his letter.

"What do I say?" he said. "How do I ask about the pay I might receive?"

"You might start by saying you worked for the Saints and the pay they gave you."

She casted on a row of gray yarn that would be a baby blanket. The soft gray yarn wound onto the needles and each added stitch reminded Ragna that she would be a mother.

Anders toiled over a letter to Mr. Brorson. She laughed when he pressed too hard and broke the nib of the feather pen.

"Now I'll have to carve another!" Anders laid the pen aside and reached over and caressed Ragna's stomach, speaking into her belly. "Did you hear that, baby? Your careless *far* must carve another pen." He rummaged for another feather in a compartment of Uncle Evan's desk. Anders pulled out his paring knife and expertly whittled a white chicken feather into a pen. "If only I had known to stop and meet Mr. Brorson in person while I was there."

"But what does Mr. Brorson have to do with the school?" Ragna turned her needle and started another row. "He's a farmer, not the mayor."

"Do you hear that, little one?" Anders laid aside the letter and pulled Ragna back onto the bed. He pulled up her skirt and pressed his ear against her bare belly. She giggled and hoped that one of the boys would not barge into the dugout unannounced. "Listen to your *far*, little baby. Your *mor* does not think Mr. Brorson is the right person to address about the school." He stroked Ragna's skin as he talked, pausing to kiss her navel, causing her skin to shiver.

The drums pounded relentlessly. Anders's presence made her feel safe. It helped that the dugout had no windows for spying Indians. It was too early to go to bed, but Anders blew out the candle.

"But your letter," she said.

Anders took the knitting needles from her hands and laid them on a flour barrel beside the bed. "*Jeg lengter etter deg,*" he said while kissing her neck and throat. "I long for you."

The drums continued long after they were finally asleep.

* * *

Ragna woke up with a start. The drums had stopped. She shook Anders's shoulder.

Anders jumped up and pulled on his pants. He grabbed the gun and looked carefully through a crack in the door before opening it all the way. Ragna pulled on her dress and tried to straighten her hair. It was early morning, the robins just beginning their song, the air heavy and misty with fog from the lake.

"The house looks quiet," Anders said. "When did the drums stop?"

"Just now."

Ragna imagined a horde of painted Indians rushing in from all sides. She willed herself to think of nothing but Anders and the baby. That's all that mattered.

Anders waved to Gunnar, who came out on the stoop of the house. "Good, he's got the gun."

"Mor says to come inside," Gunnar called in a loud whisper. The rooster crowed, quietly at first and then louder.

Anders hesitated at the dugout door, clutching the rifle barrel until his knuckles showed white in the gloom. He looked first to the right and then to the left.

"What's wrong," Ragna said. "I don't see any Indians."

"I confess, Mrs. Vollen." Anders looked at her with such affection that Ragna felt a lump form in her throat. "When I think of how your parents died . . . and our baby . . . my strength drains away."

"Come." Ragna felt courage rise within her. "We'll be fine, Mr. Nobleman."

They ran hand in hand across the open ground while Gunnar stood watch from the stoop. They had barely crossed the threshold when Milton burst into the yard on his white mule.

"*Uff da*," Auntie Inga said. Her face turned white as her nightgown. Her long hair hung in a frazzled braid down her back. "Something must be wrong for him to be in such a state."

Milton tied the mule to the butchering tree and charged into the house, his face wild with excitement.

"Indians." Auntie Inga said. She reached out to the table to steady herself. "Good Lord, help us."

"Not Indians." Milton's eyes glowed like pools of fire. "Gold!" He picked up Auntie Inga and twirled her around the crowded room as if she were one of the little boys. Auntie's white nightgown fluttered around her and Ragna was shocked to see her bare limbs showing.

"Gold right here in Tordenskjold." Milton put Auntie Inga down and reached for Ragna's hand. He pulled her into his arms and danced her around the kitchen. "Our troubles are over, I tell you. We're going to be rich."

25

IN THE WEEKS FOLLOWING DAGMAR'S DEATH, Serena's life settled into a routine. She baked in the morning, cooked meals, washed clothes, cleaned house, helped the girls with their sums and tried not to think about her future. By nighttime, she collapsed into bed.

One day Serena poured the morning milk into the churn and settled into a shady part of the yard. Churning, always her favorite household chore, allowed her time to think. She pushed the dasher up and down, finding a comfortable rhythm.

The ox carts were almost a thing of the past. Good thing they could depend on mule trains heading to the western forts or the Dakota gold fields. Serena pushed the dasher harder. It was only a matter of time before railroads expanded to more towns and villages. Serena did not know how the inn could survive.

She watched Anton chop firewood in the yard, even though the pile beside the inn reached almost to the second story windows. The larger chunks would be burned in the fireplace during the coldest part of winter when the cook stove wasn't enough. As he chopped, the girls piled the smaller kitchen wood into a huge crate.

Anton liked the girls near him, and Serena did not have the heart to refuse him.

Anton had been chopping wood every day since Dagmar's funeral, pausing only for meals. He had grown thin and gaunt, rarely speaking more than a direct answer to a question. Yesterday, he dragged a cottonwood tree into the yard, enough wood to heat the entire settlement, in Serena's estimation. He said that he would sell firewood to make up for the loss of crops.

Serena adjusted the rhythm of her churning to that of his chopping, enjoying the sounds of the girls' laughter. Churning always started out easy but grew harder as her muscles tired. She thought to call the girls to help her but instead switched hands and kept a steady pace.

Ole glowered as he crutched around the barnyard, tending livestock. Serena watched him scratch the calves' ears and check the hooves of the oxen. The first hay crop, secure in the barn in spite of the grasshoppers, would not be enough to carry the stock through the winter. He must be worried.

Ole conversed with visitors during meals. For that, Serena was grateful. Dagmar left an empty spot she could not fill. For Dagmar, cooking and cleaning had been as effortless as breathing. Her humor made the inn a welcoming place.

The inn would not have any customers over the dead of winter. What would she do when the traffic stopped for the season? Old had to be worried about that, too, and all Anton did was chop, chop, chop.

* * *

THREE WEEKS AFTER DAGMAR'S FUNERAL, Serena was serving an early supper to a crowded table of men going through with a herd of Indian ponies. They came earlier than usual and she felt ill-prepared.

"General Custer, himself, captured the ponies," a swarthy man bragged. He said something in Indian to an older man who looked like a half-breed. They laughed and looked at her, nudging each other, trying to get her attention.

"Where are you taking the horses?" Ole brought the bread basket to the table and eased himself down in an empty chair.

"Selling them to whoever will buy them," the swarthy man said with a grin. "Are you in the market for a good horse?"

The men talked about the price of horseflesh, Indian raids in Dakota, and grasshopper damage while Serena dished up huge serving bowls of boiled potatoes and fish gravy. It was a rowdier bunch than usual and though she heard Ole greet another man who came in through the door, she was so busy carrying the heavy bowls to the table that she did not look their way.

"More coffee, darling," the man who had spoken earlier said while holding up an empty cup. "No need for sweetening if you stir it with your pretty finger."

Serena felt the blood rising in her cheeks as the men burst into bawdy laughter. She looked over to the corner where Kersten and Maren washed dishes at the dry sink. Serena hated that the girls would see her treated so disrespectfully. It was Ole's job to keep the men in order. She looked toward him and felt her knees wobble.

It couldn't be.

Her brother-in-law, Julian Gustafson, looked toward her, holding his hat in his hands, and smiled. He was a little shorter than Ole. Dark curly hair hung over his brown eyes. His church suit looked rumpled and dusty from travel, and he wore a couple of days' growth of dark beard on his usually smooth face. Serena's mind flashed a map of his travels: the river boat to St. Cloud, the cars to Herman, and then north to Pomme de Terre.

"Uncle Julian!" Maren threw the dishtowel aside and ran to her uncle, flinging her arms around his waist. "Mama, look. Uncle Julian is here."

Kersten stayed at her task with a stricken expression. Serena understood how she felt. She and Kersten had both felt Old Mrs. Gustafson's scorn over the years. Julian doted on his niece but paid little attention to Serena's sister. *Stakkers liten*, poor little one. Serena felt off balance.

The other men paused briefly to watch the family reunion, and then turned their attention on the remaining food. Serena felt Julian's eyes upon her but didn't know what to say. So she said nothing and concentrated on her work as Maren chattered about the kittens. Soon the front door closed behind them as Maren and Julian went to investigate the barn and find the kittens. The herders pushed away from the table and hurried to get on the trail again. The swarthy man winked at her as he walked out the door.

Serena turned to the dishpan and washed dishes with a vengeance. Kersten dried. She thought to call Maren inside to finish her chores but decided it would be better for her daughter to spend time with her uncle. And easier for Serena to put off speaking to him.

"What's he doing here?" Kersten whispered.

"I don't know."

"I'm scared," she said and then lowered her voice to a whisper. "What if he wants Maren to live with him and her grandmother?"

"There's nothing to be scared of," Ole said from the table where he stacked dishes. "Those rough men are gone now."

Kersten placed a dried bowl in the cupboard.

"Now they were a bunch of crooks," Ole said. "Wouldn't be surprised if those horses were stolen."

Anton came in from the woodpile. "What's for supper? I'm hungry." He washed his hands at the basin and smoothed back his long gray hair with his hands. How weary and drawn he looked. Grief was a cruel master. She remembered the way her chest had squeezed after Lena's death.

"Kersten, run and fetch Maren and her uncle for supper," Ole said.

Serena had not confided in anyone about Julian's marriage proposal, not even to Dagmar. Kersten had no idea why Julian had traveled all the way to Pomme de Terre in the middle of the busy summer. Funny that she would worry about Maren going to live with him.

Serena wiped her hands on the dishtowel and fetched the pot of stew she had reserved for the family's meal. She was a grown woman without anyone to share her deepest thoughts.

She refused to confide in Jensina. She might have spoken to Dagmar had she lived. She couldn't burden her daughter or little sister.

Julian came into the house wearing a hopeful look. He was a kind and decent person, soft spoken and slow to offer his opinions. He was not a braggart nor did he think he knew everything. She had known him all her life and could trust him with her life. He was not like Gust.

Serena wondered why she always felt compelled to number Julian's good points.

They gathered around the table, and Anton led them in the table prayer. "*I Jesu navn går vi til bordså spise, drikke på ditt ord. Deg, Gud til ære, oss til gavn, Så får vi mat i Jesu navn. Amen.* In Jesus' name to the table we go, to eat and drink according to His word. To God the honor, us the gain, so we have food in Jesus' name. Amen."

Serena cast a side glance at Julian, wondering what he thought of the Norwegian blessing. Gust had always said it was time to put away the old ways and become Americans. Surely his brother thought the same. The stew caught in her throat. The coffee tasted tepid and bitter. Old feelings she had experienced when she was married scrambled to the front of her mind, the feeling of being invisible, of not having a voice.

The men made small talk about the weather, the crops, and the grasshoppers. Julian expressed interest in the Black Hills gold strikes. Ole answered his questions with politeness, if not enthusiasm.

"Delicious, as always," Julian said, pushing away from the table. "Serena, you are an excellent cook."

"Thank you." She could not meet his eyes. "My mother's recipe."

The talk turned to the inn, the progress of the railroad and Dagmar's untimely death.

"I bring sad news as well." Julian crimped his lips into a thin line. "Mother was called home a fortnight ago." He reached for Maren's hand but looked at Serena. "I didn't want to tell you in a letter."

"You mean my grandma is dead?" Maren's voice shrilled and tears sprouted from her eyes. "Bestemor and Grandma both gone?"

Julian fished for a handkerchief and handed it to his niece. Serena sat dry eyed and without emotion. She would not be a hypocrite and weep at her passing. She felt duty bound to say something, but anything she might say would surely be wrong. A small hand squeezed hers.

"Don't cry, Sistermine," Kersten whispered.

The tears came gathered in her eyes, though not for the old woman's passing. Serena sniffled tears for her ill plight with the grasshoppers, a farm that wouldn't sell, and the loss of her dear friend.

Julian's face relaxed when he saw Serena's tears. She sniffed and sucked a deep breath. She was giving the wrong impression. She searched for a handkerchief in her apron pocket.

"I have business here as well," Julian said. "I received a letter from N.W. Gardner offering to buy my brother's property. I thought it wise to come and settle the matter before taking you home."

Serena's mouth dropped open. The room turned dead silent. Serena saw his mouth move and heard the words he spoke but couldn't believe her ears.

"Jensina has need of your help with the gardens."

Surely he couldn't be serious.

"The barley crop is in but we must return to Burr Oak before the wheat is headed out." Julian pushed away from the chair. "If I could arrange for a room here at the inn, I'm sure my business will be finished by the end of the week."

"Impossible." Ole's voice carried that steely edge it did when he was angry and Serena saw the pulse throbbing in his neck. "We're filled up for tonight. You might try Gardner's Hotel."

Julian glanced around the kitchen with a puzzled look as if looking for other boarders. Serena wanted to shoo him out the door with a broom. No, she wanted to hit him with the broom. The property belonged to her. This was 1876 and women were allowed to inherit property. She could handle her own business without his help.

And the nerve of Mr. Gardner to go behind her back. Her temple throbbed and she ground her teeth until they ached.

"We're closing now to get ready for our overnight guests." Ole struggled to his feet. "Pa, you'd best do the chores before we get busy."

Anton looked at him with a puzzled expression, his face haggard beneath an unkempt beard, and his eye rheumy. He looked at Julian and then at Serena and frowned.

"Can I go with Bestefar and play with the kittens?" Kersten said.

"After the dishes are done," Serena said. She wished Julian would leave. She needed time to think. Her mind scattered in a million directions.

Anton left for evening chores, and Ole pulled himself to a standing position and steadied on his crutches. "Come, Mr. Gustafson, I'll show you to Gardner's."

Kersten poured steaming water from the tea kettle into the dish pan without taking the time to use a pot holder. The hot steam caused her to lose her grip on the handle and boiling water splashed over her hands and bare feet as it crashed onto the floor.

Serena jumped at Kersten's screams. Her mind whirled. She yanked her sister away from the puddles of steaming water on the wooden floor and pulled Kersten's wet skirt away from her legs. She tried to remember how her mother had treated scalds and burns.

Julian grabbed the water bucket and plunged Kersten's hands into the cold water, crooning to her in a reassuring voice, "Everything will be fine."

"Maren, fetch more water—hurry." Julian sat down on the chair near the sink, and pulled Kersten into his lap with her hands still in the bucket. "Put your feet in, too," he said. "It will make you feel better."

Serena stood bewildered.

"Sistermine," Kersten wailed. "I'm sorry."

"Hush now," Serena said and knelt beside her little sister, still sitting in Julian's lap, with her feet and hands crammed into the water bucket. "It was my fault."

"It's no one's fault." Julian inspected Kersten's hands and feet. "You scared us, sistermine," he said, "but it looks like you'll be fine. I've seen worse."

Ole pulled a chair closer and entertained Kersten with riddles until Maren returned with another bucket of water. By this time, Julian was almost as wet as Kersten. Julian urged Kersten's feet into the new bucket while keeping her hands into the other.

Ole chucked Maren under the chin, "You did real good, Maren."

"How do you know so much about burns?" Serena said. She peered into the buckets to examine Kersten's skin.

"Back in the war I handled artillery." Julian settled back in the chair and balanced the buckets and Kersten on his lap. "We'd shoot the big guns until they were red hot. We learned to soak our blisters in cold water. If we did it soon enough, we avoided a lot of misery."

"Smart," Ole said. "Wish I'd known that when I was shooting the cannons."

"How are you feeling, sistermine?" Serena said.

"I'm all right," Kersten said. Her freckles stood out against her white skin. Though her hands and feet had a few blisters, they seemed to be responding to the water treatment. Serena touched her forehead with the back of her hand. No signs of fever. Serena breathed a sigh of relief.

"The worst is over," Julian said. He motioned for Serena to steady the buckets while he lifted Kersten to a chair. They repositioned the buckets of water. "Keep her in cold water until she goes to bed. I think she'll be fine by morning."

"Maren, help me clean up the spilled water," Serena said as Julian and Ole left the inn. Serena felt as if the air had been knocked out of her. Exhaustion overwhelmed her.

"Why can't Uncle Julian stay here?" Maren said.

"Hush!" Serena fled to the lean-to where the supplies were kept, covered her face with her apron, and indulged in the luxury of a good cry. She knew that Julian would want an answer to his marriage proposal. All along she had told herself that she couldn't marry him because of his mother and the way he ignored her baby sister.

She no longer knew what to think.

26

EVAN HAD MORE QUESTIONS about driving mules but Old Hen slipped into a mood. At least he kept his thoughts to himself except for a few muttering rants about Ted's incompetence and disloyalty. He seemed agreeable to answer direct questions, but otherwise kept quiet. Dust gathered in Evan's nose and throat. He wished he had kept his red bandanna instead of trading it to those Indian boys.

Old Hen's silence allowed Evan time to think, something he usually enjoyed. Today, with the grasshoppers and his family back on the claim without him, Evan's thoughts drifted only to the negative. Gunnar had failed to pass his Catechization the year before, surely Evan's fault.

The father was responsible to make a son study. But how do you make a boy love God? Evan slapped a bothering fly away from his head. Do you beat him? Evan's mother would have had strong opinions about a grandson, almost grown, who was still unconfirmed and denied the Lord's Table. A man must be certain of heaven should tragedy befall him.

Evan cringed to remember the minister's words, "Those who are unwilling to learn the Catechism deny Christ and are no Christians, and neither should they be admitted to the Sacrament." He flicked the whip over a lagging mule on the right pointer.

Knut loved studying the Catechism and the Holy Bible. Knut wanted to be a minister someday. But that would take an education. And an education cost money. Evan sighed and flicked the mule again.

The straggling mule stumbled, and Evan flicked the whip again. He didn't hurt the mule, just thought to remind it to keep up with the others.

"For God's sake, put that whip away," Old Hen said. The mule regained its balance but seemed reluctant to put its weight on its hind foot. "It won't do any good to beat the poor thing. We have to stop and see what's wrong."

"Should we stop the other teams?" Evan set the brake. The two other rigs pulled out around them and kept going west on the trail. "Shouldn't we stay together?"

"*Na*," Old Hen said. "Won't take long." He jumped down from the nigh horse and walked around the front of the team. He patted the animals, speaking soothingly to them, and took a moment to feed the lead mules lumps of sugar from his pocket.

"You don't do anything fast with a mule," Old Hen said. "You let him think he's in charge." He straightened harness and lines, and when he finally got to the lagging mule, approached it from the front with soothing words. Then Old Hen lifted the hind hoof where he dislodged a pebble from beneath its shoe.

They were soon on their way but lagged behind the other wagons. Evan felt a vague uneasiness without the protection of the other drivers. He cast an anxious glance to either side of the path and wiped sweaty palms on his trousers.

Old Hen kept the same pace as before and seemed in no hurry to catch up. The flat terrain proved no challenge for the well-trained mules and Evan did not understand why Old Hen tarried.

They came to a place heavy with grasshoppers. The wheels of the great wagon crunched over the millions of hoppers until the trail turned into a slimy, stinking mess. Swarms of grasshoppers flew up into the faces of the mules. The leaders stopped dead in their tracks and refused to go forward, shaking their heads and braying a warning for the grasshoppers to leave them alone.

"Now, damn you!" Old Hen swatted grasshoppers out of his hair and beard. "Now is the time for that whip."

Evan snapped the whip over the leaders that set the pace for the whole team. Old Hen called out, his voice almost as loud as the whip's cracking sound. "Promenade all!"

The mules hesitated but obeyed. The wagon lumbered forward. Evan felt his heart rate return to normal rhythm. They pulled beyond the worst of the grasshoppers, and though they swarmed over the ground, they no longer flew up into the mules' faces. The grasshoppers had slowed the other wagons, too, and soon their rig caught up with them.

"What happened to you?" Jeppe called back. "I was about ready to send out the army."

"Nothing serious," Old Hen called back.

"Well, keep up then!" Jeppe said.

They were almost to the Chippewa River, when they met a small band of Winnebago braves riding worn-down ponies. Their women and children walked behind them beside a dog-pulled sled called a travois. The travois was heaped with furs and hide-wrapped bundles.

The Indians traveled toward Glenwood and looked peaceful enough, no war paint or feathers, but all carried bows and quivers of arrows draped over their shoulders.

Evan's shoulders tensed. He had seen too much to be comfortable around Indians.

Old Hen pulled his team to a stop and Evan set the brake. The load of boards shifted and groaned. The Indians gesticulated wildly, pointing backward along the trail, and looked very excited. Then they motioned to trade. Old Hen took off his hat and scratched his head. Then he rummaged for the rucksack containing their supplies. He withdrew the stack of pancakes and handed about half of them to the Indians. They in turn gave him a small basket and continued east without as much as a nod.

"The Chippewa River crossing is up ahead." Old Hen motioned with his chin toward the north. "We'll ford the river and stop for midday."

They bumped to a low spot on the river, heavily rutted and used by many to cross the flowing water. Old Hen climbed down and called out a "bow to your partner." He walked across the river, keeping a keen eye at his feet. Satisfied, he turned and came back to the wagon.

"Everything looks good," he said and climbed back up on the eleven-nigh wheel horse. Evan released the brake.

"Allemande left!" Old Hen called out and flicked his whip. "Promenade all." The wagon lumbered into the water while the mules pulled with all their strength. The load shifted, almost as if it were finding footing on the new ground, but crossed without incident.

"Now you, Jeppe!" Old Hen called from the far bank and waved his hat. "Look alive!"

"Pull!" Jeppe called and the crack of his whip sounded loud as a pistol shot. Their load of bricks was heavier than the sawn boards. Half way across the river, the mules stopped. Jeppe cursed and snapped his whip. Homer jumped down and waded to the front of the mules. He tugged the halters of the leaders, dusty grays with long yellow teeth. They brayed loud and long and refused to move.

Old Hen climbed down from his wagon and waded back to the river. Jeppe and Old Hen talked heatedly a long minute. Their voices rose in anger. Evan could not hear what they said but it seemed they argued about the weight of the bricks. Evan climbed down from the wagon seat and joined the other men.

Finally Jeppe slapped his hat against his leg and stormed back to his rig.

"What's happening?" Evan said.

"Two stallions fighting for position," Zeke said with a laugh. "Jeppe argued before that the load was too heavy for his team but Old Hen wouldn't listen. Now Jeppe is right and we have to either unload the bricks or hitch another team to the wagon."

"Which is it?" Unloading bricks in the middle of a river would be no picnic. Evan squinted up at the sun overhead. The hottest part of the day lay before them. He breathed a sigh of relief to see Old Hen unhitching his team. "Should I go and help him?"

"Go ahead." Zeke grinned. "It's your funeral."

Evan waded out into the river to the stalled wagon. The iron wheels had sunk until they were almost to the hub in the soft river bottom.

"This is one hell of a mess," Jeppe said. He stood by the lead mules, rubbing their noses and quieting them as best he could. "I told him so in St. Cloud but he hectored me into going along with it."

Old Hen unhitched and turned his team, and Evan was careful to watch how the pointers, sixes, and eights stepped over the chain. Old Hen led his mules into the water, still in harness. "Evan! Don't just stand there," he said. "Give me a hand."

Evan walked alongside Old Hen's team, patting their sides and speaking to them calmly in Norwegian. When he reached the lead pair, he spoke into their ears and rubbed their noses as Old Hen slipped between the mules to hitch the single and double trees to the chain of Jeppe's team. Then Old Hen looped the rope through the collar ring on the left mules.

Evan could see the problem. Attaching the extra team displaced the mules from their usual duties. A kicking hoof or a personality clash among the mules might injure mules or drivers. At least it was a straight pull up on the bank so the sixes and eights would not have to step over the chain.

Old Hen stood at the front of the twenty-four mule team. "Allemande left!" Old Hen's voice cracked out loud as a whip. Jeppe and Homer called to their leaders and signaled with the jerk line. The mules snapped to attention. "Promenade all!"

The animals strained until their muscles quivered, pulling the enormous load of bricks forward onto solid ground.

When they reached the shore of the other side, Evan breathed a sigh of relief. He waded back to his wagon while shaking his head. He had never seen such majesty in a team of animals. "Wasn't that something?" he said to Zeke. "Have you ever seen such driving?"

"Yup," Zeke said. "Let's get going. I'm starving."

Evan vowed to write a letter home and tell his sons about the mule teams and the driver who handled them like a king.

Martin veered about six feet to the right to avoid the ruts left by the wagon of bricks. The mules stumbled a little half way over, but pulled together and brought the load safely up the far bank of the river where the other wagons waited.

"We dodged the bullet," Old Hen said with a deep sigh. He blew out his breath and wiped his forehead with the back of his arm. "But a miss is as good as a mile."

They didn't bother with a fire but pulled out the remaining pancakes from Mrs. Yokum's morning labor. The men slumped under a cottonwood growing alongside the river. Jeppe propped his feet up against the trunk.

"You didn't have to give away so many to those bucks," Homer said. "Not enough left for us." He reached for several of the cold pancakes and stuffed them into his mouth.

"Here," Old Hen said and handed the basket given to him by the Indians. "These will fill you up."

Homer popped a fried bit of meat into his mouth. "These are good." He passed the parcel to Evan who took and bit into one. "What is it?"

Old Hen smiled, his eyes twinkling. "Injun recipe," he said. "Mighty good."

Martin and Jeppe reached for a sample.

"They're grasshoppers," Old Hen said with a loud guffaw after all the men had their mouths full. "They brush them into a hole filled with burning coals. Then dig out the roasted hoppers and pull off the wings and legs."

Jeppe jumped to his feet and spat, wiping his mouth. "Damn! You tricked us."

Evan swallowed hard and reached for a drink of water. It might be that he had eaten grasshoppers before at Crooked Lightning's tipi but he couldn't bear the thought of eating them now. Not when the devils had almost ruined him and might yet ruin him if things didn't turn around.

Zeke reached for another handful of hoppers. "Not too bad! I'll take your share."

"The Winnebagos brought news." Old Hen turned serious. "Looks like trouble."

Old Hen said the Indians reported Yellow Hair, General George Custer, led an army out of Fort Abraham Lincoln to go against the Sioux. Yellow Hair bragged he would wipe out the Sioux Nation.

Evan remembered the ferocity of the Sioux during the uprising. General Custer might have a harder time than expected.

"Said the Cheyenne join the Sioux and are ready for a fight."

"Where?" Martin said. "Anywhere near this country?"

"Farther west," Old Hen said. "Dakotas, maybe, or even Montana."

The mules chomped grass and weeds around a small pile of rocks next to the creek. They swished their tales against blue tailed flies buzzing around their backs. Red-winged blackbirds sang from the creek and an eagle shrieked overhead. Heat shimmered across the prairie and Evan's upper lip beaded sweat.

"The Sioux believe they were created to live in Minnesota," Evan said. His speech came out slow and halting with all the American words. "Bishop Whipple said they will never be happy unless they return."

"They won't be back," Homer said. "They're banished. Will face the army if they try returning."

Evan hoped he was right. A new worry niggled at his mind, that the Sioux might try and take back what they believed belonged to them. If they did, Minnesota would be a sitting duck. No army posts left. Everything civilized.

"We'd best get going," Old Hen said at last. "Damn that lummox, Ted. I'd like to get my hands on him for leaving us in the lurch." He stood to his feet and dusted off the seat of his trousers. "We've another river to cross and a ways to go if we want to make Gager's by dark."

* * *

THEY CROSSED THE POMME DE TERRE RIVER without incident. The men debated whether to camp by the river or press on to Gager's Station where there would be hot food and real beds.

"Daylight to burn," Old Hen said at last. "Let's press on."

By the time they drove up to Gager's Station, the setting sun showed only a ribbon of light across the western sky. Mosquitoes tormented both man and beast. It had been an exhausting day and a poor night's rest the night before.

Gager's Station was a log building with a thatched roof. A low barn stood behind the main house. Two milk cows bawled in the fenced barnyard, one with a calf on the teat. A scraggly looking geranium bloomed by the doorway. It was the only splash of color on a meadow eaten black by grasshoppers.

Evan heard a woman's screams coming from the house.

"What's going on?" Old Hen said. "Indians?"

"I won't go," a woman said in a screeching voice loud enough to make the mules skittish. "You can't make me go."

Evan braked and secured the wagon before jumping down. Old Hen and the other drivers stood on the path to the house.

"Eyes open, boys," Old Hen said. "Looks like trouble." Old Hen instructed Homer, Jeppe, and Martin to stay with the teams and motioned for Evan to go with him into the house. "Gager's is known for crooks and thieves." Old Hen hoisted his rifle. He reached into his waistband and pulled out a Colt revolver. He handed it to Evan. "Stay alert, now."

A loud crashing sound came from inside the house. Then another screech. Old Hen and Evan rushed up to the door and pushed their way inside with guns raised. The room was a huge kitchen with eight wooden tables and a dry sink alongside the wall, lit by a kerosene lantern hanging on a hook over the main table. A pretty, young woman stood waving a cast iron frying pan in her hand. Yellow hair curled around her face from a long braid that reached almost to her waist. She wore a worn dress and embroidered apron.

Ted Green cowered under a table.

"I won't go," the woman said. "You can't make me go, Ted Green, and I won't." She threw a cup at him with her free hand. It crashed into a hundred pieces on the floor. "I'll shoot myself first," she said. "I'll jump in the Pomme de Terre River before I go to Indian country with you." She threw a plate and reached for another. "I'll drown in the well. I'll stick my head in the water bucket until I choke to death." Ted cowered behind raised arms. "I'll slit my throat with the butcher knife. I'll set myself afire." She raised the frying pan higher and crashed it on top of the table where Ted was hiding. "You can't make me go."

"Well, Ted," Old Hen said, "here you are. And me worried you were killed by that outlaw." Old Hen chuckled. His shoulders shook. He burst into laughter that turned into a roar. "And you here with your pretty wife in matrimonial bliss."

"She's lost her marbles," Ted said. "Help me, for God's sake! Gertie's gone lunatic."

"You're calling me crazy?" She shook the frying pan first at Ted and then brandished it in Old Hen's direction until he backed out the doorway. "It's crazy to go to Indian country, that's what crazy is."

"Evan, fetch the boys." Old Hen wiped tears off his cheeks, gasping for breath in a fit of laughter. "This, they have to see."

27

RAGNA COULDN'T BELIEVE HER EARS. Gold in Tordenskjold Township? Impossible! The *Skandinaven* boasted of strikes in Dakota, Montana, and Colorado—but none in Minnesota.

"Just south of Turtle Lake." Milton jigged across the puncheon floor, his heels clopping out a steady rhythm on the logs. "A hunter found gold in a duck's crop." He hooked his arm into Ragna's and twirled her around the room while he hummed an old folkedanser tune. "We're going to be rich! Rich, by God. "

"How did you hear?" Gunnar said.

"Lying Jack," Milton said. He paused to catch his breath, releasing Ragna from his grip. Milton wiped sweat off his face. "And he never lies."

All the boys clamored to go along, jumping up and down and hanging onto Milton to beg his permission. Ragna realized with a start that Anders would go, too. It was only a few miles north through the woods, but still too far away for Ragna's comfort. She felt unsettled because of the drums the night before and the uncertainty with Uncle Evan gone.

"Stop!" Auntie said in a loud voice that made all of them stop talking and look at her. "*Det er ikke gull alt som glimrer.* All that glitters is not gold." Her chin tilted. "We need to know about the Indians before anyone goes anywhere. Gunnar, stand guard at the window."

Gunnar dragged his feet but obeyed. Auntie's face looked gray and haggard. Ragna felt a sharp worry. Auntie didn't sleep well with Uncle Evan on the road.

"Milton, find out where the Indians are," Auntie Inga said. "Then you can worry about gold."

"Don't be foolish," Milton said with an irritated look on his face. "The Chippewa have no interest in making war on us."

Auntie stood her ground. Milton pushed his hat on his head and stormed out to investigate the location of the Indians while Anders stood watch on the hill behind the cabin. Auntie kept the boys inside all morning. By noon Milton declared the Indians had returned to rice camp. He and Anders gathered gear for digging gold. They would not be dissuaded.

"But Anders." Ragna pulled him aside to speak to him in private. It was a hot day, steamy with humidity and not a breeze in the air. They sought the shade under the butchering tree. "You promised Uncle Evan you'd stay with Auntie and the boys." She wanted to remind him of their wedding vows but thought it better to bring up Uncle Evan instead.

"You're here," Anders said with a nonchalant wave of his hand. "There's nothing to fear." He gathered Uncle's spade and shovel. "We're only down the road a ways."

"But what if the Red Men come back?"

"They're gone. You'll be fine." Anders was giddy with excitement, his face flushed as if he had been out in the sun too long. "This is my chance to make up for the grasshoppers. Even a small strike means another start. Don't you see?"

She did see. But she didn't like it. Just that morning he had been hesitant to let her cross the yard for fear of Indians. Now the Red Men were the least of his consideration.

Ragna had heard about gold fever. Now she saw for herself how it affected people.

"I'll be back before you know it. Pray that I'll strike it rich." Anders kissed her and hurried off to load the mule.

Ragna heard Gunnar arguing with his mother before she stepped back inside the house.

"I want gold," Gunnar said. "I'm going with the men."

"*Nei*," Auntie said. "*Betre pengalaus enn aerelaus*, better be without money than without honor. Get to your chores. Listen how the animals beller for water."

"I'll run away if you don't let me go." Gunnar's brown eyes flashed sudden anger. "You can't stop me. It's gold! If Far were here, he'd let me go."

"Hush now," Auntie said without sign of wavering. "That's enough."

"But think of new dresses for you and a horse for Far. And a new plow and harrow. New books for Knut and a baby carriage for Christina. We'll have shoes and clothes. Please, Mor, let me go."

"You'll stay here and that's all that there is to it," Auntie Inga said with a firm tilt of her chin. "I'm counting on your help."

"You can't make me!"

"Gunnar," Ragna said in a soothing voice reaching out and placing a hand on his sleeve. She and Gunnar had always been close and she had learned over the years to assuage his temper. "We need your help with Uncle Evan gone."

Through the open door, Ragna watched Milton and Anders race north on Whitey. They rode as if they were being chased by Indians. They didn't look back before fading into the trees. Ragna felt like crying. "We need a dependable man in charge."

Gunnar followed her gaze and sighed. "I never get to do nothing. All I do is work."

"You can join them later," Ragna said. "Let them go first and figure it out. They'll be back and you can go next time."

Gunnar sighed and clenched his fists. "All right." He set his mouth in a thin line. "But it's not fair."

"No sassing," Auntie said. The oxen bellowed louder. They wanted water. "And no monkey business. Watch the little ones and run back to the house if you see any signs of Indians." Her voice softened. "Take a quick dip in the lake while you water the animals." The baby fussed and Auntie picked her up and laid her across her shoulder. "Cool off."

Gunnar barked at the boys to help him herd the cattle to the lake. Musky nipped at their heels as they straggled across the clearing. "Last one to the lake is a rotten egg!" The stragglers turned into racers as they met Gunnar's challenge.

"We can't stay inside forever," Ragna said. "It's hotter than blazes."

Auntie's sighed. "You're right." She changed Christina's soakers and tossed them into a bucket already filled to overflowing with the soiled rags. "Sometimes you just have to leave it in the hands of God."

The day before, Auntie had announced her plans to weave *fisketeine*, fish traps. Beaver were damming the creek that flowed into the Lake. A cone shaped trap wedged in the dam would keep them supplied in fish without the wasted time of holding a pole. Besides, if the grasshoppers came around, the fish would be too full to care about bait on a hook. Ragna had searched and found a nice willow tree along the lake and had snipped small branches, soaking them in a barrel of water to ready them for the task.

Auntie reached into the barrel and tested the branches with one hand while bouncing the baby with the other.

"I'll nurse Christiana outside in the shade. You can start on the traps. Lord knows we need something to eat."

Ragna gathered the willow branches, awl, darning needle and thread and moved outside to the shade of the butchering elm while Auntie Inga sat against the tree trunk and nursed the hungry baby.

"That's a man for you." Auntie circled a finger through the baby's sweaty hair. "Milton is as useless as teats on a boar."

Ragna smiled but swallowed a guilty feeling. After all, Anders had made the same promise. She pounded a willow branch with a rock until the bark peeled off. She separated the pulpy strands and piled them for Auntie to weave into a cone. Ragna's mouth watered at the thought of fried fish. Extra would be dried and salted for winter.

"How soon do you think they'll be back?" Ragna reached for more willow branches. The sun stood high in the afternoon sky. The men had only a couple of miles to travel, going north through the woods. "How long does it take to strike it rich?"

"I don't know," Auntie said with a sniff, unlatching the sleeping baby from her breast and laying it on a blanket beside her, "but from what I know about human nature and the male of the species, I expect it will take longer than it should."

Ragna's heart sank.

"They'll be home soon," Auntie said with a sneaky grin as she reached for the willow strands. "I noticed they took only spades and shovels—not a bite of food along." Auntie twisted a fibrous strand into a small, tight circle. "I thought to tell them but decided to let them get good and hungry. Serves them right."

Ragna burst out laughing and Auntie joined in. The laughter was a welcome release from the worry over grasshoppers, Indians, and gold.

Ragna didn't want to sleep in the dugout alone, was afraid of centipedes without Anders there to take care of her, and remembered only too clearly how Migwans had looked at her white skin.

"Wouldn't it be wonderful if they found it?" Ragna said. "Gold would solve all our problems." She pounded another willow branch with the rock, hitting her thumb by accident. "Ouch!" She stuck her thumb in her mouth and sucked away the pain. The willow sap bitter on her tongue.

"Money rarely solves problems," Auntie said. "Causes more, usually."

Auntie hesitated a while, then looked around to make sure no one was within earshot. "I married a rich man, you know." Auntie lowered her voice and told about marrying Ingvald Ericson after the death of her first man.

"He had money," she said, "and I thought that would solve everything." Her nimble fingers looped wet willow strands through the base of the net. "I learned the hard way that money rarely makes people happy."

The boys splashed in the lake as the cattle drank their fill. Farther out on the lake, a heron landed, its blue wings like a fan as it settled onto the rippling water. An eagle screeched overhead, circling for prey. It suddenly dove straight down into the lake, not far from the heron, and came up with a fish dangling from its claws. Its majestic wings stretched wide as it carried the catch away to feed its young.

"But maybe God will send a gold strike to help us."

"I believe in the goodness of the Lord but it seems unlikely that He would hand us a gold strike on a silver platter." Auntie pulled another strand. "Even the eagle has to work for its food."

Ragna hoped Auntie was wrong. She hoped that Anders would burst into the yard with a sack of gold hung over his shoulder, enough money to take away all their worries. As she pulled the willow strands, a strong dread fell upon her, making her morose and anxious.

Ragna prayed under her breath, turning away from Auntie so that she would not see her moving lips. *Thy kingdom come. Thy will be done. On earth as it is in heaven.*

The men did not return for chores. The evening sunset was a glorious explosion of red and purple. Ragna left the door unlatched until the moon was full over the water. Wolves howled in the distance and Auntie asked Gunnar if he was sure the cattle were all safe in the barn and the chickens penned in the coop. Gunnar nodded and Auntie pulled in the latch and settled the cabin for the night. She checked the boys for wood ticks.

"Red sky at night, sailor's delight," Auntie said looking through the window. "Looks like rain tomorrow."

Ragna would sleep with Auntie and the baby until Anders returned home. Maybe a change in weather might bring the men home sooner than expected.

The next morning dawned cloudy and overcast. Thunder rumbled in the sky and across the lake jagged lightning pierced low, dark clouds. Ragna poured milk for their porridge and hoped with all her might that Anders would ride in on Milton's mule before the storm.

"Hurry with the chores, boys," Auntie said.

Gunnar and Knut ran to herd the stock to the lake for water while the twins took empty water buckets to the spring.

"Uncover the rain barrel," Auntie said to Sigurd, still dawdling at his mush. "Hurry now, before the storm."

Musky barked in the yard and Ragna saw him chasing Fisk up a tree. Before she could call out to him to stop, the little dog turned and ran into the bushes by the barn while barking furiously. Something was in the bushes. She remembered the gray wolf they had seen in the brush.

"What's the problem?" Auntie Inga picked up the baby and settled by the table to nurse.

Ragna reached over the door for the muzzleloader. "It might be a wolf skulking around the hens." A wolf pelt meant two and a half dollars. Enough money to get them through for a while. "Anders says Lying Jack pays good money for pelts." She had not fired the ancient gun in a long time but knew how to do it. Anders would be pleased if she took down such a valuable creature.

As she left the cabin, thunder rumbled and lightning flashed over the lake. The storm would be upon them any minute. Musky barked and jumped beside the bushes, more furious than before.

"Who's there?" She raised the gun. "Tell me if anyone is in the bushes." She took aim but before she could get anything in her sights, a bolt of lightning sizzled in a pine tree beside the barn and thunder crashed.

Ragna jumped and fired by accident. It was a wild shot that hit nowhere close to the bushes. A black-and-white skunk ran out and turned to spray. Musky ran between Ragna and the skunk and took the brunt of it. Before Ragna could get away, a choking mist settled over the clearing. Scared by the noise of the gun and thunder, Musky ran straight at Ragna and rubbed against her legs.

"No," Ragna said. "Get away from me!" Her eyes burned and she coughed and choked. "You stink!"

Another crash of thunder and the twins raced from the spring toward the house in a flurry of buckets and driving rain. The dog dashed after them and ran into the house through the open door before Ragna could say a word to stop it.

The storm released its fury. Ragna's apron blew straight out from her body as drenching rain fell from the sky. She hurried into the house where the boys chased Musky around the cabin. The dog hid under Auntie's bed and refused to come out. The house reeked of skunk. Ragna's eyes watered and the baby cried. It might have been funny except for Auntie Inga's rage.

"Get that dog out of here!" Auntie's voice roared louder than the thunder. She climbed half way up the loft ladder holding the baby out of reach of the skunky dog. "This very instant!"

The boys knelt on the floor and coaxed Musky from underneath the bed. Sigurd grabbed the dog but it wiggled out of his grasp and ran across the floor. Knut finally cornered Musky behind the wood box. He grasped the dog and held it straight out in front of him to keep the stench off his clothing. He was about to take the dog outside when the door opened.

Migwans walked inside, rain streaming down his face and hair. Outside the storm roared. Thunder clashed and lightning pierced the air.

"Missus." He pointed to Ragna, nodding. "Migwans." He tapped his chest.

He stood regally with his arms crossed in front of his naked chest, water dripping down his legs and puddling at his feet. He carried nothing. Perhaps he sought shelter from the storm. He stood silently and looked at them. Curiosity sparked his eyes and sudden humor. "*Zhigaag.*" He laughed and pointed to the dog as he held his nose with his fingers. "*Haag.*"

Auntie climbed down from the ladder and stood behind Sigurd, holding the baby with one arm and Sigurd's shoulder with her free hand. Her knuckles showed white from her grip. Ragna worried that Auntie was near the breaking point. Uncle Evan gone, the drums, the men leaving to seek gold, the skunk, and now Migwans. It was too much for any woman to bear.

Ragna looked around the room, searching for something to give the Indian to appease him.

"Milk." Ragna lifted the milk jug from the table and gestured for him to drink.

"Milk," he repeated. Migwans nodded his head and tipped the jug to his mouth. He drank a long draught and burped loudly. He handed the jug back to Ragna and pointed to the kettle of porridge on the stove. Ragna scooped some into a dish and handed it to him. He blew on it to cool it and ate rapidly with his fingers while the boys gaped in amazement. He licked his fingers and placed the empty bowl on the table.

"*Migwetch.*" He nodded at Auntie Inga.

"He didn't use a spoon," Sigurd said.

"Hush!" Auntie squeezed his shoulder tighter. "Be quiet now."

Outside the wind died down as quickly as it had started. The rain turned into a steady drizzle and thunder once more rumbled in the distance. The sounds of songbirds filled the air. Migwans nodded again, then walked out through the open door and stepped over puddles in his path.

The trees swallowed him.

28

S ERENA DRIED HER TEARS, left the storeroom and returned to the dishpan. Dirty dishes heaped on the table and dry sink. The slop bucket filled almost to overflowing and the water pail near empty. The stove died down and the kettle boiled almost dry.

"Maren!" Serena said. "I need your help." Tears sprouted in spite of her best efforts to swallow them.

"What's wrong, Mama?" Maren carried a stack of dirty plates from the table. "Are you sad about Grandma Gustafson?"

Negative words filled her mouth but Serena stopped herself. It was wrong to speak ill of the dead. Tommy Harris had once told her that only good deeds and successes were remembered in heaven and that we were wise to do the same.

Old Lady Gustafson had lived a miserable life with a mean husband. She had watched all her boys, except crippled Gust, go off to war. Arne was killed at Fredericksburg and Lars wounded at Wilson Creek. Serena would not speak ill of her mother-in-law although the negative words curled in her mouth ready to jump upon her tongue.

Maren wiped the good platter and placed it on the shelf.

"Sistermine," Kersten said in a whisper. She sat at the table soaking her hands and feet. "You can cry if you want to." Her eyes looked so much like their mother.

To think Mr. Gardner had gone behind her back trying to get her land! Dagmar had named him a low-down louse. She had been right.

Serena scrubbed the dishes in record time and dumped the dirty dishwater over what was left of the potato patch. Maren had a mound of dishes yet to dry. Serena knew she should return to the kitchen to help her, but felt so overwhelmed that she decided to sit outside a while. She lowered herself onto a large rock by the garden. Flowers had bloomed there before the grasshoppers. Now only a few stray weeds sprouted in the dirt.

Night was falling on Pomme de Terre. Crickets and frogs sang from the slough. Junebugs slammed against the window panes to get at the light. Serena welcomed the cooler air. Anton, still doing chores, lit the lamp in the barn. Its feeble gleam glowed through the single window pane. Bats swooped in the sky, diving for mosquitoes and gnats. A whippoorwill chanted its call until it was breathless, then caught its wind and started again. Whip-poor-Will! Whip-poor-Will!

Serena felt whipped. Everywhere she looked she saw the dimpled earth where grasshoppers had laid their eggs. She didn't know when they would hatch but knew when they did hatch, it would be the same torture all over again.

Gardner offered so little for her land that she would never be able to strike out on her own. Her options were to return to be her sister's housemaid or marry Julian. Either way meant she must surrender her will and sound judgment to another. Even if she remained at the inn, she would be dependent on someone else.

If only the grasshoppers had stayed away until she could have found a buyer for Hungry Hollow. The perfect name for that jinxed parcel of Minnesota dirt.

Dear Lord, why are you sending this plague upon us?

"A penny for your thoughts," Ole said in his deep voice.

Serena jumped and let out a small shriek. "You scared me half to death!" She hadn't heard him come up behind her. She hurriedly wiped tears off her face. She hadn't realized she had been crying, so intent was she upon counting her troubles. "You need to warn people you are coming, not just sneak up on them!"

Ole threw aside his crutches and sat on the ground beside her. The neighbor girl herded their geese into a small cage. Her cajoling and the geese's hissing sounded louder than the whippoorwill's call. The neighbor girl called goodnight to them and slammed her door as she ran back into her house. Cows lowed from the barn, the sound of a baby's cry from down the lane, and the smell of frying meat wafted from across the way.

"Your brother-in-law," Ole said at last. He plucked a strand of green from beside the rock and chewed on it. "Seems like a nice enough man."

Serena sighed. She did not have the words to say what was on her heart.

"What's he really doing here?" Ole said. "Why does he care where you live or what you do?"

Serena shifted her weight, trying to find a more comfortable place on the rock. She slapped a mosquito buzzing around her hair, catching it in her palm and smashing it on the surface of the rock. "It's a long story," Serena said.

Anton came out of the barn carrying the lighted lantern in one hand and a bucket of milk in the other. He blew the lantern out as soon as he left the dark log barn. He walked over to the garden.

Anton handed the bucket to Serena. "Needs to be strained."

Serena got to her feet and steeled herself to finish this last chore before bedtime. Exhaustion sucked the air from her lungs.

"You've got yourself some fine girls, Serena," Anton said. "I couldn't be prouder of them if they were my own."

Serena looked up in surprise and a smile curled her lips. "They're keepers," she said.

"You're a good mother," Anton said. "Don't let anyone tell you otherwise. Dagmar said the same and you know Dagmar—never said anything she didn't mean."

It was the most Anton had said in one conversation since Dagmar's death. Serena impulsively kissed his whiskery cheek. "*Takk skal du ha,* dear friend," she said. He smelled of cow barn and sweat and Serena felt a sudden longing for her far. "Thank you very much."

* * *

IN THE MORNING, SERENA WOKE up on the wrong side of the bed. She should have been overjoyed that Kersten's burns were minor. She had Julian to thank that Kersten's skin blistered only on the tops of her feet and hands.

Before Serena had finished the breakfast dishes, she looked through the window and saw Julian coming up the path to the inn. If only there were somewhere she could go. She debated hiding upstairs but then he saw her through the glass and waved.

She sighed. The grasshoppers had eaten the hollyhocks that once shaded the window from view. Without the hollyhocks, Serena was caught flatfooted. The last person she wanted to see was Julian Gustafson and yet there he was.

The kitchen fire stoked hot for baking and it already felt too hot for comfort. Good. Maybe he wouldn't stay long.

Serena pulled open the door with a frown. "I have my morning work to do," she said without greeting. "Perhaps you could come back later in the day."

She could tell it was not the greeting he wanted. He fingered his hat, tracing his fingers around the brim. Julian was clean shaven and his hair neatly combed. A dab of shaving soap showed behind his ear.

"Walk with me," he said. "Take me out to your property and let's see how it fared with the grasshoppers." He flashed a shy smile. "Don't you owe me that much?"

Ole crutched up the path from the barn with the girls on either side of him. Kersten carried the milk bucket and Maren the egg basket. Maren ran toward her uncle as soon as she saw him.

"Would you excuse Serena from today's work?" Julian said while squeezing Maren's shoulders with one arm. "We need to go out to the property and see what remains."

Ole paused, balanced on his good leg and pushed his hat brim up from his eyes. He looked at Serena without comment or expression. "Of course," he said. "The girls can take care of the chores for one day."

"I want to go along," Maren said jumping up and down and hanging on Julian's arm. "Please! Take me along!"

Serena was about to say yes when Julian spoke. "Not this time, Maren." He kissed the top of her head. "You have chores."

Serena fetched her plainest bonnet and did not change out of her oldest dress and apron. She found her barn shoes, the ones she used for outside work, and put them on. They looked as clumsy and ugly as what a man would wear. She had a long walk ahead of her, a mile and three quarters if they cut through the woods, longer if they went by the road.

She straightened her shoulders and strode out into the yard. Without waiting for Julian, she headed in the direction of Hungry Hollow. At least she would see for herself what was left. She had wanted to make a trip out to the old place but hadn't found the time with Dagmar's sickness and funeral.

Julian caught up with her and chatted about the news from Burr Oak. Jensina had fallen behind with the berry crop when her youngest suffered croup. His cousin had been injured in a fall from a ladder. Old Mr. Ingram had suffered a heart attack while chasing a runaway horse. His funeral had been the day after his mother's. The barley crop had been the best ever and the wheat looked promising. A German family had moved into town and was building a brewery. There was talk of a seminary being built.

Serena listened half heartedly. She and Gust had traveled this very path. Old ruts showed in the trail, perhaps ones that Gust had made with his ox team. Betty and Betts had been the sweetest animals. Serena remembered their soft lowing and gentle eyes. Tommy Harris had ridden out to their shanty to drop off the mail.

Sparrows and shrifts sang in the grove along the path and a blackbird warbled. Squirrels chattered from their nests. A prairie hen skirted a patch of grass missed by the grasshoppers.

As they walked through the woods, the landscape changed from desolation to green vegetation. Gardner had lied to her. It was a miracle. Serena's pulse quickened.

"Look!" she said. "The grasshoppers haven't been here."

They walked in silence until they came over the rise and looked down at the old homestead. Beside the old oak tree, the renegade Sioux had killed her husband, surely the same Indian who had scared her half to death as she wrote a letter home to her mother. He had stolen her pen and ink. Even after all these years, Serena marveled at the miracle of it. She should have been killed. Maren would never have been born.

Only charred timbers and a partial chimney remained of the shanty. The barn tumbled into a pile of rubble and ash. Wild grasses filled the meadow, a potential hay crop.

The fields burst with weeds but held potential. Beyond the ruins lay the meandering Pomme de Terre River.

"You're not listening," Julian said and took her hand in his.

"I'm sorry," Serena said. "You may not know—this is the first time I've been back since Gust's death."

"I'm sorry." He let go of her hand. "It must be hard for you."

They walked in silence around the former buildings and Serena found an old clothespin lying in the weeds. She placed it in her apron pocket. A keepsake. She sat on a fallen log in a shady place where the woodshed used to stand and Julian sat beside her.

Bumble bees buzzed on wild roses. How sweet they smelled. Dragon flies flitted around ox-eyed daisies. Ovenbirds chirped from the grove, reminding her of the brown bird story. Serena felt like a brown bird, invisible and with a very average song.

"Serena," Julian said with a trace of a stammer. "I don't know how to compete with a dead man. I have something to say and not a lot of time to say it."

Such weariness filled Serena that she thought she might die. How could she explain her feelings when she didn't understand them herself?

"I've come a long way. I need your answer."

Dagmar had said that she needed to get on with her life. Tommy Harris had said that truth sets people free. She took a deep breath and chose truth.

"Your brother was neither a good husband," she said as she twirled a corner of her apron with her chapped fingers, "nor a good person." She looked up to see if he was shocked by her words but he looked at her without expression. "He lied to get reparation payments from the government after the uprising." She lifted her face to the breeze blowing in off the river. "Said Lena was murdered by Indians so he could cash in on her death. He lied to me, too. And lied to your parents and caused great agony by keeping me away from my parents without explanation." The pace of her speech quickened as the memories rushed in. "And he was mean and domineering and spiteful and arrogant."

"So because Gust was a son-of-a-bitch you'll deny me?" Julian said. "I know what a bastard he could be. None of this surprises me. I've always known."

"I loved him." Serena thought back to their honeymoon across Minnesota and a fierce need to defend her dead husband rose up in her. "But he broke my heart and then left me alone." She bit her lip to stop it from quivering and sniffed back a tear. "Maybe I am afraid to try it again."

"I'm not my brother." Julian took her hand in his and knelt down on one knee in the damp ground in front of her. He lifted her chin with his other hand and forced her to look at him. "I won't mistreat you, or leave you—and I won't lie to you."

"But don't you see," Serena struggled to find the words. "I felt invisible as a married woman. When you said last night that you were here to manage my business, I felt myself shrinking back . . ."

"Not so," he laughed. "You'll be the queen of my house. The mother of my children. You'll be a respected married woman. You won't have to put up with any guff like I heard last night." He kissed her hand and Serena knew that he would have swept her into an embrace if she had given any indication of consent. "Living in a roadhouse is no place for Maren. Or you either. You deserve better."

"I vowed to raise Kersten as my own."

"Jensina wants her," he said. "Needs help with the children."

"Damn Jensina!" Serena stood and stomped her foot, knowing she was acting like a child, not caring. "Don't you see that it has to be about what *I* want for once? Not what you want or Jensina wants or anyone else."

"Wait! Don't be upset!" He chuckled, which only made her angrier. "Kersten can live with us, if you want. She'll be my sister, too, when we marry." Julian stood and drew both her hands to his chest. He looked down at her with such devotion that Serena felt her cheeks flame. "I thought with Mother gone you'd have a change of heart. I know she was difficult. I understood your hesitancy—but now you have no reason to decline my offer."

Serena shook her head and started to speak.

"Wait," he said and kissed her softly on the forehead. "I own my farm, free and clear, with a good crop in the field. I've a little savings and have every reason to believe I can provide you with a good living. We'll be a real family." It had been so long since she had been that close to a man. She felt confused, mixed up. "Think about it and give me an answer tomorrow."

They walked back to town, Julian talking the whole time of hog prices and bushels per acre. She tried to imagine being Julian's wife, listening to him every day for the rest of her life, sharing his bed and bearing his children. She had been alone for so many years. His kiss had reminded her of what she had been missing. She tried to imagine what kind of father he might be. He wasn't a bad person. He had been kind to Kersten the night before. She could make it work if she tried.

She was still young enough to start over but the years were passing by. Maybe this would be her only chance. Julian would provide a good living. The girls would have an education. Jensina wouldn't be so bossy if Serena were married with a home of her own.

So what if Julian wanted to manage her business? She'd never cared before. The smart thing to do would be to marry him and get on with her life as Dagmar had said she needed to do.

If only she could hear a voice from heaven.

29

EVAN AND THE OTHER MEN LAUGHED to see Ted put in place by his woman. The more they laughed, the angrier his missus became. Evan stepped out of the way in case she might heave the skillet toward him. Finally, Ted scooted out from under the table and stood in the doorway, ready to make a quick getaway.

Mrs. Green, stomping and muttering threats of death and mutilation, cooked a meal in the cast iron pan instead of using it as a weapon.

Ted hung back from the group and kept his distance while his wife fried potatoes. Either he was ashamed of deserting his job or afraid of being brained with the frying pan. Finally Ted ambled over to the muleteers who were arguing about whose turn it was for swamp chores.

"I'm sorry about leaving you boys," Ted said. "I don't know what came over me. Addled, I guess."

"I thought you took off with the highwayman," Old Hen said. He fastened bright eyes on Ted as if waiting for a reaction.

"You're mistaken," Ted said. "I left right after dark. Did you say you were robbed? I don't know nothing about that, nothing at all."

The men looked at each other and rolled their eyes.

"What mount did you ride?" Old Hen said. "Surely you found a horse to carry you this far."

Ted didn't answer and Evan waited for Old Hen to say something, maybe quirt him with the blacksnake whip or shoot him. Surely, Old Hen wouldn't put up with such treachery.

"You might as well make yourself useful, Ted," Old Hen said at last. "Water and grain the mules—make amends for your recent misjudgment."

"Thank you. Thank you, kindly." Ted smiled a fawning smile, rubbing his hands together and bowing slightly forward in Old Hen's direction. "I'll do all the chores. Every single one of them—if you just believe me." Ted almost tripped over his feet in a hurry to get out the door.

Evan trudged to the nearest lake to wash off the trail dust. The water felt cool after the day's heat, though it floated algae and tadpoles. Evan dove in and came up spouting water from his mouth as Ted brought the first mules to drink.

"I don't know why I have to do all the work," Ted said. "Isn't fair." He pushed the mule, trying to hurry it. He pushed again and the mule kicked, just missing Evan's leg.

"Careful!" Evan stepped out of range of the strong hooves and combed back his wet hair with his hands. He bit back a smile. "You deserve it," Evan said. "And you know it." He felt almost human again after ridding himself of at least some of the trail dust.

"But it wasn't my fault," Ted said as Evan went back into the house where the muleteers were still talking about Ted.

"We looked for him everywhere," Jeppe said. "Never dreamed we'd find him hiding under a kitchen table with a frying pan aimed at his head."

The men laughed and Mrs. Green gave them a withering glance from the cook stove. Evan had promised to write Inga often and by God, he would keep his promise. He had mailed a letter to her in Glenwood but was glad to see another post office, called Potosi, at Gager's Station. It was a wooden box with leather hinges and though it didn't look official in any way, Old Hen assured him his letter would go through.

"Why is it called such a strange name?" Evan expected Potosi to be another American word for post office.

"A Spanish name," Old Hen said. "Meaning great riches. Out here a letter is most treasured."

Evan hurriedly scratched out another letter to Inga. He shoved it into the Potosi when Mrs. Green called them to the table. The food was plain but good. The men shoveled it in without speaking. Through the open window they could hear Ted swearing at the mules. From time to time a mule brayed back. Evan marveled that such a poor excuse for a man could find a job anywhere.

Three rough looking men ambled into the station as the teamsters finished their supper. One was dressed in miner's clothes, faded and ragged. He was long legged and his hands dangled almost to his knees. He pulled out a chair from a table and stretched a leg over the back of the chair. He held a deck of cards in his hand and reached for a cigar with the other.

"Care for a friendly game?" he said. "Hank Gager hired us to run this farm for him." He gave his partners a wink and a nod. "But we take time for a little game of chance now and again." His friends clattered around the table and made themselves comfortable.

"No, thank you," Old Hen said. "Have work to do."

"Gertie," one of the men called. "Bring a bottle."

"You know what they say about all work and no play," the man said as he popped the cork and filled a dirty glass.

Homer and Jeppe snooped around the card table until Old Hen motioned them outside with a quick jab of his chin. Ted had almost finished tending the mules. The wagons clustered together at the front of the building.

"We've got to stand guard," Old Hen said while looking around to make sure Ted wasn't listening. "It's no time to slack."

Evan was surprised at Old Hen's caution since the station had a pen with sturdy fences and Ted was with the mules. Evan looked forward to a night of uninterrupted sleep.

Old Hen eyed the corral and wagons. "We're up against it, boys," he said. "Those men inside are scalawags and horse thieves."

Old Hen told them that they would cross the Big Muddy the next day and then face twenty-five miles of prairie before they reached Toqua Station. He was afraid the men might follow and rob them once they were away from the settlements.

"By God," Old Hen spit a stream of tobacco into an ant hill at his feet. "I told Captain Van der Horck we needed a military escort." He swore a streak of words that would have made a preacher blush.

"They stopped and talked with Ted on the way inside," Homer said. "I saw 'em through the window. Pointed to the mules in the corral. Means he's in on it."

"Don't play cards with them card sharps," Old Hen said. "You'll lose the shirts off your backs."

Evan remembered his mother's admonition to stay away from liquor and gambling. Mostly he had followed her advice. These men were trouble. He would stay as far away from them as he could.

"Watch for the highwayman we met by Glenwood," Old Hen said. "He's around here someplace. I can smell him."

They paired up for guard duty. Evan and Martin took the first stint. Evan searched in the wood pile, hoping to find a basswood log for clogs. The closest he found was a chunk of willow, probably cut from the banks of the Pomme de Terre River. He sat on a stump by the corral and pulled out his knife.

Mosquitoes swarmed in the darkness, catching in his nose and flying into his face. Martin built a fire. By sitting or standing in the smoke, they avoided the worst of the pests.

In addition to the hum of mosquitoes was the chomping of grasshoppers. Minnesota farmers would have a hard time finding fodder for their animals next winter if the grasshoppers didn't let up. He might sell extra from his fields for a tidy profit. His thoughts drifted to home.

He had little expectation his farm would be spared while others weren't. Evan sighed. *Annan manns skade er lettast ae loere av.* It is easier to learn from the damage of another.

Night hawks swooped through the evening sky and an owl hooted from the barnyard. Evan glimpsed a great horned owl swooping down to catch a mouse running through the grass, its majestic wings snapped like sails catching the wind.

The noise startled Evan and reminded him that he must keep watch as he carved shoes. He figured Gunnar, the most reckless of the boys, would be most in need of a new pair by winter. Confirmation would be in the fall and Gunnar couldn't attend barefooted. Dear God, let him learn his lessons this time.

Evan determined to write a letter to Gunnar, urging him to take Catechization seriously or face a whipping. But then he remembered something his father used to say. *Age og ris gjer neppe guten overlag vis.* Great fear and spanking hardly make the boy extremely wise.

If Evan had compassion on Gunnar because of his struggle with learning, he surely could expect no less from the Heavenly Father.

Evan lay aside the carving and pulled a paper and pencil from his pocket. The pencil stub needed sharpening. Evan used his carving knife to hone the point. Then he wrote a quick letter to Gunnar. Evan feared he was giving his son license to laziness. In his heart of hearts, Evan knew he was doing the right thing.

When he was finished with the letter, Evan picked up the carving again. He could not afford idleness.

The mules twitched their tails against the mosquitoes, a small slap on hide that reminded Evan of cleaning carpets for a wealthy nobleman back in Norway. One of his most hated chores had been to drag the heavy carpets outside, hang them on a line and beat them with a carpet beater. Just thinking about it brought a dusty smell back to his nostrils and a feeling of hopelessness to his spirit. Thank God he had left Norway when he had the chance.

Evan counted the mules, then counted them again and dug his knife into the soft wood. Thirty-six beautiful animals. He would give them names if he were to stay on as muleteer. He would name the gray jack, a header on Old Hen's team, after an old wolf, smart and cautious. Something about the way it lifted its nose into the wind before it stepped out in Old Hen's promenade. A white jenny on Jeppe's team reminded him of a goose wing.

Martin nodded and Evan thought he had fallen asleep. Evan's eyes drooped, too, and he fought to stay awake, adding columns of numbers in his head, counting the stars overhead and finding the shoe hidden inside the block of wood. These shoes wouldn't be fancy, but better than going barefoot.

"He rode in balloons," Martin said suddenly. Evan thought he hadn't understood the American words.

"Custer," Martin said. "He rode in observation balloons during the war."

Evan remembered the newspaper article he had read about hot air balloons used for spying on the rebels. He had been captivated by the idea of rising above the earth like a bird.

"I fought under Custer," Martin said out of the darkness. "In the War Between the States." The fire had died down to glowing coals and Martin stood up and threw another leafy branch onto the coals. He slapped a mosquito away from his face and moved into the smoke and sat down again. "Never saw such a dandy."

"How is that?" Evan said. If the truth were told, he would have conversed with anyone about any subject in order to stay awake. The day had been long and arduous. He was exhausted. It must soon be time for others to relieve them at watch.

"Custer was reckless," Martin said. "He'd put his men in harm's way to make himself look good. Rumor had it he wasn't very smart—graduated dead last in his class at West Point."

Evan laid the chiseled wood on the ground and marked around his foot with the tip of the knife. Gunnar was growing so fast that he wore the same size shoe as Evan did. Evan wondered how Inga was faring. Lord help her.

Martin said that Custer was wild about being photographed. "He pushed his face in front of every camera within five miles. Papers said he was the most photographed officer in the Union Army." Martin spat on the ground. "And believe me, that was no accident—he worked real hard at it."

A wolf howled and the mules skittered. Evan counted them—all thirty-six in their proper places. The wagons loomed like sleeping giants in the shadows behind them. One thing for sure, the wagons wouldn't go anywhere without the mules.

"He'd preen like a woman," Martin said. "By God, worried more about his looks than he did the soldiers under him."

"My *far* said to stay out of a rich man's war," Evan said. "I almost joined up a few times but something held me back."

"Good sense, I suspect." Martin grew quiet and Evan thought he might be dozing. It didn't matter. The others would soon be out to relieve them.

"Can you imagine Custer's long yeller hair flying on a Sioux lance?" Martin said.

Jeppe and Homer came out of the house for their turn at watch, yawning and stretching. It was the middle of the night, the moon rising high in the sky cast enough light to see their tired faces.

Evan couldn't get the image of Custer's hair out of his mind. Suddenly, he felt wide awake. He and Martin trekked into the house and threw their bedrolls on the hard floor. Martin started snoring the minute his head hit his blanket roll but Evan tossed and turned, trying to get comfortable on the hard station floor, and finally gave up. He dragged his blanket outside and wrapped up by the smudge fire.

When he finally slept, Evan dreamed of Custer's scalp, blood dripping off yellow curls.

30

AFTER THE STORM, AUNTIE PLOPPED down on the bench by the table, still holding Christina. "Ragna, thank God you were here." Ragna felt a surge of relief go through her, strong enough to weaken her limbs. She sat down beside Auntie and took the baby.

"You knew what to do," Auntie said. "I couldn't think of a thing."

Auntie could not know how shaky Ragna felt, how fearful and weak.

"Boys, go to the lake for a bath," Auntie Inga said. "And take the dog." She fetched a jug of vinegar from the shelf and handed it to Gunnar along with the jug of milk. "Rub down with milk and vinegar then jump into the lake." She handed Knut a bar of soap. "Knut, you're in charge of the hard soap—no wasting, it, mind you. It's our last bar. Scrub everyone head to toe, including the dog, and don't lose it."

"Do we have to?" Sverre whined.

"Yes, you have to. No foolishness, now," Auntie said. "And leave your dirty clothes on the shore. Don't even touch them. Run to the house for clean clothes after you've washed. Nobody will see you."

Then Auntie poured a hot cup of water from the tea kettle on the stove and sprinkled a few tea leaves over the water and placed it before Ragna on the table. She sat beside her and reached for the fussing baby.

"Hush now." Auntie sighed and settled the baby to her breast. "Sometimes I think all I do is feed this baby." The baby latched onto the nipple with a greedy slurp. "It's the only time a woman gets to sit down."

The last drops of rain dripped from the roof. The boys splashed in the lake. Ragna opened the door wider and breathed in the fresh washed air. The rain was a godsend for the berry crop.

"I hate that dog and I hate when the Indians come and I hate when Evan's gone." Auntie's face curled down into a frown. "Lord knows but your baby might be marked with a skunk on his forehead or a stripe down his back." She blew across the top of her cup. "And I hate the gold strike in Tordenskjold. I'll change my mind, of course, if they find anything." She patted Christina's head as the baby guzzled at her breast. "But today I hate the gold strike as much as I hate the smell of skunks . . . or as I hate the grasshoppers."

"I know." Ragna didn't know. She put a protective hand on her abdomen, hoping her baby wouldn't be marked. She could only imagine what Auntie was feeling. But it seemed best to her to offer tea and sympathy. She had nothing else.

Ragna reached for a scrub brush and a scoop of ashes from the ash barrel, saved for this year's soap making. She'd scrub every inch of the cabin and pray that God would deliver them from the stink of skunk. It might take a miracle.

Gunnar herded the stock in the far pasture and the other boys went berry picking to allow the women privacy to bathe and wash their clothes. Auntie said that the fresh air and sunshine might sweat the stink off the boys—if nothing else it allowed the women a little peace and quiet.

Ragna ripped the beds apart and did an extra washing, boiling the clothes in soft water from the rain barrel with soap and vinegar. She and Auntie scrubbed their hair and bodies and changed into their oldest clothes. The yard soon flapped with sheets and covers.

Her auntie looked around the dismantled house. "We may as well air the mattresses while we're at it," she said. "We'll call it an early fall cleaning. I'll be busy enough with the harvest."

Ragna and Auntie Inga dragged the lumpy bed ticks outside into the sunshine, carefully unraveled a seam in the ends and dumping the old straw into a pile. Straw absorbed summer humidity, leaky roofs and leaky boys. Mildew was a problem without regular airing. Ragna spread the lumpy straw into a thin layer that would dry quickly.

Then something moved. Ragna bent to examine the straw.

"Auntie." Ragna's heart sank. Her skin crawled and she checked her arms for evidence of bites. "Bedbugs."

"*Nei!*" Auntie shrieked. "I noticed the boys had a few bites but I blamed mosquitoes," Auntie said. "Once they get in . . ." Her face drooped into a mournful frown and

Ragna worried she might cry. "And in our new cabin." She clenched her fists and rubbed her eyes with the backs of her hands. "We'll boil the bed ticks, treat the bedsteads and refill with new straw."

"I'm sorry, Auntie."

"Nobody's fault. Just another trouble to this terrible day."

Ragna added wood to the fire until the kettle bubbled again. The mattress ticks soon scalded in the cauldron of boiling water. Ragna poked them down into the water with a stick and let them cook a long while. Then she used the stick to haul the wet bed ticks to the lake to rinse. They steamed and sizzled into the cold lake water. When they cooled enough to wring out, she then draped them over the hazelnut bushes by the lake to dry in the afternoon sun. Thank God the rain had passed over and the sun blazed hot again.

Ragna and her aunt began the tedious job of scalding the bedsteads and rubbing them with a small measure of quicksilver mixed into lamp oil. Ragna used a feather to dip the solution into the cracks of the bed frame, the floor, and the loft where the boys slept.

"Good drying weather," Ragna said. "I think we're getting rid of the skunky smell."

Auntie rolled her eyes but didn't answer.

It was afternoon by the time they had finished treating the house. They had yet to refill and stitch the straw ticks. Ragna and Auntie Inga checked the empty mattresses and found them nearly dry. They turned them inside out to allow the hot sun to dry the seams. Any dampness would only breed mildew. The boys were still picking berries but were expected home soon.

"We'll sup on berries, if the boys found any." Auntie sighed and turned the last bed tick. "We're short on everything until Evan sends money home. Let's hope the fish traps catch something tomorrow. "

Christina's wailing sounded from the cabin.

"I'll get her," Ragna said. As she ran to the cabin, Ragna spied something lying on the front stoop. It looked like an animal of some kind. Her heart quickened. Someone had been to the cabin while they were at the lake. A fat doe lay on the step.

Migwans.

31

J ulian did not return to the inn for supper, as Serena expected.

"Where's Uncle Julian?" Maren asked for the hundredth time.

"That's enough, Maren!" Serena said. "Set the table."

"But when is he coming back?"

"I said, that's enough." Serena sawed bread with the old butcher knife. She must ask Ole to put a new edge on the blade. "He'll be back tomorrow."

"Where's your uncle?" Ole said at the supper table. He spoke to Maren but looked at Serena. "Thought he'd be here for supper."

"I've five cords of wood for sale," Anton said, clearly changing the subject. "Ole, do you know of any takers? I'd like cash money but would trade for grain or hay." He took another bite of bread. "Heck, I'd trade for pigs or lambs or apples. Anything."

"I have hay," Serena piped up. "Hoppers haven't been to Hungry Hollow yet. The meadow has grass standing ready for the hay knife."

Anton's eyes lit up. "Now that would be fine," he said. "Close enough to manage."

"We can't pay," Ole said quickly. "We already owe you for helping us out."

"Didn't ask for pay," Serena said. "You're welcome to it."

She felt foolish, giving away her only asset, but she could hardly put the hay crop up herself. Although Serena had known women who worked fields alongside their men, Serena had never worked much outside. She had helped in the garden, of course, and picked potatoes and stones, and helped with the flailing of the wheat. She had no idea how to scythe a meadow.

"I'll start cutting tomorrow," Anton said. "*Mange takk*, many thanks."

No muleskinners stopped at the inn that night although Serena had glimpsed a small train of wagons pulling into Gardner's as she and Julian returned from the farm. Maybe for the best, she had been gone too long to fix a decent meal. Besides she was too exhausted to deal with a house filled with men and the clean up afterwards.

Kersten and Maren washed the dishes. Serena set a sponge for tomorrow's bread and went to bed. It was still light, the days stretching well into the evening this time of year. Looking out the small window of her upstairs room, Serena watched the evening stars pop out one by one. Fireflies glowed in the meadows.

Serena prayed as she looked out toward the little village of Pomme de Terre. She asked God for wisdom, not only for herself but for the sake of the girls. Responsibility settled heavy on her shoulders.

That night Serena dreamed about Hungry Hollow. She dreamed of blooming fields of blue flax and orioles warbling in the grove beside a little cabin built along the Pomme de Terre River. In her dream she sewed new dresses for the girls while a man worked in the fields. It was too far away to see his face but Serena knew that it was someone she loved.

* * *

THE NEXT MORNING, THE GIRLS FOLLOWED Anton and Ole to the hay field, carrying hay rakes over their shoulders and wearing sunbonnets to guard their complexions. Anton toted the hay knife and a lunch basket that Serena had prepared. Ole hobbled with his crutches. Serena watched them through the back window, wondering what Ole would say about her decision.

Her thoughts were interrupted by a knock on the door. She opened the door to Julian and motioned for him to sit at the table. The coffee pot sat half-filled on the back burner. She poured a cup and set it before him.

She wished she were angry. Anger would make it easier. She tried to drudge up the emotions from his first day at Pomme de Terre when he rode roughshod over her feelings, but her anger had gone.

Tillie Swanson squealed as she ran away from the hissing goose on her heels. The girl ran up on the steps of the inn and yelled in the door, "Can I come in? He's after me."

Before Serena could answer, the girl ran off to the barn with the goose flapping its wings and hissing close behind.

"Never could abide a goose," Julian said. "I'll not have them on our place. Ducks maybe, but not geese. I'll buy you all the feather pillows you want. "

"Julian," Serena said. "I'm not going to marry you."

Julian's jaw dropped open. When Serena saw the disbelief on his face, she realized he had fully expected her to become his wife. Waves of guilt and relief swept over her. She was a terrible person to hurt this decent man who had no interest in anything except making her happy. But the words were spoken and it was too late to take them back. Relief washed over her to have them out in the open.

Julian took a sip of scalding coffee hot enough to burn his lips, blew on it and sipped again as if to bolster his courage. He set the cup on the table, swirling his pointer finger in the drops of coffee that had spilled over onto the table.

"Why?" He looked at her with such anguish in his face that Serena had to look away. "Am I so terrible?"

"It's not that." Serena tried to think of the words that would make it easier for him. "It's me. Maybe I'm afraid to risk being hurt again."

"You going back to Jensina's?"

Serena shook her head. "Not for a while."

Julian looked around the inn and Serena saw it through his eyes. This town, blackened by grasshoppers, had nothing to offer his niece . . . or her.

"I could make it hard for you," Julian said. "You living with men who are not your relatives. Not a pot to piss in." Tears gathered in his brown eyes. "Any judge would listen to a concerned uncle." He stood and put his hat on his head. "Why, there's not even a school for the girls to attend."

"Please, Julian," Serena said. Panic rose in her throat. It was unlike him to be vindictive.

"You're being foolish." He walked to the threshold and turned toward her. "It's a hard world, Serena. You've always had your parents to fall back on. Think about the girls if something were to happen to you. What would they do?" He turned to leave. "Do you know what happens to young girls without parents?"

Serena scrambled for words. "I'm sorry, Julian. Please don't . . ."

"Mother always said you were trouble," he said. "Blamed you for Gust's foolhardiness. I defended you, all these years. I took your side."

"Julian," she said. "I'll always take care of the girls, you know that."

"Don't worry. I won't make trouble." He was half way out the door before he spoke again. "I wouldn't do anything to make your life any harder than it will be."

As she watched him walk away from the inn, Serena hoped she wasn't making the biggest mistake of her life.

32

THE NEXT MORNING AT GAGER'S STATION, Evan and Old Hen were hitching up the mules when Ted approached them with hat in hand. "I'm sorrier than I can say," he said while twisting his hat until it twirled like a hay stick ready for the cook stove. "You can see how it is with Gertie," he said. "I couldn't take it anymore—took off without telling you for worrying about her."

Old Hen pursed his lips and spat a stream of brown tobacco juice at Ted's feet, fastening his eyes on Ted until he squirmed. Evan held his breath for Old Hen's answer.

"You worried about your wife so much that you ran off with outlaws who would have just as soon killed your comrades as looked at them." Old Hen spat again. "And now you're so worried about her welfare that you want to haul her off to the gold fields to be scalped by the Indians."

"You don't understand," Ted said. "I didn't have nuthin' to do with them boys."

"You left in the middle of the night without so much as a by-your-leave." Old Hen motioned for the men to hitch up the mules. "On the very night we were almost robbed." Old Hen smashed his hat down over his ears and reached into his pocket to retrieve coins to pay for their board and lodge. "I don't have time to find the sheriff and see justice done. But rest assured, Captain Van der Horck will get my full report. You'll not teamster again."

Evan nodded to Ted who stood gaping in the yard as they drove off. Of course, Ted was guilty of falling in with the robbers. But Old Hen was right. There was no time to find the sheriff and see that he was brought to justice. And of course there was the matter of proof.

Betre at ti skuldige slepp fri enn at ein skuldlaus blir doemt. Better let ten guilty ones go free than judging an innocent man.

* * *

They veered southwest toward Frisby's Grove. The morning waxed hazy and humid with an ominous line of gray on the western horizon. Evan scanned the skies for portents of bad weather. A red sky the night before had been the first warning but weather omens were often wrong.

A flock of blackbirds busied themselves with leaping grasshoppers and a brood of prairie chicks scurried after their mother through the long grass in the ditch. The mother hen reminded him of Inga and how she watched over their children. *Dear God, keep them safe from harm.*

Jeppe stopped his team and jumped out of the wagon. "Wait up!" he called. Old Hen looked back and stopped his mules with a loud, "Bow to your partners."

"What's the hold up?" Evan called from his wagon at the back of the train. He felt drained with the heat and humidity and reached for a canteen stashed under the seat.

"One of his mules is limping," Old Hen said. "Didn't you notice?"

Evan's face warmed. He hadn't noticed. He should have been paying more attention.

Jeppe worked his way around the team until he came to the mule that stood on three feet with the other lifted partly off the ground. Jeppe eased himself closer to the animal and lifted the hoof. He frowned and reached for a pocket knife in his pocket. He balanced the hoof on his knee and picked with the knife.

Old Hen and Evan climbed down to see what the trouble was.

Jeppe worked for a short while and then released the hoof and stepped away from the team, holding something in his hand. He swore a long string of cuss words, awesome in rhythm and variety.

"What is it?" Old Hen said.

"Look," Jeppe said and held out his hand with a shiny carpet tack on his palm. "Someone thought to slow us down." His face flushed and he clenched his jaw. "Sabotage, pure and simple." He thrust the nail toward Old Hen. "Tapped alongside the shoe into the soft part."

Old Hen examined the nail with its peculiar square head and shiny shaft. "Ain't nothing used on horseshoes." He pocketed the nail in his shirt pocket. "Damage to the mule?"

"Found it in time, I think." Jeppe climbed back on the nigh horse and took up his whip. "Could have been bad."

"Ted?" Evan thought it impossible Ted would be smart enough to think of such a thing.

"Whoever it was overstepped himself," Old Hen said. "Wanted us to break down so they could ambush us. We'll be ready. Check your mules, boys. Every hoof."

The storm hit just as they pulled into Frisby's Grove. The weathered inn stood between two small lakes. A western gale blew waterspouts on the water as the rain poured down in curtains. Trees surrounding the inn bent and swayed. An ancient cottonwood snapped in half, its leafy top crashing on top of the woodpile.

Beside the inn stood a large barn and empty corral, the barn door banging in the wind. Clothes flew straight out from the clothesline. Chickens scurried for cover.

It was far too early to stop for midday but with the Big Muddy Crossing just ahead and the downpour of rain, it seemed they had no choice.

Old Hen insisted a driver stay with the teams at all times. Homer took first watch and herded the mules into the corral. Old Hen refused to come in until he had personally counted every animal. Evan and the others dashed into the inn, holding onto their hats and shielding their faces as hail pounded down.

Evan snatched a few hailstones. It had been such a hot day. He popped them in his mouth, delighted at the treat. The melting ice tasted like dust.

"We're rich," Zeke said with a laugh as he grabbed handfuls of pellets from the air around him. "Poor men get ice in winter but rich men have it in the summer."

Evan always counted his family as riches, the way his father had back in the Old Country. His thoughts turned to Inga and the children back home, wondering if the storm stretched up to Tordenskjold, hoping the roof didn't leak.

Mrs. Frisby, a stout, jolly woman with gray hair and a toothy smile, welcomed them at the door. She wore a faded calico dress that strained across her full bosom. "Come in, come in, before you drown like rats." The kitchen was smaller than Gager's, but cheerful, and smelled of something baking in the oven.

Mrs. Frisby kept up a lively conversation. As she talked, she pulled out tin cups and motioned the men to the table. She bent to reach a plate from a lower cupboard and her skirt rode up, showing stockings and garters.

Martin and Jeppe jabbed each other in the ribs with a laugh, pointing at her large behind. She didn't seem to notice but kept talking about the weather and the unfortunate folks caught on the trail.

Still talking, Mrs. Frisby fetched a plate of biscuits. Then she dragged a frying pan from the shelf and cracked eggs in melting grease. She had a meal on the table in astonishing quickness.

"You're following a wagon train heading out to the Black Hills," she said. "Nicest people you ever saw. Just left. Bound to strike it rich."

"Not worried about grasshoppers?" Old Hen said from the door. "We've met quite a few heading east to get away from the hoppers."

"No," Mrs. Frisby said as she put the food on the table in front of the men. "Not planning to farm. Just strike it rich. And I hope they do. Such nice people."

"Any riders coming through the past day or so?" Old Hen said. "Wearing an old army jacket and tall leather boots. His beard white around the edges and salt-and-pepper hair. Wore a big hat." Old Hen held his hands around his head to mimic a wide brim.

"Sounds like you're talking about Clay Brady." Mrs. Frisby crossed plump arms across her chest and twisted her face into a puzzled frown. "He lives mostly at Gager's Station but I haven't seen him for a few days."

"Does he ride with a sharp faced man?" Old Hen said. "Skinny man."

"Why yes, he does." Mrs. Frisby's face relaxed into a smile. "Nice boy by the name of Elias Lake. Left for the gold fields. More biscuits?"

"How about Ted Green?" Evan said. He surprised himself by speaking up but it was as if the words popped out of his mouth before he had time to think about them.

"Of course," Mrs. Frisby said, "Ted works for Gager's, too." She seemed to search for words but found none. "Has for years," she finally said and turned back to the stove without saying anything more.

"And his wife, Gertie?" Evan said. "Do you know her?"

Mrs. Frisby busied herself at the stove, turning suddenly quiet.

"And Mrs. Green?" Evan repeated, thinking maybe his American words had been unclear.

"I heard you the first time but I have nothing to say," Mrs. Frisby said with a sigh and a firm crimp of her mouth. "My mother taught me to speak only good about people or say nothing at all."

"Storm's letting up," Old Hen said. "One of you go out so Homer can come in and eat."

Evan stood and pulled on his cold, wet hat. He felt chilled to the bone with his clothes wet and clinging. Might as well get his shift over so he could undress and dry his clothes overnight. He felt a longing for his home, his own bed, a change into dry clothes.

Mrs. Frisby followed Evan out the kitchen door. At first he thought she needed another bucket of water from the well or something from the shed. When he was on the steps leading out of the house, she grabbed his arm.

"Wait," Mrs. Frisby said and leaned in closer. Her breath smelled of coffee and felt hot on his cheek. "You asked about Gertie Green." She hesitated only a second and then spoke quickly, as if she might lose her nerve if she waited a minute longer. "She's a bad one," Mrs. Frisby said. "Stay away from her."

Then she turned and went back into the house.

33

nders crept into the cabin long past dark. "Phew!" he said. "Where's the skunk?"

"You're home!" Ragna said and lowered her voice to a whisper so she wouldn't wake up the rest of the family. "What happened?" She climbed out of bed and tucked a pillow beside the sleeping baby to prevent Christina from falling out of bed. Ragna slept with Auntie Inga while the men were gone, the baby tucked between them.

"Nuthin." Anders whispered. "Not a grain of gold dust. Anything to eat?"

Auntie threw back the quilt. "I told you it was foolishness."

"Don't get up," Ragna said. She felt for her wooden clogs and wrapped a shawl around her nightgown. "I'll find something."

She rustled in the kitchen, finding clabbered milk and a dish of berries that the boys had picked. "There's milk in the dugout."

She touched a dried branch into the fire box of the cook stove. When the end lit, she passed it to her husband. She carried the food in one hand while clutching her shawl ends with the other. They hurried to the dugout, slapping the mosquitoes drawn by the flame.

"You should see it," Anders said as he pushed the dugout door open. As the light pierced the darkness, centipedes raced back into their hiding places. Ragna squelched a small scream as a dangling spider web touched her face. The dugout smelled of earth and sour milk but was much cooler than the stuffy cabin.

He told how miners flocked to the area and makeshift tents dotted the hills. Ragna had known it was only a dream of riches, but her heart fluttered anyway. Any kind of strike would have helped.

Anders reached for the milk jug and emptied it with greedy slurps. "Folks shoving and shouting, knife fights, men wild to find gold." He sprinkled berries on top of the clabbered milk and shoveled the food into his mouth with a wooden spoon. "Tents sprang up across the prairie like white flowers. Sounds of shovels clinking on stones night and day."

"Where do they come from?" Ragna said.

"From all over," Anders said as he wiped his mouth with the back of his arm. He pulled off his boots and flopped back on the bed. Ragna tried not to think of the clean linen under his dusty clothes. "The dregs of society, I tell you. Criminals. Gamblers. Good thing Gunnar didn't go along—it's no place for a boy."

"Sounds like it is not place for a grown man either," Ragna said. She told him about the skunk and Migwan's visit during the storm. She didn't want to pressure her husband, but Ragna had to ask. "Will you go back?"

Anders didn't answer. He was already asleep. Ragna covered him with the blanket and nestled close beside him. He reeked of dust and sweat.

The next morning, Anders milked the cows before breakfast was on the table. He brought the frothing buckets into the cabin along with three fat fish from the trap. It was a lovely morning with white daisies scattered across the yard and loons calling from the lake. Mourning doves cooed and an eagle shrieked over the lake as it caught its morning food. The air outside smelled sweet and fresh after yesterday's storm but inside lingered the horrid smell of skunk.

"Where's Milton?" Auntie said as the family gathered round the table. The boys looked red as Indians from their berry-picking day in the sun and bug bites sprinkled across their arms and backs. "Did he go back to his claim?"

Anders shook his head. "Still there. Won't give up." Anders entertained the family with tales of miners, the trials of tenting on stony ground, and then demanded a full account of Musky's tangle with the skunk.

"I've an idea." Anders spooned the last of his porridge, scraping against the sides of his bowl. He told of his plan to cut hay in the small meadow across the lake. "I'll build a raft to haul it back to the barn."

"Now that's not so dumb," Auntie Inga said. "Saves time and distance going over the water."

"Do you know how to build a raft?" Ragna said.

"That would be easy," Gunnar said. "Grape vines would hold the logs."

Anders directed the twins to gather grapevines and the older boys to finish their rows in the garden patch. Sigurd would herd the cows. Ragna offered to clean the fish while Auntie dried meat strips from the deer left by Migwans.

"Ragna, come home with me instead," Anders said. "Our garden needs tending and we have to see what is happening with the hoppers."

"But the chores," Ragna said and looked at her auntie.

"Chores will wait," Anders said. "We'll be back by mid-afternoon if we leave right away."

Ragna hurried to finish the dishes as Anders waited impatiently. He had that determined look on his face, and Ragna knew it was no use to try and dissuade him. Anders got an idea in his head and that was the end of it. Maybe all men were that way.

As they walked out of the yard, Ragna hurrying to keep up with her husband, Anders called out to the older boys in the garden. "Start pulling logs from the wood pile. They need to be about the same size. Nine or ten should be enough. We'll work on the raft this afternoon."

It was going to be another hot, humid day. They traveled the footpath through the woods and when they came to Evan's south field, they stopped in horror. The prairie crawled with hatchling hoppers. They crawled up Ragna's skirts and spat tobacco juice on her apron.

Anders slapped whirring hoppers away from his face. "March like an army from hell, eating everything."

"And the wheat looked so promising," Ragna said. A lump formed in her throat and tears filled her eyes. "What will we do now?"

Anders didn't answer right away. "Hurry." His voice turned husky. "I've missed you."

Ragna hated the way the grasshoppers scrunched under her shoes and crawled under her skirt. She hesitated and Anders reached for her hand and pulled her towards him. "It's all right, Mrs. Vollen," he said. "Let's run!"

The grasshoppers thinned out when they reached the next patch of woods. They slowed to a walk, still holding hands.

"This settles it," Anders said while catching his breath. "I mailed the letter to Cold Spring and I've decided to accept the job if it is offered." He tipped Ragna's chin and kissed her lips. His face felt scratchy with stubble, and he smelled like sweat and barn. "There's nothing to keep us here."

"But Auntie and Uncle," Ragna said. "We promised to help them out."

"Hush now," Anders said. "We'll go to Cold Spring and someday when the grasshoppers ease up, we'll move back to Alexandria."

Ragna drew in a quick breath and her heart beat hard in her chest. "Really?"

"Ja, ja," Anders said. "The grasshoppers won't last forever."

He told her about a man at the gold field who said that grasshoppers usually follow drought years. "He said they'll leave when the rains are steadier."

"I'd like to live on my farm again." Ragna thought of the family cemetery where her parents and baby brother were buried. "Maybe you could find a teaching job in Alexandria."

Anders kissed her again and nuzzled her neck. His face, covered with a week's worth of stubble, tickled against her skin and she pulled away.

"I asked about Alexandria last winter when I was with the Saints." Anders took her hand and they started toward their cabin. "They have teachers enough." They walked out of the trees and grasshoppers covered the meadows. "It was the first place I tried."

Ragna remembered the Roman Church in Cold Spring. It would be her chance to study the Catholic religion. She refused to think about the millions of grasshoppers crunching under her feet.

"We have nothing to harvest," Anders said. Ragna could tell that he was trying his hardest to make the best of it. "As soon as we get word from Cold Spring, we'll pack up and leave."

"But we promised . . ."

"We have to be settled before the school term begins." Anders quickened his pace as he walked into the yard. "Besides, there's nothing to harvest." Anders unbuttoned his shirt and headed toward the lake. "Come for a swim, Mrs. Vollen."

Only a few green weeds remained in the garden plot. A pair of otters played on the far shore of the lake. Everything looked the same as they left it. Ragna walked toward the water as she removed her apron.

Anders dove under and came up spouting streams of water. "Hurry!" he said. "The water is glorious."

She removed the hairpins holding her braids and shook her hair loose. The water sparkled in the bright sun. She unbuttoned her dress, noticing her rounding belly where the baby grew. Anders watched her undress and she wondered if he noticed, too, and what he thought about the changes in her body. She turned her back to him as she kicked off her petticoats.

How lazy to bathe in the middle of a work day. Auntie Inga would have strong opinions if she knew! There was nothing she could do but follow her man. It was what she had pledged and she would not go back on her word. Ragna ran to the lake, the pebbles along the shore sharp on her bare feet, and squealed as the cold water slapped against bare skin.

Anders laughed and reached for her, pulling her into the water, and kissing her. She pulled back and dove under the water. He swam after her.

34

SERENA WASHED THE LINENS and hung them out on the clothesline. While they dried, she ironed the girls' dresses. She forced her mind to think about other things, anything except the slump of Julian's shoulders as he had walked away from the inn.

She had hurt Julian. She made Julian feel as Gust had made her feel.

One thought intruded whenever she let down her guard. Julian never said that he loved her. It was all she and Gust had talked about while courting— but they had been only children. Babies, really.

She was thirty-two years old with girls to raise. She was well past her prime. If she did not marry soon, she would end up alone. Dagmar had said that Ole was fond of her but Serena could not read him. He always seemed angry. His wounds from the war went deeper than his missing leg.

Serena dusted the cupboards and scrubbed the top of the cook stove with a wire brush. She chopped vegetables for a pot of soup, chopping so hard that the knife left marks on the bread board. She cut lard into flour. The men and girls returned from the hayfield just as the biscuits came out of the oven.

"Smells good!" Anton said and his dirty face broke into a smile. "I'm starving!"

Ole mumbled something about washing up at the horse trough. Maren and Kersten giggled as they held out the empty lunch basket for Serena to look inside. The basket held a family of five baby rabbits found in the meadow. Maren picked up a bunny, no bigger than a mouse, its eyes still closed. It squirmed in Maren's grimy hand.

"*Stalkers liten*," Serena said with a shake of her head and a sigh. "Poor little ones won't survive away from their mother."

The truth of Julian's comments pushed into her thoughts. Maren and Kersten would be as vulnerable and helpless as these bunnies without her.

"But we'll feed them with a milk-soaked rag," Maren said. Her blue eyes pleaded. "We'll take care of them."

Serena dreaded the tears and regrets sure to follow. Life was hard. The bunnies would not last the week.

"All right," Serena said at last. "Just this once."

The girls ran to the storage room to fetch milk and rags. Anton looked after them and shook his head.

"Such energy they have." He reached for the water dipper. "Makes me feel old."

"Anton," Serena said. "Mr. Gardner talked of a school starting in the fall. Have you heard anything about it?"

"*Nei*," he said. "You want me to find out?"

The girls interrupted before Serena could answer. She gave a quick nod and smile to Anton and returned to the task of putting supper on the table. Ole came in and slumped down in his chair.

"Nice property you have," Anton said after they finished the table prayer. "Good water and plenty of wood." He wolfed the food on his plate. "I'm looking for a place. Hungry Hollow might fit me just right."

"It's for sale." Serena's heart pattered in her chest.

"Don't you have enough work?" Ole said. "We can't keep up as is."

Anton cleaned his plate and pushed away from the table with a vague remark about running an errand before bed. Ole wore a questioning expression at his father's abrupt departure but didn't say anything. Ole glowered through the rest of supper.

Kersten and Maren chattered about the bunnies and the rabbit hutch they would build in the barn. Maren begged to be excused from dishes. Serena nodded and the girls took the bunnies to the barn.

Ole reached for his coffee cup while Serena stacked the plates in the dishpan. She was thinking about Julian and wondering if he had reached Herman in time to catch the cars. The steamboat left tomorrow afternoon. He would be home in two days if all went well.

"Where's your brother-in-law?" Ole's testy voice made Serena bristle. "Expected him to be here tonight."

"Went home to Iowa," Serena said as she poured boiling water over the dirty dishes.

"What answer did you give?" Ole tipped his cup and blew across the coffee, then took a tentative sip, looking at her over the rim of the cup. He blew again.

Serena dipped a bit of soft soap from a gourd on the window sill and dropped it into the steaming water, swirling it with her hand. "About what?"

"I'm not a fool," Ole said. "He wants to marry you. What was your answer?"

"I'm sure it's not your business," Serena said. She straightened her posture and tried to control her temper. "He came and left. That's all there is to it."

"You could do worse," Ole emptied the cup in a long swallow. "He's a decent person. Good with the girls. He'd take care of you. Give you stability."

Serena scrubbed a dirty plate with the dishrag and scraped a sticky spot with the back of her fingernail. He had a lot of nerve to ask such questions. She was sick and tired of people giving her advice. She had a brain. She would make her own decisions. She rinsed the plates and reached for the dirty cooking pot.

Through the window, the sun dipped behind the barn, leaving a gleam of light beneath the purple sky. Like her life, she thought. The best over and only shadows and gloom left behind.

"Well?" Ole said. "What did you tell him?"

"It's not your concern," Serena said and made a conscientious effort to be more cheerful. "Not unless my work is unsatisfactory."

"It's not about the work," Ole said and set his jaw in a stubborn thrust. "You need to find a man and settle down. You weren't born to be a charwoman."

"I've hoping to enroll the girls in school," Serena said, trying to change the subject. "Mr. Gardner said there would be a school this fall."

Maren and Kersten burst through the door. Kersten held a bunny in her outstretched hand. It didn't move.

"Sistermine," Kersten said. Tears filled her eyes and her lips quivered. "It's dead."

"I told you," Serena said. An image of her girls, orphaned and penniless, flitted through her mind. "They won't survive without their mother."

"Where are the others?" Ole said. "The cat'll get them if you don't watch."

"No!" Maren said. The girls ran out of the inn, Kersten cradling the dead rabbit in her hands.

Ole pulled himself to a standing position and balanced on his crutches. "I've got to finish the chores." He was almost out the door when he turned and said, "Where did Pa go?"

Serena shrugged and returned to the dishpan, relieved to avoid further questions. After the dishes, she swept the floor, startling a mouse under the cook stove, filling the dustpan with wiggling grasshoppers. She thought to fetch another bucket of water from the spring but decided instead to set a sponge.

Anton came in while she was wiping the table, bringing in the pail of milk from the barn. She need only tend to the milk. Then this horrible day would be over and she could go to bed.

"I want to buy Hungry Hollow," Anton said as he set the milk bucket on the table. He reached for the wooden strainer and poured the milk into the milk pans. "I've made up my mind."

"What does Ole say?" Serena said. She emptied half the milk into the butter churn and left the other half in the pan. In the morning she would hang the curds in a cheese cloth bag to drain. By the day after, there would be cottage cheese.

"Any buttermilk left?" Anton slumped into a chair by the table and pulled off his cap. "Ole doesn't know." Anton looked at her. "All the while I chopped wood I thought about it. Finally, I've made up my mind."

Serena reached for the buttermilk jar and poured him a tall glass. She sniffed it until she was confident it had not spoiled. "What will you do?"

"I talked to Gardner tonight," Anton said. He emptied half of the glass in one long swallow. "He made an offer and I'm taking him up on it. I'm selling the inn."

Serena gasped a quick breath. She would have money for a new start. Then doubt removed the first wave of excitement. If she failed, her girls would bear the brunt of her mistake.

They discussed Hungry Hollow and agreed on a fair price. Anton said that he always wanted to run a country store with a few trade goods. Hungry Hollow would be the perfect place, far enough out of town to attract farmers.

"Gardner will let us live here until spring as long as we quit the mule trains." Anton pulled out his pipe and tamped tobacco in the bowl. "Says we can take in long-term boarders as long as we send the overnight trade to his hotel."

* * *

THE GIRLS BURIED THE DEAD BUNNY under the lilac bush and decorated the grave with sprigs of cedar pulled off a tree in the Swanson's yard. It was late and the mosquitoes were bad. Fireflies dotted the yard like burning stars. Anton, Ole, Tillie Swanson, and Serena attended. The girls carried on as if it had been a relative.

Afterwards, Serena shooed the girls to bed. They looked sodden and bedraggled after their emotional outburst. Kersten carried the box of remaining bunnies upstairs to their bedroom to guard them from the barn cat, arguing with Maren about who would stay up with the rabbits through the night to watch over them.

Anton and Ole sat at the kitchen table. Serena picked up a wet dishtowel and hung it over the back of a chair to dry.

"It's a losing battle," Anton said, lighting his pipe and leaning back in his chair. "Rabbits won't last another day."

Ole crutched over to the stove and rattled the coffee pot. Serena excused herself and went to bed. From her room upstairs, she could hear the men's voices though she couldn't hear what was said. Later, Serena woke up to arguing.

"You tell her . . . or I will," Anton said in a loud voice.

"Stay out of it," Ole shouted and slammed something, maybe his crutch, against the floor. "Damn it! You'll just make it worse."

"We both care about her," Anton said. "It has to be settled." His voice lowered and Serena strained to hear the words being spoken.

She crept from her bed and stepped to the top of the stairs in her nightgown. The floor squeaked and she froze, hoping the men below hadn't heard. They didn't speak and she thought for sure they had heard her creeping around and would say nothing more. She was just about ready to turn back to her room when Anton spoke.

"She deserves to know."

35

E VAN CLIMBED UP ON THE WAGON SEAT as Old Hen finished checking the traces. Then Old Hen painstakingly lifted the hoof of one of the lead mules. Only then did Evan notice the men of the other two rigs doing the same. Evan hurriedly climbed down and did his share. Only after they examined every hoof of every mule did they proceed on the journey. They would not be caught by the same trick again.

Once underway, Evan glanced back. Three riders had ridden up to the door at Frisby's Station. One of the men resembled Clay Brady, something about the way that he sat on his horse. Evan called to Old Hen and pointed out the riders.

"Twenty-five miles of prairie and no military escort," Old Hen groaned. "Going through the worst patch of outlaws in Minnesota. Good God, we might as well give up now and be done with it."

The vast prairie stretched before them. Instead of blooming flowers and green grass, bleached skulls and old buffalo bones dotted the landscape. The rain was a godsend for the parched ground. Already sprigs of green showed against the white bones.

"My God," Evan said. He flicked the whip over a nipping mule. "Grasshoppers bad these parts."

"Yup, they've got us by the short hairs." Old Hen searched in several pockets for his tobacco plug before he found it. "I've seen Injun wars, blizzards, floods, hail, and twisters. I've seen hoppers before but never like this. These devils are second only to prairie fires in my book."

Evan's thoughts shifted to Inga and the children. He had no reason to worry. Milton and Anders were well able to handle emergencies that might arise while he was gone. If there were a prairie fire at home, they need only go into the water to survive.

"See those hills against the horizon?" Old Hen said. "Coteaus des Prairies, old timers called them the Shining Mountains."

Evan shaded his eyes with his forearm and squinted at a row of low hills on the western horizon. They looked nothing like the mountains of his homeland.

"If you look close, you can see all the way to Toqua." Old Hen explained the peculiar circumstances of this region. "Some call it mirage—but there's not a wisp of smoke or a single tree. Nothing to mar the view."

The afternoon sun on the soaked ground created steamy waves of heat across the trail. The hours dragged by. Cicadas buzzed near Evan's ears and flies bothered the mules until they kicked and brayed. Evan swished flies off the animals with the tip of his whip. Behind him, boards shifted and bumped over the rutted trail.

Evan silently recited the Catechism to himself to keep awake. All his life, Evan had turned to the Catechism for direction. It had helped him choose the right path during the difficult days when Inga was still married to Ingvald Ericcson. A worry stabbed through his thoughts, of Gunnar growing up without the comfort and help of the ancient words.

"Watch, boys," Old Hen called out. "Pull closer together for defense and draw your weapons." He pointed to a few dots moving toward them from the northwest. "Indians."

Evan pulled the mules to a halt and pulled the brake as Jeppe's team pulled up beside them and Martin came close behind. Sweat gathered on Evan's neck, and he took several deep breaths to collect himself. The dots moved too quickly to include women and children.

"A war party," Evan said. The words thickened in his dry mouth.

"Looks like it," Old Hen said and spat over the side of the team. "Hard to keep the young bucks on the reservation."

"Sioux?"

"Most likely. Chippewa come from the northeast but they might be coming back from a raid on the Sioux," Old Hen said as he climbed down from the nigh horse and crouched between the mules. "Indians mighty fond of mules. For both meat and pack animals."

Evan cast an anxious glance toward the approaching Indians, their horses almost visible, and reached for his gun beneath the seat. He threaded the lines under the seat and tied them to the wagon frame. He secured the brakes. The last thing he needed was a runaway team. There was no place to hide. He knelt down in the wagon seat, stacking the supplies around him for protection and propping the gun on top of the boxes. Dear Lord, spare me for my wife and children's sake.

The sound of war whoops came with the sound of pounding hooves. They were close enough for Evan to see their painted faces.

"Wait until you get a good shot," Old Hen said. "It might be young bucks feeling their oats. Might blow over into nothing."

Suddenly, the Indians stopped and pointed east. The Indians parleyed with each other, pulling the ropes on their ponies and gesticulating toward the mules and then toward the eastern trail. Finally, they turned and raced away to the northwest. War whoops faded into the distance.

"What happened?" Evan said as he wiped sweat off his neck.

"Look," Old Hen said in a grim voice while dipping his head toward the back trail. "Keep your defensive positions, Boys!"

Evan craned his neck around the load of lumber as five riders galloped toward the caravan. They soon positioned themselves around the cluster of wagons. Although the prairie stretched for miles in every direction, Evan felt as if walls were pushing in, making him feel trapped. He gripped his gun and aimed it at the man Mrs. Frisby had named as Clay Brady.

"Looks like we got here just in time." Clay Brady pulled hard on the reins of his panting horse. The horse grimaced, showing yellow teeth and a long tongue.

The horse was a fine bay, maybe sixteen hands. Evan admired the way its nostrils flared and the way its muscles rippled.

Old Hen raised his buffalo gun from where he stood between the mules and calmly pointed it at Clay's face. "We don't want your help," Old Hen said. "Move on now."

Clay Brady and Old Hen stared at each other until Evan's hackles rose on his neck. No one spoke. Evan could almost see the wheels turning in Clay's head as he calculated the risk of Old Hen's weapon.

"Our hearts are in the right place," Clay said. His eyes were cold and his voice a grating whine. "We got you out of a bad scrape." His mouth twisted in a weak smile. "Let's travel together, watch each other's back until Toqua."

"Not this time," Old Hen said. He raised the gun barrel in a threatening gesture. "Now get."

"You're making bricks without straw."

"Maybe so," Old Hen said. "It's none of your concern what we do."

"We fought in the war," Clay said as his eyes flitted across the load of cargo and the mules. "Know how to manage."

"From the looks of your jacket, you were on the losing side," Old Hen said. "Didn't know as much as you thought."

Clay Brady's eyes sparked fire though his expression remained calm. He motioned to his men with a sharp whistle and a quick jab with his hand. Evan gripped his rifle, now slippery with sweat.

"Have it your way," Clay said. "We'll meet again."

"I doubt it," Old Hen said.

Evan let out his breath in a low whistle as the three men road to the west.

"Quit your dawdling, boys!" Old Hen called out. "We've got to get moving now if we hope to keep your lives. We've a good three miles before camp."

Evan swallowed his disappointment. He didn't know why they couldn't camp where they were. It's not like there was anywhere to go to—Old Hen had said they traveled through empty prairie to Toqua. Evan's stomach growled in protest. Fatigue washed over his body. He licked dry lips and reached for his canteen. Old Hen climbed back on the nigh-horse.

"Well, loose the brake, Evan!" Old Hen said. "It's time to fish or cut bait." He snapped his whip over the heads of the lead pair. "Promenade all!"

36

RAGNA FELT A SURGE OF RELIEF when Anders declared he would not return to the gold field by Turtle Lake. He seemed resigned to earning a living rather than striking it rich and had already turned his energies to the hayfield across the lake. Anders and Gunnar planned how they would cut and haul the hay over an early breakfast.

The sun rested over the lip of the eastern sky. Gunnar and Anders had been up before dawn finishing the raft while Knut and the twins did the morning chores. Ragna wondered how they could accomplish as much as they planned in a single day.

"I'll help," Ragna said. "I could use some sunshine."

"Then you'll wear a hat," Auntie said as she burped the baby and refastened her blouse. "In your condition . . ."

Ragna grumbled but agreed as she packed a lunch. If nothing else, the hat would keep her from turning brown as an Indian. Anders often complimented her on her complexion and she did not want to disappoint him. At the same time she chafed over being treated like a girl. She was fully grown, a married woman. It wasn't right that she must obey her auntie and a husband.

Ragna suppressed a guilty twinge leaving Auntie Inga alone with the housework. But only Auntie could nurse the baby and the tipping raft was no place for them. Besides, Sigurd must herd the cows and could not be left alone.

"Hurry up, boys!" Anders said as he stacked rakes, scythe, and tarp on the raft. "The dew is burned off the grass and time is wasting."

"It's not fair," Sigurd said with a pout as his brothers scrambled onto the raft. The dog sat on Sigurd's feet. "Why do I have to stay home?"

"Don't fuss," Ragna said. "You can help make the stack when we get home."

Sigurd dragged his feet toward the sounds of the tinkling cow bells with the dog nipping at his heels. Ragna listened to the cowbells as she boarded the tippy raft, wishing they could have taken the little boy along. It was a hard truth that someone in the family always had to stay home and watch the animals.

Water splashed up through the splices as Ragna stepped on the corner. Her weight pushed it down enough to wet her feet. The boys clutched the logs. She hoped the rough raft was large enough to hold the four boys and two adults.

"Watch out," Knut said. "You'll tip us over."

"When is Uncle Milton coming back?" Sverre lisped. "Does he know about the hoppers on his field?"

"Not yet," Anders said. "He'll find out soon enough."

They poled and paddled across the narrowest part of Long Lake. It was a glorious Minnesota morning with blue sky and puffy white clouds overhead. Otters played in the water. A moose dipped its nose into the lake and came up with green weeds draped from its mouth. It eyed them for a long moment and then splashed to the shore and loped away with a long stride. Not until it was on shore again did Ragna see its calf hiding in the brush. She pointed it out to the boys.

"A creation of God," Knut said. "Just as we learned in Confirmation."

"Maybe you learned it," Gunnar said with a sigh and sad shake of his head. "I'll never be confirmed."

"You will," Ragna said. "I'll help you."

"You will, with the help of God," Knut said. "Don't forget that part. The arm of flesh will fail you."

"Shut your mouth!" Gunnar said.

"Boys!" Ragna said. "It's nothing to fight about."

Gunnar and Anders scythed the hay while Ragna and the twins spread it into thin layers that would dry in the sunshine. The wild grass was not the highest quality hay but it would do in such hard times.

They worked until into the early afternoon when they finished scything. They ate their simple lunch and the boys and Anders swam. Ragna waded along the shore, the icy water comforting after the heat. Then they returned to work.

They turned the hay and raked it into uneven rows. After they finished, they turned the hay once again. The prairie grass quickly dried into sprigs of straw-like material.

Late in the afternoon they raked the rows on top of the tarp that had covered their wagon on their journey to Tordenskjold. Then they dragged the tarp to the raft.

"Let's get a big enough stack to make it worth our time," Anders said. He looked at the sun, scratching his neck. "It's getting late. I wanted to finish today."

Ragna scratched her back, too. The chaff caused a fierce irritation.

"I think we had best start with a smaller load," Gunnar said. "Try it before we risk a bigger stack. It would be a shame to lose the whole crop."

"By golly," Anders said. His eyes brightened and he clapped Gunnar on the back. "You're not as dumb as you look."

Ragna stared at Gunnar, for the first time noticing a fuzzy shadow across his upper lip and chin. He was almost grown. How she loved this almost-brother. Some people boasted being book smart but Gunnar was work smart. Always figuring out better ways to do things. The one to turn to in a crisis.

By evening, they had hauled five small stacks of hay across Long Lake, the hay mounded into a pile beside the dugout. They were tired, itchy and sunburned. The calf bawled in its pen.

"Let's take another swim before supper," Anders said. His eyes drooped and small blisters formed on the back of his neck from the burning sun.

"I'll fetch Sigurd," Ragna said. She scanned the barnyard but saw no sign of the cows or oxen. No tinkling bells either.

"Auntie Inga," Ragna said as she entered the cabin. "Where's Sigurd?"

Auntie Inga was nursing Christina in bed. She raised up with a start. "*Uff da!* I fell asleep." She unlatched the baby and moved her to the center of the bed. Then she swung her legs over the edge and fastened her shirtwaist.

"It's suppertime," Ragna said. "Anders and the boys went for a swim to wash off the dust." She reached for a dipper of water and took a long draught.

"Isn't Sigurd in the pasture? I heard the cowbells a while ago."

"I'll fetch him," Ragna said. "Can't be far away."

Ragna waved to Anders splashing in the lake.

The cool water looked inviting but Ragna determined to find Sigurd before she indulged. Besides, the boys' clothes littered the shoreline and they were growing up. It would be better if she waited until they were finished.

"Sigurd!" Ragna called. It was always hard to get Sigurd's attention. He didn't hear out of one ear and sometimes it seemed he didn't hear out of the other ear either. Her auntie said that Sigurd heard what he wanted to hear. Ragna paused and listened for cowbells.

She hiked east across the pasture and when she didn't see the little boy, she walked through the woods to the southeast, following an old game trail that led to another meadow on the far southern border of Uncle's property. A doe and twin fawns grazed by the side of the path. The doe looked at Ragna and sniffed the air before turning and bolting away. The babies leapt after their mother, stretching their short legs.

A pair of striped gophers skirted through the grass and a porcupine waddled into the trees. Ragna kept her distance from its prickly quills.

"Sigurd!" No answer. No tinkling bells. Where could he be? Her pulse quickened and she hurried her pace. "Sigurd!" she called again.

As she left the trees, she saw the open prairies. The hoppers had devoured the rolling meadows, leaving only a few scattered patches of green weeds. Ragna scanned the wide meadow that blended into Milton's property but did not see Sigurd or the cattle. Holy Mary, Mother of God.

Ragna turned and headed straight west, coming out on the shores of Long Lake near Milton's dugout. His place was little more than a hole in the hillside covered with a wooden door. She knew Milton was not home but knocked on the door anyway and called his name. When he didn't answer, she opened the door and peeked in. No sign of Sigurd, but of course, there was no reason for Sigurd to be at Milton's dugout. Dear Jesus, where was her little brother?

On a sudden impulse she turned south and headed to their cabin. Maybe he lost his way. He was just a small boy. Maybe he strayed this far and thought to stay there until someone found him. She ran on the path through the trees, feeling eyes upon her, afraid—but knowing she was being foolish. She pushed out of the trees and saw their little cabin sitting in the clearing.

It was like seeing an old friend. She opened the door and startled to see Migwans standing in the middle of their cabin.

"Missus," he said and pointed to her. He acted as though it were the most ordinary thing in the world to be inside their cabin while no one was at home. "Migwans," he pointed to himself.

"I know who you are," Ragna said and bit back angry words. "I'm looking for my little brother," she said and made a sign for a short boy by holding her hand flat about his height and then put her hands by her head like horns and made a mooing sound. "My little brother."

Migwans said something in his language and pointed southeast. Then he motioned for her to follow. Ragna hesitated but obeyed, praying the whole time that she was doing the right thing and that she would find Sigurd.

Almost at the top of the hill, Ragna heard tinkling cow bells. The air had softened and the light dimmed to dusk. She picked up her skirts and ran toward the sound, not looking to see if Migwans followed or not. From the top of the hill, Ragna saw the oxen and cow grazing in a patch of swampy ground at the bottom. They bawled when they smelled her and started plodding in her direction.

Then she saw a large group of Indian children picking berries. In the midst of the black haired children, one lighter child stood out like sun on water.

"Sigurd!" Ragna called. He turned his sunburned and bug-bitten face toward her and waved.

"Thank God, Thank God." Ragna ran down the hill.

She slowed and caught her breath. He was picking berries. Everything was all right. Migwans caught up to her. He spoke in his language and pointed to the children with pride. Ragna thought that the children, or at least some of them, belonged to Migwans. A plump boy had a droopy eye. He smiled at Ragna with berry-stained lips. The boys wore leather loin cloths or britches. The girls wore leather dresses. All were barefoot.

Migwans spoke to the children in their language and the boy with the droopy eye ran over to him and told him something while gesturing toward the north. Ragna got the impression that Droopy Eye was Migwans' son.

"Ragna," Sigurd said holding up a gourd filled with plump, red berries. "See what I found."

"Good boy, Sigurd. It's time to go home, now," Ragna said. It was late. Auntie Inga would be worried. Ragna pushed down the anxiety she felt being among the Indian children. She did not need to be afraid of them. Migwans had led her to Sigurd, after all, and seemed trustworthy—even though he had been snooping around their cabin. She did not know what to think about that. "It's past milking time."

She took his hand and pulled him toward the cows. Sigurd squirmed and tried to call out to the children but Ragna marched him firmly away, following the animals who headed toward home. The cow bellowed, its udder swaying side to side, dripping milk as it lumbered toward home and its calf.

She was almost to the end of the glen when she remembered her manners.

"Migwans," she turned and waved. He twisted toward his name. "*Migwetch!* Thank you!"

* * *

ON THE WAY BACK TO THE HOUSE, Sigurd told her about playing with the Indian boys. "They can spin a hoop with a stick like nothing," he said. "And they're fast runners."

"But berry picking," Ragna said. "Why did you leave the cows?"

"Migwans told us to."

"How did you understand him?"

"He told us." Sigurd raised a quizzical eyebrow. "That's all."

"Your *mor* needs you to stay closer to home," Ragna said. "With your *far* gone, we need your help."

"But I like playing with the red boys," Sigurd said. "And the hoppers have eaten the best grass by our house." He flicked a switch at the cow to guide it back on the path.

"What would Far say about it?"

"All right," he said after a long pause. "Don't tell him."

They trudged home, Ragna weary beyond description. She scratched at the itchy chaff on her back. She longed to dive into the cool water and decided she would do so as soon as she got back, even if she missed supper altogether.

But when they came over the last rise, she saw Milton's white mule wading in the lake. The cow loped toward its stall and relief. The calf bawled and butted against the pen, hungry and anxious to nurse. All weariness left and Ragna picked up her skirts and ran to the house.

"Hurry," she said to Sigurd, who trailed at her heels. "Maybe he found gold!"

37

SERENA'S FIRST THOUGHT the next morning was about the conversation she had heard in the night. "She deserves to know," Anton had said. They must have been speaking of her. Nothing else made sense. Maybe they had decided against buying her land and hesitated to inform her.

Anton and Ole ate their eggs in silence at the breakfast table. What she deserved to know remained a mystery. The sky grayed overhead and humidity hung in the air like a wet towel. The men were heading back to Hungry Hollow after chores. They hoped to finish the haying before it rained.

As Serena sliced bread for their lunches, she debated about asking Anton's plans to purchase her land. She didn't want to stir up a hornet's nest but needed to know where she stood. If Anton had changed his mind, she would approach Mr. Gardner and try to renegotiate a price. It didn't matter who bought the land. She opened her mouth to ask but loud wails erupted from upstairs.

"Dead rabbits," Ole said around a bite of porridge. His mood was as gloomy as the weather. "I knew they wouldn't live."

Although Serena agreed, she bristled at Ole's negative words. He was always moody, always angry. There was something about the man that drove her crazy. Gust had been the same way. Negative. Something she abominated. Yes, Ole had suffered in the war, but everyone had suffered. It was over. He needed to forget and start over.

Dagmar had said the same about Serena. The realization surprised her. She had not understood what Dagmar had meant. Serena had suffered during the uprising and needed to go forward with her life. It sounded so simple.

The girls ran into the kitchen. "Sistermine!" Kersten held out three dead bunnies. "They were alive in the night."

Maren cradled the only remaining rabbit. It lay lethargic in Maren's hands, but its sides moved with every panting breath.

Serena groaned. She could not bear the thought of another dramatic funeral—especially since the other rabbit would surely be dead by evening. "Set them in the store room," Serena said. "We don't have time for a funeral until tonight after supper."

"Make hay while the sun shines," Anton said when the girls protested. "Come, girls. The sooner we get started, the sooner we finish."

Ole started up from his chair but Anton shook his head. "Finish your coffee. We'll head out to the field if you take care of the milking. Join us later."

Strange, the day before Anton had been adamant that they all go out to the farm together. She shrugged it off. Maren filled an empty tin can with milk and tucked it into the lunch basket alongside the bunny and a clean rag.

"Be good now," Serena said. "Mind your *bestefar*."

Serena watched them leave the yard, bedraggled and sad about the dead pets. "I knew those rabbits would only cause heartache," Serena said with a shake of her head. "I've seen enough dramatics to last a long while."

"Hmm." Ole seemed distant and preoccupied.

"You didn't grow up with sisters," Serena said with a chuckle. "With girls it's always that way."

Ole drained his coffee cup and shook his head when Serena held out the pot. She would bake bread, finish the ironing and start the mending. She had enough scraps saved to start a patchwork quilt but she wanted the girls to learn how. The mending would keep her busy until they got home again. Of course, the funeral would be uppermost in their minds.

To think the rabbits would have a better funeral than that of her baby, Lena Christine, who died during the uprising. It was an obscene thought, one that sent a stab of grief through her chest as if it had happened yesterday instead of fourteen years ago.

"You must have heard Pa and me talking last night," Ole said. He stared out the window. "Had words."

"What about?" Serena said. She reached for her crocheting. "Heard voices but couldn't understand what you said." She thought it safer to put it that way. Let him do the telling.

"I'm leaving for the gold fields," Ole said. "Pa's selling the inn and I'm setting out on my own."

Serena took in a quick breath and forgot to crochet. She hadn't seen it coming. "What brings this about?" She looped yarn around the hook.

"I'm a grown man and have no reason to stay in this godforsaken place." Ole finally looked at her, his expression unfathomable. His voice dropped to near whisper. "It's time I go out on my own. I'm leaving as soon as the hay crop is in."

Serena's chest felt heavy. "We'll miss you," she said. Her voice trembled and she took a deep breath to steady it. She stabbed the hook into the garment. "The girls. All of us."

The tea kettle steamed on the stove and a wasp battled the corner of the window pane. The sponge set the night before filled the room with a yeasty smell.

"Pa wants me to tell you something." He picked up a cloth napkin lying on the table. "No, I have something to say." Ole twisted the corner of the napkin in his hands, twirling it into a corkscrew of cloth. "There's nothing for you here. You have a future back in Iowa."

"I don't think . . ." Serena felt anger surge inside of her and words press into her mouth.

"Hear me out." Ole took a deep breath. The goose from next door flew onto the stoop, flapping its wings and hissing. Tillie Swanson chased it away with a stick. Serena swallowed her words and watched the girl herding the mean old goose away from the garden patch.

"Listen."

Serena looked back at Ole. He opened his mouth to speak but licked his lips and closed it again. "Nothing is perfect in this life. Not a single thing. You have a chance and you need to take it."

The look on his face reminded Serena of someone from her past. She thought of several names but couldn't pinpoint the one with a similar expression. He wore a hopeless, agonized expression. Then it came to her. Ole's eyes reminded her of the Indian who had taken her pen and ink, but spared her life. His eyes had been black holes without a bottom.

"I don't understand," she said.

"It has to be this way. I can never . . ."

Serena waited for him to speak while planning what she would reply. She would tell him to mind his own business, that she was a grown woman, that she didn't want his advice.

"The war ruined me." Ole blurted out the words.

"Lots of people live without a limb," Serena said. "At least you're alive . . ."

"Listen to me, God damn it!" He slammed his fist on the table. Anger blazed in his eyes. It smoldered in the curl of his mouth. "Do I have to spell it out to you?"

"I don't know what you are talking about." Serena searched her mind for a clue, something she was missing.

"It took more than my leg." His face flushed bright red and the words tumbled out in a rush. "I can't be a husband—or a father." He pulled himself to a standing position and jabbed the crutches into the floor, his mouth crimped into a hard line. "I'm half a man. I'd be better off dead. Do you understand now?"

Her face flushed as she realized what Ole had said. Ole clomped across the room, his crutches sharp thumps against the wooden floor, and slammed the door behind him. There must be something she could say that would make it better. She could not think of what it might be.

She paced to the window and watched him walk to the barn, the rigid tilt of his head, the angry way he used his crutches. When he reached the barn door, Ole leaned against the frame with slumped shoulders. He turned his face briefly toward the house and even from that distance she could see the tears on his face.

Ole hadn't mentioned love although Serena suspected he loved her. Ole told her his tragic story because he thought Serena was in love with him. He blamed himself that she refused Julian.

It wasn't true. Serena didn't love Ole—but maybe she had harbored the hope that someday she might.

It was as if a door closed. A door that hadn't looked all that inviting in the first place, Serena admitted, but nevertheless, a door closed for good. Though she would sell her land, she didn't know which direction to turn.

Serena didn't exactly know what growing up meant but she saw clearly that she was not there yet. Her petty arguments with Jensina, her selfishness about sharing her father's house, and her wallowing in self-pity for more than a decade were sure signs that Serena had not yet grown up. She had much to learn.

She had made a mess out of her life. Life wasn't perfect. Ole was right about that. Life was messy and stinky and far from pretty. Ole's problems wouldn't go away if he went to the gold fields. She wouldn't be able to run away from hers, either.

38

EVAN STRUGGLED TO KEEP HIS EYES focused on the trail. They had been on the road more than twelve hours and still they traveled west on the Wadsworth Trail. The long evening turned into dusk and yet Old Hen kept pushing them forward. Evan heard complaints from Jeppe and Zeke behind him. Evan wanted to complain, too. He was exhausted by long days on the trail and short nights interrupted by guard duty.

Though the men tired, the mules kept pace as if they had just started the day. Mules were stronger than horses, showed more gumption and never tired. Slower, maybe, but magnificent, all the same.

Someday Evan would buy a pair of mules to work his farm. Of course, he'd prefer a horse for riding but if his farm produced as he hoped, he could have both. The fertile black soil would yield again once the grasshopper plague ended. He would write to Inga and tell her about his dream for mules.

The daydream kept him awake. Finally Old Hen waved them off the trail.

"It's a buffalo circle," Old Hen said. His face a wrinkled worry. "Not many defensive positions here on the prairie but at least we can put the mules in the center and put guards in the declivity around them."

"You think they'll be back?" Evan had long passed mere hunger and his stomach churned with an urgent need for food.

"Yup," Old Hen said. "Sure as shooting."

"And the Indians?"

"We were lucky." Old Hen spat a stream of tobacco juice into the weeds. "The closer we watch, the luckier we get."

As luck would have it, Evan and Old Hen drew the final watch. Evan relieved Zeke who yawned, flopped down on the ground beside him and immediately fell asleep while Old Hen kept watch on the opposite side of the mules.

Evan hated the last watch. He always slept better toward morning and had the hardest time staying awake in the quiet of predawn. Evan hunched in the groove of the buffalo circle, scanning the surrounding area for anything unusual.

Old Hen said the buffalo circle was made by herds circling their young to keep them safe from predators. Over the years, they always came back to the same places until large grooved circles showed in the prairie. Evan had seen buffalo, of course, in his early years of driving stage. It was rare to see one in Otter Tail County anymore with so many people settling the area. Anywhere people settled meant the demise of wild game and Indians.

Owls hooted. Evan knew Indians sometimes imitated owls or other animals. He kept close watch on the spot where the sound came from until gray wings flapped up from the ground. Evan blew out a breath of relief. Maybe they'd get through this night without incident.

On the eastern horizon, a sliver of light pushed against the darkness. Purple and red tints gathered around the brightest spot of light. He breathed the damp, heavy air and felt chilled in spite of the rough blanket thrown over his shoulders. A faint whiff of skunk. Frogs croaked and in the distance a pack of coyotes greeted the dawn.

Suddenly the mules skittered. A rustling started at one side and rippled across the herd like wind over water. It was more a reaction than an actual warning, but it was enough for Evan to toe Zeke's back with the tip of his clog.

"What's the matter?" Zeke said in a groggy voice.

"Wake up," Evan said. "Something's in the mules."

They were upon them before Zeke could leave his blanket. A shout and a rush of boots on stones. Evan fired in the direction of the noise as Zeke struggled into position. Evan didn't dare shoot in the direction of the mules lest he kill one of the animals by mistake. Jeppe and Martin called out. Old Hen barked orders.

"Watch the mules," Evan shouted. "They're coming from the west."

A dark form rose in front of him and without thinking, Evan fired. The man fell forward over the lip of the ridge. Not enough light to see his face but Evan knew that he had killed him. His thoughts flitted back to the Abercrombie siege and their desperate fight against the Sioux. He had always suspected that he had killed during the battle but had never been sure. Now he had killed another human being and it was beyond dispute.

How would he tell his sons?

Another shape rose up before him and Evan pulled the trigger again. This man fired a round from his pistol before he fell at Evan's feet. Hot lead grazed Evan's ear and the side of his cheek. He reached up and when he pulled it away from his face, it dripped something warm and sticky. Evan slumped down to the ground and leaned against the edge of the buffalo circle. He felt fuzzy. When he tried to speak, the words refused to form.

"Mules all here," Old Hen said from somewhere behind him. "But they got the saddle horse." It was over as quickly as it had started. "Is everyone all right?"

"Damn! They got my horse." Zeke crawled over with his gun still in his hand. "Evan, are you all right?"

The sun peeked over the horizon enough for Evan to see the two men he had killed. Ted Green's twisted face stared up at him with gaping mouth and rotten teeth. Behind the circle another man wearing a rebel army jacket and tall boots lay face down on the ground.

Clay Brady, by the look of his clothing.

Zeke grabbed his shoulder and asked again how Evan was. Evan tried to answer but a black mist clouded his eyes and stopped his words. He lifted his hand again to the side of his head where something felt on fire.

He reached out to steady himself but felt himself falling.

39

RAGNA BURST THROUGH THE DOOR but bit back her question when she saw Anders and Milton at the table. Dust covered every inch of Milton's hair and clothing. He slumped in his chair, his face set in an expression of despair. Their glum mood told her everything.

"Bad luck follows me like a cloud," Milton said. "I'm cursed. Andersonville, hoppers, bank failure, and no gold. "

"Let's walk over and take a look," Anders said in a soothing voice. "I'll go with you."

Milton shook his head. "I know what they look like." He pulled three letters from his pocket and the *Skandinaven*. He slapped them down on the table. "Almost forgot your mail. Dollner came by today."

Anders handed a letter to Auntie Inga who was changing the baby on the edge of the bed and another to Gunnar.

"For me?" Gunnar said. He looked at the letter in his hand as if it might bite him. "I've never had a letter before."

"It's Far's writing," Knut said and snatched it out of Gunnar's hand. "I'll read it to you."

"*Nei*," Ragna said and plucked it out of Knut's fingers and returned it to Gunnar. "It's against the law to open another's mail."

Gunnar carefully opened the sealed letter and smoothed out the page. He frowned over some of the words, reading silently though his lips moved. Finally he shoved the letter to Ragna and asked her to read it to him.

"His handwriting is bad," Gunnar said. "Hard to make out in this light."

Ragna's heart ached that Gunnar struggled with learning of any kind. Uncle's penmanship was his usual neat script.

Dear Gunnar, I've been thinking about Confirmation. I do not believe God will judge you harshly if you try your best. All I ask is that you work a little every day and then I give you permission to quit worrying about the test. Some things are best left in the hands of Almighty God, the loving father who takes pity on his children. Not everyone has a gifted memory. You have strong talents in other areas and no doubt will succeed in whatever path you take. I take comfort in knowing you are there to help your mother.

Your *far*

"That's not what the minister says," Knut said and looked ready to pontificate on the doctrines of Martin Luther when Auntie Inga spoke up.

"Your *far* is the head of this family," Auntie Inga said. "Not Martin Luther nor the Lutheran priest." She nodded at Gunnar and tears made her brown eyes shine. "Your *far* is right. We will abide by his wishes." She walked over and kissed Gunnar on his forehead and gave him a quick hug.

Ragna stared open mouthed. Such display of affection for an older child was unheard of in their family. Only babies were showered with hugs and kisses.

Gunnar stood in the middle of the room with a dazed expression. Ragna reached over and placed the letter into his hand. "Keep it safe, Gunnar," she whispered. "Keep it always."

Auntie Inga had opened her letter. She read it silently and then tucked it in her apron.

"It's time for chores and no monkey business," Auntie said. "I'm writing a letter tonight and you don't want me tattling."

"I'm filthy," Milton said and rose heavily. "I'm going home for a swim."

Ragna held her breath as Anders opened his letter. His face darkened. He threw it on the table, stood abruptly and stalked out of the cabin.

"What was that all about?" Auntie said, looking up from the newspaper.

Ragna picked up the letter and as she read it, her heart sank.

Dear Mr. Voller, We have already found a teacher for our Cold Spring school term. Thank you for your interest.

Weston Mueller, School Board

"Cold Spring has a teacher," Ragna said. She sniffed back tears. What would they do? No crops and no job.

Auntie searched the *Skandinaven*, following the small row of print with her pointer finger. The *Skandinaven*, written in Norwegian, was the one thing Auntie could read without help.

"Look here," Auntie Inga pushed the newspaper across the table and pointed to the middle of a page. "They're looking for a teacher in Pomme de Terre. That's a lot closer than Cold Spring."

* * *

Anders and Ragna stayed up late talking about the job at Pomme de Terre. The dugout felt cool and clammy after the hot sunshine of the hayfield. A small candle stub glowed on the holder but the dugout remained dark as a grave. Ragna snuggled close to Anders, trying to keep her mind from centipedes and spiders.

"But where would we live?" Ragna said. "You could board with a family, but I doubt anyone would take a teacher with a wife and baby coming."

"Evan has friends at Pomme de Terre," Anders said. "What's their name?"

"The Estvolds." Ragna worried about the baby coming. She needed Auntie to help with her lying in. Suddenly life seemed complicated.

As she drifted off to sleep she tried to be positive about a move to Pomme de Terre. It wasn't easy.

The next morning, Ragna found a note from Milton tacked to the front door of Auntie's cabin. It was addressed to Auntie, but Ragna read it before bringing it inside.

> Dear Inga, I hate to disappoint but I have taken off for the Black Hills. No gold in these parts and the hoppers have ruined me. Sorry to leave you in the lurch but I must go while there is a chance. Milton

Ragna dished up the porridge as Auntie Inga wiped her hands on her apron and took the scrap of paper. By the time Auntie finished reading, her voice was as tight as a Hardanger fiddle string. Her chin thrust and she crimped her lips.

"Where is Uncle Milton?" Sigurd said. "I don't want him to go."

Lewis reached over and grabbed Sigurd's dish. Sigurd let out a squeal. Auntie Inga cuffed Lewis on the side of his head.

"Boys, there's a lesson to be learned," Auntie Inga said. The baby wailed from the bed, and Ragna picked her up and nestled her close until she quieted.

"I abominate an oath breaker." Auntie Inga said. "A man doesn't break a promise to take off after some pie in the sky."

"What's a pie in the sky?" Sverre asked with a lisp.

"It's a gold mine," Lewis whispered.

"It's as good a time as any to tell you my decision," Anders said.

The boys quit eating and no one said a word. All eyes were on Anders.

"I'm leaving for Pomme de Terre today with the mail carrier." He looked at Auntie Inga. "I'm breaking my promise, too, but Lord knows I need a job."

No one said anything. Ragna wanted to ask if Anders meant to leave her behind but she didn't care to speak in front of the family.

"School won't start until after harvest," Auntie said "Evan will be home by then."

"I won't risk the mail," Anders said. "I'll go in person with my letter of introduction from the Saints."

Christina gurgled in Ragna's lap. The baby smelled of dirty hair and sour milk. The boys returned to their porridge.

Auntie's face flushed and she opened her mouth to say something but snapped it shut and crimped her mouth tight. Ragna held her breath and looked at her husband. She had seen her auntie's anger enough to know when it was about to erupt. Anders didn't know what was coming.

A strange energy built up in the room and then fizzled away.

"Go, then," Auntie Inga said with a decided tilt of her chin. "Do what you want."

40

SERENA PLODDED THROUGH the following days, working hard to focus her mind on the girls and the many tasks to do. Ole avoided her like the plague. Perhaps that was best. Too much had been said for things to be as they were before.

Against all odds, the remaining rabbit lived. The girls named it Scatterbunny and it soon nibbled on clover and green grass.

One night after supper, Ole pushed away from the table and announced he was leaving for Fort Wadsworth in the morning.

"Hay crop is in the barn and I must be on my way."

"But Ole," Kersten said with alarm. "You can't leave us." She gathered Scatterbunny into her arms and snuggled him close to her cheek.

"I must, Sistermine," Ole said. "I'm going to strike it rich and bring you a china doll."

"Me too?" Maren's face lit up. "I'd like one, too."

"Girls," Serena said with a click of her tongue. "You're too old for toys and Ole has better places for his money."

"Tell you what," Ole said. "Uncle Ole will bring new dresses to Iowa when I come and see you. Dresses pack easier in a saddle bag."

"Really?" Kersten said with such a happy expression that Serena did not have the heart to tell her it would never happen. "You'll come to Burr Oak?"

"I will," Ole said with bright eyes. "Because you girls are the closest thing I have to nieces and I'm not going to let you get away." He reached over and took Kersten's hand. "And I know for a fact, Sistermine, that you don't have another uncle."

"You'll be my uncle," Kersten said. "Always and forever."

"That settles it then." He leaned back in his chair and opened the newspaper. Though the girls tried to keep him talking, they were unable to get more than a mumbled reply to their questions.

In the morning, he was gone.

Anton said that he left with Milton Madsen from Tordenskjold Township.

"They'll travel together," Anton said with relief in his voice. "I'm glad. Hated to think of him riding through Indian country alone."

"He has only one leg," Kersten said with tears flowing. "How will Uncle Ole get away from the Indians?"

"Hush now," Serena said. "God will take care of Ole as he cares for us."

Serena was exhausted by the time the day was over and the girls finally asleep. She planned to go to bed early but a strange restlessness pulled her downstairs. It was she who had driven Ole away, after all. Except for her presence at Pomme de Terre, everything would have gone on as before.

Anton sat at the table with the newspaper spread out before him, a cup of coffee on the table and his lighted pipe in his hand. A curl of smoke rose over his head like a chimney.

"Anton," Serena said as she slipped into a chair at the table. "Mind if I sit a while?"

"Of course not, Serena," Anton said. He looked up from the paper with bloodshot eyes. A bolt of guilt stabbed through her. "Could use the company."

"It's my fault Ole's gone," she said.

"What are you talking about?" Anton snorted. A swirl of smoke came out of his mouth around the pipe stem. "Ole is a grown man. It's about time he struck out on his own. Would have left long ago except for his mother."

They sat in silence listening to the whippoorwills, owls, and the whine of mosquitoes. A June bug slammed against the window pane.

"He never told his mother," Anton said. "And Ole made me promise to keep my mouth shut." Anton puffed on the pipe again and Serena shooed the smoke from her face with a wave of her hand. "Would have spared him from a lot of harping. Dagmar wanted him to get married and give her grandchildren." He took another puff on his pipe. "I felt bad not telling her, but it's not the kind of thing a man likes to talk about."

"Maybe it wouldn't matter," Serena said. She felt her color rising at such frankness but continued on. "There's more to a marriage . . ."

"It would matter to Ole." Anton folded the paper and slapped it on the table. "It would kill him. A grinding reminder every day that he's less than a man." Anton stood to his feet. "Ole made his decision. He's gone and won't be coming back."

* * *

THE NEXT DAY ANTON AND SERENA signed papers and exchanged money. Hungry Hollow belonged to Anton. Serena placed the money in the small wooden box that had previously held the deed to the property.

Serena shed a few tears to see Gust's signature on the old deed. He had such strong, beautiful penmanship. Such a waste. Yes, he had faults but she still missed him. She liked to imagine that if he had lived they would have known a happier ending. She was sure that things would have been just like he promised. But then his death.

Anton talked of nothing but his plans for a store at Hungry Hollow. "I'll trade with the country folks who don't have time to come into town." He said that he would hire a boy to help him get a cabin up and help around the place. "I'll sell eggs and milk, trade goods for pelts and cranberries. Maybe take game in trade if I can find the time to dry it. People going west would trade for jerky."

Serena listened. Anton was older than her father had been and though he had lost his wife and had seen his only son go to the gold fields, he seemed positive about the future. She thought to ask if she and the girls could go along to Hungry Hollow. They could manage the store.

She opened her lips to say as much but something stopped her. She knew Anton would welcome them.

It was time to grow up. She was alive and where there was life, there was hope. It had seemed the world ended after Gust's and Lena's deaths. But then, the world came back.

If only Auntie Karen were there to give guidance now. Serena didn't know what to do. And so, Serena did nothing.

The evenings were quiet without muleteers or ox carters. Serena's workload lessened without the extra washing and cooking. Anton entertained the girls with stories of trolls and bears from the Old Country while Serena taught them to quilt. One night they had just finished the first square of a log cabin design when a knock sounded at the door.

Serena opened the door to a tall young man with a chipped front tooth and a missing index finger. "May I help you?"

"I'm Anders Vollen." He stretched to shake her hand. "The new teacher. Mr. Gardner said my wife and I might board here over the winter."

41

E VAN WOKE UP WITH A POUNDING pain in his ear and a sour clench in his stomach. He lay on the damp ground, struggling to remember what had happened. The sun, low on the horizon, caused a searing stab. He clamped his eyelids shut and tried to will away the swirling motion in his head.

"Don't move!" Old Hen's voice sharpened with what Evan hoped was more worry than anger. Something cold pressed hard against the side of his face. "You've been shot. Lost part of your ear."

"Good Lord." Evan tried to sit up. Strong arms pushed him down on the ground and forced a bottle of whiskey to his mouth. Evan sputtered. The liquor like liquid fire.

"I said don't move," Old Hen said. "If you even think about dying, you'll answer to me. We need every man."

The memory of what happened, the shots in the darkness, the thud of flesh falling to the ground, returned and Evan shuddered.

"Lay still. I'm packing the wound with mud to stop the bleeding." Old Hen said. There was a sound of cloth ripping and the tight feeling of a bandage around his head to hold the mud in place.

"Ted," Evan mumbled. The smallest movement jarred his skull and sent lightning bolts to his closed eyes.

"You got him," Old Hen said in a gentler voice. "The lousy snake. Got what he deserved. Clay Brady, too."

"Both dead?"

"You did good, boy," Old Hen said and patted his arm. "Looks like Ted was with them from the beginning."

Old Hen and Martin lifted him to the wagon box and propped him upright with their bedrolls. Evan couldn't eat but managed to swallow a dribble of water now and then. He clamped his mouth tight against the fiery liquor no matter how the others cajoled him.

The hard truth of the matter was that it took more than one man to drive a mule team of that size and load. Ahead lay the Coteaus des Prairies, the most difficult stretch of the trail.

Evan never considered leaving the job. He had signed on and would work until he no longer had breath—but he felt so weak he doubted he could pull the jerk line.

Old Hen propped the rifle on the seat beside Evan with the barrel stuck into a rolled blanket. "There's a doctor at Toqua."

Evan tugged his hat over his eyes to keep out the blinding sun and braced himself with his feet.

"Allemande left!" Old Hen said. "Promenade all!"

Each turn of the wheels felt like a knife poked in Evan's ear. Good Lord, what would Inga say? If he died or became too sick to work, his family would never make it.

He remembered too clearly the hardships his family had faced in the Old Country after his father's death. They had scrabbled and scraped for every mouthful of food. He could not bear the thought of Inga and the children going through such hardship. It was bad enough with the grasshoppers.

Lord, have mercy.

＊　＊　＊

THEY TRAVELED LATE INTO THE EVENING and pulled into Toqua just as the mosquitoes were bad enough for a smudge. Evan had dozed in the wagon seat most of the day. It came to him that he had been mostly out of his head.

"Deliver these boys to the sheriff," Old Hen said to Zeke and Jeppe, pointing to the bodies of Ted and Clay draped over their horses. "Tell him how it happened. If he has questions, he should come here to the camp."

"Don't worry," Jeppe said. "Me and Homer'll get everything squared away."

"Might be a doctor around," Zeke said. "I'll post our letters and fetch one."

Evan pulled a half-written page from his pocket but couldn't sign it for the spots dancing before his eyes. Instead, he shook his head and tried to put the paper back in his pocket.

He didn't have the strength. Zeke helped him, as gentle as a woman with a sick person. Old Hen and Martin eased him down from the wagon box and propped him beneath a willow tree alongside Lake Toqua.

The gentle waves lapping against the shore lulled him almost to sleep. The smell of lake and fish. Ducks floating on the water, bobbing up and down with each wave.

Something niggled at the back of Evan's brain but he couldn't place his finger on it. He thought maybe it was something about the men he had killed. He had no choice in that, and many witnesses to prove he had acted in self-defense. No, something about this place demanded his attention. He had almost dropped back to sleep when he realized what it was.

They had driven out of grasshopper country. The land around Toqua lay green and verdant with big bluestem grasses waving around the lake, wild rye and prairie dropseed. Milkweed and shooting stars flowered beside him. Beyond the campsite bloomed oxeyes and alumroot. No sign of grasshoppers anywhere. The joy of it brought tears to Evan's eyes. There was a world without grasshoppers. There was still hope.

Zeke brought the doctor. Evan woke from a dream about Gunnar's Catechization. The dream felt so real that at first Evan could not remember where he was. Then the doctor jerked the bandage off his face.

"Mud stopped the bleeding," the doctor said. He wore a filthy waist coat and had long hair pushed behind his ears. His gray beard curled under his chin and flared into puffs of mustache. "Your ear is about gone." When he leaned over Evan's face to sniff the wound, his breath smelled of alcohol, and Evan noticed a tremble in his gnarled hands. "I fear putrification."

"What does that mean?" Evan felt the hairs rise on the back of his neck. He had never liked doctors or sick people. He could not stomach even a hammered thumb or a stubbed toe.

"I'll sear it with an iron," the doctor said. "Still time before you mortify."

Evan grabbed the whiskey bottle from Zeke's outstretched hand and guzzled as fast as he could. The doctor poured lake water over Evan's face. The cold water stabbed like knives and in spite of his best efforts, Evan cried out.

The doctor pulled a metal instrument from his bag and wiped it on his pants leg. "Good thing I was in town," he said. "Saw a lot of this type of grazing wound in the war." He blew on the instrument and scraped a fleck of dried blood with the back of his thumb nail. "Good thing you turned your head or you would have lost an eye." Then he probed into the wound. Evan bit his lips until blood tasted on his tongue.

"Lucky," the doctor said again. "You'll lose your looks but probably live. Bullet furrowed your cheek. Beard has to come off."

Evan drank another swig of whiskey and the doctor pulled the bottle out of Evan's grasp and drank a long swallow himself, emptying it. Then he pulled scissors from his vest pocket and cut Evan's beard close to the skin. Evan felt naked as a sheared sheep.

"Helps to know barbering." The doctor chuckled and pulled a rusty straight edge razor from the same vest pocket. "You a married man?"

"*Ja*, I'm married." Evan nodded through the whiskey haze as the doctor scraped the dull blade over his face. Evan felt like he was losing the top layer of his skin.

"Good thing," the doctor said. "In my experience, a wife sticks by a scarred man but a sweetheart will leave forthwith." He pushed an iron rod into the campfire, adding a dried branch to build the flames. "I could tell you stories about the boys I tended in the war. A female is a temperamental creature when it comes to looks." He repositioned the rod closer to the hottest flame until the metal tip glowed red.

"This will hurt considerably," the doctor said as if he were discussing the weather. Evan decided he disliked the man, disliked him intensely.

"Hold him down, boys."

Jeppe and Homer each took an arm and Martin lay across his legs. Old Hen steadied his head and chin. The doctor brought the glowing rod. Evan clamped his eyes shut and steeled himself for the sake of his family. For Inga.

A blazing pain shot through his head. Evan lurched but they held him tight. "Hold still," the doctor said. "You don't want to lose an eye."

The sizzle and smell of burning flesh. A tortured scream that did not stop.

42

I T SEEMED TO RAGNA THAT ANDERS had been gone forever. One day, Ragna woke up with a bout of morning sickness and tripped over Musky on her way to the outhouse.

She yelled at Sigurd for allowing the dog on the porch. The cat streaked under the bed and stayed there. Then Ragna slapped Christina's fingers for reaching into the slop bucket. Christina had learned to scoot across the floor and was into everything. Ragna jostled the wailing baby on her hip and was about to scold Knut for not fetching the water quick enough when she glanced out the open door.

Lying Jack and Many Beavers rode along the shoreline.

"*Uff da!*" Ragna said. "It's Lying Jack!" She was still in her nightgown and wrapper. "Company always comes at the worst time!"

"I know," Auntie said. "Always when the house is in an uproar or I'm in the middle of something."

Ragna pulled a dress over her head and tied a kerchief on her hair. She and Auntie scurried to clean off the breakfast table and make themselves presentable.

"But I'm glad he's come. I need needles and thread," Auntie said as she nervously patted her braids into place. "We're out of flour. And sugar. Vanilla. I guess we're low on everything. I was hoping Evan would send money by now."

"Is anyone to home?" Lying Jack called as he and his wife climbed down from their horses. Musky ran nipping and barking to welcome them. "We's comes with goods at grasshopper prices. Yes, ma'am, we's bring bargains."

"Well, hello there little dog," Lying Jack said. He knelt to rub the dog's ears and neck. "Good puppy!"

Many Beavers toted the full packs into the cabin and spread them across the table. She nodded at Ragna but didn't speak. The woman's eyes seemed to soak in the entire situation, the cat under the bed, the crying baby. The boys jostled round the table and stared with wide eyes at the sacks of candy and sugar, the pocket knives and fish hooks.

"Sigurd," Auntie said. "Take the cows out to pasture. Hear them beller?"

Sigurd whined and cajoled. Finally Auntie relented. "Just for a minute then. Don't touch," Auntie said. "Only look."

"What will you take for these shoes?" Gunnar pointed to a pair of heavy work boots. His voice started out low but ended in a squeak at the end. The other boys laughed at his cracking voice. "I've twelve muskrats and three beaver skins," he said, completely ignoring his brothers. "I could use a good pair of work boots."

They haggled over the price of shoe leather while Ragna examined bolts of flannel and cotton batting. She fingered a paper of needles and embroidery floss. If she only had money, she could begin sewing for the baby.

Gunnar presented his pelts, but Lying Jack refused to budge from his price. He declared that he would need at least a half-dollar cash money in addition to the hides.

"They're fine boots. You did good work with them hides," Lying Jack said. "Nice and clean. But I've gots to make a living."

"How many more hides would you need?"

"Lots of skins these parts but not much money." Lying Jack scrunched his mouth into a frown as if he were thinking hard. "Gots to have cash moneys with the hides."

Auntie Inga examined everything and picked up a small sack of flour.

"How much for the flour?" Auntie said.

"A dollar a sack. Cheaper to buy it by the barrel, missus," Lying Jack said. "Dollner's Store gets $3.88 a barrel."

Auntie Inga looked at the flour a long time and then put it back on the table. Instead she chose a sack of cornmeal. Ragna noticed she chose the cheaper grade. "Ragna, fetch a dollar from the writing desk."

Ragna pulled herself away from the trade goods and came back with a silver dollar. Lying Jack counted out change into Auntie's hand. "They're paying bounty for grasshoppers," Lying Jack said. "Three cents a bushel."

Auntie seemed to be adding figures in her head.

Lying Jack told how the government was buying grasshoppers to help out the farmers. He pulled a stack of folded burlap sacks from a remaining pack. "Lots of folks looking for gunny sacks to tote the hoppers into town. These are nice and sturdy and scarce as hen's teeth. Hold five bushels." Lying Jack patted Sigurd's head and chucked under his chin. "Even little ones can fill a sack. Bounty only crop this year for most folks."

Anders burst through the doorway and interrupted the trade. A smile stretched broadly across his stubbly face. His clothes wrinkled and stained with sweat. Ragna knew he got the job before he said a word. He tossed the mail on the table and greeted everyone.

"We're moving to Pomme de Terre, Mrs. Vollen." Anders pulled Ragna close and planted a kiss on her lips right in front of everyone. "I'm the new teacher."

Ragna had never lived away from Auntie and Uncle since the uprising, except for the few weeks she and Anders had lived on their claim. One could hardly count that since it was within shouting distance. Going to Pomme de Terre would mean really moving away from them. She wouldn't know anyone. Her lying-in loomed. A sinking feeling of dread mixed with the excitement of going off on their own

Ragna plastered a smile on her face. That's what a good wife would do.

"And more news," Anders said. "There's a job for Gunnar if he wants it. Cash money plus room and board." Anders explained how Gunnar might work for Anton Estvold at Hungry Hollow. "He might even attend school in bad weather."

Gunnar looked like a popcorn kernel about to explode. Ragna breathed a sigh of relief and hoped with all her might that Auntie would say yes. It would be easier if one of her brothers were along.

"Gunnar is needed at home," Auntie Inga said with a tilted chin. "He's just getting old enough to be useful and now you want him traipsing off to Pomme de Terre?"

"Please, Mor!" Gunnar said. "We need the money."

"Out of the question," his mother said. She turned to Lying Jack. "Would you take a quarter dollar along with the hides for the shoes?"

"I would, missus," Lying Jack said. A wide grin split his dark face. "I would indeeds."

"Then add three cent's worth of peppermint drops." Auntie looked at the coins in her hand. "And a paper of pins and a spool of white thread and two pounds of sugar."

Ragna wondered at Auntie's free hand with the money. Uncle Evan had left strict instructions that it was to be held back for emergencies.

Gunnar tried on his new shoes with a bewildered look on his face. Disappointment washed over Ragna. She wanted Gunnar to go along more than anything. It was out of her control. Everything was out of her control. Ragna was having a baby and must depend on strangers to help at her child bed. She must follow her husband to Pomme de Terre in spite of her own wishes.

"How much for the sacks?" Auntie said, fingering the burlap material and holding it up to the light.

"A dollar a dozen," Lying Jack said. "They're good material and sturdy. I'll make it a baker's dozen for you, missus."

"Sold," Auntie said. "Ragna fetch the other dollar."

Ragna went back to the writing desk and pulled open the drawer with a shaky hand. Inside rested a single silver dollar and coins totaling seventeen cents. It was all they had.

"Uncle Evan said to keep this for emergencies," Ragna whispered into Auntie's ear. She feared insanity had fallen upon her aunt to cause such extravagance.

"This is an emergency," Auntie Inga said in a low voice. "I know what I'm doing."

"I'll take a dozen sacks," Anders said. "And a licorice whip." He pulled a half dollar piece from his pocket, two quarters and a penny. He winked at Ragna and gave an encouraging nod. "One thing we have plenty of is hoppers."

Ragna scribbled a quick letter to her friend, Bertha. Lying Jack would be stopping by the Wheelings' place later in the week. It seemed like only yesterday Ragna had sent messages to Anders while he taught school at the Branch of Zion.

Ragna tried to think of something to say to her friend and finally wrote a vague report of doing fine. It was the truth after all, only not all of it. Ragna listed Pomme de Terre as her new address.

She handed the letter to Lying Jack who lingered near the door as if he wanted to say something while Many Beavers packed the trade goods. She meticulously stacked spools of thread on top of the bolts of cloth, making every item fit exactly into the pack.

"Something on your mind?" Auntie Inga said to Lying Jack.

"Saw Milton Madsen," Lying Jack said, "over Pomme de Terre way."

Ragna saw the muscles clench in Auntie's jaw.

"Said he was off to the gold fields and asked me to checks up on you when I's in dis country."

"I'm fine." Auntie swooped Christiana from the floor where she was about to touch the stove. "Surely you can see we're all fine."

She and Ragna walked with them to the horses. It was only mannerly to say goodbye again as they left the yard.

"I'd like to give you a bit of advice," Lying Jack turned serious and dropped off his usual dialect. He climbed onto his saddle. "Collect hoppers while you can. The bounty money won't last. Nobody in these parts has nuthin."

As Lying Jack and Many Beavers rode away, the family made plans. They would all gather hoppers. Even Auntie. The baby would nap alongside the field. The grasshoppers were everywhere—it wasn't as if they had far to go. The biggest problem was how to get the sacks to Dollner's Store to collect the bounty. Lying Jack had said Charlie Dollner would burn the hoppers as they came in so folks could reuse the gunny sacks.

"We sold the wagon too soon," Ragna said.

"Don't worry. I'll build a travois like the Indians," Gunnar said. "We'll be rich."

The boys streamed toward the fields like water pouring from a bucket. Each carried an empty sack.

"Fetch the rake and broom, Ragna," Anders said. "We'll sweep the hoppers onto the tarp and scoop them into the sacks. It will go faster."

By nightfall, twenty-six gunny sacks stood against the barn, stuffed with grasshoppers. Ragna and Auntie stitched the sacks shut. Ragna's back ached and her belly growled with hunger. She hoped she could keep her eyes open long enough to eat.

"Just think," Anders said. "Almost four dollars for one day's work."

"We'll do it every day." Gunnar pounded the last nail on the travois. "Tie the sacks on tight. We'll be ready to leave at sunup."

Ragna felt exhausted. They finished the evening chores and supped on milk and mush. Then they collapsed into bed. Ragna longed for sleep but sleep would not come. It seemed impossible anyone would pay for grasshoppers. She thought how many grasshoppers filled a bushel. The number of bushels in each sack and the number of sacks ready for Dollner's Store. It seemed most likely to her that they would bring their new crop to the store and find it a cruel hoax. But Lying Jack was most reliable. He wouldn't spread a false rumor.

Her hands scratched from the sharp grasshopper wings. Her back ached from lugging the heavy sacks across the field. Her legs jumpy and pained.

When she finally slept, Ragna dreamed that a flock of passenger pigeons descended on their fields and ate the entire harvest of grasshoppers before they could collect a cent of bounty money. In the dream, Milton watched the flock descend and said, "I'm cursed. Andersonville, hoppers, bank failure, and now pigeons."

43

M R. GARDNER CALLED ON SERENA one afternoon when she was alone in the house. Anton and the girls had walked out to Hungry Hollow to plan where the new house would be. Serena had almost gone along but decided at the last minute to stay behind. A quiet day in the house was too wonderful to resist.

Serena needed time to think, time to figure out her next path of action. She planned to hurry through her chores and spend the remaining time in serious contemplation. But then Mr. Gardner showed up.

Serena hesitated. She wanted nothing more than to pretend she hadn't heard his knock. Instead, she patted her hair and straightened her skirt. She opened the door and invited the man inside. It was only polite.

"Mrs. Gustafson," he said and removed his hat. "It's nice to see you again."

"Please take a chair," she said. Serena added a piece of kindling to the fire box and stirred the coals with the poker until the wood burst into flames. She pulled the tea kettle over the hottest burner. "I'll fix a cup of tea."

Mr. Gardner was dressed in a nice suit and bowler hat. Though his clothing was impeccable, his nails were chewed down to the quick. He smelled of boiled cabbage and stale cigars.

"How may I help you?" Serena rummaged in the cupboard for cups and saucers. She placed them on the table beside Dagmar's blue teapot.

"It's this." Mr. Gardner combed fingers through his greasy hair until it stood straight up, reminding Serena of a wild Indian. She stifled a smile. "Another cook has left for the gold fields. I'm desperate."

Serena considered his statement. She had few options. If he was desperate, he would be more agreeable to her demands.

They discussed the position as the kettle boiled. Serena excused herself and poured the hot water over a measure of tea leaves in Dagmar's favorite blue pot.

"I won't do the laundry," Serena said while the tea steeped. "And you'd have to find a dishwasher. After supper, I'll need to return to my girls."

Mr. Gardner thought for a long minute. "The girls could work, too. Kitchen helpers and dishwashers." He mentioned a fair wage. "You could work together."

Serena thought it over as she filled their cups. Ole had said it was not a suitable place for her or the girls. Ole was gone. It was her decision now.

"I'll try it. But I won't tolerate disrespect toward me or my girls." Serena said firmly. "I'll expect you to keep the men in line. Any problems and we'll quit."

Mr. Gardner wrung his hands and smiled. He was about to speak but Serena interrupted him.

"We won't do anything outside the kitchen. Won't do the laundry or clean the rooms or anything else."

"But our last cook," Mr. Gardner said and was about to say more when Serena interrupted.

"Maybe overwork convinced him to leave," Serena said. "Only kitchen work and the girls must attend school." She was determined to make her demands known lest she find herself in an impossible situation.

"I'll advertise for a maid and laundress," Mr. Gardner said. "Maybe an immigrant girl."

"Then we'll start tomorrow."

"Pomme de Terre will be the biggest town on the river," Mr. Gardner said as he settled back into his chair. He sipped tea. "The railroad will follow the old Red River Trail, right through the old fort. This inn will be the railroad depot—in a few years or less. You won't regret settling down in Pomme de Terre."

While Mr. Gardner drank his tea, he touted Pomme de Terre's rosy future and its link to the railroad. Serena found her mind wandering. She smiled politely and tried to force herself to pay attention to Mr. Gardner's rambling monotone.

The clerk from Gardner's store ran up the path and pounded on the door. He was a man named Hopkins, middle-aged and bald.

"Something must be wrong," Serena said. She opened the door and the storekeeper burst into the room.

"Mr. Gardner," he said, panting for breath, his face beet red after running from the village. "You'd best come back to the hotel. There's trouble."

"What kind of trouble?" Mr. Gardner said. He stood to his feet and replaced his hat on his head.

"General Custer." Hopkins gasped for breath and wiped his face with the back of his hand. "Wiped out by the Sioux in Montana." He took a dipper of water from Serena's hand and bobbed his head in thanks. "Indians heading this way."

"What do they want with us?" Mr. Gardner said. "We've no quarrel with the Sioux."

"It seems they have a quarrel with us," Hopkins said.

"Oh no! My girls went out to Hungry Hollow with Anton." Serena looked out the window expecting a painted horde to sweep down upon them any minute. "Where are the Indians now?"

"Don't know where they are," Hopkins said. "Just got word that the Sioux are heading this way and folks should prepare."

"Come to the hotel, Mrs. Gustafson," Mr. Gardner said. "We'll mount a defense."

Serena shook her head. She wouldn't leave the inn until Anton and the girls were back. "Later. I'll wait for my girls."

Serena stood in the kitchen as the men left the inn. She remembered the stories told about the uprising. Captives scalped and raped. Horrible things happened. Hundreds killed. Her girls were at such a tender age.

What could they do? Anton had guns but the stockade around the old fort had mostly been burned for firewood. No soldiers for miles. She remembered how it had felt to be stranded inside the fort walls with hostiles surrounding them.

Then, Gust had stood between her and the savages. Soldiers stood guard. Now she and the girls were defenseless. No husband. No soldiers. She saw clearly that her decision to linger in Pomme de Terre had placed Maren and Kersten at risk.

She dropped to her knees beside a chair. *Dear Lord, bring the girls and Anton back to the inn. Protect us from the Indians.*

44

E VAN GREW FEVERISH. The mule train waited an extra day in Toqua but Evan did not improve. His right eye swelled shut and the skin pulled over the fresh scar every time he moved his jaw. He was too weak to walk.

Old Hen paced around the camp, fretting about the schedule, and barking orders at the men. Evan blamed himself for the delay but there was nothing he could do.

"I'm sorry," the doctor said after he examined Evan on the second day. "I thought I got all the mortification, but it seems I didn't. You're burning up with fever. You'll have quite a scar—if you live."

"I'll live," Evan mumbled, trying not to move his jaw and stretch the tender skin. "How much do I owe you?"

"Two dollars ought to do it," the doctor said. He pulled from his bag a tin of mule salve and a bottle of laudanum. He wiped his hands on the back of his pants and dipped his index finger into the salve. He smeared it generously across Evan's wound. Evan pulled away in a burst of pain.

The doctor tucked the tin into Evan's shirt pocket and told him to apply it twice a day to keep the scar supple. Then he dosed laudanum into Evan's mouth. Evan choked the bitter liquid down and reached for the whiskey bottle to wash the taste away.

"Keep the salve," the doctor said, "I won it off an army sutler in a friendly card game." He held up the laudanum bottle to the light to examine its contents and frowned. "But I'm short on laudanum and won't part with this unless you have another two bits."

Evan wasn't sure which was worse. The pain or the treatment. He shook his head. He would have to make do.

The doctor held out his hand until Evan drew money out of his pocket. He was down to nothing. Although the laudanum made him not care about anything, Evan reminded himself of his family back home, forcing himself to care.

"Think you'll make it?" Old Hen said with a worried look. "You could stay here until you mend."

Though his head reeled and fever weakened his knees, Evan shook his head. "I'll be fine." He would set his mind to it and that was that. He couldn't afford to lose pay. His family needed every cent he could bring home.

The sheriff came by the camp just as the doctor was leaving, asking Old Hen to repeat the story of how the two robbers were killed. Evan listened through a laudanum induced haze. When Evan heard himself named as the man who had shot both of the outlaws, Evan tried to explain but felt too ill to speak. It seemed Old Hen blamed Evan for their deaths.

The sheriff was a short, skinny man with a leather vest and tall boots. His clean-shaven face showed pox marks. He carried in his hand a bank draft for one hundred dollars.

"Reward for Clay Brady," he said and handed the bank draft to Evan. "He was wanted in Dakota Territory for horse thieving and general devilment."

Evan tried to clear his head. He must be dreaming again. The sheriff repeated the story and Evan realized he was serious.

"We'll divide it," Evan mumbled. "We're all in this together."

"You shot him. Shut up and take it," Old Hen said. "We don't have time to argue."

A hundred dollars. A godsend. But Evan remembered Gertie banging pans at Gager's Station. He wondered who'd tell her her man was dead. Evan was relieved that chore would fall to someone else. He imagined Gertie's face crumbling into weeping and tried to remember if they had children. Evan couldn't.

Clay Brady was a hardened outlaw. Evan had to admit that he had little regret over killing him. But Ted was someone Evan had known from his very earliest days in Minnesota. Although Ted had been a poor excuse for a man, Evan knew that regret over his death would linger a long time.

But one hundred dollars! What his wheat might have yielded if the grasshoppers had stayed away. Evan must mail it to Inga. He scribbled a note of explanation. He told Inga that he had been shot, then rubbed out the words and wrote hurt instead. He told her the money was reward for two outlaws that he had killed. As he wrote the words, he realized that he was saying both too much and not enough. Inga would worry. It was too late to change it.

Old Hen was ready to leave and had waited for Evan long enough. Evan scribbled his love and signature. He didn't have the strength to explain anything else. Zeke posted the letter as the mule train left Toqua. Evan prayed it would arrive intact. Surely Milton would assist Inga to travel into town to the bank. It was a comfort knowing his good friend and neighbor was there to watch over his family. The relief of the reward money brought tears to his eyes. Or maybe it was the pain of his wound.

The fresh air of the trail cleared Evan's head. The bandage covered half of his face and one eye but Evan need not see to drive the mules. Old Hen told him when to brake, when to pull the jerk line and when to snap the whip over the leaders. Evan settled back in the seat, draping the lines through his fingers, trying to ignore the pain.

They had traveled less than five miles when they came upon several covered wagons. Evan squinted. The wagons clustered without horses, mules or oxen, stranded in the middle of nowhere. A ragged group of people huddled around a campfire, families mostly. A woman stirred something in a large kettle.

"Arm yourselves, boys." Old Hen called back for Evan to pull the brake. "Looks like trouble."

"What's wrong?" Jeppe called from the second wagon.

"We're not going in 'til we know for sure," Old Hen said. "Might be a trap."

They stopped about a hundred yards from the Conestogas. Old Hen stood up and waved a white rag. Evan watched two men walk across the prairie toward them. One hobbled on crutches. The other man looked familiar.

"Milton?" Evan said. "Something wrong at home? What're you doing here?"

"Evan?" Milton said. "What happened to you?"

* * *

THE TRAVELERS WELCOMED THE MULETEERS to their fire for the noon meal.

"Jeppe and Martin," Old Hen barked. "Stand guard." Old Hen climbed down from the nigh horse and helped Evan down from the wagon box. "We're not out of the woods yet, boys. Keep a close watch."

Evan hoped he could walk the hundred yards to the fire. The smell of boiling coffee added incentive to keep going. Milton and Zeke walked on either side of him, grasping Evan's elbows and holding him upright. Evan heard everything as through a roaring waterfall.

"Inga and the children?" Evan said. Fever gave the strange sensation he had forgotten something, was missing something important. Sweat poured from him.

"Everyone's doing fine back home," Milton said as they walked over the uneven ground toward the campfire. "Don't worry."

Evan slumped to a rock by the fire and took the tin cup handed to him. Evan used his shirt tail to wrap around the hot cup handle.

"We were caught flat-footed night before last," Milton said. "Outlaws robbed us clean out. Took the horses and mules. The cow. All the weapons and ammunition. Took our flour barrels and food stock. Stole rings, silver and folding money folks had tucked away."

"What did they look like?" Old Hen said as he took a cup of coffee from the woman by the fire. "How many?"

"Three men and a boy," Milton said. "Boy driving the buckboard not old enough to shave."

The others described the outlaws as Evan listened. Evan thought the outlaws sounded a lot like the men who had been playing cards at Gager's Station. He hadn't seen a boy with them back at Gager's.

The coffee revived Evan. He realized what he had been trying to remember. Milton had promised to stay back with the family while Evan was on the road. Evan mulled the broken promise. He didn't like it but decided to let it go—after all, Evan's family was not Milton's responsibility, in spite of their agreement.

The men languished around the fire in near despair, agonizing over lost time in the gold fields. The women busied with everyday tasks, as women always did. Evan had never known a woman to idle and these had plenty of work to do. One boiled dirty soakers in an iron pot, draping the wet cloths over the wagon wheels to dry. An older woman with gnarled fingers and snow white hair rocked a fussing infant, patting its back and singing a tuneless lullaby in a strange language. Several older children worked sums on the top of a flat rock using charcoal for chalk. Their mother, at least the woman who instructed them, looked ready for childbed. A young woman pulled feathers from a prairie hen, reminding Evan of Ragna's wedding and the pigeons she had plucked.

"They took everything but the Conestogas," one man said. "If we could only tow the wagons back to Toqua, we might recoup a little of our investment." He gave Old Hen a hopeful look. "We need to borrow a few mules."

"We're on contract with Fort Wadsworth and can't delay," Old Hen said. "We'll send someone back, though."

"We need help." The man who seemed to be the leader of the group spoke. "Buried a child yesterday. Two more children down with measles in that tent." Evan looked toward a small tent pitched in the shade of a big rock. "We've few supplies and no ammunition or weapons. Boys chucked rocks at prairie hens this morning so we'd eat."

Evan thought of the coffin he had left with Inga and prayed a desperate prayer that it would still be empty when he returned home. Children died. It was a fact of frontier life. They sickened and died in a hundred different ways. The faces of his children pressed into his memory. *Dear Lord, keep them healthy.*

They calculated the number of animals needed to haul the heavy wagons. Evan drank a second cup of coffee as the travelers argued whether they should go with the muleteers or wait for help. They finally decided to wait for help.

"You may think us foolish," the leader said, "but Conestogas go for a good price. They're all we have left. Enough for us to reach the Black Hills."

Milton and Ole asked to ride along with Old Hen and the mule train. "We've nothing to hold us with these folks," Milton said. "We were just riding along, trying to get to the gold fields."

"Walk along back to the wagons," Old Hen said. "We'll talk about it."

Zeke and Milton again positioned themselves on either side of Evan. Ole crutched behind them.

"Looks like you were both soldiers." Old Hen looked at them closely, no doubt noticing Milton's ancient uniform blouse and Ole's missing leg. "Know anything about mules?"

"Both of us in the artillery," Milton said with a nod. "Handled mules moving the big guns."

"Come with us, then, and welcome," Old Hen said. Evan heard the relief in his voice. "We're short of man power and a man down sick. Robbers hit us twice already."

Milton climbed up onto the wagon seat and reached down to help Ole. Ole threw his crutches onto the wagon and grasped Milton's hand. Somehow he managed to climb up in the box. Old Hen said that he recognized Ole from Pomme de Terre and asked about his parents. It was then Evan realized who he was.

"I knew your folks," Evan said. "Used to drive the stage through Pomme de Terre. Good people."

Ole grunted. Evan couldn't decide the grunt's meaning. Ole slipped into a dark mood as the conversation shifted to Pomme de Terre and grasshoppers. Ole slumped back on the seat and seemed content to let Milton do all the talking.

"Hoppers took everything," Milton said. "Nothing left to harvest."

Although Evan had suspected as much, the news still hit him like a sock in the stomach. "The family?" Evan knew bad news would have been said at the beginning but feared Milton had held something back. "Inga and the children?"

"Fine, just fine." Milton scratched his head with a wry grin. "I'll tell you straight— Inga wasn't too pleased that I left for the gold fields."

Evan weighed Milton's statement and grinned. The stretching skin made him wince but Evan couldn't hold back the smile. Inga, no doubt, had been mad as a wet hen. She hated when people didn't keep their word. Evan would have loved to have been there when Milton broke the news to her.

The prairie stretched out around them, filled with blooming ox-eyed daisies, Indian paintbrush, and purple cone flowers. Wind rippled over the grasses until it rippled like a vast ocean. Not a tree in sight. Nothing but endless grass and the blue hills ahead of them. Soaring eagles swooped down to grasp field mice with strong talons. A covey of prairie hens skirted into the weeds.

Milton told about the Tordenskjold miners, the gamblers hoping to win pay dirt, and how tents had covered the hills like a flock of white cranes resting in the grass.

"You didn't get enough of mining camp?" Evan said between half-closed lips. His wound felt better if he didn't open his mouth.

"Guess not," Milton shook his head and said. "Nothing holding me back. I'm off to the Black Hills and fame and fortune."

"But your claim. All you've worked for."

"Farming is too much work," Milton said. "Even Anders is looking for a teaching job."

"*Alle vil vere herre, ingen vil bere sekken,*" Evan said with a chuckle that brought a sharp pain to his ear. "Everyone wants to be a gentleman, nobody wants to carry the sack."

"And you?" Evan said to Ole, more to be polite than to seek information. "What are you leaving behind?"

"Nothing," Ole said. "Lost everything in the war. Nothing left to lose."

Evan was struck by his bitterness. Knowing Ole's parents made this attitude harder to understand. Dagmar and Anton had been cheerful through all of life's difficult times. Evan would have thought their son would inherit the same mindset. Evan blamed the war. War changed people.

Evan decided to speak to his boys about war when he saw them again. They needed to learn their *bestefar's* advice and how it had spared Evan from untold grief. They were growing up so fast. He hoped he had taught them what they needed to know to make it on their own. He thought how they needed to know the dangers of bragging and overconfidence, the cautionary tale of Ted Green. They were good workers but how important they learn to find joy in daily tasks. They must seek wives who would help and comfort, be industrious and thrifty.

Evan was far from home. He could easily have been killed by the robbers. Only the kindness of God had spared his life. He would write a letter with all the important things he wanted to tell them. Foolish or not, he could not risk leaving them unsaid.

45

S TARS BLINKED IN THE SKY as Ragna cooked breakfast for Anders and Gunnar. They
would head to Dollner's Store as soon as it was light enough to see the trail. Robins
and chirping horned larks welcomed the day. The rooster crowed its first sleepy alarm.

Marta Sevald had always compared birdsong to nuns singing their morning *Angelus*.
Marta had spent her childhood next door to a convent and described how songs echoed
from its open windows every morning, like clockwork. Ragna loved starting the day with
Angelus followed by *Lauds*, morning prayers.

As Ragna stirred the porridge, she tried to imagine how it would feel to be a veiled
nun, totally dedicated to prayer and service.

Though Ragna was a *kjerring*, she prayed her own *Lauds*: prayers for relief from
the scourge of grasshoppers, for Uncle Evan's safe return, Anders's teaching job, their
move to Pomme de Terre and the baby growing within her.

Surely the softness of the air and the first gentle rays of light were God's answer
of approval and blessing. With praise I will awake the dawn.

"Ragna," Anders called from the front stoop. "Hurry! Bring needle and thread."

Ragna hurried to obey her husband, pulling the porridge to a cooler part of the
stove where it was less likely to scorch and tucking her prayers away for later.

"Look! They've chewed clear through the burlap," Anders said. "Let's hope we can
get them to Dollner's Store before they all escape."

Anders hit the sacks with the back of a shovel to kill the offending hoppers while
Ragna patched the holes. Gunnar fussed about the travois. In spite of several tries, only
twenty-three sacks would fit on the travois.

"If I had wheels," Gunnar said. His dark eyes smoldered with frustration. "I'd build a wagon. I could do it!"

"It's all right," Ragna said. She reached over and patted his hand before returning to her sewing. "We'll make another trip later."

Ragna encouraged Gunnar to eat his breakfast but Gunnar refused to stop until he contrived a rope harness that fastened a sack to the back of each ox. Anders and Gunnar would take turns carrying the remaining sack across their shoulders.

"We'll get all twenty-six sacks to Dollner's," Gunnar said with a grin. "I knew I'd come up with something."

"Be careful with the basting thread when you empty the sacks," Auntie said. Her brow knitted into a furrow between her eyes. "Snip at the ends and bring every thread to use again. We can't afford to waste a thing."

Auntie Inga roused the boys from their beds. The rooster's crows gained strength as day broke. The men ate breakfast. Ragna tucked needle and thread into Anders' pocket in case they had another breakout and kissed him goodbye.

Anders and Gunnar left just as the sun peeked over the horizon, Goldie and Ryder dragging the travois behind them. The calf bawled from the pen, anxious to be turned in with its mother. The boys were already heading out for chores, Musky nipping at their heels, Fisk streaking after a gopher.

"Need anything from the store?" Anders said as they passed by the cabin. He spoke to Ragna but Auntie Inga answered.

"Mail from Evan," Auntie Inga said. "And bounty money for the hoppers."

After the chores, Ragna, Knut and the twins began the tedious job of harvesting more grasshoppers. Auntie said that if they gathered enough for another trip into town, there would be a special treat for all of them.

"What does Mr. Dollner do with the grasshoppers when he gets them?" Lewis said. "Haul them to the Capitol?"

"Lying Jack said that they empty the sacks into a big pit and burn them," Knut said. "Of course, he keeps tally of the bounty money spent to report to Governor Pillsbury."

Knut dug a pit near the barn while the others raked grasshoppers onto the tarp. The hoppers flurried up into Ragna's face, spat their evil excrement on her arms and apron, cut into her skin with their sharp wings.

She and the twins dragged the loaded tarp back to the pit. Knut covered the hole with layers of pine boughs to keep them confined.

Auntie stood watch with the rake lest the hoppers get away. Baby Christina napped on a blanket in the shade. Auntie loosed the cow into a patch of weeds behind the barn and said that she would watch Bossy so Sigurd could help with the hoppers. Sigurd whooped with joy.

Ragna found it was easier to rake the hoppers than lug the heavy tarp. Her back ached as she and the boys dragged their strange harvest to the pit. Ragna thought again of the nuns and determined to set her heart into a similar mode of sacrifice and duty. *Our Father, which art in heaven, hallowed be they Name, thy kingdom come, thy will be done on earth as it is in heaven.*

Ragna and her brothers toiled all morning and filled the pit by early afternoon. It was difficult to gauge how many hoppers would refill the sacks but it seemed they had enough.

Anders and Gunnar returned early-afternoon, jubilant with cash money in their pockets. They turned the oxen loose to wallow in the lake and graze among the cattails. Without stopping to eat, Anders and Gunnar began the difficult job of refilling the sacks. Ragna and Auntie stood by to patch holes and close the sacks. They used the threads saved from the first batch, sewing with a quick running stitch.

Three cents a bushel was almost too good to be true. Ragna darned the bottom of a sack. Of course, wheat would have brought as much as thirty-five cents a bushel, maybe fifty cents this year while the grasshoppers were bad in other areas. Ragna pushed away the numbers multiplying in her head. They had planted three acres of wheat. Thirty bushels an acre at fifty cents a bushel would have meant a lot of cash money. Enough to keep them on their claim.

Instead, three cents a bushel. Better than nothing.

Ragna pricked her finger and popped it in her mouth.

"It's late for another trip to Dollner's today." Anders paused from scooping hoppers into the sacks. He scratched his head and squinted at the sun trying to determine the hour. "We'd be coming home after dark and the oxen are tired."

"Go anyway," Auntie Inga said. "I have a premonition." Auntie stabbed her needle into a sack and pulled the thread. "Feel pressed that you go again and not delay." She had a desperate look about her that almost frightened Ragna. Her auntie was usually calm and collected. "Lying Jack didn't know how long the money would last." She pulled the thread so hard that it broke.

Ragna looked at the exhausted faces of her brothers. They had spent the last two days working like grown men. There were still chores to do. Two people were needed to carry the extra sack. "I'll go with Anders," she said though her back ached and she felt fatigued to her very bones.

She had no choice. She was a grown woman now. Uncle Evan was gone, Milton was gone, and the boys still too young to bear the burdens of the family. "I'd enjoy a trip to the store."

"You'll ride the travois on the way home if you're tired, Mrs. Vollen," Anders said. He yawned and stretched his arms over his head. "I'm hungry."

"I should go." Gunnar frowned. "Ragna isn't strong enough to carry a sack."

"Then I'll carry it alone," Anders said. "Or we'll take only twenty-five sacks this time." Anders yawned again. "Not the worst thing to lose fifteen cents."

"I'll come up with something," Gunnar said with a scowl. He fiddled with the straps of the harness. "Fifteen cents is a lot of money. I'll find a way."

"Grain the oxen while we eat," Anders said to the younger boys, "and finish refilling the sacks."

"I'll do it," Auntie Inga said with a determined tilt to her jaw. "Ragna, put food on the table for you and the men. Keep an eye on Christina until she wakes from her nap. Sigurd, care for the oxen. Twins, hold the sacks open and Knut and I will fill them. We'll work together and be done in no time."

Ragna realized that today Gunnar had become a man. She grinned at her favorite brother. "Come along, men. You must be starving."

The twins grumbled and dragged their feet.

"Be good," Anders said over his shoulder as he walked into the cabin. "I'll bring licorice whips."

"And fetch a barrel of flour," Auntie said. She spoke firmly, as if she had thought long and hard about her decision. "It will take my share of today's money but I'll rest easier knowing my family has bread. I'm thinking the price might rise if wheat is scarce."

* * *

ANDERS AND RAGNA WALKED BESIDE the loaded travois, heading into the afternoon sun. It was steaming hot, cicadas zinging past their ears and sweat dripping down their backs. Goldie and Ryder strained against the yoke, chewing their cuds and flicking their tails against the flies.

They passed through patches of green weeds and sprouting grasses as they traveled around the reedy shore of Long Lake. Only sky and lake remained unchanged.

While they walked, Anders talked about where they would soon live.

"Why, Mr. Gardner, a local businessman, assures me the railroad will go right through town," Anders said. "You know what that means."

Ragna didn't answer. She had no idea why a railroad would be so important to a town.

"It's because of trade." Anders picked up a flat stone and skipped it across the water of Long Lake. "Farmers bring goods to the train depot. It changes everything for country folks. Markets opening up all across the east."

"Not every town will have a railroad," Ragna said. "Surely trains can't go everywhere."

Anders skipped another stone before the trail turned away from the lake. "Those towns without railroads won't last," Anders said. "But Pomme de Terre will get one— Mr. Gardner says it's a sure thing."

Goldie and Ryder plodded slower than molasses in January. Ragna didn't mind. She was tired and enjoyed the slower pace. She liked the time on the trail, the peace of leaving behind the little brothers and crying baby. She liked having her husband's attention to herself. Mostly, Ragna listened as Anders talked.

"I'll teach the school children to read American books, how to understand the differences between European and American cultures."

As he talked, Ragna felt a strange cramping in her lower back. She rubbed it with a closed fist and felt a little better. She mustn't overdo, she reminded herself. She must think of their baby.

"I'm going to keep studying even if I can't go to college." Anders kicked a stone out of the path with the toe of his boot. "Read every book I can find. Every newspaper." He slapped the lines against the backs of the oxen in a futile attempt to hurry them. "There's so much to learn, Ragna. Will I ever learn it all?"

Ragna smiled at him but had no answer. The first time she had seen Anders, he was carrying *The Last of the Mohicans* and eating a licorice whip. Maybe that's what had intrigued her. Someone who cared enough about books to tote one around with him.

As they came closer to Dollner's Store, Ragna saw a cluster of horses and buggies. Ragna had never been to Dollner's before and felt a little apprehensive about going into such a public place. The women were always left to tend the animals and children while the men did the trading. The store was smaller than Ragna had expected, a log building surrounded by a split-rail fence.

"Looks like Berge Lee's horse," Anders said. "And that buckboard belongs to Hans Juelson."

A row of young cottonwoods stood as a northern windbreak and a pot of red geraniums bloomed in the window. Chickens scratched in the dirt and an old rooster crowed a challenge as they plodded into the yard. A hissing goose flapped its wings and rushed toward them until Anders kicked it away with the side of his foot. A whiskey keg propped the open door. Mourning doves cooed in the shadows.

"I'm surprised so many people are here this time of day," Ragna said. "You'd think the farmers would be home doing chores—unless they're trying to get a jump on the bounty money as we are." *Dear Lord, don't let us be too late. Give us this day our daily bread.*

She reminded herself that though their crops and gardens were gone, Uncle Evan was earning cash money. He was smart to take the teamstering job when he had the chance. No matter how hard it was for him to be gone, Ragna knew he had done the right thing. And Anders was doing the right thing, too, in taking another teaching job. The bounty money would tide them over until everything else fell into place. She had no reason to worry.

Anders drove the oxen to the water trough and tied them to a post. "Come, Mrs. Vollen, look over the dry goods," he said with a reassuring smile. "Pick out flannel for baby clothes."

They were hardly over the threshold when Charlie Dollner rushed over to them. "Did you hear?" Charlie held a rifle and his hair stood out like a white puff of dandelion. "Mailman just brought the news." Sweat dripped off his face in steady rivulets.

"What news?" Anders said.

"Custer. Sioux wiped out Custer's Seventh Cavalry." Charlie Dollner said. "Two hundred sixty-five soldiers massacred." He gripped his rifle so hard his knuckles showed white. "And the Indians are heading this way."

* * *

GOLDIE AND RYDER STUMBLED HOME in the dark of the moon. Ragna's heart raced with anxiety. The newspaper said the Sioux were in Fergus Falls, attacking Breckenridge, and making war all across the countryside.

"It can't be true," Ragna said. Her thoughts fixated on her parents, her baby brother and little sister. Surely she hadn't come this far only to meet the same fate.

"Dollner has no reason to lie," Anders said. "It's in the paper."

"Then what do we do?" She walked as close to Anders as she could, hearing strange noises in the darkness, afraid that Indians would leap out with war whoops and scalping knives. "Should we go to Pomme de Terre?"

"No soldiers there anymore," Anders said. "No stockade left though I suppose there's safety in numbers. But Inga and the children couldn't walk all that way."

Ragna stuffed a knuckle into her mouth to still the trembling of her lips. Anders hadn't been in America during the uprising. Only someone who had known the terror and violence could understand what the news meant. Ragna remembered the face in the window, being stolen by the Indians, Camp Release and finally Uncle Evan's rescue. She remembered the violence of Birdie's death.

Just when she thought she was finally grown up and had moved past the old fears and memories, she must face them again. *Pray for us now and in the hour of our death.* She laid a hand over her belly. She must protect her baby.

"It will be all right." Anders reached over and took her hand and squeezed it tight. "First we go home. Then we'll eat supper and get some sleep." Anders sounded calm although something about the timbre of his voice made Ragna realize his anxiety. "You heard Hans Juelson and Berge Lee. They're building fortifications south of Turtle Lake. We'll go there if trouble comes near us."

"No." Ragna squeezed here eyes shut against the tears that filled them. Her voice shrilled. "You don't understand. We have to go to the fortifications before the Indians come. Otherwise it's too late."

"You're right," Anders said. "Don't worry, Mrs. Vollen. I'll take care of you. Maybe it will be like the Chippewa drums—turn out to be nothing." The oxen bawled and swished their tails at annoying blue flies. "We'll go tomorrow."

Ragna's father had trusted reason and civility. It was a disastrous decision. Anders did not understand. She did not know how to instruct him. She did not know how to explain the terror that roared through her imagination. *Our Father which art in heaven.*

Instead she quieted her racing thoughts and focused on her responsibilities to her family. Her brothers and little sister. Her auntie. Her baby.

"What do we say to Auntie Inga?"

"The truth," Anders said. He reached into his pocket and took out two licorice whips. He handed one to Ragna. "She's stronger than you think."

Lamplight spilled from the open door of the cabin. Auntie's face flushed with excitement when Anders hefted the flour barrel inside the cabin. Her smile stretched across her face, revealing her missing tooth. For once, Auntie was too excited to remember to cover her mouth with her hand.

"Thank God. Put it in the corner." Auntie said. "Pancakes for breakfast. Bread again."

Ragna looked for the boys but they were asleep, no doubt exhausted from their day of grasshopper harvest. Christina slept in Auntie's bed.

"It's really true." Auntie said. "We traded grasshoppers for flour. And another batch ready for tomorrow. If we bag them right away in the morning, we can send another load tomorrow—maybe two."

Anders cleared his throat. "There's bad news." Ragna watched Auntie's face turn white, like a brush of paint across a wall. Auntie reached out and grasped Ragna's hand. "Not Evan."

"*Nei*, not Evan." He paused before speaking. "The Sioux are on the warpath. Wiped out General Custer in Montana. Now, they're heading this way," Anders said. "It's in the papers."

Auntie gasped and slumped into the chair. "Indians? Where?" her voice reedy and tremulous as a whippoorwill. "Tell me they're not at Fort Wadsworth."

"Papers say Breckenridge and Fergus Falls," Anders said.

"Fergus!" Auntie said, loud enough that the baby stirred in the bed. "What will we do?" Her voice lowered again to a whisper. "And Evan and Milton both gone."

"Hans Juelson and Berge Lee are building fortifications south of Turtle Lake," Ragna said. "We'll go there—it's only a few miles through the woods."

"Now? In the dark?"

"Not tonight," Anders said. "We'll get some rest and leave at first light."

"We'll be killed in our beds," Auntie said. She picked up the baby and held her close as if to shield her from the savages. "They'll swoop in as we sleep."

"*Nei*," Anders said. "I'll stand watch. You've nothing to fear."

Ragna could tell how tired he was by the slump of his shoulders and the gray circle around his mouth. Anders reached for the gun over the door and checked its prime.

"How long has Gunnar been asleep?" Anders said. "Maybe he can take first watch."

"A little while," Auntie said. "He and Knut studied the Catechism before bed. They wanted to stay up until you brought the licorice but fell asleep."

"Don't wake Gunnar. I'll stand watch," Ragna said though fatigue pushed hard behind her eyes and her back ached. She would stand guard and let the others rest. She would pretend she was at *Matins*. Marta said the nuns prayed for the whole world during midnight prayers. Ragna would do the same. She would ask for the protection of the Holy Angels. She could sleep later.

"Are you sure?" Anders looked at her with such intensity that Ragna felt a flush rising in her cheeks.

Ragna nodded. She wouldn't mention her aching back. It was nothing, after all.

"I'm beat." Anders stretched and yawned. "And starving." He reached for a bowl of porridge. "Almost forgot your letter, Inga."

Inga's hands trembled when she opened the envelope Something fluttered to the floor. Ragna picked it up and saw that it was a bank note for one hundred dollars. She had never seen that much money before. She read it again to make sure she had seen correctly, holding it closer to the candle light.

"He's been hurt." Auntie's voice rasped. "Nothing else. Just that he's hurt and received this bounty for killing a horse thief." Auntie laid the letter on the table and picked up the draft. "Good Lord, Evan killing someone, even a thief. So soft hearted he can hardly do the butchering."

Auntie looked at the bank draft a long while. "I hope it was worth it."

Anders ate while Ragna fetched the writing desk. Auntie tucked the bank draft in its drawer. Then Auntie Inga placed the box high on the kitchen shelf, out of reach of curious boys or other mishaps.

"A hundred dollars. Enough to keep the family a year if we're careful." Auntie's lips trembled and her voice took on a hard edge. Ragna saw her mouth crimp. "But not enough for his life." Fat tears dripped down Auntie's face, something Ragna had rarely seen in all her years with the Jacobson family.

"Dear God, I couldn't bear to lose him."

46

SERENA TRIED TO PRAY but old memories intruded.

Images of the Sioux Uprising swirled in vivid clarity. How she and Lena hid in the tiny cellar under the cabin while Indians pilfered their possessions above them. The smell of earth, the spider webs tangling in her hair. The taste of flour sifting down through the cracks in the floor and her desperate need to sneeze. The scours exploding from Lena's bowels. How she had pressed her hand over Lena's mouth to keep her from crying out. That was the hardest memory of all. That she had been rough with her baby, cruel. The fear of the Indians greater than her love for her daughter.

Serena should have been the one who died instead of Lena. But even as she thought these words she knew it was impossible. Without her mother's milk, Lena would have starved. Nei, in spite of the pain of the memory, Serena had to admit that God knew what he was doing. Lena died, Gust died, but she had lived. She was grateful she had survived to birth Maren, to care for Kersten—even though alone without a husband.

Serena stayed mostly on her knees until Maren burst through the door. Maren carried Scatterbunny in her apron pocket. Her face streaked dirt and her dress hem torn loose.

"Mama," Maren said. "We're back. Can we make pudding tonight?"

Serena struggled to her feet, wiping tears away from her face. "Where's Anton?" she said. "And Kersten?"

"Coming," Maren said. She dipped water from the bucket and took a long drink. "I think there are enough eggs. Kersten found six behind the hayrack."

Anton and Kersten straggled into the kitchen. Anton removed his hat and was about to speak when Serena interrupted.

"It's General Custer," she said and was ashamed at the tears in her voice. She was a grown woman, after all, and must set a brave example. "Sioux wiped out Custer's army and are heading this way."

"When did this happen?" Anton's voice was calm though Serena saw his expression turn hard and sharp. "How do you know?"

"In the papers. Folks are gathering at the hotel."

"When do we go?" Maren said. Her voice rose in panic. "I'm taking Scatterbunny along. And the kittens."

Anton paused a long moment. "We've been through Injun trouble before," Anton said. "No sign of Indians on our way home so we have a little time." His face twisted into thought. "This building is the most defensible around. I wouldn't trust the town site—on low ground, too close to the river."

"Will the Indians attack?" Kersten's eyes widened into blue saucers. "Give me a gun and I'll fight like Bestemor did. I'll shoot as good as any man."

"Girls," Anton said. "Hurry now. Fill the water buckets and bring in a stack of kitchen wood. Then stay in the house with your mother." He replaced the hat on his head.

"We will go with you to the barn," Maren said. "What if the Indians get the kittens?"

"No argument," Anton said. "Start your chores. Of all times for Ole to leave." His usual calm was replaced with a firmness that Serena had not seen before. She remembered how Old Hen had described Anton as an Injun fighter from way back. The remark comforted her. She chose to rest in his judgment.

"I'll watch until the girls get back in the house. Then I'll finish chores. Serena, bar and shutter the windows—and keep the doors locked." He reached for the water dipper and took a drink from the tin dipper. "Fix extra food. It don't hurt to prepare."

The girls slammed out through the side door in a flurry of buckets and aprons. Anton turned to leave the inn. "I'm taking the rifle. Leaving you the pistol." He handed her a revolver. "Careful, it's loaded. Don't hesitate to use it."

"Hurry back." Serena lowered her voice to a whisper so the girls wouldn't hear but they were already out of earshot, arguing about who would be the best shot. "I'm afraid to be alone."

"Nothing to worry about yet," Anton said, looking out the door after the girls.

* * *

THEY ATE SUPPER IN SILENCE. Serena kept one eye turned to the door and her ears to any unusual sounds. Once Swanson's goose flapped against the stoop and Serena's heart clutched in her throat.

"Are the Swansons home?" Serena tried to sound casual.

"*Nei*," Anton said. "They've gone to the hotel. I'll pen their goose."

Serena stood at the door with the revolver in hand while Anton chased the goose into the wooden pen and closed it in for the night. Everything was calm. Owls hooted from the grove. A chattering squirrel scolded from an oak tree. A warm breeze carried the sweet smells of earth and lake. Only the absence of people was unusual.

"Should we join the others?" Serena hated the way her words sounded, like she was questioning Anton's judgment, but she was fearful.

"You can do what you want," Anton said. "I won't leave this place—know how to defend it. Can't imagine how they could defend the town. Too many windows, too much cover on the river banks where a sneaking Injun could hide."

Serena looked toward the town, almost a mile away. She didn't dare walk there alone. Instead she went back inside and strained the milk and prepared to churn. The girls washed dishes. Anton locked the doors and blew out the lamp.

"No sense drawing attention to ourselves," he said.

Serena settled in a chair and started plunging the dasher when someone pounded on the front door.

"*Uff da*," Serena said and quit moving the dasher. She jumped to her feet and felt the blood drain from her face. She looked at the girls who were doing their knitting while Scatterbunny hopped around the kitchen floor. "Who can it be?"

Anton answered the door with the gun in his hand, peeking behind the shutter. He let out a sigh of relief and flung the door wide open.

"*Velkommen!* Come in and welcome, old friend."

Olaus Reirson swept in through the door like a winter wind, laughing and lighting up the room with robust exuberance. His white hair floated around his florid face like a halo and he carried a rifle and had a sack slung over his back.

"By God, Anton," he said and tossed the sack on the floor and leaned the gun against the corner. When he spoke his mouth was a black maw in the midst of a white storm of beard. "We've whipped them before and we'll do it again."

"Have a chair," Anton said. "Serena, fetch Olaus a plate."

As Serena scurried to fill a plate for the visitor, she heard Anton ask Olaus his reason for coming to Pomme de Terre.

"By God, Anton," Olaus said. "Every time there's been Injun trouble I've come here for refuge. I'm not about to change now."

"I must admit I'll rest easier tonight with you under my roof," Anton said.

Olaus lifted a heaping spoon of stew and smacked his lips around it. "Ole and his friend stopped at Chippewa Station on their way to the Black Hills." He reached for a slice of bread. "He asked me to keep an eye on all of you." The bread disappeared into his mouth in two great bites. Olaus reached for another slice.

"You shouldn't feel obligated," Anton said and was about to say more when Olaus interrupted him.

"There's injun trouble and I'm here. That's all there is to it."

Serena breathed a sigh of relief. Olaus inspired confidence wherever he went. Surely he would be a stalwart defender against the savages. She smiled an encouraging smile to the girls who had set their knitting on their laps to gawk at the visitor.

"I've tied my horse in the woodshed," Olaus said in an apologetic manner. "Injuns got mine back in the uprising. By God, they won't get this one without a fight." He looked toward Serena and the girls. "Excuse my language, Mrs. Gustafson."

"Put aside your knitting, girls," Serena said. "Time for bed." She returned to the churning and listened to the men's conversation as she pushed the dasher up and down. The girls dragged their feet upstairs.

"Mailman says the papers are filled with the news of Custer's defeat." Olaus ate the second slice of bread and reached for a third. "Talk of closing down the railroads until the Sioux are settled."

"What did the papers say?" Serena said. She wished she had a newspaper to read the details herself. "Where are they?"

Olaus pushed away from the table and wiped his mouth with the back of his hand. His belly pushed forward like an expectant mother. No doubt he ate well in Chippewa Station, even without a wife to cook for him.

"Mrs. Gustafson," he said, "that's the rub. Papers say Pomme de Terre is under attack as is Fergus Falls and Breckenridge. No sign of Indians here that I can see."

"You mean the newspaper has it wrong?" It seemed impossible. Jensina spouted that newspapers were filled with lies and false advertising but Serena had always put full confidence in the printed words.

Serena had a sudden flash of insight. She had taken the opposite view just to spite her sister. Warmth started in her neck and spread up her cheeks. She had acted like a child.

"Maybe, maybe not," Anton said. He pulled his pipe out of his pocket and tamped tobacco into the bowl. "We'll keep watch." He pulled a wood splint out of his pocket and lighted it from the stove box. He puffed until his pipe drew. Then he used the burning sliver to light a lamp. "Dr. Cormonton comes back from Fergus Falls tomorrow. He'll know first hand what's going on."

47

THE MULE TRAIN TRAVELED WEST toward the Shining Mountains.

As the laudanum wore off, the pain in Evan's head intensified. Finally he handed the lines to Milton and lay back on the seat, covering his eyes with his hat to keep out the light.

Milton entertained with war stories, the peculiarities of the immigrant train and the fizzled gold rush at Tordenskjold. Evan listened as the sun beat down upon him. Finally Evan propped his feet against the wagon edge, pulling his hat lower over his face, thankful for the bandage that protected his tender wound. He napped like a cat lying in the sunshine.

Evan awoke much later with his cheek on fire. He sat up and wiped his mouth with the back of his shirt sleeve, trying to get his bearings. It was almost dark. Directly ahead of them flickered a few lights.

"Browns Valley," Old Hen said from his nigh-wheel horse. "We pushed through to make up lost time."

"How are you feeling?" Milton said at his side.

"Better," Evan said in a croaky voice. "Thirsty."

Ole handed him a worn canteen. The water, brackish though it was, eased Evan's parched throat.

"You slept so hard, we thought you'd died," Milton said. "I held a feather in front of your nose to see if you breathed."

The men laughed and jostled each other. "You snored loud enough to wake the dead," Old Hen said. "No worry about you dying."

They pulled into Brownsville at the southern end of Lake Traverse.

"To the northeast lie the Breckenridge Flats," Old Hen said. "Lake Traverse and the Boise de Sioux River run north to the Red River of the North at Breckenridge and empty into the Hudson Bay." He took a chaw of tobacco and handed the plug to Evan. "Just south of here, Big Stone Lake flows into the Minnesota River and down toward the Gulf of Mexico."

Evan thought of several comments he might make but kept silent and shook his head in response to Old Hen's generous offer of tobacco. The less he moved his mouth the better.

"This a no man's land?" Milton said.

"Something like that," Old Hen said. "Folks gather at Lovett and Lowry's Store for whiskey and music."

They pulled their wagons into a meadow beside the lake, not far from the store. A corral was built alongside a campsite. The faint sound of fiddle music came from the store.

"Take it easy," Old Hen said to Evan. "There's enough help without you and I'd just as soon not have to stop for a funeral."

Evan felt too weak to protest. He found his bedroll and spread it out in the shade of a cottonwood tree, enjoying the sound of music from the store. Odd to lie there watching the others work. Ole Estvold busied with a cook fire. A great racket of thirsty mules braying for water and grass. The men unharnessed the teams and led them to the lake.

Old Hen squatted down on the grass beside Evan. Evan rose up on an elbow, thinking Old Hen was there to give him a new command.

"Don't get up," Old Hen said. "Just wanted to talk a minute." He spit a long stream of brown tobacco juice into the weeds. "You're not pulling your share right now." Old Hen spat again. "But you've earned your rest and your pay won't be docked. Consider it your reward for stopping the thieves. You'll be back on your feet in a couple of days and carrying your weight soon enough."

"I think I'm better. I could . . ."

"No, rest yourself."

Evan watched the mules splashing in the water as darkness settled down over them. Clouds of mosquitoes came out of nowhere.

"We're not out of the woods yet, but I think we'll make it. We're on the home stretch," Old Hen said.

Evan appreciated his kindness. He did not know the American words to express his gratitude so he said nothing. He pulled the blanket up over himself to keep the mosquitoes away.

"You've learned a lot," Old Hen said. "Army pays two hundred a month for teamsters willing to risk their necks going out to Dakota forts." He spat again, pulled the plug from his pocket to bite off another chew. "Good money but risky." He rolled the wad of tobacco around his mouth as if measuring his words. "Less risk doing mail routes and short runs on the Minnesota side of the border."

"Any chance I could get that kind of work?" Evan said. He would be more content working closer to home.

"I'll put in a word for you." Old Hen stood to his feet. He stretched his arms over his head and commented about the smell of coffee coming from Ole's fire. "I'm not one to give advice but if you asked me, I'd say go home to the family and come back next year."

As Old Hen walked away, Evan mulled his words. He was earning one hundred dollars a month on this trip. It was top money. From the sounds of it, there would be no harvest at home this year. He tallied the price of flour, yard goods, animal fodder, cornmeal, and shoes. No matter how he figured, it wasn't enough.

Rather than agonize over the high cost of living, he pulled out a pencil stub and paper to write a letter to Inga. The words of explanation came with great difficulty but he finally got them down on the page.

> Dearest Inga,
>
> I hope you are doing well and that all of you remain strong and healthy. I think of you and the children and send prayers for your safety and protection. Tap the lucky horseshoe when you go past it—we need all the luck we can find.
>
> I'm feeling better but I'm afraid I will carry a scar for the rest of my days. The doctor assures me wives are less likely than sweethearts to abandon a husband if he loses his looks. I'm counting on that.
>
> My heart is heavy since I took the lives of those men. I had no choice, but still I remember the commandments and must come to grips with the hard truth that I have killed two men. It lingers over me like a dark shadow. I fear I have grown cold hearted with the weight of it. Please pray that I find forgiveness and peace.
>
> At the same time, the bounty money will carry us through this rough spell with the grasshoppers. It's a mystery how something so terrible can turn into a blessing. Please use the money with great care. I have carved new shoes for the boys. I can only imagine how tall they must have grown while I am gone.

You will not believe who I ran into out here on the prairie. Milton Madsen and Ole Estvold are on their way to the gold fields. They ride with us and have taken over my work while I mend from my injury. They tell me our crops are lost.

Don't worry, dearest wife, the Lord will see us through this hard time. There's a chance for me to have more work next season.

Evan signed his name and printed large letters across the top of the page. DO NOT LET THE CHILDREN READ THIS LETTER. Inga would understand. He felt better for telling her.

Zeke saw him writing and offered to post the letter along with one he was sending to his wife. "There's a post office in the store."

"Supper is ready," Ole called from the fire.

Before Evan could get to his feet a soldier raced toward the store from the west, riding a weary horse, lathered with sweat. The soldier leapt off his mount and stormed into the store. The music stopped.

"What's that about?" Evan said. "Must be bad news to abuse a horse that way."

"I'll find out," Zeke said, "and mail these at the same time." He snatched Evan's letter and sprinted toward the store.

Evan and the others gathered around the fire for supper. Darkness settled over them like a setting hen on her chicks. They ate their meager fare, slapping mosquitoes and waiting for Zeke to return with the news.

Zeke was gone less than five minutes.

"Old Hen!" Zeke gasped for air. "Indians!" Even in the darkness his face gleamed pale with fear. "They want you inside to hear for yourself. Custer— wiped out by the Sioux."

48

RAGNA FELT THE FIRST PAIN about an hour before morning. She thought she must have had something that disagreed with her, maybe the licorice eaten so late in the day.

She had stood at the dugout door all night, watching the bats dip across the water in the moonlight, hearing the loons and the bitterns. Through the long night she recited the rosary, counting the prayers bead by bead. She prayed it for Anders and their baby, then again for deliverance from the Red Men. With a start she realized she had been neglecting to pray for the grasshoppers. So she prayed the rosary through the third time for the hoppers. Between prayers she scrutinized every inch of the lake and trees around the house.

No signs of Indians but she knew that did not mean they were not there. She prayed again for the Holy Angels, asking God to place them at the four corners of their property to protect them. Once she glimpsed a flashing wing and thought it an angel—but a gray owl swooped down upon a scurrying mouse.

When the second pain slashed her abdomen, Ragna knew it was more than licorice. She leaned against the doorframe, keeping as still as possible, not wanting to bother Anders who snored from the bed. He had worked so hard. He needed rest for the day ahead.

The third pain made her cry out. She couldn't help herself. She felt something warm between her legs.

"What's wrong?" Anders said in a groggy voice. "Indians?"

"*Nei*, I'm sick," Ragna had been praying all night for their safety. Could it be that God had not heard?

It was pitch black in the dugout but Ragna imagined Anders's face etched with concern. "Let's get you into the house to Inga." She felt the welcome weight of a wrap thrown around her shoulders as a sudden chill shivered and chattered her teeth. The sound of striking match and smell of sulphur as Anders lighted a candle stub.

Ragna held the candle as they stumbled to the cabin. Anders held her with one arm and the rifle with the other.

It was almost morning. Nighthawks swooped after mosquitoes. Heavy dew tickled Ragna's bare feet and chilled her even more. The rooster made its first feeble crows. She stepped on a sharp grasshopper wing and yelped in protest. Musky barked and ran to them, jumping on Ragna's legs, sniffing and pulling at her wrapper with sharp teeth.

"Go away!" Ragna said. The dog yipped and pulled on her nightgown. "What's wrong with him?"

"The blood on your nightdress." Anders said. "It smells your blood."

Ragna looked down in dismay. A dark splotch bloomed on her white nightgown. Hope drained away as she realized she was bleeding. Women bled when they lost their babies. She was losing her baby.

Auntie Inga met them on the stoop and Ragna handed her the candle. The light splashed through the darkness and Ragna wondered if her auntie had heard Musky or if she had been up all night.

"What's wrong?" Auntie Inga gasped out the words, her hands trembling so the light moved up and down in front of her. "Not Indians!"

"*Nei*," Anders said. "Ragna is sick."

"Oh, *nei*," Auntie Inga lifted the candle and looked at Ragna's face and down at her nightgown. "Crawl into my bed," she said. "*Stakkers liten*, you're white as a ghost."

"I felt a pain on the way to Dollner's Store," Ragna confessed on her way to the bed. Guilt and blame filled her. It was her fault if they lost their baby. She had overdone. She hadn't cared for herself as she should have.

"You didn't say anything," Anders said. Ragna knew he did not mean to blame her but his words felt accusatory. "I wouldn't have let you walk had I known."

"It was nothing." Ragna felt another cramp and sat on the edge of the bed.

Auntie helped her into bed, pushed rags under Ragna's bottom, fussed with the blankets, fluffed the goose down pillows, and proceeded to prop Ragna's feet on a rolled blanket.

"Anders!" Auntie whispered. "Fetch a sack of salt from the dugout."

Anders ran out of the cabin, forgetting the gun.

Dear Jesus, protect us from the Red Indians. Deliver us from evil.

Ragna touched her abdomen. With each cramp, a spew of blood left her body. Her baby at risk, maybe already dead. She tried to feel something, anything, but she felt only emptiness.

She tried to pray the rosary but the words slipped away.

Auntie lifted her head and urged a sip of water. Only then did Ragna notice her auntie's tears. "I'm sorry, Ragna," she said. "It's my fault. I shouldn't have insisted on that second load to Dollner's Store."

"*Nei.*" Ragna must be strong. She must believe in God and have faith something good would come from this. Even as she thought these lofty thoughts she felt the cold hand of doubt choking her throat. "It's not your fault, Auntie."

Ragna felt another pain. Auntie repositioned the rags under Ragna's hips.

"Did I lose it?" Ragna said. "I need to know." Her voice took on a fierceness she did not intend. "Tell me—is my baby gone?"

Auntie shook her head. "Not yet." She knelt by Ragna's side, and when Anders brought the salt, she positioned the cool sack against Ragna's abdomen. Anders paced between the door and Ragna's bed, muttering about fetching a doctor, assuring Ragna that she would be all right in the morning.

When the sun peeked into the east and the rooster crowed, the boys crept down from the loft, yawning and rubbing their eyes.

"What's wrong with Ragna?" Sigurd said. His curly hair tousled around his face and Ragna noticed how tall he had grown that summer, how he had lost the babyish roundness of his face.

"She's sick," Auntie said without further explanation. "Run and do your chores—Knut, stay with Sigurd. Gunnar, stay with the twins." Auntie bit her lip and wrung her hands together. "Listen, now. There's talk of Indian raids. If you see anything at all, you run back into the house." The boys left in a shuffle of bare feet on wooden floor.

Ragna watched tears well in her auntie's eyes, the way her lips trembled, the paleness of her face. Even the gap in her smile from the missing tooth seemed dearer. Ragna had never loved her auntie as much as she did at that very moment. How much she owed her auntie and uncle. They had never failed to love and care for her. They had raised her as their own.

Tears dripped down Ragna's cheeks. She would be like Auntie Inga. She sent a desperate prayer for God's help and the prayer became a promise. *Let my baby live and I'll be the best mother in the world.*

"Anders," Auntie Inga said. "Take the gun and guard the boys while they do their chores."

Anders nodded, looking toward Ragna with worried eyes. Ragna fought a panicky feeling rising within her. She was losing her baby and would lose her brothers, too. The Indians would kill them and then come into the house for her and Auntie and Christina.

"Anders!" her voice quivered. "Stay by me."

"Mrs. Vollen," Anders grinned a teasing grin, "you can surely see I have work to do." He squeezed her hand and kissed her forehead. The faint smell of sweat and cow manure on his clothing. "I'll be back soon," he whispered. "Just rest."

Christina fussed until Auntie Inga gave her a wooden spool to play with. Christina sat on a blanket on the floor, throwing the spool and giggling as Fisk chased it across the room. Auntie stirred the porridge and stuffed another small piece of wood into the firebox. From time to time she opened the door and scrutinized the woods and field, keeping an eye on the boys.

"Sweet Jesus," Auntie said. Her voice sounded heavy, like the nuns who interceded for the world. "If it's not one thing, it's the other."

"I should help you," Ragna said. Never in her life had she lain in bed while Auntie worked alone. "We must ready to go to the fortifications."

"*Nei!* We'll stay right here," Auntie said with a tilt of her chin. "Your baby has a chance if you stay in bed with your feet up."

"But we have to go," Ragna said. Her pains had slowed. Maybe it was all a big mistake and nothing bad would happen after all. "Think of the children," Ragna pushed down a wave of panic. "I won't be responsible for their deaths."

Musky barked and Lewis ran into the house. "Riders coming from the south," he said. "Lying Jack and Many Beavers."

"Are they in a hurry?" Ragna said. "Bringing warning?"

"*Nei,*" Lewis said. "They're taking their time."

"Out trading hides in the middle of an Indian war!" Auntie blustered around the kitchen like an angry hen. "Always knew the man didn't have a lick of sense." She patted her hair and straightened the sheet over Ragna.

Auntie took the coffee grinder out of the cupboard. She had told Ragna before that she was saving the last of the beans for Evan's homecoming.

"We'll have real coffee this morning." Auntie said. Her face drooped into lines of fatigue as she turned the handle of the grinder. "We could all use a good strong cup."

She stirred an egg into the coffee grounds and scraped the mess into the coffee pot. The fragrance of fresh brewing coffee filled the cabin.

* * *

"Didn't see no Indians," Lying Jack said with a serious voice. "Neither Chippewa nor Sioux neither." He said something to Many Beavers in her language. Many Beavers shook her head emphatically and pointed to the west.

"No warriors, no smoke signals," he said and shrugged.

Many Beavers pointed at Ragna lying in the bed. She spoke to her husband who translated. "Her wants to know what's wrong with Badger."

Ragna startled to hear her Indian name. While she and Birdie were in the Sioux camp during the uprising, Many Beavers had given Ragna the name of Badger because of her protectiveness over her little sister. The name reminded Ragna of being taken, of her families' death, of all the suffering and loss. She knew Many Beavers waited for an answer but Ragna felt helpless in the flood of old memories.

"She's sick," Auntie said. "The baby . . ."

Auntie's words trailed off and Many Beavers bustled outside. Ragna watched through the open door as Many Beavers rummaged through a sack tied to the packhorse.

"Juelson and Berge Lee are building fortification south of Turtle Lake." Anders told Lying Jack about their plan to go there for protection as soon as Ragna could travel.

Many Beavers returned with a small pouch. She made signs for boiling water and stirred a pinch of herbs into a cup of water.

Gunnar burst through the door. His chin stubbled and pimples sprinkled across his forehead. "There's smoke to the west of us. Maybe Dollner's Store."

Anders and Lying Jack stepped outside. Ragna craned her neck but could see nothing from her bed. The men returned with grim faces.

"Something's burning to the west," Lying Jack said. "Might be Injuns after all."

"Good Lord." Auntie picked up Christina from the floor. She held her so tightly that Christina yelped in protest.

"Get ready to leave." Anders spoke to Auntie but looked at Ragna. "We can't risk staying here."

"Ragna can't be moved," Auntie Inga said and her chin tilted.

"She'll ride the travois," Anders said. "Lie down all the way."

"I won't go," Ragna said. A strange wisdom rose up within her, an understanding that any movement meant her baby's certain death. "The bouncing travois would be the end of it." She would be shielded by the angels. "You go and I'll stay behind."

"Mrs. Vollen," Anders said. "I won't leave you at such a time."

Many Beavers brought the teacup and Ragna downed the bitter concoction in one swallow. Many Beavers nodded approvingly and planted herself in a chair beside Ragna's bed. Many Beavers spoke something in her language. Lying Jack seemed to argue but Many Beavers stood firm on whatever she had said.

"My woman says she'll stay here with Badger while us men takes Inga and the children to the fortifications." Lying Jack looked at Anders with a helpless shrug. "Her says the folks won't welcome a Sioux woman during an Indian scare anyway and she might as well stay here."

"Of course," Ragna said. "Many Beavers will take care of me while you're gone." Ragna felt unseen hands directing their paths. "If the Sioux come, Many Beavers will explain that we're here in peace."

"Anders, take them to the fort." She grimaced as another pain jabbed through her belly. "Keep your promise to Uncle Evan. Then come back to me as fast as you can."

Faith rose up within her. Or else she felt the presence of the Holy Angels. The answer to her prayers.

49

SERENA AND ALL OF POMME DE TERRE waited for the Indians to appear.
Tormenting dreams woke her several times that first night after the warning, making her heart pound and sweat dampen her nightgown. In her dream, Indians snatched Maren and Kersten and dragged them across the fields. Serena floundered to find a rifle that worked. Each one she picked up refused to fire. Finally she found a loaded gun but when she aimed it at the fleeing savages, she could no longer see them. They had escaped over the hills.

Serena checked on the girls so many times that she finally climbed into bed with them, nudging Maren closer to Kersten to make room. She dreamed the dream again toward morning but reached a hand, touched the girls and knew they were safe.

Once during that fitful night, Serena felt she would scream with fear and anxiety. She felt as if she were losing her mind. She breathed deeply, reminding herself that the girls needed her to be sane and in control. Like the bunnies without a mother to sustain them. When she peeked out the window, she saw Olaus standing guard by the barn door. The sight of him standing there, armed and ready for danger soothed her.

She finally slept.

In the morning, Serena awoke to a day that felt mostly normal. Olaus, tired from standing watch, climbed to the top of the hill for one last time and reported no Indians in sight. They ate breakfast together and then Olaus crept into Ole's empty bedroom for a nap while Anton left for barn chores.

Birdsong filled the morning and Serena opened the door for a moment to allow fresh air into the inn. She admired the ovenbirds, those little brown birds with their most ordinary songs. Serena busied herself with her kitchen tasks and tried to forget the murdering savages.

The girls were churning butter and squabbling over whose turn it was for the dasher. Someone knocked on the door. Serena hesitated. Anton was in the barn. It could only be bad news. She comforted herself that Olaus, asleep in Ole's bedroom, was within call if she needed him.

Another knock. The girls looked out the window and flew into a fit of giggles, elbow jabbing and snickering behind cupped hands.

"It's Torger Torgerson," Kersten said. Her squeals were shrill enough to burst Serena's eardrums.

"Maren! Kersten!" Serena had seen the young Torgerson around town. He worked at the grist mill and the girls believed him to be the most handsome boy around. "That's enough. You'll wake Mr. Reierson."

Serena opened the door with pistol in hand. At least it wasn't an Indian. The girls huddled behind her, no doubt hoping for an opportunity to speak to the good-looking young man.

"Mrs. Gustafson," Torger said while holding a black cap in both hands. His blond hair flopped over his eyes and curled around his neck and ears. His face speckled with freckles and a bright red pimple bloomed on the tip of his chin. He wore dusty britches and a food-stained shirt. His boots ran down at the heels.

He glanced at the girls, turned red and then looked into the air as he recited a memorized message. He quoted in a sing-song cadence. "Mr. Gardner asks why you have not come to work as you agreed. He says the Injuns will scalp you all unless you come to the hotel for protection by the city militia. Dr. Cormonton never came back from Fergus Falls—he must be killed. Hurry up and come so you can cook dinner."

Torger finished the last sentence with a triumphant nod of his head. He broke into a big smile and returned to normal speech patterns. "Good morning, Mrs. Gustafson, Miss Maren, Miss Kersten."

"Good morning, Torger," the girls said in unison.

"Mr. Gardner says I should escort you to the hotel," Torger said. He waited expectantly. "Are you coming?"

Serena looked at him in confusion. The Indian raids had so consumed her thoughts that she had forgotten all about her agreement with Mr. Gardner. Dr. Cormonton dead! He only wanted to help people.

A fierce anger toward the Indians boiled within her. Why couldn't they leave ordinary people alone? Their argument was with the government, after all, not with women and children.

It was a long walk to the village—through an unprotected place. Torger was just a boy and without a weapon. The girls looked at her eagerly.

She could not risk it.

"Please send my regrets to Mr. Gardner and tell him I am unavailable for employment until the Indian situation is settled."

"You mean you're not coming?" Torger said. "Everything is fine. I just saw the mailman coming from the south."

"No thank you," Serena said. "Not today." She said goodbye to the young man and closed and locked the door.

"Sistermine," Kersten wailed. "It would be more fun at the hotel. There's nothing to do here."

"There's always something to do. Finish churning and fetch your knitting." Serena felt very old. She picked up her crocheting and found comfort in stabbing the needle into the loops of thread.

It was hard being both mother and father, especially as they grew older. Why, they would be marrying soon, she realized with a start. Most girls married by seventeen or eighteen. Not that many years away, really. Then what would she do? She turned the half-made sweater and began another row.

She regretted her attitude toward Julian. He deserved better. She had known him her whole life. In all those years he had never been unkind to her. He even defended her to his witch of a mother. No small attribute, to her thinking. She unrolled a length of crochet thread and turned the row again.

Serena felt a sudden longing for Jensina. Serena had been uncharitable toward her only remaining sister. She had been jealous when Jensina became the woman of the house, the job Serena had known since her mother's death. Serena's actions had been childish. She saw it clearly in the face of Indian danger and felt ashamed of herself.

Pomme de Terre felt lonely. She no longer wanted to move to a strange place where she didn't know anyone. As a new bride, Serena had been dragged to a lonely place. When tragedy struck in Hutchinson, they had been without family to turn to. She saw clearly that she must not put her girls in the same situation.

Family was precious. She had almost forgotten. Maybe that was the reason God had led her back to Pomme de Terre. To learn the lesson of family.

Another knock on the door. Serena pulled the curtain, ready to give the young man a piece of her mind. She'd said no, after all, and he should respect her decision. But as she pulled the curtain back, Julian Gustafson looked back at her.

She opened the door. "Julian," she said. To her surprise, she threw her arms around his neck and burst into tears.

"What's wrong?" Julian said.

Serena shook her head but was crying too hard to speak. He held her, patting her back and letting her cry.

Finally she pulled away. "What are you doing here?"

"Newspaper said Indians were attacking Fergus Falls and Pomme de Terre." He wore a sidearm, no doubt from the war. She had never known him to carry a weapon. The sight of it made her feel safer. "I came as soon as I heard," he said.

The girls gathered around and he laughed and lifted Maren up into his arms although she was so tall her legs dangled almost to his knees.

"I took the first boat and caught the train to Herman. Tried to rent a horse but they wouldn't rent any kind of rig for folks heading this direction." He set Maren down, squeezed Kersten's shoulder. "I caught a ride with the mailman."

"But why did you come?" Serena said.

"The papers are full of wild stories. I wouldn't leave you here alone. I couldn't live with myself if something happened to you and the girls."

Serena looked at him as if seeing him for the first time. He was starting to gray around his temples. His church suit was still wrinkled and he had the beginning of a paunch. His hands were farmer hands, thick and callused and his face sprouted a thick dark beard. He smelled of honest sweat. The brown eyes looking at her were as they had always been—kind and gentle.

Gust had left her alone during dangerous times. Maybe not intentionally, but Gust had never placed her safety ahead of his plans. He had left her at the cabin while he visited Olaus Reierson in the dead of winter, back when the Indians were still on the rampage. Even Ole had left—of course he had his reasons, but Serena wished that Ole had at least given her the opportunity to work something out with him. They might have been happy.

But here was Julian. Coming all this way again though it was harvest time. He said that he could not live with himself if something happened to her or the girls. Girls. Both of them.

"Serena," he said. "Aren't you going to invite me inside?"

50

E VAN LISTENED TO OLD HEN and the others discuss what they should do in
light of Custer's defeat. The moon rose, a bright orb above the black fringe of
shoreline, touching the water with sparks of fire. Evan's thoughts drifted back
to the uprising. It had been a moonlit night when he had come face to face with his
Sioux friend, Crooked Lightning.

"I say we vote on it." Zeke's loud demand disrupted Evan's thoughts and brought
him back to the present.

"You're yellow," Jeppe said in an equally loud voice. "Scared, that's all."

Only a fool would face a Sioux war party without fear. Jeppe was a newcomer and
hadn't been in Minnesota during the uprising. Evan remembered the six-week siege at
Fort Abercrombie only too well. The surrounding Sioux had picked them off one by
one if anyone tried to leave the fort.

Zeke grew up in Breckenridge and was a young boy during the uprising. Of course he
would be afraid, Evan thought. And it was only natural that Zeke would want to return to
care for his young wife and new baby back home.

"We signed on for this job and by God, we'll finish it," Old Hen said. "We're almost there. There are three soldiers at Lovett's who are heading back to Fort Wadsworth
in the morning. They'll ride with us. We'll stock up on food and ammunition."

"But the Sioux wiped out Custer," Martin said. "What will they do to us? Even
with an armed escort."

"The way I figure, we'll push straight through," Old Hen said. "We won't stop at
the agency, just keep going until we arrive at Wadsworth."

Zeke glowered and mumbled, muttering about going home anyway and no one could stop him.

"You'll not receive your wage until we get to the fort," Old Hen said. "Besides, the biggest danger is for a lone rider on the prairie."

"It's only another day or two," Evan said. "We'll pull together and make it." Evan had to admit that he spoke braver than he felt. He tried to push away the image of painted Indians attacking the mule train. Dizziness swirled through his head. "You'll see. We'll make it."

Old Hen posted double guard and directed Ole to fix extra food for the trip. "We won't be stopping long enough to build camp."

Ole got right to work putting a kettle of mush over the dying fire. Then he started a batch of sourdough flapjacks. "I'll fry these up in the morning before we leave."

Evan's head throbbed and he was about to return to his bedroll when Zeke walked by on his way to stand watch by the mules.

"Zeke, how are you getting home after we deliver this freight?"

"Damned rustlers got my horse," Zeke said. "It's a long walk."

"I've been thinking we could travel together," Evan said. He laid his head on the rolled blanket. He hoped he was making sense. Everything felt very strange. "Go home through Breckenridge Flats on my way back to Otter Tail County."

They talked a few minutes about possible routes. Coyotes howled in the distance— at least Evan hoped they were coyotes. Everyone knew Indians used animal calls to signal each other before attack. As Evan fell asleep, he dreamed he was riding across the prairies on a blood-red steed.

* * *

OLD HEN AWAKENED EVAN and the muleteers before light. Another soldier agreed to travel with them, the messenger they had seen racing into Browns Valley the night before. As they harnessed the mule teams and dismantled their camp in the darkness, Evan comforted himself that four armed soldiers would ride alongside the freight wagons.

Evan felt ill. The doctor in Toqua had urged him to keep his wound covered from the sun and to change the bandages often. Evan had put off the bandage change as long as he could. The cotton strips gummed to his wound and he feared it would hurt like blazes to remove it.

He rolled up his bedroll, surprised at the weakness in his limbs, and ate a hurried breakfast. Surely the food would strengthen him.

The more he moved, the more the world whirled around him. Evan staggered to the lake and knelt down by the water's edge. He wet the crusted bandages and pulled it away as fast as he could, and then smeared salve onto the wound. He had an extra shirt along and though it pained him to destroy it, he ripped it into strips of bandage. Weakness made even this small chore difficult, and Evan pushed down a feeling of alarm. He should be getting stronger, not weaker.

Evan awkwardly wound the bandages around his ear and face as the soldiers led their mounts to the lake for water. Evan paused to regain his strength and walked over to the horses as they dipped their noses into the water.

He leaned against the one closest to him, letting his body rest against it. Evan loved horses, even their smell. Loved the way their soft lips wrapped around a sugar lump, the swish of their tails and dainty hooves.

Evan would own another horse someday, a roan maybe, or dapple gray. Surely life would get easier after the grasshoppers.

"That's my horse, Grayback," Bo Mitchell, one of the soldiers, said. "Not much to look at—but dependable."

Bo was not that much older than Gunnar. Evan doubted he shaved every day.

"What are you doing at Browns Valley?" Evan said, carefully choosing the American words.

"Chasing horse thieves," Bo said. He led his horse out of the water and threw the blanket over its back. Then he reached for the saddle. "Bad nest of them out of Gager's."

Before Evan could ask more about the thieves, Old Hen whistled from the mule train. "Time to hit the trail!"

They scrambled to their positions. Milton and Ole sat on the wagon seat and scooted over to allow Evan a spot. Dizziness made Evan glad to let Milton handle the lines.

"We've nothing to worry about," Old Hen said in a loud voice. "It's a long way to Montana. We'll be at Fort Wadsworth before the Sioux can travel this far."

"Fort Sisseton," Bo Mitchell said. "They've gone and changed the name on us."

The men laughed and murmured about the foolishness of governments and armies, making Evan contemplate the unifying act of complaining.

Splashes of red and purple painted the dawning. They were getting a good start. Surely they would make it to the fort in safety. Evan rested his swirling head on his hands and closed his eyes.

"Promenade all!" Old Hen called.

* * *

The mule whackers pushed themselves and pushed their teams, stopping only to water the animals and give them each a measure of oats. The men ate cold flapjacks, jerky, and dried prunes.

Evan dozed and dreamed of the letter he must write his children before he died. He couldn't remember if he had written the letter or if he was writing the letter. He looked around for pen and ink but saw only the backs of the mule team, his comrades, and the shining mountains just ahead.

"Evan," Milton said. His face serious with concern. "Are you all right?"

Evan roused himself and drank from Ole's old canteen. He choked on the water as dizziness swirled through his body, making him clutch the wooden seat for support. He drifted back to sleep but woke up with a start, thinking he was back home and Indians were attacking. Sweat drenched his shirt. His wound burned like fire. He called out for Inga.

"Wake up!" Milton said. "It's only a dream."

More murmuring voices. Evan heard them speaking as through a huge tunnel but was too sick to speak. He had never known such weakness. *Dear God, let me live for the sake of my children. For Inga.*

"We'll leave him at the agency," Old Hen said. "I think there's a doctor."

51

RAGNA WATCHED THROUGH THE OPEN DOOR as the family left the claim. Goldie and Ryder pulled the travois holding bundles of blankets and food. Christina sat in the middle, laughing as she bounced over uneven ground. Musky yipped underfoot.

Auntie Inga walked directly behind the travois to watch Christina, carrying the writing box tucked securely under her arm. Anders and Gunnar drove the oxen. Sigurd and the twins herded the cow and calf. Lying Jack rode his horse and led the pack animals.

Only Ragna, Many Beavers, Fisk, and the chickens were left behind.

Anders and the family turned to wave and Ragna swallowed tears as she waved back. It seemed they took the air with them and she forced herself to take long, deep breaths. She focused on their faces, memorizing their features. She did not know if and when she would see them again. If all went well, Anders would be home by dark.

The last time Ragna experienced an Indian war, she had been dragged from her home never to see her family again. It's different now, she told herself. Anders would be back soon and Many Beavers would take care of her. Even so, Ragna wished that she could climb to the top of Leaf Mountain and see for herself if Indians came from the western prairies.

Many Beavers brought a bucket of water into the cabin and closed and barred the door. It was hot without the fresh breeze blowing in and Ragna wanted to complain, but it was only sensible to take precautions. Although Ragna was exhausted, she felt too agitated to sleep. Fisk purred from his post on top of the flour barrel. Flies buzzed against the window skin. Outside the sounds of mourning doves, ovenbirds and screeching jays.

Ragna twisted from side to side, restless and teary. She touched her abdomen and then removed her hand lest she jinx herself. She wondered where the family was, if Christina rode the travois without bouncing off, if the dog would get lost chasing rabbits along the way. She tried to sleep but could not.

Then she woke up. She had slept after all, the exhaustion of the previous day and sleepless night catching up with her. By the position of sun on the window skin, she judged it late afternoon. Many Beavers dozed in the chair by her side. Ragna touched her stomach. She felt no cramping. She checked the pads under her. Only a small drop of blood.

She felt again the strong conviction that if she only stayed off her feet, everything would be fine.

Many Beavers woke up and fixed another cup of herbal concoction. She handed it to Ragna with a quick nod of her head. Then Many Beavers opened the door and walked out toward the chicken coop.

Ragna dozed again in the comforting blanket of summer heat. She heard a step on the stoop. She opened her eyes to see an Indian brave.

"Migwans!" A wave of relief washed over her. Migwans was a familiar face in a troubled time. They were almost neighbors.

"Missus." He looked at her curiously, as if wondering why she was in bed in the middle of the day.

Many Beavers came into the cabin carrying two eggs in her open hands. Many Beavers looked first at Migwans and then at Ragna.

Migwans's scowling face reminded Ragna of the eternal feud between the Sioux and Chippewa.

"Many Beavers is my friend." Ragna pointed toward Many Beavers and lightly touched her chest to show what she thought was a sign for friendship.

Many Beavers placed the eggs on the table. She handed one to Migwans. He hesitated only a moment and then accepted the egg and cracked it into his mouth. Many Beavers watched him with sharp eyes and moved closer to Ragna's side.

After Migwans swallowed the egg, he made signs with his hands. Many Beavers responded with hand gestures while Ragna watched, trying to figure out what they were saying to each other. Many Beavers pointed toward the west. Migwans shook his head and signed his reply. Many Beavers touched fingers to her forehead like horns, and pointed to the north.

Migwans made a scoffing sound and shook his head again. He signed again and turned up his nose at Many Beavers, holding himself proudly aloof.

Many Beavers handed him the remaining egg. Migwans nodded politely to Ragna before leaving the cabin.

"What did he say?" Ragna said.

"Him says no Indian war."

"But the fire to the west?"

"Roasting grasshoppers for feast." Many Beavers propped the door to catch the southerly breeze. "No war party."

Yesterday Charlie Dollner had emptied the collected grasshoppers into a hole filled with fire. Perhaps he burned hoppers again this morning. Though it sounded rational, Ragna felt uneasy in spite of Migwans's report. She wished Many Beavers would close and bar the door.

Many Beavers fanned herself with the back of her hand and reached for the water dipper. She looked at Ragna for a long time before speaking again. "Him says his warriors will keep the snakes away from this country." Many Beavers remained expressionless but Ragna could tell that his words had offended her.

Sioux was a derogatory word that meant snake. Another sign of the ancient feud.

"Thank you, Many Beavers," Ragna said. "For staying here with me and for rescuing me so long ago. I'm ever so grateful."

Many Beavers's lips curled into a smile. "Badger will be mother of great warriors." She pointed at Ragna's belly. "But maybe this time girl-child like Little Bird."

Ragna smiled back. She had not had any cramping for a long while. Deep inside of her she knew the baby was safe. A little girl with blond curly hair and blue eyes named for her sister, Birdie.

An unwelcome memory of pregnant women abused by the Sioux during the uprising intruded into her thoughts. She chided her faithlessness and began again the litany of prayers that sustained her. *And lead us not into temptation but deliver us from evil.*

52

SERENA'S MIND WHIRLED.

She had just been thinking about Julian and suddenly he appeared at the door. She had read about people who claimed to have second sight, that supernatural gift that knew things before they happened. Auntie Karen had known many things by reading the coffee grounds. It didn't seem Christian, and a vague discomfort flitted through Serena's mind.

"Come in," she said. She took Julian's hand and pulled him inside the room, then closed and locked the front door. "What was I thinking, to leave you standing there?" Serena felt the blood rush to her cheeks. "Take a chair. I'll pour coffee."

The girls crowded around him, both talking at once.

"Sistermine," Julian said. "Did your burns heal?"

Kersten showed him the backs of her hands and feet. Serena noticed his kind attention and the use of her sister's pet name. Maren pulled Scatterbunny out of her apron pocket and placed him on Julian's lap. They chuckled as the rabbit bounced off his lap, climbed down his pant leg and hopped across the kitchen floor. Maren explained how the bunny was the only survivor of the rabbits they had found in the meadow.

"How is the family?" Serena said as Julian drank his coffee.

"Jensina is unwell," he said. "Sick headaches keep her in bed more than she's up and around." He paused for another sip of coffee. "She's in the family way." Julian's cheeks reddened and he seemed to take a sudden interest in the bottom of his coffee cup.

"Another baby! We should help her!" Kersten said.

The foolishness of cooking for Mr. Gardner while her sister needed her swept over Serena.

"Where's Anton?" Julian said looking around the inn. "And Ole?"

Serena explained that Anton was in the barn and Olaus Reierson slept in the downstairs bedroom. She hesitated a brief moment. "Ole left for the Black Hills a few weeks ago." She hurried to the stove and returned with the coffee pot although Julian's cup remained half full. "We don't expect him back."

Julian gave a slight nod and his face relaxed. He fingered the tablecloth with his thick fingers and then twirled the cup around in its saucer. "Good thing I came." He looked at Serena and she noticed the gentleness of his brown eyes, almost like looking into the eyes of a favorite dog. Trustworthy.

Serena felt the smile inside of her before it showed on her face. She heard Anton clatter into the storage room. Olaus stumbled out of the downstairs bedroom, rubbing sleep from his eyes and pulling up his suspenders.

"Good God," Olaus said. "Sounded like screeching savages. Enough to wake the dead."

Serena introduced Julian, and the men discussed the Indian situation while Anton washed up at the dry sink.

Then another knock at the door.

They all looked at each other. It was as if everyone knew there could only be more bad news coming. Serena looked at Julian and held her breath.

"I bring you news," Torger Torgerson said in the same singsong, memorized chant. "Dr. Cormonton came back from Fergus. He wasn't killed. Just taking care of the Hogue family in Erhard. They got the Scarlet Fever but they'll be all right. Says he didn't see no Indians anywhere. None in Fergus and none in Erhard and none in Pomme de Terre." He paused for breath and began again. "Dr. Cormonton says it's a false alarm." Torger beamed like a child winning the spelling bee. "I said it all."

Serena felt like weeping. Thank God! A false alarm. Nothing to worry about.

"*Mange takk!*" Anton said. "We appreciate you bringing the news." He closed the door and returned to his seat at the table with a huge sigh. "It's over."

Serena glanced over at Julian. Gust would have been furious had he left his harvest and made a trip for no reason.

"Thank God," Julian said. His voice was calm and quiet. He seemed genuinely happy and showed no signs of temper. He looked at Serena. She did not look away. "We're spared," he said.

Olaus declared that he would take a little sashay over to Breckenridge to be sure. "If there's no Indians in Breckenridge, we'll know it were all a wild goose chase." He slurped down his coffee, grabbed a slice of bread and smashed his hat onto his wild, white hair. Then he was out the door.

Anton looked at Serena and then at Julian. "Come girls," Anton said. "Help me in the barn."

The girls threw down their knitting and followed Anton outside, talking the whole time about Torger Torgerson's good looks and the kittens. Scatterbunny hopped after them as if it were a pet dog. Swanson's goose flapped its wings at Maren's heels until she squealed in fright.

Serena and Julian sat at the table. Serena's heart fluttered in her chest. She didn't know how to say it but she knew that she had to speak. She was ashamed of herself, pure and simple.

"Julian," Serena said. "I owe you an apology."

"No, you don't," Julian said. "You owe me nothing."

"I was rude." Serena bit her lip and looked down at her lap. Her hands were rough and work-worn, the nails broken and ragged. "I'm sorry."

"You weren't ready, that's all."

Serena looked up in surprise. Julian was right. She hadn't been ready to leave Gust behind, sell the farm, forget the past, and face the future. But now she was. "Anton bought the farm," she said. "Nothing holds me in Pomme de Terre."

"Then we should go home before school starts." Julian pushed away his coffee cup and reached toward Serena's hand, holding his palm up on the table. "The girls need an education."

Another knock at the door. Serena felt a strong irritation that they were interrupted and hoped with all her might that it was not someone looking for a boarding house.

Torger Torgerson stood at the door with his hat in his hands. "I forgot something. Mr. Gardner told me to hightail it back here and say it all or I wouldn't get paid."

"What did you forget, Torger?"

"Mr. Gardner says that you had best get over to the hotel and start cooking or you can forget about working for him at all." Torger said it all in a rush and finished with a breathless gasp. "There. I did it."

Serena looked at Torger and thought how the girls would miss him when they moved back to Iowa. Of course, there were boys back home, too. And they would have more time to enjoy life if they weren't slaving in Mr. Gardner's kitchen. She didn't know what to say, the words escaped her somehow. She opened her mouth to speak to Torger but nothing came out. She looked helplessly at Julian.

"Thank you for the information," Julian said in his calm, gentle way. "But Mrs. Gustafson has had a change of plans and will not be working for Mr. Gardner after all."

"He's not going to like it," Torger said. He put his hat back on his head and as he turned away Serena heard him muttering Julian's words in a sing-song fashion, "Mrs. Gustafson has had a change of plans and will not be working for Mr. Gardner after all."

Serena thought of the map to Burr Oak. The long journey, though much shorter by train, still traveled the same ground. As a girl, she had been dragged to Pomme de Terre against her will. It had been the darkest moment of her life. After Gust's death she had returned home to her parents' house seeking refuge and healing. She had chosen to come to Pomme de Terre to help her dearest friend. And now she chose to return to Burr Oak, not as a daughter running home to her mother, but as a woman returning to her own future.

Serena reached out and took Julian's hand in hers.

53

E VAN WOKE UP IN MRS. TOWNER'S boarding house when Dr. Hawse pulled the
bandages away from his wound. "Ouch! That hurts!"

A single candle lit the dark room. A crucifix hung over the door and a wash basin
and pitcher stood on the commode. Evan realized that he must have been carried into the
house because he could not remember leaving the wagon.

Dr. Hawse stood thin as a broom handle. His narrow face looked down at Evan,
reminding of a ghost from a childhood story. Long fingers reached toward him.

"Nasty wound," Dr. Hawse said. "Hold still."

"Will he live?" Zeke spoke from the other side of the bed.

"I'll live." Evan inched away from Dr. Hawse's prodding fingers with a squeal of
pain. "I've got to live for my children."

"That's the spirit," Dr. Hawse said in a calm, deceptive voice. "A strong will to live
is the best medicine. Hold him down."

Evan felt a great dread fall upon him.

"Mr. Jacobson, I'm cleaning your wound and applying a poultice to draw out the
infection. It will hurt, but you must endure for your children's sake."

Evan gritted his teeth as Zeke's strong arms pushed him into the sagging mattress.
Then a blinding pain.

* * *

E VERY TIME EVAN OPENED HIS EYES that first night, he saw Dr. Hawse napping in the
rocking chair in the corner, his long legs stretched before him. Zeke snored from his side
of the double bed. At first light, the doctor jumped up and changed Evan's poultice.

"It's looking a little better," Dr. Hawse said as he removed the old dressing and smelled it. He reached for another already soaking in a metal pan. "I doubt you would have lived had you arrived a half day later."

"Where's Old Hen and the mule train?" Evan said.

"Quiet now," Dr. Hawse said. "Save your strength. They went on without you but left you in the care of this fine companion."

"But my job," Evan said.

Zeke sat up, jostling the bed. "Don't worry." He stretched his arms and yawned. "Milton and Ole are taking our places for the last day of the journey. Old Hen said he'd stop back here with our pay in a couple of days." Zeke pulled on his pants and boots. "I'm starving. Think I'll go down and see if Mrs. Towner has anything for breakfast."

"But . . ." Evan tried to sit up.

"Sir," Dr. Hawse said and gently pushed him back down on the bed. "Stay put. I've saved your life but you must cooperate."

* * *

Evan TRIED TO REMEMBER if he had ever spent more than a day in bed. Not since he and his sister had measles back in Norway. He slept through the first day as his body fought the infection.

By the second day he felt a little stronger. He propped himself up in bed and attempted to write the letter he had dreamed about, the one to his children. It was more difficult than he had thought. The advice and lessons learned sounded stilted and formal on the page.

Finally, he set aside the letter to his children and instead wrote one to Inga. He told her that he was safe at the Sioux Agency, his wound improved day by day, and he would be returning home as soon as he received payment for his time on the road. Zeke wrote lengthy missives to his wife and baby son and seemed content to lounge in the boarding house except for daily jaunts to the post office.

Zeke brought back news of the little village clustered around the Indian Agency. He said the town was abuzz with worries about safety in light of Custer's defeat. The Indians usually in the vicinity had disappeared without warning. The storekeeper had already left with his family for Fort Wadsworth along with the saloon keeper.

"You going to Fort Wadsworth?" Evan said to Mrs. Towner when she brought his dinner to his room. "Don't want to hold you back."

Mrs. Towner was a matronly woman, about the age of Evan's mother, had she lived. She had the figure of a pudding bag wrapped in a feed sack apron. Her gray hair pulled back into such a tight bun that her skin pulled away from her teeth.

She shook her head. "I'm too old to leave on a wild goose chase." Mrs. Towner set the tray on a small table by Evan's bed. "The army is still here. I'll leave when they do."

On the third day Zeke went to the post office and Evan got out of bed and dressed. His arms and legs wobbled but he was relieved to be without dizziness. Evan peeked into the mirror over the commode but could see only a ragged red beard on the left side of his face and the bandage on the right.

Evan washed his face and hands and found his way downstairs to the kitchen where Mrs. Towner was peeling spuds for dinner.

"What are you doing?" Mrs. Towner said. "You belong in bed."

"I'm hungry," Evan said. "Could I bother you for something to eat?"

Mrs. Towner scurried around the kitchen and found a slice of bread and a small jar of honey. She put the butter dish on the table and motioned for Evan to sit down. Then she poured thick coffee from the pot on the stove.

Evan had just sunk his teeth into the fresh bread when someone rapped at the back door. Old Hen entered and stood awkwardly by the doormat, shifting his weight from one foot to another. He held a newspaper in his hand.

"Old Hen," Evan said. He stood beside the table, a little wobbly on his pins but definitely on the mend. "How did it go?"

Old Hen stared at Evan without saying a thing. Finally he passed the newspaper to Evan and watched him read the headlines: Savages in Breckenridge, Fergus Falls, and Pomme de Terre.

"I've got to get home," Evan said. He threw the newspaper down on the table and pushed the rest of the bread in his mouth. "How much do I owe you, Mrs. Towner?" He stood thinking all he must do before he left. Evan had little to pack. The small sack of wooden shoes and his extra change of clothes.

"Captain Van der Horck sends regrets for your injury." Old Hen pulled a wallet out of his pocket and counted greenbacks for Evan. Then he handed another bill to Mrs. Crowner. "Army's covering your expenses while you're here." Old Hen cleared his throat and shrugged a shoulder. "But I couldn't finagle a horse no matter how hard I tried."

"I'll ride shank's mare," Evan pocketed the money. It looked like a lot but he knew it had to carry the family through lean times. "Leaving right away."

"You're weak—would be better if you waited a few days," Old Hen said. "But kin is kin and I can't say I'd do it different in your shoes."

"Sit down," Mrs. Towner said. "Fill your stomach before setting out. I'll fix you a lunch parcel." She sniffed and wiped a tear with her apron. "To think after all we've been through to settle this country and now the Sioux would take it back."

Zeke came into the kitchen. When Old Hen handed him the newspaper, Zeke turned wild-eyed and frantic to leave for home. "Good God!" he said. "Sioux in the streets of Breckenridge! I'll never forgive myself if something happens to my wife and son."

"Sit and eat," Mrs. Towner said. "You'll need your strength."

Old Hen said he had one more person to ask about horses. He left the kitchen, slamming the door behind him in haste. Zeke and Evan sat at the table.

The food that had smelled so good before tasted like cardboard in Evan's mouth. He imagined Inga and the children surrounded by painted warriors. He could almost smell the smoke and gunpowder of battle. He ate as much as he could force down and gratefully took the cloth wrapped parcel of food from Mrs. Towner's hands.

"You let me know how it turns out," she said with a sniff and another swipe at her eyes. "I'll be praying for you."

The two men walked out of the boarding house and started east out of the agency. Zeke carried his saddle and bridle. The robbers may have taken his horse but at least he had kept his gear. Evan considered how far it was to the Breckenridge Flats and how heavy the saddle would be to tote all that way. They would make it somehow.

Evan sent up a desperate prayer for Inga and the family, then for strength and health. His legs wobbled though his head no longer swirled. He felt weakness to his very bones.

"Wait up!" Old Hen called from the stable. "Found some animals for sale."

The men veered to the stable. Inside was a ragtag assortment of oxen, mules, Indian ponies, and a large white mule. It looked familiar. "A patrol took these animals off a band of renegades."

"Whitey!" Evan snitched a corner of bread crust from his lunch and held it out it to the mule. He rubbed between its ears and nuzzled its nose. "This one belongs to Milton Madsen."

"Too bad," Old Hen said. "He's left for the Black Hills. Him and Ole signed on to freight. It's suicide, but they was glad for the work."

Evan shook his head. If Milton had only kept his promise to stay back with Inga. Instead he was getting himself killed in Indian country. Evan shrugged it off. What's done was done. He thought of the price of a mount and how little he would have left to show for his time on the road.

"It's starting to make sense," Old Hen said. "Army found the bodies of three men and a woman near the Black Hills. Indians got them. Woman dressed as a man—didn't realize she was female until they looked through her pack and found her dresses."

"Anyone we know?" Evan said.

"Gertie Green," Old Hen said. "The soldiers found letters addressed to her. Descriptions of the others match the three gamblers from Gager's."

"Good Lord." Evan said. "Gertie with the robbers." He remembered the look in her eye as she pounded Ted with a cast-iron skillet and Mrs. Frisby's warning.

"That's the way I figure it," Old Hen said.

The sun had climbed half way up the morning sky. They needed to haggle for mounts and get on their way. An idea wiggled through Evan's mind. It was a wild scheme but the only solution that would save his hard-earned money.

"How about I take possession of Whitey?" Evan said. "Milton will be back to settle his claim eventually."

Old Hen kicked the dirt with the toe of his boot, fiddled in his pocket for his tobacco plug and took another chaw. "If he lives to come back," Old Hen said. "Custer poked a stick in their eyes and the Sioux are mad as hornets."

Old Hen rolled the tobacco wad around in his mouth and wiped his lips with the back of his sleeve. "Wouldn't be right to sell the mule, knowing its owner. Army would have to pay board and found—and Milton would have to repay the army to get it back." He spat a stream of tobacco juice into the weeds. "It seems my civic duty to spare both the army and Milton the expense."

"My horse ain't here." Zeke said. "It's only fair I get one of these in exchange."

Old Hen thought for only a moment. "Go ahead," he said. "Pick what you want. I'll explain to the captain."

Zeke chose a sturdy looking dapple gray and saddled it. The horse rolled wild eyes and skittered away as he tried to mount. When he finally succeeded in climbing up on the saddle, Zeke held on. The horse crow-hopped across the yard.

"I'm leaving," Zeke said. "Don't dare get off!"

Evan clambered up on Whitey. Old Hen handed Evan a gun. "Take it. You can return it next time you see me."

"I hate to inconvenience you." Evan felt the cold steel in his hands and smelled the faint odor of gunpowder and gun grease. He dreaded the thought of turning a weapon on another human being. He had seen enough killing.

At the same time he knew he needed to arm himself to return to Inga. He would do whatever it took to protect his family.

"Not safe to head into Indian danger without a weapon," Old Hen said. "I'll see you next season. Grasshoppers still bad—you'll need the work."

"*Mange tusen takk*," Evan said. "I'll take good care of it."

Evan urged Whitey forward but the mule planted its feet in the street and refused to move. Maybe it didn't like the smell of the rifle. Evan slapped the reins against its neck and jabbed his heels into its side in frustration.

"Damn stubborn mule," Evan said. "You're doing me no favor letting me take the blasted animal." He might have to walk home after all. His legs trembled.

"I'll handle him," Old Hen said.

Zeke was already a half mile down the road and Evan knew the man was in such a frenzy to get home that he would not wait for him. Evan gripped Whitey's flanks with his knees.

Old Hen walked around to the front of the mule and murmured a soothing flow of words. He patted Whitey's shoulder and scratched between his ears, all the time murmuring sweet endearments to the stubborn beast. Old Hen opened his palm holding a scattering of oats before its mouth. Its ears perked forward. Whitey pulled back his lips and stretched a long tongue to lick the grains out of Old Hen's hand.

Old Hen stepped away from the animal.

"Promenade all!" Old Hen said in his loud, mule-skinning voice.

Whitey stepped lively. Evan hung on for dear life.

54

NDERS AND LYING JACK STUMBLED into the cabin after dark with Musky at their heels. Ragna let out a sigh of relief and reached for the matches beside the bed. She lit the candle stub as Anders came directly over and knelt beside her bed.

Musky barked at Fisk who hissed back from its place on top of the flour barrel.

"Hush!" Lying Jack slapped the dog on its nose and chased the yelping dog outside.

"How are you?" Anders smelled of sweat and campfires. He pulled Ragna's small hands into his larger ones and kissed her knuckles. His bristly face tickled her skin. "I worried, Mrs. Vollen."

Many Beavers, who had been sleeping in the loft, climbed down the ladder and left the cabin without a word. Lying Jack came back inside and sat down at the table. He lighted his pipe and the smell of sweet tobacco filled the room.

Anders's gentle voice caused tears to sprout in Ragna's eyes. Her bravado evaporated and the seriousness of their situation washed over her. "I'm feeling better." Ragna looked toward Lying Jack and lowered her voice to a whisper. "The bleeding has stopped. I think I'm going to be all right."

"Thank God." Anders buried his face in her hands and Ragna felt his tears on her palms. His voice cracked. "I was crazy with worry. I couldn't bear to lose you."

The flickering candle flame reflected off Fisk's eyes. A plume of smoke spiraled above Lying Jack at the table. It was the middle of the night. A mouse rustled in the corner and Fisk jumped down from the barrel to investigate.

"Any news?" Ragna said. "Auntie Inga . . . and the children?"

"Musky tangled with every dog at Fort Juelson." Anders said with an attitude of disgust. "Inga told me to bring it home and spare her the humiliation of owning the worst-behaved dog in the township."

"Said it was a good thing her childrens mind better than that dog," Lying Jack said with a hearty chuckle.

Ragna smiled in spite of her anxiety. "I meant about the Indians."

"Nothing." Anders got up and stirred the porridge on the stove and dished up a bowl for Lying Jack. "Not a trace. Smoke came from Charlie Dollner burning the heaps of grasshoppers brought in for bounty."

"What do the papers say?"

"Same. Indians in Fergus and Pomme de Terre."

Ragna's heart dropped. So close. "Migwans stopped by," Ragna said. "Said there were no Sioux anywhere in this country."

"There's something strange about all this." Anders finished his porridge and scraped the sides of the bowl with the wooden spoon, the clack of wood on wood. "Don't you think we'd hear something besides newspaper headlines?"

"Lots of folks upset but peoples gets that ways," Lying Jack said. His voice stretchy and mellow in the darkness. "I won't believes it till I sees it."

Many Beavers returned with a handful of fresh eggs and the jug of milk kept in the dugout. Silently she stoked the fire and pulled the cast iron skillet over the flame. Ragna started to get up to help but Many Beavers motioned for her to stay in bed. Ragna watched her dip into the jar of muskrat fat and rub it on the pan, then drop the eggs into the sizzling fat.

"I'm goings to Pomme de Terre and sees for myself," Lying Jack said. He spoke to Many Beavers in her language. She nodded and slipped the eggs onto plates. She began gathering her few belongings as the men wolfed down the food.

"It's the middle of the night," Anders said. "Stay until morning. You can sleep in the dugout."

Many Beavers gave Ragna another cup of the bitter herbs before she and Lying Jack left for the dugout. Anders ate and collapsed in the bed beside Ragna. He was asleep before his head hit the pillow.

Ragna lay awake. She prayed the rosary through and made special efforts to thank God for protecting them from the Indians and for sparing her baby. As she prayed, she laid a hand across her belly, willing the baby to live. She petitioned God for Bertha and her new baby, Uncle Evan and his recovery from his injury, for Auntie Inga sleeping in a strange place with all the responsibility of the children. She prayed herself to sleep.

In the early morning hours, Many Beavers shook Ragna's shoulder. Anders slept like a stone beside her though the rooster crowed outside their window, first at half strength and then another at full measure. Many Beavers handed a steaming mug of the bitter herbs to Ragna. Ragna choked it down. Each dose seemed worse than the one before. But it was working. The bleeding had stopped.

Many Beavers took the cup back to the table. "We go." She held up five fingers. "You stay in bed this many days. Then get up."

Ragna pushed back a jab of fear. What if the bleeding started again after Many Beavers left? "Don't go."

"Badger will be good mother." Many Beavers nodded and left the cabin.

Ragna thought to rouse Anders and tell him Lying Jack and Many Beavers were leaving, but hesitated. Anders needed his rest. Surely he need not stand watch as long as the Holy Angels guarded them. She prayed the morning *Angelus* with the birds singing in the background. Then she began the morning *Lauds*.

As she prayed she had the sensation of being protected by unseen witnesses around her. Her mother and father's presence, her baby brother, and Birdie. The communion of saints, according to Marta. Those in heaven interceding for those on earth. Her heart almost burst with the joy of feeling her family close to her.

Ragna laid a hand across her stomach. As she prayed over her unborn baby, she felt it move. Ragna held her breath. Could it be true? Had God truly answered her prayers?

The baby kicked.

55

THE WEDDING WAS A SIMPLE AFFAIR. Reverend Holton, the Lutheran minister, was in town only for a day. They could marry now or return to Iowa and get married there.

"What do you think, Serena?" Julian had not quit smiling since she had agreed to marry him the day before. "Will you marry me today?"

Serena thought for only a minute. Being married in Pomme de Terre would mean one less day away from the harvest. Julian's wheat waited. It was more practical to marry now and travel as man and wife.

Serena nodded. The minister agreed to come to the inn at mid-afternoon.

Serena wore her best dress and the crocheted snood from Auntie Karen. She sponged and pressed Julian's suit. Julian and the girls walked out to the old farm and returned with bouquets of wild flowers: Indian paintbrush, ox-eyed daisies, purple phlox and coneflowers.

"It's providential I'm in town," Reverend Holton said. He was a small man, short and balding with a square forehead and icy blue eyes. "Had an unexpected order for hard soap from Van Dyke's Store in Alexandria. Brought me this way sooner than expected."

It was hot and stuffy in the inn and smelled faintly of last night's fish chowder. Serena opened the windows and propped the door before pulling on her white gloves and taking her place beside Julian Gustafson. Anton stood witness.

Cows lowing from the barnyard and the singing birds outside the open door provided the only music.

She had married Gust in a fever of emotion that changed her life forever. She doubted this marriage would be so tumultuous. She would live a stone's throw from her childhood home and would still be Serena Gustafson. This pleased her.

Julian smiled at Serena and looked at her with such devotion that tears welled in her eyes. He had not once spoken of love. She smiled back at him. He didn't need to tell her what she already knew.

Serena only wished that her parents could be there with her. Somehow Serena knew that they would be happy for her. Her father had always liked Julian.

She took a deep breath and took Julian's hand.

"This is a wedding but we would be amiss if we neglected to pray for those suffering from the grasshoppers." He looked at Serena and Julian as if for permission to continue.

Julian nodded.

"I'd like to share a prayer written by a Roman priest in Dakota Territory," Reverend Holton said. "You might think it strange but I doubt the grasshoppers know the difference between a Roman priest and a Lutheran minister."

Anton chuckled and the girls giggled. Serena glanced at Julian and stepped a little closer toward her groom.

"Pray with me."

They bowed their heads. Serena felt the rough wool of Julian's suit against her wrists, smelled the fragrance of his shaving soap. She remembered again how it felt to be a wife. Dagmar had taught her well. This time she would not lose her voice.

"I bid you depart, animals of destruction. Leave our fields and plains immediately. Live no longer in them but pass over into places where you can harm no one." Pastor Holten paused for a breath and spoke in a clear, strong voice. "I call God's wrath upon you, and diminishing from day to day, may you disappear except where you serve the health and good purposes of mankind. May no trace of you be found."

Silence filled the room. Julian reached his arm around Serena's waist. "Amen," he said and Serena felt the vibration of his voice against her arm.

"Now we can get to the wedding," Pastor Holten said.

After the vows were said and the bridegroom had kissed his bride, Serena invited the minister to stay for coffee. She and the girls had baked a raisin cake. Maren and Kersten fluttered around the kitchen, grinding coffee beans and boiling water for tea. Maren laid the spoons and the best linen napkins. Sunlight reflected off the gold band on Serena's left hand as she made tea in Dagmar's best teapot.

Serena could feel Julian's eyes upon her as she busied around the kitchen. They would spend the night at the inn and leave for Iowa tomorrow.

The minister blessed the repast and Serena was about to cut the cake when someone rapped at the open door.

"Well, look what the cat drug in," Olaus said and pushed a man into the room ahead of him. The man looked unwell and wore a filthy bandage over half of his face, the other half a scraggly red beard. Serena hurried to bring a chair.

"It's Evan Jacobson," Olaus said. "More dead than alive, but it's him. Found him at Breckenridge."

"Mr. Jacobson?" Serena looked at him more closely. It was the stagecoach driver who had been so kind to her after Gust's death. "How nice to see you again. Won't you join us for wedding cake?"

Julian shook Evan's hand and proudly introduced himself as Serena's husband. This made the girls giggle and laugh. Serena shot them a warning glance and urged everyone to the table. They had just started to eat when another rap sounded.

"Come in and welcome," Anton said. "You're just in time."

Lying Jack, the trader, and his Indian wife entered the inn.

"Maren Rose," Serena said. "Fetch more plates."

56

E VAN PLODDED THE LAST FEW MILES to his farm. He trembled with weakness but pushed himself to go forward. Thank God for a faithful mule. He patted Whitey's back and promised a pound of sugar when they finally got home. He smiled and the stretching skin reminded him of his healing wound. As if Inga would ever allow such a waste of good sugar.

His mind flitted to Milton mule-whacking in Indian country. The war affected some men that way. Made them careless and devil-may-care. As if surviving the war made them infallible to other dangers.

He rounded the south shore of Long Lake and eyed something against a rock pile. It looked like a pile of rags or maybe a dead animal. A flutter of red cloth prompted him to investigate.

It was Little Wolf, the young Indian boy who traded the pup for a noggin of milk and the red bandana still tied around his neck. When Evan helped him sit up, he saw a bloody wound on his chest and remembered how the drums had sent the young men out to battle the Sioux. He recalled the soldier's report of the Chippewa war party with the stolen horses. Could it be that this young man was the only survivor?

The boys' eyes blazed with fear.

"Don't be afraid, Little Wolf," Evan said in the same crooning voice he used with animals or small children. "We're almost home."

Evan boosted the boy onto Whitey's back but was too weak to crawl up behind him. He must lead the mule on foot for the remaining mile. Evan had come too far to stop short of home.

They passed Anders's empty cabin and Evan was pleased to see popcorn growing on top of the roof. Grasshoppers had missed the popcorn. The thought encouraged Evan more than anything. That something could remain after the grasshoppers had dealt their worst.

They were almost to Milton's property line when the sound of a splitting mall echoed through the woods. Anders was fencing.

Evan didn't know if he had the strength to call out but Anders heard him and came running.

"By God," Anders said. "You don't look so good." He pointed at Little Wolf with his thumb. "Him neither."

Evan was too weak to answer. Anders boosted him up on the mule behind Little Wolf and patted Whitey's rump. "Don't worry. I'm right beside you," Anders said.

Evan gasped at his ruined fields. He wanted to curse the dirty grasshoppers but stopped himself. He would think instead of his safe return. He would be glad for the greenbacks lining his pocket and the bounty money that would get them through this coming year in spite of the ruined crops.

Hoppers or no hoppers, they would survive.

* * *

INGA LOOKED ASKANCE AT EVAN'S FACE and then at the injured boy. Then she tilted her chin and barked orders. Anders and Gunnar were to lay the boy under the butchering elm.

"Won't risk lice in the clean beds," Inga said. She called Ragna to put the kettle to boil and tend the boy's wounds. "Fetch a gourd of *melk*, but don't let him drink too fast."

Evan was about to join the Indian boy under the tree but Inga steered him into the cabin. "Bought hard soap at Dollner's Store," Inga said to Evan. Her gentle hands caressed his arm and stroked his ragged beard as she led him to their bed. "He got it off a preacher in Pomme de Terre." Evan slumped down onto the rustling cornhusk mattress.

Inga kept a steady conversation of small talk while she unwound the bandage. She bent over and sniffed the wound. "Doesn't stink." She let out a sigh of relief. "Thank God."

The boys stood gawking with their mouths hanging open.

"What happened to your ear," Sverre said from the doorway.

"Are you going to die?" Lewis said.

"I was hurt," Evan said encouragingly while Inga probed the wound. "I'll be all right but will have a scar." He winced and pulled away but Inga would not be dissuaded.

"Don't just stand there, boys." Inga's voice had lost its sharp edge reminding Evan of the first time he had heard her calling the cows. It was long ago, back when she was still married to Ingvald. Her alto voice had floated over the pasture like a stringed instrument.

"Lewis, fetch a bucket of water and Sverre, run out to the coop for eggs." Inga looked down at Evan, her brown eyes welling with emotion. "Gunnar, help your sister with the Indian boy and tell Anders to fetch Migwans. Knut, bring Sigurd home from the pasture. Tell him his *far* is home."

As Whitey trotted east toward the Indian village and the boys scrambled to obey their mother, Evan stretched out a hand to Christina. She held back. Either she didn't remember him or else didn't recognize his strange appearance. Tears of disappointment and relief flooded his eyes. He reached to wipe them away but Inga was already wiping them with the corner of her apron.

"You're safe now, dear husband," Inga said. "Christina will know you soon enough." She unbuttoned his shirt. "Take off these dirty clothes and get under the covers." She was all business again. "That filthy beard has to come off."

Evan protested but Inga shaved his beard anyway and trimmed his hair. He felt younger and lighter with it gone. She brought hot water and soap to the bedside and cared for him as if he were a baby lamb without a mother. It hurt when she rubbed in the salve but Inga's vigilance could not be deterred.

"*Jeg har savnet deg,*" Evan said when Inga knelt over his wound. Love choked off the words. Lying Jack had told him how she had fled with the children to Fort Juelson. How frightened she must have been. "I've missed you."

"*Mange takk* for the letters." Inga bent to kiss him.

Evan didn't answer but pulled her closer. Christina howled holding a burnt finger after touching the hot stove. Inga's face wreathed in smiles.

* * *

ON AUGUST 28, ST. BARTHOLOMEW'S DAY, the family gathered at the log church for Catechization. The breeze blowing in through the open windows carried the first crisp hint of autumn. Evan's family filled the entire pew. Inga and Christina sat to his left and the boys, scrubbed pink and wearing new clogs, beyond them. Anders and Ragna sat in the pew ahead of them.

Evan crossed his legs and admired his new, leather moccasins. They were the most comfortable shoes, a gift from Migwans. Evan pushed down a guilty feeling. He had done little to deserve such an extravagant gift. Ragna, after all, had been the one who tended Little Wolf's wounds.

Christina climbed over to Evan's lap and played with his remaining ear lobe. She poked her finger into his mouth and fingered his scar while they sang the opening hymn, "Who is on the Lord's Side." Evan pushed her hand away and turned his daughter around to face the front as the Confirmands marched to the altar and stood before the congregation.

Evan held his breath and reached for Inga's hand.

The minister turned first to Knut who answered his questions quickly, almost pridefully. Evan must remember to speak to Knut about the pitfalls of arrogance.

Evan squeezed Christina tighter at Gunnar's turn. The question from Luther's Small Catechism sounded through the small church, "Our Father who art in heaven. What does this mean?" Gunnar thought a long moment before speaking and Evan almost despaired. Gunnar couldn't remember and would not be confirmed. The congregation squirmed.

Then with deliberate and careful pronunciation, Gunnar answered the question in complete accuracy. "God would by these words tenderly invite us to believe that He is our true Father, and that we are His true children, so that we may with all boldness and confidence ask Him as dear children ask their dear father."

"Very good, Gunnar," the minister said. His voice jubilant. "And would you please share with the congregation the verse that holds special meaning for you in relationship to this passage?"

Gunnar looked blankly at the pastor. Then he looked at Knut as if for assistance. Then Gunnar looked at Evan. Their eyes locked. Evan smiled and nodded.

"Like as a father pitieth his children, so the Lord pitieth them that fear Him. Psalm 103:13," Gunnar quoted with sure and steady voice. His face burst into a smile that carried the light of heaven.

Evan's heart pounded in his chest and he wiped his eyes on the back of Christina's bonnet. Inga squeezed his arm. He did it. The Confirmation service was immediately held after the questions and answers. Evan thought how happy his parents would be for his oldest son to become a member of the church, free to partake of all the sacraments. He felt their presence, though they were both gone these many years.

Afterwards friends and neighbors came to the house. Ragna, with rounding belly, helped Inga serve the meal. Bertha and Elijah Wheeling came with their new baby son. Hans Juelson and Berge Lee brought their families. Charlie Dollner rode in on his old nag.

Lying Jack and Many Beavers did not attend the church service but came early to watch the animals while they were gone. Migwans and his three sons came for the dinner. Little Wolf proudly wore the scar on his chest like a war trophy. The twins and Sigurd rushed to look at his wounds and play with the younger boys. Little Wolf held himself aloof like his father. He had proven himself as a man.

Gunnar supplied venison for the meal. It was his last day at home. Tomorrow he would leave for Pomme de Terre with Ragna and Anders where he would work for Anton Estvold. Inga was reluctant to let him go but Evan had taken the young man's side in the debate. With times so hard, everyone must contribute to the family coffers.

Knut was needed at home. Someday he would go off to school. Surely there would be a way once the grasshoppers ended.

While everyone was eating, Charlie Dollner waved Evan over to the butchering elm and handed him the *Skandinaven* and a letter. "Brought your mail."

"*Mange takk!*" Evan said. "I've been so busy getting up wood that I've not even thought of picking it up."

The letter was from Old Hen. Evan ripped it open and read the scrawled lines.

Dear Evan, Bad news from Dakota. Indians killt Milton Madsen and Ole Estvold on their trip out to the Hills. I told them it were suicide to go.

Keep the mule. Old Hen

Evan felt the air suck out of his lungs. Milton had traveled with him to the Saints that first year the grasshoppers had taken his Alexandria crops. Milton had cared for the twins when measles threatened Sigurd's life. Milton helped build the first Tordenskjold dugout and loaned him the use of his mule to get the teamstering job. He wasn't ready to lose him yet. He doubted he would find another friend and neighbor like Milton.

"Bad news?" Charlie said.

He was quiet after Evan told him about Milton's death.

"I guess life goes on," Charlie said. He plucked a twig and chewed it into a tooth-pick as he headed back toward the table. "We don't have to like it."

"Life goes on," Evan said, mostly to himself. Anton Estvold had lost his entire family in the New World and was completely alone. It put things in perspective. A man with a family knew true riches. A fierce gladness rose up in Evan, stronger than the grief of a moment before. Ragna and Gunnar would be with Anton over the coming months. Evan's children would bolster Anton through his grief. A loss to the family back home, but a blessing to a friend in need.

Evan would not share the bad news until the party was over. Today was a day to celebrate. Sounds of laughter and celebration drifted across the yard.

"Everything all right?" Inga came up beside him. She always seemed to know when he needed her.

"*Ja*, the horseshoe holds our luck." Evan took her hand. "We are blessed." Evan's voice cracked. "We've good land, a real cabin and six healthy children." He glanced over to the picnic area where Anders bounced Christina on his shoulders. "We have our health and strength to work. What more could we want?"

"And you're home," Inga said with a laugh, forgetting to cover her missing tooth.

"*Borte bra, men hjemme best*," Evan said. "East-west, home best."

They turned and walked back to the celebration hand in hand. Whatever happened, they would face it together.

Epilogue

1879

SERENA'S SISTER FLUTTERED AROUND the stove, adding a bit of water to the pan as she tucked potatoes around the meat. The rich smell of beef filled the room. "Should I add turnips and onions?"

Serena read a letter while rocking her fussy baby and did not answer Jensina's question.

"Bad news," Serena said. "Ragna Vollen writes that Anton Estvold broke his arm while chasing a runaway bull." She shifted the infant in her arms. "He sends congratulations on our new baby and many thanks for naming her after his wife."

Serena settled the newborn to her breast as Jensina sliced onions into the roasting pan.

"Although he reminds me that Dagmar would be more concerned about a healthy child than a namesake."

Jensina chuckled. "Wish I could have known her."

"Ragna says her brother, Gunnar, the young man who works for Anton, saved enough money to buy his father a horse," Serena said. "Imagine that." The baby arched away from the nipple and howled in protest. Serena pushed the floor with her toe and rocked harder until the baby quieted. "Ragna and her family are moving back to Alexandria now that the grasshoppers are gone. Says Anders found a teaching position. She says her two babies, Birdie and Ann Elin, keep her busy." Serena kissed her baby's head. "I know what that's like."

Jensina dropped the cover of the turnip bin and the loud thump startled Baby Dagmar.

Serena hoped this little one would grow up to be just like her old friend—well maybe without the profanity. She hoped she would be plucky and determined and would weather all trials with an unbroken spirit.

The infant drifted off to sleep and Serena picked up a small pamphlet that Ragna had tucked inside the letter. She read quietly as Jensina pared carrots and turnips. Her sister screeched the roasting pan into the oven, closing the door with a bang.

"Everything's ready," Jensina said. "There's wood in the firebox. You shouldn't have to do a thing." She gathered the peelings into the slop bucket for the hogs and wiped her hands. "What are you reading?"

"It's a Gospel tract," Serena said. "Telling how the grasshoppers left Minnesota after Governor Pillsbury's day of prayer."

"What happened?"

"After the day of prayer the grasshoppers flew away without laying their eggs."

"Where did they go?" Jensina reached for her shawl. "They couldn't just disappear."

"A Boston woman says she saw them fly overhead as she hung clothes on the line." Serena turned the page. "A few grasshoppers fell into her clothesbasket." Serena shuddered. She would never forget the chattering horde that had descended onto Pomme de Terre. "Then the noisy cloud flew over the ocean and was not seen again."

"A miracle," Jensina said. "Why haven't we known this before?"

Serena thought of Tommy O'Hara. "Maybe miracles don't look like miracles until time passes." She remembered Reverend Holten's prayer that ordered the grasshoppers to leave forever. "It's in looking back that we see God's perfect timing."

Jensina kissed Serena's cheek.

"How can I thank you, Sistermine, for all your help?" Serena had felt so weak since childbed. Especially with Edward old enough to get into everything.

"That's what sisters are for." Jensina tied her bonnet strings with a laugh. "Will you be all right until Julian gets in from the field?"

Tears welled in Serena's eyes. They were best friends now, neighbors and confidants.

"I'll be fine." Serena swallowed a lump in her throat. "Little Eddy should nap until the girls get home from school. Dagmar and I will stay right here in the rocking chair."

The house quieted after Jensina left. It looked very different since Serena's marriage. She had replaced the heavy curtains with gingham frills. Serena and the girls had painted the walls and moved Auntie Karen's old trunk beneath the window next to her father's favorite chair. She and Julian slept in the downstairs bedroom that had once belonged to his grand-parents. Serena chose not to sleep in the room where Gust had slept growing up or the room that belonged to his parents. It was Serena's house now. No longer her mother-in-law's.

Serena rocked Dagmar, humming a Norwegian lullaby.

"How are my girls?" Julian came in through the side door. Sweat and dirt streaked his face and chaff covered his overalls. He smiled like the cat that swallowed a canary. "Your color is better today." He leaned over and kissed the baby and then tipped Serena's chin and kissed her. "Feeling any stronger?"

"I'm fine," Serena said with a laugh. "Spoiled with being waited on hand and foot."

"Do you remember what day it is?" Julian wore an expectant, hopeful look.

"Our anniversary." Serena flushed in embarrassment. With the new baby, she had completely forgotten. "I'm sorry. I haven't a gift—not even a cake."

"You're holding the best gift," Julian said. "A daughter as beautiful as her mother." His face wore the same expression as when he had purchased the organ for Kersten's music lessons. "A son and a daughter. What more could a man want?"

"I've presents." He knelt down beside the chair and stroked Baby Dagmar's cheek. "And I bring the newspaper. Which do you want first?"

"You silly man!" Serena giggled. Julian showed his affection with gifts and acts of kindness rather than words. "Presents, of course."

He tossed the *Skandinaven* on the table and held out empty hands. "Here it is." He looked at her expectantly, his dark eyes sparkling.

Serena didn't understand.

"For you on our anniversary." His voice soft and teasing.

"Tell me," Serena said. "I'm a little dense from lack of sleep."

"I've found a young couple looking for work," Julian said. "Immigrants from the Tronderlag of Norway." Julian paused to find the right words. It was something Serena admired about him, the way he tried always to find the words most gentle, least likely to offend. "You're queen of this house," Julian said at last, "and only if you approve." He looked at her again. "Empty hands—someone else doing the heavy work so you have more time with the children."

"But the expense," Serena said with a gasp. She worried about his extravagance sometimes. The harvest looked good but surely there were other places to spend the money. "The girls will help me."

"Maren and Kersten have their studies." Julian turned serious. "I don't want them missing school."

They talked about what room the couple might have, how Serena would direct the housework and vegetable gardens, and the possibilities with another man in the fields and barnyard. Additional help would benefit the farm operation as well as the household.

"Only if you approve."

She nodded and could not hold back the tears.

"Good. It's settled. And now the other gift." Julian reached behind the wood box, withdrew a paper-wrapped package and laid it on her lap. He took the baby from her arms. "For you, dearest wife."

"Julian," she said. "Kitchen help is more than enough."

"Open it," Julian said. He tucked the baby close to his chest and twirled around the kitchen in a waltz. "I'm starving."

Serena untied the string, careful to roll it for reuse. She unfolded the wrapper and gasped to see a leather-bound Steilers Handatlas. Although the words were written in German, the maps portrayed oceans, rivers, and countries of the world. Hand colored, the pages glowed like works of art.

No one had ever before understood her fascination with maps and geography.

"Husband!"

Edward cried out from the upstairs bedroom. "I'll get him." Julian and the baby disappeared up the stairs.

Serena turned the pages until she found North America's map. She swept her hand across the mid-section of the continent, from the Canadian prairies down into Texas where the grasshoppers had caused such havoc. She touched Hutchinson where Lena Christine had been born and the lonely spot along the trail to Fort Snelling where she was buried. She followed the Mississippi River to St. Cloud, the railroad route to Herman and the trail to Pomme de Terre. Then she traced it again, remembering how Julian had followed to rescue her and bring her to her senses. She found Burr Oak and planted her finger on the spot.

Kersten and Maren sounded at the door. Julian came down the stairway with a baby in each arm. The kitchen filled with the homey smells of beef and onions. Serena reached for her sleepy son and snuggled him on her lap as Maren laid the plates. Kersten played "The Anniversary Waltz" on the organ as they gathered around the big oak table.

Serena didn't understand life at all. She didn't know why she had gone through such hard years. She didn't know why people suffered and died. She didn't know what God had planned for them. But as she sat there in the midst of family, Serena knew that somehow, everything would be all right.

As they recited the Norwegian table prayer, Serena held squirming Edward on her lap. Across the table, Julian snuggled Baby Dagmar against his chest, patting her back with his burly farmer hands. A few strands of silver gleamed in his dark hair. Edward banged a spoon on Serena's plate and Julian looked at her. Their gazes locked. She could see the love in his eyes.

THE END

Sources

Harvest of Grief: Grasshopper Plagues and Public Assistance in Minnesota, 1873-1878 by Annette Atkins, Minnesota Historical Society Press St. Paul, 1984.

The Wadsworth Trail by Grace Cynthia Hall, Stevens County Historical Society, 1938, 2nd edition 2007.

Pomme de Terre A Frontier Outpost in Grant County by William Goetzinger, 1962.

The Red River Trails by Gilman, Gilman and Stultz, MN Historical Society Press 1979.

Fort Juelson and the Indian Scare of 1876 by Clifford Knutson 2011.

Ever the Land, A Homestead Chronicle by Ruben L Parson, Adventure Publishing 2004.

Book Club Discussion Notes are available online:
www.candacesimar.com